I0670460

# THE DICTATOR

# OF BRITAIN

## BOOK TWO: THE DIRTY WAR

PAUL MICHAEL DUBAL

Copyright 2014 Paul Michael Dubal
ISBN: 9781311549693

The Dictator of Britain
Book Two: The Dirty War
All Rights Reserved
Copyright © 2014 Paul Michael Dubal
Published by Paul Michael Dubal
ISBN: 9781311549693
eISBN: 9781520833019

Discover other titles by Paul Michael Dubal at www.paulmichaeldubal.com

*"True Liberty consists in the privilege of enjoying our own rights, not in the destruction of the rights of others"*

(Dr. George Pinckard, 18th Century English scholar)

# CHAPTER 1

If Harry Clarke possessed a mirror, he would have been shocked at his appearance. His once lush, wavy brown hair had thinned and greyed, the optimism of his youth long since faded as if it belonged to a different, untroubled soul. His formerly vigorous physique had diminished; his body was more slender and gaunt. In the three months since he had escaped the compound in Kent, he figured he had lost at least thirty pounds. His face was thinner, the cheeks more hollow. The stress of living rough had aged him, he was certain of that.

Since the escape, Harry had become unrecognizable from the man ruthlessly hunted by the authorities. This was partly because of his enforced Hermit-like existence, but the new appearance served him well to avoid detection. The police often carried small mobile devices that carried built-in face recognition software. They only had to point it at the face of a suspect and the device would instantly trawl the vast police database of offenders to match the image.

His lank hair was now long and straggly, dirty and matted from lack of care. A grey-streaked unkempt beard covered the bottom half of his face. He normally liked to keep even, neatly groomed stubble, in vogue with today's fashion but lacking the most basic amenities, he had little choice. He had to be careful his beard did not become home to a host of unwelcome squatters. Even with the unruly hirsute mass around his face, there were no guarantees he would avoid detection if by chance he was scrutinized by the facial device. It worked on a number of parameters, including facial contours, which the beard cloaked efficiently, but there were others, such as eye shape, that were less easy to disguise, and the devices worked from long range. He had to remain vigilant when he ventured into the town.

Harry emerged from the makeshift shelter set in the base of a huge fallen oak tree that he now called home and shivered in the still morning air. Although it was only the middle of October, his breath was already condensing in front of him, the chill a portent of a long hard winter ahead. The weak sun filtered through the trees, creating sparkling diamonds of light as it reflected off the dew on the bushes that surrounded his tiny encampment. The birds no longer sang, as if they too had been silenced like so many dissidents who had protested against the authoritarian regime that had swept to power and imposed chaos and violence of a magnitude never before seen in this country.

He surveyed the densely wooded area around him, crouching low as he had conditioned himself to do, alert for signs of movement. He had stayed off the grid for several months, but he remained a hunted man. Every day was a matter of survival. He had avoided several close calls, narrowly escaping the clutches of the State Secret Police that patrolled the woods in the hope of finding wanted 'criminals' hiding out in places like these. They stalked the woods dressed all in black, even their faces covered in black ski masks. The SSP, or the *'Blackhearts'* as they were often called in the bourgeois press, had become a highly feared and reviled offshoot of the People's Independent Army, the PIA, the paramilitary organization with a reputation for violence all too familiar to many broken families.

Although it had been over three months since Prime Minister Lawrence Pelham's government forces had issued a warrant for his arrest, Harry knew he remained high on their wanted list. On the occasions he was forced to walk into town for essential supplies, usually in broad daylight where he hoped to remain inconspicuous amongst crowds of people, he saw the media screens placed at the corner of every main thoroughfare. The screens blared out Pelham's propaganda to the masses, his engaging features filling the twenty foot screens like a benign shepherd watching over his flock. His words resounded across the city centres and town squares of the country, forcing his subjects to listen to his twisted vision for a New Britain.

Often the screens would cut to the faces of the government's most wanted, the 'terrorists and criminals' who, he thundered, were the enemy of every citizen of this great country. The faces of these 'saboteurs of a better society,' cleverly portrayed with wild eyes and sunken cheeks, would peer down at the masses like a macabre roll call. Scrolling beneath the mug-shots in large black letters were the 'crimes' of these wanted men, followed by Pelham returning to the screen, urging his faithful, loyal subjects to do the right thing and flush out these extremists. He promised a substantial reward to those who turned them in to the State Secret Police, followed by a barely disguised threat of severe repercussions to anyone failing in their civic duty.

About a month ago Harry had looked up at the screen and an icy tremor stabbed through him as he saw his own face peering back. His grim visage filled the entire twenty-foot screen, his crimes, including murder and treason, scrolling across the image. Glancing around in panic, he found that people merely brushed past him, heads down and ignoring him. He spotted an Order Police armoured truck in the distance, leisurely patrolling the street, too far away to bother him. Even so he had hastily gathered his supplies and left town.

He brought his mind back to the present. Keeping low, he hurried through tall grass to the nearby stream to wash. The tinkling of the tiny stream brought a false feeling of peace and tranquillity, and the water was cold but refreshing. Harry felt the first pangs of hunger in his stomach, and filling his water bottle, he headed back to his tiny concealed shelter that housed his meagre provisions, currently goat's cheese and bread. He was desperate for a cup of tea to stave off the morning chill, but decided against it. Boiling water would require a fire that would almost certainly attract unwelcome attention. Only on rare occasions when the craving was too great would he be foolhardy enough to risk detection by lighting a fire, always some distance into the woods away from his shelter. He was tired of living in fear, a fugitive from the perverse justice that held sway over the country, the rule of law now merely a distant recollection. As temperatures dropped later in the season, a fire would soon become a necessity not a luxury; but lighting a fire to survive could be the very thing that could trigger his demise, he thought ironically.

Harry finished his breakfast, forcing the stale bread down, not knowing when he would eat next. He needed to head back into town, a four mile hike, avoiding the roads and people until he reached his destination. He had become adept at stealing and shoplifting, but he knew he was on borrowed time. The Order Police would discover who the dishevelled vagrant really was. He still recalled the ordinary police forces patrolling the streets to serve and protect the ordinary citizen. The patrol cars had been replaced by military style armoured jeeps and the uniform by full body armour and sub-machine guns, so this new breed of police looked and acted like an occupying force. They were just another part of the government machine designed to harass and intimidate citizens. As a political offender, Harry would be handed over to the paramilitary State Secret Police, and then.... he did not wish to contemplate. The stories of what the SSP did to dissidents sometimes filtered through to him despite his enforced absence from the media. Getting caught was not an option.

As he wandered toward town, passing the tiny village of Charlton-All-Saints, its fire-bombed church spire a twisted wreck silhouetted black against the hazy sky, he reflected on that fateful day back in July when the compound had been destroyed and he had narrowly escaped with Julianne. He could picture the day like a movie running inside his head, every detail sharp and distinct. It was the last time he had seen Julianne, and he had to admit to himself that he missed her terribly. Since the demolition of the final structured resistance, weak as it was, Pelham had kept the country in a tight stranglehold. His government was determined to quash any insurgency before it gained traction. There was little organized opposition either in Parliament or on the streets. Since the passing of the U.K. Enabling Act, a law which gave the Cabinet authority to enact new legislation without Parliamentary approval, the regime's power had increased steadily. Allied to that was the growth in Pelham's personal dominance. He now ran the country like his own personal fiefdom, impervious to challenge. His warped vision for Britain had changed the political and social landscape even faster than that envisaged in his leaked Cabinet memo *'Giving Britain Back to the British – A Five Year Vision For Restoring Power,'* the document that had been the originator of Harry's current plight.

On that scorching hot day in July, from the relative safety of the hill overlooking the sweeping valley, they had witnessed army tanks thunder into the compound and raze the farmhouse and its outbuildings to the ground. There would have been few survivors and he had to acknowledge that Julianne had saved his life by guiding them through the old, stinking tunnel that led them clear of the devastation. Even so, he had told her that he had to move on, to somehow try and rescue his family from the deportation camp. She had cried but understood, yet he still felt compelled to engage in one final act of cruelty on her, as if to justify his exodus from her. He shook his head with guilt at the memory as he ran through that terrible July day in his mind.

"I heard you in the house Julianne."

She stopped crying and blinked in surprise, her beautiful hazel eyes blotchy and bloodshot. Down in the valley, the carnage was subsiding, but the rumble of the tanks and the solid boom from their turret guns still resounded through the stifling summer air.

"I was there by the window before sunrise. You were with Sean and Luka - plotting to kill me."

Julianne visibly flinched, as if stung by his accusatory tone. "You've got it wrong," she protested. "It wasn't like that." She tried to slip her hand back into his, but he jabbed it away like hot metal.

"What was it like then?" he sneered.

Julianne had an edge to her voice, a cross between defensiveness and indignation. "I had to go along with it or I would have betrayed us both. You know how Sean felt about you. Sticking up for you would have probably got me killed too. He was becoming more un-balanced with every passing day. You saw how paranoid he was. You cannot reason with the type of person Sean had become and Luka was just as volatile." She let out an exasperated sigh and rubbed her eyes. "I saved your life, remember?" she snapped.

Harry foolishly snapped back and instantly regretted his impetu-ousness. "You betrayed me. How can I trust you now?"

She shot him a wounded look, her chin quivering. Harry thought she was going to burst into another flood of tears and he bit his lip, wishing to take back his accusing words. However, Julianne did two things he least expected. First, she delivered a stinging blow across one side of his face, her expression shifting from sorrow to pure anger as she did so. A white light flashed across his vision and he clutched his raw cheek, surprised at the ferocity of the strike, as if all the anger at his cruelty had been channelled into one blow. He almost welcomed the throbbing hurt, pleased that Sean's fierce treat-ment had not blunted her feisty edge.

He had little time to react to her second unexpected action. She swiftly pulled out a small revolver from around her hip, concealed by her long, baggy linen shirt, and pointed it directly at Harry's chest. He instinctively raised his hands in a placating gesture and noticed her hand trembling. Beads of sweat had formed on her forehead, mixing in with the dirt that still clung to her face from their tunnel escape.

"Maybe," she began, half sobbing, "You can't trust me but I sure as hell could never trust you!" Julianne paused, her chest rising and falling under her filthy white shirt as if she were trying to catch her breath. "Perhaps this way it's for the best."

Harry stared at the tiny revolver, a shudder of apprehension piercing through him. "What on earth are you talking about?" His voice was unsteady.

Julianne said nothing, but the tiniest crease of a smile formed on the corner of her mouth. Her grip no longer wavered, and her smile broadened as she raised the gun. She was clearly enjoying his discomfort.

"You don't have to do this Julianne," he pleaded. His voice was high-pitched and he swallowed hard to relieve the knot in his stomach.

"Yes I do," she replied resolutely. Then she laughed and flipped the gun in her hand and held it out to Harry handle first. "Jesus, Harry did you think I was going to shoot you? I could never do that despite the fact that you are an insensitive, callous bastard. It was amusing to watch your expression for a minute there."

Harry tentatively took the weapon, too confused to reply.

"If you are going to embark on a suicidal mission to try and save your ex-wife and child, you'll need this more than me. It's loaded with several rounds of ammunition but it might keep you safe for a while. I would wish you luck but it's a miracle you'll need to avoid getting killed."

Harry took the gun and mumbled his thanks. In the awkward silence that followed he knew he had to depart quickly to avoid causing Julianne any more heartache.

He recalled the feel of her soft lips, cool against the burning cheek she had slapped only a few minutes before, as they made their sad, unspoken farewell, both silently contemplating whether this would be the last time they saw each other. What he wouldn't give now for the feel of human contact, the tender touch of her delicate hands. She had urged him one more time to stay with him, but he was too stubborn to listen. She never revealed her plans, and he had not asked, but he sincerely hoped that she was still alive somewhere plotting the downfall of this malevolent regime. She had been right about one thing. It was a dangerous, reckless mission to go after his former wife Tamara and their son Byron. He was not even certain they were still at the deportation camp. Even if they were he had no idea how he would rescue them. He had tried once before, and had been fortunate that the guards had merely interrogated him and kicked him out of the camp.

Since Pelham's defining speech at Wembley when he had set out his vision for the nation, there had been a subtle shift in the mood of the country. He doubted the camp leaders would be so lenient if he was caught again, but he had convinced himself it was his only option. He had to do something positive rather than sit back waiting to be hunted down while the nation around him collapsed.

So with the conviction of a man committed to his cause, he had set off across the valley, palls of smoke rising into the air from the shattered compound, the roar of the tanks still audible, punctuated by the odd chilling scream. He did not realize at the time that Julianne's pessimistic assessment of his prospects would be so intuitive.

# CHAPTER 2

A chilly autumn mist hung in the air as Harry continued walking to Salisbury. The distant drone of a vehicle invaded his thoughts and he instinctively sought cover in the unkempt undergrowth by the roadside. The straggly bush was unyielding and pressed painfully at his skin, but Harry dived in, oblivious to the sharp thorns until he was completely concealed. Although his route was set back from the road, he dared not risk being seen. The traffic into town had reduced considerably since the regime had introduced compulsory road blocks for cross county travellers, but the odd vehicle still passed by on this minor road, and even civilian cars could not be trusted. A vagrant walking alone on the side of the road was sure to attract suspicion and the public had been seduced by the promise of reward for turning in potential opponents to the regime accompanied by threats of reprisals for failure to do so.

As he peered out he saw an army jeep pass by occupied by three armed soldiers and the driver, its wheels squealing as it swerved to avoid a pothole. It quickly roared off into the distance and Harry emerged, again able to enjoy the relative peace, a rare commodity in this chaotic land. His thoughts turned again to the terrible events three months before that unfolded after he left Julianne.

Grasping the gun that Julianne had given to him, he continued to lope across the valley, half jogging, realizing he had no plan how to reach the deportation camp. He also had no transport, and as he reached a small side road that skirted the valley, he began to consider his mission. His aim was to rescue his family and reach the ferry to Ireland, where he still had some distant cousins living in the suburbs outside Dublin, or so he assumed. It had been ten years since he had heard from them, and it would be necessary to track them down when he reached Ireland. His more immediate problem was to seek transport, and as a dirty white van appeared in the distance he turned the gun over in his hands and made his decision.

With no other traffic around, he slipped the gun into his pocket and stepped out into the road. He began waving frantically at the van and as it bounded along over the small rise in the road. It was a huge risk and Harry prepared to swiftly jump out of the way. To his surprise the van slowed, and Harry could see the driver inside despite the shadows flitting across the windscreen. The van had a roof rack and its big black letters on the side suggested a local tradesman. It looked like the driver was alone, which made life easier. The vehicle pulled over to the side, brakes squealing.

Harry raced around the side of the vehicle and saw the driver. He had an open, friendly face, his pale features framed by a shock of dark curly hair. Even from his sitting position in the cab Harry could tell he was tall and gawky, his long legs forced to squeeze tight in the cramped footwell. When he spoke it was in a broad Geordie accent, a man far from home. "Is everything okay?" he said, his caramel eyes crinkling into a frown of genuine concern.

"Oh thank God you stopped!" cried Harry. "My car was set

upon by a group of youths. I barely got out alive! Can you drive me into town?" It had been a long time since Harry had acted at the Cambridge footlights, and he had not even been good at lying to Tamara when he strenuously denied having an affair. The driver hesitated before he nodded. "Get in."

He reached over to the passenger side of the cab and unlocked the door. Harry gratefully jumped in and expressed his thanks. The driver noticed Harry's dishevelled appearance and wrinkled his nose. "The name's Joe. Whoa, did they throw you in a sewer? I would shake your hand but I am not sure what I might catch," he laughed, giving a disarming smile.

Harry smiled weakly, embarrassed by his condition having made his escape through the dirty tunnel with Julianne barely an hour earlier. "It's a long story," he muttered softly. He fumbled in his pocket and glanced in the rear windscreen. He was relieved to see no traffic or pedestrians on the small side road. Before Joe could move off, Harry pulled out his small revolver and pointed it squarely at the driver, whose friendly expression froze. He stared at the gun apprehensively and then at Harry, his eyes registering an unspoken fear.

"Don't be afraid," Harry reassured him. As long as you listen and do what I say I have absolutely no reason to use this. I need you to drive me to Salisbury. If you do then you and I will get along fine but be warned; I am a little nervous right now and this trigger does not need much pressure."

"Salisbury? That's nearly a hundred miles away! We'll never get through with all the Army checkpoints. Please don't shoot. I have a family," he pleaded, eyes wide with fright.

Harry had to reluctantly admit to himself that Joe was probably right. If the checkpoints had already been set up, they had little chance of reaching Salisbury. What the hell was he doing pointing a gun he did not know how to use at an innocent man? He wasn't a criminal, but desperate times called for desperate measures. "Just drive. I'll figure out how we get past the checkpoints," he replied. "Stay on the side roads as much as you can. I will direct you."

Joe glanced from Harry to the gun, clearly regretting his attempt to be a good Samaritan. He gunned the engine and the van raced forward, occasionally bouncing on the uneven road surface. Joe kept the windows open, and the warm, sultry air blew into the cab. The wind felt refreshing to Harry after the claustrophobic tunnel he and Julianne had used to escape from the carnage when the compound was attacked. They spoke only briefly, Joe explaining that he was a carpenter on the way to a job. "My gaffer's going to be furious," he complained, a little calmer.

For a while they encountered little traffic and lapsed into silence, Harry holding the gun as steadily as possible, trying to calm his trembling hands. There was no way he could keep the gun pointed for the duration of the journey and his captive realized that, occasionally stealing furtive glances in his direction. Then Joe broke the heavy silence. "You look familiar. Have I seen you before?"

"No you haven't," replied Harry curtly. "Shut up and keep driving."

Joe got the hint but continued to cast sideways glances at Harry as they continued along a number of small roads under Harry's guidance. They were the only words exchanged between them until Joe asked, "Do you mind if I turn on the radio?"

Harry shrugged. "Be my guest. It's probably the usual propaganda crap anyway."

They had encountered light traffic, but so far there was no sign of any militia. Harry remained alert, keeping his gun low and concealed from the outside. He suddenly felt an overwhelming tiredness. It was not even midday but he had not yet eaten, and as warm air blew in from the window, the humidity seemed to sap his strength. Joe pressed the digital dial and the numbers flickered until they found a news station. The newscaster announced in perfectly enunciated BBC English the breaking news that one of the key terrorist camps at a farmhouse near Sevenoaks had been destroyed. He declared it a glorious victory for the military in their continuous fight against the malevolent forces that sought to resist Prime Minister Pelham's great vision for the nation.

Joe listened intently as he negotiated a deep pothole and then turned to Harry, a glint of suspicion surfacing in his eyes. "That's not far from where I picked you up. I saw smoke rising into the sky from the valley."

Harry said nothing but his expression betrayed him. He always found it difficult to conceal his true feelings, as Tamara had often reminded him during their divorce proceedings.

The BBC announcer continued in his faultless English. Harry could imagine him sitting there in a tuxedo and bow tie, slicked back hair, addressing the nation in his dulcet tones, speaking into the large boom microphone. Only that image belonged to another time, the era of Pathé News and the Queen's coronation. The reality was that he had probably been given a script and surrounded by soldiers to encourage him not to slip up. "There are unconfirmed reports that the murderer of the Cabinet Minister Graham Matheson was hiding out in the compound, but he is unaccounted for and it is believed he may have escaped. Harry Clarke is considered armed and dangerous and residents in the area are asked to remain vigilant. There is a reward for information leading to his capture."

Joe turned again to look at Harry, but this time it was a full, piercing stare, as if his mind had suddenly grasped the situation. "You're Harry Clarke, aren't you," he said accusingly, a tremor in his voice.

Harry waved the gun threateningly. "Keep your eyes on the road. It doesn't matter who I am."

The tall Geordie turned back to the road just in time to swerve away from the wreckage of a burnt out car abandoned by the roadside. The carcass of the vehicle was still smoking, as if the damage was fairly fresh, but Harry could see no sign of anyone around.

Joe, eyes now fixed on the road, said, "Please don't kill me. My two young boys don't have anyone else. That bloody politician probably deserved it, but I'm just an ordinary guy trying to get by."

Harry snorted with derision. "You can't believe everything you hear in the media you know. Most of what the Press feed us is a parody of the truth, especially now the Tories are in power."

"So you didn't kill him?" Joe's voice held a tinge of relief.

"You can believe what you like. I'm not interested. I just need you to get me to Salisbury and we go our separate ways and no one gets hurt."

"Why Salisbury?" enquired Joe.

"They're holding my ex-wife and our son at the deportation camp there."

"I'm sorry to hear that but you will never get in. I've heard security is tight, especially with the strange outbreaks there."

"Like I said, don't believe everything you hear in the media," Harry retorted.

They continued in tense silence. Harry watched Joe fidget nervously, wiping sweaty palms on his khaki pants and then gripping the steering wheel tightly. His face was a grim mask, and the sweat trickling down his greasy forehead was clearly more than from the heat and humidity. Traffic remained light, even on the wider highway south of the M25 motorway that skirted the southern edge of London and through Reigate and Dorking.

Harry was uncomfortable taking the main road, but there appeared few options, and as they rounded a curve onto a long, straight section a little east of Guildford, his worst fears were confirmed. Apart from the heat haze shimmering above the road, visibility was clear in the cloudless sky, and far ahead of them the road was divided by a makeshift barrier with two green military jeeps parked across the road so that access was limited to one line of traffic. Joe uttered a small cry of panic.

"Calm down Joe," Harry admonished him. "Pull over, quickly."

Joe stopped on the side of the road and Harry climbed over the seats and squeezed into a tiny alcove behind the driver's seat, making himself as small as possible. "Remember I'm right behind you and I still have the gun. If you keep it cool and don't arouse their suspicion we will get through." Harry did not sound convincing even to himself. "If they decide to search the van we're done for anyway," he added.

Joe pulled back onto the road and approached the barrier slowly. It was too late to turn back. "What shall I say?" he said, voice trembling.

"Use your imagination. Just don't tell them the truth." growled Harry, twisting his body with discomfort in the tiny space. The soldiers waved two cars in front through after a brief stop and then it was their turn.

A surly looking soldier, barely out of his teens, cigarette hanging out of his mouth, stepped in front of the van and motioned for the driver to open his window. Joe obliged and the soldier stepped to the window and took the butt from his mouth, blowing stale smoke into the van's interior.

"Where ya goin'?" he asked in an arrogant voice clearly intended to convey his authority.

Joe hesitated for a second. "I'm a carpenter. I have a job in Farnham."

"Oh yeah? Got any papers?" Harry could see the soldier's serious expression from a tiny gap in the seat.

Joe hesitated and then pulled out a couple of twenty pound notes. He leaned forward conspiratorially, pressing the money discreetly into the young soldier's hands so his nearby colleagues could not see. In a low voice, he said, "Look, between you and me it's a cash job. Got to make a living any way we can right? If the client gives me papers I have to declare it. You know what I mean?"

The young soldier hesitated, picking at an acne spot and staring at the cash. The silence hung heavy for several seconds before the soldier resolved his inner conflict and relented. "Alright, mate on your way." The soldier stubbed out his cigarette, pocketed the cash and waved at his colleagues. They raised the temporary metal barrier and the van passed through. As the checkpoint receded into the distance, Harry clambered into the passenger seat, his limbs stiff. Joe let out his breath in one long sigh. "Whoa, that was close," he gasped.

"You did amazingly well."

"Yeah and you owe me forty quid. Are you sure you want to go to Salisbury? There will be more checkpoints. Please mate can I let you off here? I won't say anything to anyone I promise."

Harry gave a guilty sigh. "I can't, I'm sorry. I have to get to Salisbury quickly. You're my ride."

# CHAPTER 3

For the next several hours the drive was uneventful as they skirted past Farnham and Winchester south-west toward their destination. Taking several back roads, they encountered no more checkpoints. The tension eased a little and they even made some small talk. Joe had convinced himself that whatever his assailant was, it was not the cold-blooded murderer portrayed in the media.

"Yes I am a fugitive," Harry said in answer to a question Joe raised. "But we all are in some ways. If they discover you've been driving me they'll arrest you too as an accessory," he warned. "They won't listen to your protests that you were taken at gunpoint. That's just unnecessary detail."

It was mid-afternoon by the time they reached the outskirts of Salisbury and Harry directed Joe south of the town toward the village of Nunton, near to where he knew the deportation camp was situated. As they got closer to the area the traffic almost died, and that somehow felt ominous to Harry.

"We have to avoid the town as far as possible. Follow the A30 as far as you can and then we will take the side roads heading toward the New Forest and pick up signs for the village," instructed Harry. Joe complied and presently they turned onto the side road, which was degraded and full of potholes, even worse than when Harry had recently driven on his first attempt to rescue his family. Only the odd car kept them company, and even the farmhouses set back from the side of the road appeared empty. They passed a local pub, the *Greyfriars Inn*. By this time they were both hungry and Harry craved a pint of beer to stave off his thirst in the heat. However, the parking lot was empty and the sign, a head-shot of a shaven headed monk dressed in coarse grey robes, hung still and lifeless. They pressed on, hoping for more positive signs of life. As they turned a bend in the road, large cedar trees pressing in on either side, a large flatbed truck with a tall rusting iron cage in the back appeared in front of them. Joe gave a gasp as he saw the filthy, hopeless occupants crammed into the metal cage, squeezed tighter than a London subway at rush hour. Dirty fingers wrapped themselves around the square metal fencing and desperate eyes peered out from the small gaps.

As the vehicles passed in opposite directions, Joe caught only fleeting glimpses of their faces, young and old, but it was enough. "I heard about these but I refused to believe it."

Harry was less shocked. "This is the barbarity I want to rescue my wife and son from."

Harry glanced at Joe. His face registered revulsion. The guy was clearly a decent, ordinary family man, totally disinterested in politics. It was his own citizens, people like Joe that Pelham's regime was deceiving. Most of them would be appalled if they witnessed the government's actions first hand, no matter how much spin Pelham weaved about it being for the future benefit of the nation.

Harry directed them to turn off onto another side road which ran, as far as he could recall, very close to the village of Nunton, near the camp's location. The road undulated until they entered a forest where the trees formed an archway, the canopies providing a wel-come relief from the hot afternoon sun. The road began to descend steeply and Joe slowed down as the road twisted and turned through the woods, each bend tight into another corner until the road evened out and they had descended into the valley floor. It turned rapidly darker despite dappled shafts of sunlight piercing through the foliage.

When their eyes finally adjusted to the gloom, it was too late. Emerging from the shadows was another checkpoint and this time it was much closer. The soldiers on guard immediately stood alert and Harry knew it was too late to turn back. The soldiers waited ex-pectantly as the van slowed. "Stick to the same story and keep a cool head like you did last time and we may get past," he hissed.

There was no time for Harry to hide, and as the van crawled closer to the checkpoint, an acidic feeling of apprehension rose in his stomach. The soldiers here were older, grim-faced, and at least five of them marched vigorously to the van to surround it, as if they were happy to be called into action after a long period of inactivity. Harry doubted they received much traffic on this small road in the woods, yet this checkpoint was bigger than the one they had encoun-tered earlier.

Joe wound down his window and forced a weak smile. "After-noon," he said, trying to sound casual.

The soldier at his window looked in his late forties. His fuzzy moustache had been badly trimmed and was flecked with grey, the same colour as his dead looking eyes. His weathered, lined face was set like alabaster, devoid of any expression. "Papers?" he demanded curtly, his cold eyes peering into the cab, appraising them.

Harry stayed silent but knew Joe's next response would be critical. "We're carpenters and we have a job for a wealthy client. It's a….a cash job if you know what I mean?" Joe winked conspiratorially but the soldier was unmoved. "You don't pass here without proper papers. Don't you know this is a restricted zone? Where are you going anyway?" His gruff voice conveyed a hint of irritation.

Harry intervened, leaning toward the window. "It's okay, we'll turn around. The client was a tosser anyway."

The lifeless eyes flickered. "It's not as simple as that," he warned them.

A younger soldier joined him at the van's window, curious at the delay. As he looked into the cab his eyes locked with Harry's and Harry quickly looked down but it was too late. The younger soldier continued to stare. "Here," he said tersely, "Don't I know you?"

Harry avoided his gaze. "I doubt it. We're from London. I have never been here before."

The soldier was unconvinced and in the heavy silence, his thin lips moved wordlessly with the effort of recall. Then without warning his expression turned darker, bushy eyebrows knitting together in a deep frown. "I remember now. You're the idiot that broke into the camp a few weeks ago." A cold anger spread across his features. "Get out of the vehicle!" he barked at them.

Harry knew the charade was over. He prodded Joe hard with the gun. "Go go go!" he screamed at the driver. With a deafening screech the wheels spun and the van jolted forward as Joe hit the accelerator. The van careened through the metal barriers with a hefty thud, forcing two soldiers to dive for cover, and the van broke free, dragging a broken section of the barrier before it clattered away on the road as Joe fought to stay in control. They heard the shouts and curses of the soldiers behind them and an engine quickly starting up. Harry glanced behind and in the gloomy forest spotted the dark green shape of a military jeep racing behind them.

"Faster Joe!" screamed Harry. The rear windscreen shattered and a bullet whizzed past Harry's ear, pinging off the dashboard. Harry dived down into his seat and Joe cried out in panic, trying desperately to keep the van in a straight line as it slipped and lurched around on the debris in the road.

Another bullet ripped through the headrest where Harry's head had been a second earlier and Joe swerved, now hollering in panic. Harry, crouched low in the seat, could see the military jeep in the passenger wing mirror, its lights flashing rapidly and weaving skilfully around the debris in the road so that it gained on them fast.

"Move it! They're nearly on us!" Harry yelled.

The van suddenly veered to one side and Joe fought to stay in control. Harry felt the van career crazily as if they had shot out a tyre. Joe realized it too but before he could correct the van's wild lurching, he let out a small grunt and slumped over the wheel, his head resting on the horn so that its ear splitting howl bounced around the confines of the cab. As Joe's head flopped forward, Harry saw the entry wound, a gaping hole pumping out blood, framed by bone and ragged tissue. The vehicle swerved off the road and bounced along the uneven forest floor, bushes slapping against the side, the undercarriage hitting hard against protruding tree roots on the ground. Harry was jolted around and Joe's lifeless body slumped down in the seat, head lolling at an unnatural angle, the light gone from the wide open, frightened eyes.

The van was still travelling at speed when a huge oak tree materialized in Harry's field of vision. He swung open the passenger door and rolled out of the van onto the rough ground a second before it slammed head on into the tree and crumpled like a concertina, rolled over and burst into flames. Harry immediately sprinted off into the forest, sharp brambles tearing at his skin, stumbling blindly forward. He took one quick glance around him and saw that the jeep had stopped close to the shattered van, the flames blackening the painted white metal of the chassis. No-one appeared to be chasing him, at least not yet. The van's chassis had shielded his exit, buying him precious time. He kept moving fast however, taking no chances. His breathing was laboured but his escape was fuelled by adrenaline, and only when he reached a small, sheltered clearing did he finally drop to the ground, utterly exhausted.

He scrambled into a sheltered cove hollowed out under the cover of a huge oak tree and concealed himself under a bed of leaves, his body shaking uncontrollably. He fought to stay motionless, and within a minute he saw a pair of soldiers storm past at a light jog, scanning the area, rifles poised. Harry dared not breathe as they passed within ten feet of him but they were soon gone. He stayed there all night before venturing out in the humid morning air, alert for any signs of his pursuers. When he was sure the area was clear, he dropped to his knees and allowed himself the luxury of breaking into bitter tears of frustration as guilt over Joe's death overwhelmed him.

# CHAPTER 4

Although Joe's death had been three months ago, the guilt and outrage still tore at Harry like a festering wound that wouldn't heal. The man had been an innocent victim of Harry's selfish desire to reach the camp again on a reckless, hopeless mission. Harry rarely slept for long but there were times when he tossed and turned on his woven mat of leaves that served as a mattress in the sturdy 'A' frame shelter he had built. His nightmares woke him, and a recurring dream was of him telling Joe's two boys that they were now orphans, the children howling uncontrollably as they blamed Harry for killing their father. He would never know or see those children, yet his actions had probably destroyed their lives in addition to that of a good man. He felt a mild repulsion as he recalled Joe pleading with Harry not to shoot him. What was it he had said? *I'm just an ordinary guy trying to get by.* Harry was not a criminal but he had felt like one. After the killing he had fallen into a deep trough of depression, which had evolved into an emotional passivity, his actions fuelled by the will to survive.

Harry had escaped and wandered in the forest far from any army or police patrols, until he had found a suitable hiding place and built a primitive shelter in the blackened, gnarled hole of a fallen oak tree using branches and leaves. He had not intended to stay long. It was a temporary shelter as he contemplated his next move and waited for the clamour surrounding his escape to die down. At the time he was still convinced he could break into the camp. Instead Harry had spent the last three months living like a vagrant, staying off the grid, petrified that one day he'd be found, while observing the nation deteriorating under the despotic rule of the Conservatives.

He shivered in the chilly October air but reached Salisbury town centre without further incident, though he remained alert. There were plenty of beggars sitting listlessly in doorways, and the general level of poverty that had permeated through society meant his appearance was not in itself startling. He had refused to sit on a street corner and beg like so many people whose pride had deserted them in the effort of survival.

It was incredible the lengths people would go to just to survive, but street begging was not a wise option. In the desperate daily struggle across all sectors of society, people's compassion had been eroded to the point where a beggar located in the same place day after day could starve to death and remain virtually unnoticed. They became invisible after a while, except to the gun-toting Order Police, who occasionally enjoyed sadistically beating these poor unfortunate homeless dropouts. It was a peril of being on the streets. These beggars were often people who in better times were respected family men and women with homes and jobs, before Pelham had targeted the immigrant population, forcing thousands of families to flee. Not all were immigrants, however. Many were an unfortunate by-product of his policies, the very people he had promised greater jobs and prosperity. Harry also noticed an increasing incidence of children appearing on the streets.

Harry's strategy was risky but generally more productive. He had become quite adept at shoplifting from local stores, but there had been several close calls. In the last few weeks he had been recognized by several storekeepers and chased out, a few of them shouting at the top of their lungs for the police, forcing Harry to flee. This lifestyle only had a limited duration and soon he might be forced to beg for food along with the feckless vagrants drifting aimlessly, at the mercy of the kindness of strangers or the random beatings of the Order Police.

He still retained some pride, although appalled by his own appearance. He remained vigilant, particularly when the People's Independent Army or the SSP were in town. It was now late morning and people went about their daily business, heads bowed, afraid to stay out longer than necessary in case they were accosted for interrogation by the police or paramilitary forces. At both ends of the High Street a small collection of jeeps belonging to the Order Police were assembled. Officers patrolled the area, gripping their Heckler & Koch assault rifles menacingly as they arrogantly strolled along the sidewalk. They did not expect any trouble but revelled in their intimidating presence, glaring at passersby who dared not catch their eye. The irony was not lost on Harry. Only five months before he had complained about the lack of a police presence on the streets. Pelham had promised in his manifesto to put the nation's police back on the streets, and he had certainly done that. Now they were a ubiquitous presence, their style of policing very different from those forces from which they had evolved.

However the Order Police represented a wholly less sinister

and threatening presence than the other authoritarian forces which controlled the citizens through fear and intimidation. The People's Independent Army had evolved from the roughneck organization known as FREE, the Fight to Return England to the English. Its members were openly racist, proud of their neo-Nazi tendencies, and at first the government had superficially condemned the organization. However, after its successful boycott of foreign businesses both online and physically, and the attempted assassination on the Prime Minister at Wembley last June, Pelham had used them to develop his own private army under the direction of the 'thug in a suit' Adam Griffiths. FREE flourished as a result, to the extent that it had now become a mainstream national organization; a reviled street force that had also taken over from the army as the chief administrators of the deportation camps.

The State Secret Police also consisted of FREE members. They were its interrogation and investigation arm, examining acts of treason, espionage, sabotage, terrorism and criminal attacks (such as harbouring immigrants) against the Party and the nation in general. The SSP also reported to Griffiths, but what made them so despised by society at large was that they were not subject to judicial oversight, following a special parliamentary decree that the Party had forced through during the crisis in the summer when Pelham declared martial law. This meant they could act with impunity and never be called to account for their actions in a court of law. Griffiths had summed up the rationale by stating that "as long as the SSP carries out the will of the leadership, it is acting legally." This was open to interpretation, and the SSP's reputation for violence had spread rapidly, able to attack with impunity. In their all-black uniforms and black ski masks, their chilling presence meant that their colloquial name of the *Blackhearts* was well deserved.

Harry shuffled down the street, acutely aware that his dishevelled appearance was likely to attract more attention, despite the anonymity it afforded him. He stayed in town only as long as necessary to replenish his supplies, and as far away from the police as possible. Overhead the media screens screamed at the people below, spewing out its propaganda, the presenter, a former game show host with slicked back hair and a ponytail, lecturing the people that their quality of life had never been better.

Harry headed for the store, his senses alert as always at these times of potential danger. He surveyed the street. There were piles of rubble and broken concrete at various points along the street, where mortar bombs had taken out buildings. Here and there those buildings had not collapsed completely and stood like empty skeletons of steel, pieces of concrete hanging from them like ragged flesh. Even the Tudor buildings, with their timber cross beams and white facades that added character to this attractive tourist town were showing severe signs of neglect and depreciation. Like the people, the whole street now looked shabby and unkempt. However, it was the gallows standing in the market square that really defined how the nation had degenerated.

Harry was well aware from his occasional forays onto the social media circuit that Salisbury had not suffered as much as those towns and cities with a greater density of ethnic residents. Most of them had become urban battlegrounds in which pockets of resistance had been ruthlessly crushed, the militia's methods brutal and direct; the extensive property damage was an unfortunate by-product of the militia's activities. The media, now almost entirely controlled by the government, heralded the great victories and sacrifices of the British military machine as it rid the country of the scourge of insurgents. Most large towns were still occupied by the threatening presence of soldiers as well as Order Police, a deterrent to anyone who stepped out of line.

The nation had only recently lifted martial law, and the Order Police had assumed the role of keeping order on the streets previously entrusted to the army. The army remained in the background to help deal with any sporadic trouble, although such incidents had decreased recently, hence the lifting of martial law. With the loyalty of the Armed Forces, Pelham's power was unassailable.

Although Harry was aware that they sometimes patrolled the woods where his tiny encampment lay, the SSP also made the odd appearance in town. It was usually when they were investigating a specific report, maybe of a dissident on the run, or an escaped immigrant from the deportation camp. Harry recalled the first time he had seen them in town. They had swept through the town in a battered Toyota pick-up truck, all of them apart from the driver riding in the back, perched on the edge of the trailer's side walls, guns visible but faces hidden behind menacing ski masks. Only one of them was lacking his mask and Harry happened to catch his eye as the truck breezed past. Quite stupidly, on reflection, Harry found himself staring. The soldier was hardly more than a boy, twenty at most but his shaved head and metallic grey eyes radiated hostility. As they locked eyes, he raised his weapon, a small Beretta style handgun, and pretended to reel off a number of shots at Harry, making inane popping noises as he did so. As the truck cruised on, Harry continued to gawp until a bony but surprisingly firm hand grasped his shoulder and shook him fiercely.

He turned to see a gaunt-faced old man of at least seventy, with a shock of unruly white hair, his wild eyes round like marbles in their hollow sockets. His thin mouth moved wordlessly as he struggled with his dentures. "What are you doing, staring at them like that?" he finally spat out. "D'ya have a death wish?" He paused, chewing like a cow. "You never look them in the eye. They'll take you away and they'll beat you 'til there's nothing left. They're itching for a fight. Don't give 'em a reason." He turned and lifted his shirt to expose his bare back. The skin was purple with contusions and an ugly, ragged scar, still fresh, ran diagonally from his right shoulder to his left hip. Harry recalled how he had gasped in shock but before he could respond, the man had quickly disappeared, afraid to remain outside while the SSP was patrolling.

Today a similar pick-up full of SSP agents roamed the street, headed in Harry's direction. People began to disperse quickly, afraid they might be randomly targeted by these masked thugs. Harry stepped back from the roadside, watching the vehicle carefully. Their presence caused a stir amongst the people that wasn't there when the regular Order Police patrolled. The crowd began to anxiously drift away when a projectile was hurled at the truck. It looked to Harry like rotten fruit, and it splattered harmlessly on the side of the vehicle, leaving a streaked red mark on the white chassis.

Although the ski masks hid their expressions, Harry had no doubt the SSP agents were enraged. Immediately five of them jumped off the back of the truck and went racing toward the source, guns raised. The small crowd scattered in panic, and the agents ran toward a young man who, realizing he had been spotted, fled down an adjoining street, pushing past several confused people also trying to escape. His pursuers cut through the small group, lashing out with their guns at anyone who blocked their way, and sprinted toward the young man. Harry saw their target's wide-eyed, frightened expression as the man looked back, stumbled on a pothole and fell to the ground. Harry watched in morbid fascination as his the SSP agents pounced on him like feral animals, beating and kicking him as he lay prone on the ground. No one dared challenge the attackers, and the crowd continued to disperse, anxious to avoid having to witness the savage attack.

Satisfied the man had been subdued, the agents pulled him up and dragged him by his hair to the market square. Harry saw the man's face streaked with blood and his body limp, legs dragging on the ground as they pulled him along. Several of them continued to beat the man's back with their rifles and as they did so his body twitched and went into spasms. He was hauled like a sack of potatoes up the five wooden stairs of the gallows where the hangman's noose gently swung in the light breeze. The man was forced to stand upright and one of his attackers quickly placed the noose around his neck. Even in his pain and misery the young man realized with rising panic their intentions. He struggled hard but was too weak and unable to fight. The platform was fitted with a trap door that sprung open when a lever was pulled and one of the agents gripped the lever.

A few curious people gathered around the gallows, gaping with macabre fascination as the victim cried out in terror. The rope tightened around his neck and his eyes bulged and face turned blue, but the trap door did not open. The man was being slowly strangled as the rope bit into his neck, compressing his windpipe. He made unintelligible choking sounds as he clawed desperately at the rope in a futile effort to ease the pressure. Then without warning the rope was cut and he fell heavily to the wooden floor of the platform. He lay prone on the platform before he was hauled up by his arms and roughly thrown into the back of the truck. The SSP agents jumped in behind him, and the vehicle roared away with their prisoner. Harry suspected it was unlikely the young man would be seen again.

Harry quickly headed back to his encampment following another successful foray into town. He had filled his old canvas bag with supplies of food and water and even a torch he had pilfered, satisfied with his booty. As he reached the edge of the forest the skies turned a leaden grey, and the first spots of rain began to fall. Harry had so far been lucky he had not encountered too much bad weather in his shelter, but when winter closed in he knew he'd have to move on. A while ago he found an old tarpaulin to protect against the rain and would have to set it up tonight. As the gloom descended he reached the densely wooded area where the fallen oak tree housing his crude home was situated. He knew the area so well he hardly needed the light to move around. He knew almost every tree, every root and overhanging branch. He could easily navigate his way in the dark, almost sensing his way forward. His intimate knowledge of this small area had equipped him with a keen awareness if something had changed, and he quickly sensed the area had been disturbed. In the failing light, he saw the unmistakable evidence of trampled leaves and snapped twigs.

Harry quickly headed toward his shelter, carefully checking the crushed vegetation and, heart sinking, realized it extended directly to his hideout. Even as he reached the fallen oak tree, alert to the possible presence of intruders still in the area, he saw that his home had been dismembered, his possessions scattered indiscriminately on the ground, exposed to the steady drizzle.

He stared at the ruins of the shelter. He recalled the time he arrived back from the deportation camp to his apartment in London to find his home ransacked and the incriminating disc at the heart of his troubles gone. His time for introspection was brief, however. He had let his guard down and did not hear the quiet rustle in the bush until the cold steel of a large handgun was pressed into his neck.

# CHAPTER 5

The atmosphere of fear that permeated the Cabinet meetings had been cultivated by Pelham from the early days of his administration. Chamberlain recalled the first meeting of the newly formed Conservative Cabinet, when they had introduced the *Five Year Plan*, prompting the resignations of two Cabinet members. It was no coincidence that Graham Matheson was dead and Anil Khan was languishing in a deportation camp. Lance Pelham had considered them as traitors to the cause; and enemies of the Prime Minister tended to have a short future.

Chamberlain held himself out as a staunch supporter of Pelham's philosophy and as his Deputy and official spokesman, had defended that philosophy many times to the world's media. Yet in the five months since the Conservatives had swept to power, he had witnessed Pelham become even more narcissistic and domineering. Chamberlain had detested Pelham as a person before, but since the failed attempt on his life at Wembley Stadium back in June, the man had become insufferable. He was paranoid and obsessive about his security, to the extent that even a Cabinet meeting required the attendance of two PIA agents.

As the Cabinet shuffled into the room to sit around the spectacular polished oak War Rooms table, Chamberlain stole a glance at the two bodyguards. Their faces were impassive, set like stone, and both had neatly shaved heads. They could have been Epsilons created through Bokanovsky's process, bred to serve the higher ranking castes as envisioned in Huxley's *Brave New World*. The analogy was appropriate because Pelham was trying to fashion a homogenous society modelled on the type of social structure envisaged in the classic novel.

The two agents had been sculpted into highly-trained killing machines, their natural aggression and thirst for violence as former members of FREE honed into an intimidating ferocity that radiated like heat from them. While the pair stood like sentinels in the corner, there was little dissension to Pelham's views, instead a cursory discussion followed by meek deference to their leader. It was ironic that FREE, the organization criticized by Pelham's regime, had evolved into the mainstream movement of the People's Independent Army. His private army of personal bodyguards was drawn from the group, which had grown into the most powerful and vilified paramilitary force in the country. It was at the front line of the fight against insurgents, but reviled more amongst immigrant dissidents because of its administration of the deportation camps.

The government had only attacked FREE because it was convenient to do so at the time. The new administration could not be seen to support such an organization and Chamberlain had made sure they made the right noises in the media. However, now they controlled all branches of the media, social, online, TV, radio and print, it no longer mattered. There was no longer any need to bow to the media. The power base had shifted in an extraordinarily short period of time. The media acted as a government propaganda machine, its power greater than at any time in history. Pelham had restricted entry into the country by foreign journalists so that only the selected few were allowed to report on events. Those journalists were carefully vetted and once in the country were forced to surrender their passports. This was a highly effective way of keeping them in check. One French journalist had broken the unwritten protocol by publishing a disparaging article which criticized Pelham's attempts to control the population and tacitly supported the underground insurgency. As if a damned Frenchman had the right to criticize this great nation. The French had so many social problems they sent the boat people across the Channel to the U.K.'s shores.

The journalist had met his demise in an unfortunate accident, and despite the protests of the French Ambassador, no explanation or body was forthcoming. Afterwards foreign journalists in the country became even more restrained, but that did not stop the intelligence agencies from having them closely followed. The surveillance was not always discreet but served its purpose. It was useful for the journalists to be reminded every so often that their activities as a guest of this country were being monitored.

Control over the media was, however, only one aspect of controlling the population. The immigration problem was a long term one, and since the government had broken the cell that was indirectly responsible for the attempted assassination of the Prime Minister, new bands of insurgents, often ill-equipped but extremely determined, had taken their place. Although martial law had been lifted, the iron grip that Pelham sought was still not as solid as he wished.

The list of critical issues facing the country seemed to grow day by day, yet Pelham's autocratic leadership style did not tolerate a free flow of discussion amongst Cabinet members. The weekly meetings had a curious atmosphere to them, and had settled into an odd routine. One of those idiosyncrasies was that no one spoke before Pelham did. As the buzz of conversation died amongst the Cabinet members, all eyes turned expectantly to Pelham to kick off the formal proceedings.

The Prime Minister peered down the long table at his team. His luxurious leather chair was raised higher so that he peered over them. His smile was affable but his eyes betrayed thinly disguised contempt.

"Good morning everyone," he began, helping himself to a glass of water from the crystal decanter in front of him. "Let's get down to business."

There was a chorus of sycophantic "Good morning Mr. Prime Minister," part of the weekly ritual. It reminded Chamberlain of a class of schoolchildren before a benevolent teacher. He found it hard to suppress his own contempt.

The routine of the meetings had developed into a one way discussion. All reports from each Cabinet member covering areas that included Defence, Homeland Security, Health, Justice, Energy and Climate Change, Jobs and the Economy were prepared in advance on the tablets in front of each Minister, available at the touch of a button. Chamberlain had to admit that Pelham read each report assiduously, with a remarkable ability to absorb and memorize information. More than that, however, was his ability to analyze the reports as he read them and formulate probing questions that really dug deep to the heart of the matter.

It was these questions that struck fear into the hearts of his Ministers. Pelham's questions were often difficult to anticipate and the Minister had to be ready with an answer. Chamberlain knew that secretly the Ministers prayed they did not get picked on. If the reports they presented did not prompt any questions, they knew it was complete and the Prime Minister was satisfied. However, that rarely happened. Chamberlain could sense the discomfort of the Ministers and he enjoyed watching them shift in their chairs anxiously as the P.M.'s eyes flicked over them.

Today it was the turn of the Homeland Security Minister to feel the heat of Pelham's intense glare. "Minister Shaw, your report does not make for comfortable reading. The internal security situation is clearly deteriorating yet I fail to see any firm proposals in your report about how to eradicate the problem. How can you assure me you have the situation under control?"

Minister Angus Shaw, a portly man in his late forties whose shock of flame-coloured hair betrayed his Scottish descent, adjusted his thick glasses and coughed with embarrassment. He looked around the table for some moral support but found only blank stares.

"Mr. Prime Minister, we have had a couple of security issues but I assure you we are making great progress in rooting out the insurgents," he began limply. "The Order Police have made a significant number of arrests, and we have a record number of informants; in fact our prisons are getting overcrowded."

"Yet, Minister Shaw, the protests and the attacks on our forces seem to be growing in intensity. We arrest two dissidents and two more appear to take their place. Why haven't you found the hornet's nest? You can't rest on the glory of breaking the terrorist cell in Kent forever you know."

A few stifled laughs rippled around the table. Shaw had taken the credit for having directed the operations that located the cell which supported the Muslim would-be assassin, but since that time there had only been sporadic victories against resistance forces.

"But Mr. Prime Minister, this is not a traditional war. We're fighting against separatists who rarely come out in the open," he protested meekly. "They only emerge from their rat holes when they attack our troops and they disappear just as fast. We know they are predominantly Muslim but we know there are many other creeds fighting us as well. There is a range of disparate rebel forces. It's impossible to recognize who these people are. They could be standing next to you in the street and you would never know. They will always have the element of surprise."

Pelham's eyes blazed with fury but he said nothing, and an awkward silence hung in the air. When he spoke, his voice carried the condescending tone the Cabinet had become all too familiar with. "That is a pathetic excuse Minister Shaw. We have created two of the finest intelligence organizations in the history of this nation. The State Security Service has a huge network of informers; we are arresting dissidents every day. The SSS reports to you so if they're not doing their job properly then I hold you accountable. You need to be working more closely with the State Secret Police."

"But Prime Minister, they rarely share information with us. Adam Griffiths has passed a clear directive to the SSP that their intelligence network functions independently of the SSS." The distaste in Shaw's voice was evident as he uttered the name of the Head of the People's Independent Army and its intelligence and investigation arm, the State Secret Police, the SSP. Griffiths had been the leader of FREE before it metamorphosed into these two branches of internal security, and he retained the leadership of both branches. Although he was not a Cabinet Minister, his organization supplied Pelham with his personal bodyguards and he reported directly to the Prime Minister, thereby circumventing the usual lines of political protocol. Griffiths was far more likely to secure a private audience with Pelham than someone like Shaw. The bodies under his control were like an unofficial task force, working outside the familiar police and army structure, and with their activities free of judicial review, their loyalties lay squarely aligned to Griffiths and his in turn to Pelham. That made Griffiths an extraordinarily powerful man in Pelham's unique constitutional structure.

Pelham's voice carried a threatening edge. "Then you will have to try harder to make it happen, Minister Shaw. Mr. Griffiths has my complete confidence. You, Minister Shaw, do not."

The Homeland Security Minister's corpulent features turned as red as his hair in humiliation. He took off his thick, round spectacles and wiped his brow. "Yes, Prime Minister."

"Let me make this easier for you Minister Shaw," continued Pelham. "You will recall that I was particularly anxious to locate Harry Clarke, the tabloid reporter, when the army raided the terrorist compound in Kent. Your intelligence networks suggested that Harry Clarke was in the compound, but we found no trace of him, dead or alive. He has information that could harm all of us. Given your intelligence failures in the past, I am not prepared to accept any more mistakes. I want you to find him and quickly, and if you do you may just keep your job."

"Thank you Prime Minister. I won't let you down," Shaw grovelled.

"For your sake, I hope you are right."

The next object of the Prime Minister's wrath was the Secretary of State for Economic Affairs Stewart Mills, whose department oversaw the nation's jobs and pensions. The employment situation had declined steadily since Pelham had taken over but much of it was due to the way in which the statistics were collated. The official rate was now showing at 32%, but Mills had included in the calculations those members of the workforce who had been sent to deportation camps, losing their jobs as a result.

"Are you completely incompetent?" yelled the Prime Minister. "How can you include these immigrants in your analysis? They ceased to become part of the working population when they were taken to the camps. The numbers eligible to work have shrunk and that is inevitable in the short term, but those jobs are still there. The percentage should be decreasing not increasing! Go back and revise the figures and have a more realistic report on my desk in the morning."

Mills was a tough, wiry character, an old war horse on the political circuit, his athletic six-foot five frame a substantial presence in the corridors of power, but even he seemed to visibly wilt under Pelham's verbal onslaught.

Pelham was not finished, however. "Why is my program of direct investment not yielding the desired results? I came to power on a tide of expectation that I would repair our crumbling infrastructure. I have seen very little to convince me that we have made any progress. Your report explains new road building projects, construction of power plants and military installations. Yet I look around and still see our highways full of potholes and our streets with shabby buildings that need demolishing. Half the country is still suffering daily power cuts and the other half severe water shortages. Explain."

"But Prime Minister, we are already running at a significant budget deficit and the International Monetary Fund has refused further funding unless we meet strict conditions regarding human rights for immigrants. We have sought funding from the Private Finance Initiative program but companies are unwilling to invest in infrastructure projects in the current uncertain climate."

"What about the tax revenues?"

"I am sure my honourable colleague from the Treasury can answer more fully," Mills replied, glancing down the table at the Chancellor of the Exchequer, Baron Edward Young. "But I know tax revenues have reduced considerably since we came to power. Many of the jobs that paid taxes were held by immigrants and those have been lost in the short term, until we can find local people to take over the jobs. Although we're starting a program of getting the unemployed into those jobs vacated it will take time for us to see any tax revenue stream. The Pensions crisis that the Labour administration left us shows no signs of abating. In fact it's getting worse. The taxes barely cover the government's pension commitments, never mind revenue for investment. We are getting deeper into debt."

Pelham began scribbling on a notepad. This surprised Chamberlain because he knew Pelham had a phobia against writing anything down. This extended to his email and social media correspondence. He hardly ever responded to these personally. "Then we reduce our pension payments, make more people ineligible. We blame it on austerity measures."

Baron Young, an Old Etonian with an aristocratic style that suited his immaculately groomed features, leaned forward and coughed discreetly. "Mr. Prime Minister, does that not contradict our direct investment programme? We can hardly expect the population to understand our austerity measures when central government spending is at a historical high."

The Minister in charge of the nation's purse strings was one of the few Cabinet members that Pelham did not detest. The man was almost as charismatic as Pelham himself, but not so smooth that he did not know his place.

"Edward," began Pelham patiently. "It's hardly the same. We need the public to understand that the investment we are making is in jobs, industry and our nation's future. The people who are claiming pensions are the nation's past, sucking the lifeblood from the economy. Their sacrifice will be a noble one. Anyone who lives beyond working age is a burden on the State in any event, and this country can no longer afford to carry passengers."

Pelham turned back to Mills, his voice once again dismissive. "Look into the pensions issue and have a proposal on my desk along with the jobs report. We also need to work the immigrant chain gangs harder. We have a huge pool of labour in the deportation camps. We need to maximize our efficiency in deploying this resource."

Another gentle cough sounded from the far end of the table. Pelham glanced down the line of men to the token woman on his Cabinet. "Yes, Miss Beaufort."

"Mr. Prime Minister, I am a little concerned that we are continuing to use the deportation camps as a pool of surplus labour, especially as we're not paying them. It is a clear breach of their human rights and is tantamount to....slavery." Miss Eleanor Beaufort, the Secretary of State for Health, an elegant woman in her late fifties, had long been an advocate for human rights, and had been a consistent thorn in his side over his policies. Pelham had a grudging respect for her, because unlike most of her male colleagues, she was not as submissive; her resistance was firm but moderate, never aggressive.

"Your concern is duly noted Miss Beaufort. But I strongly believe these people will benefit from working as they wait for deportation. They are providing a valuable service to us as we try to rebuild our infrastructure, a small price to pay for their residence in our country over the years. They're being well fed, housed and fully employed. What possible breach of human rights could there be? I think your use of the term 'slavery' is inflammatory, Miss Beaufort, and I would ask that you do not refer to it as such again."

Beaufort bravely persisted. "May I ask then Mr. Prime Minister, if these people on the chain gangs have volunteered for this work? Are they doing it willingly and without pressure?"

Several Cabinet ministers bowed their heads, inspecting their tablets, not wishing to be associated with their colleague's comments. It was becoming increasingly rare for the Prime Minister to be challenged so openly. Pelham said nothing for a few moments but when he did his voice was surprisingly calm and measured. "Miss Beaufort, we are all equally responsible as representatives of the government. We shall all be held accountable in the end for what we did and we did not do. If you have concerns over the way immigrants are treated, please feel free to investigate further and report to me. In the meantime, please concentrate on your job. May I have your report?"

Eleanor Beaufort nodded, stung by the rebuke. She perched her half-moon spectacles on the end of her nose and glanced at her tablet. "Thank you Mr. Prime Minister. Today I want to concentrate my report on the health situation in the deportation camps. I believe that the situation is deteriorating rapidly and we are woefully under-resourced to address the problem. The conditions are a cause for concern, particularly with the spread of water-borne diseases. At the very least we need to install water-filtration systems in all the camps."

Pelham sipped his water and merely looked bored. "Should we not be more interested in the health of our people? The deportees will cease to be our problem before long."

Miss Beaufort looked appalled. "Mr. Prime Minister, they are still human and deserve our care," she said indignantly.

Pelham's tone was conciliatory. "I am not saying they don't, however we have to prioritize. We are facing a funding and man-power crisis in the National Health Service. The system is under huge stress. We cannot afford to allocate any more resources to the camps. As you know we dispatched a highly qualified medical team from the Health Protection Agency to one of the camps and they are making a preliminary assessment. We would be ill-advised to move without their recommendations."

"Yet in the meantime people are dying. The mortality rate for this new mystery disease is over 80%. We don't know what we're facing. This disease is unlike anything else we have seen," countered the Health Secretary.

Pelham sighed, as if he were lecturing a child. "This is precisely why we must not panic and allow the team from the Health Protection Agency to finish their assessment."

Eleanor Beaufort persisted, wiping away loose strands of white hair that had flopped down from her neatly tied bun. "How long are they going to be? They've been on site for over five days and I cannot get any information out of ...." She hesitated, unsure how to phrase it, "Your man Griffiths. He simply refuses to engage with me, says that he reports only to you."

Chamberlain observed this exchange with detached amusement. Pelham said nothing but Beaufort was in her stride. She looked around the room, all eyes now fixed on her. "Colleagues, I want to show you what we are up against." Her fingers danced over her tablet and within a few seconds the image appeared on the screen of the tablet in front of each Minister. There was a chorus of gasps from the assembly. On the screen was a picture of about twenty corpses piled high, as if they were waiting to be thrown into a funeral pyre. The high resolution photo was close enough to show some of the faces, which were ashen grey, eyes turned up into their sockets. However, it was the angry red blotches on the faces and bodies of the corpses that really disturbed the Cabinet members. It was if the skin on the corpses had been stretched tight, and the blood was about to burst through. Here and there the skin was already torn, with hideous black lesions around which purple, bruised skin hung loosely. Dried blood was caked around the faces of the deceased, as if they had leaked blood from the ears, mouth, eyes and nose. The corpses looked as if they had been beaten with a branding iron.

"It's horrific I know, but the external signs of trauma are minor compared to the war raging inside their internal organs. As far as we know, the pathogen attacks them through the bloodstream. The accumulation and retention of fluid around the organs causes a huge build-up of pressure around them, causing swelling, and in different cases, has caused pulmonary edema and consequently fatal heart attacks, or liver and kidney failure, but in the worst case cerebral edema, resulting in fatal haemorrhaging of the brain. The incubation period ranges from seven days to nearly thirty days, depending on the health and fitness of the patient."

"Miss Beaufort you've made your point," Pelham said with mild admonishment.

However, the Health Secretary was not easily deterred. "If I may, Mr. Prime Minister. These outbreaks have occurred at all but three of the deportation camps. The pathogen is spreading and we don't yet know how it is transmitted. For anthrax, the nearest type of disease we have to this new pathogen, the infected body is the most hazardous source, most likely because of the infected fluids exuded through body cavities. It is important that corpses are isolated and quarantined as quickly as possible, but that has clearly not been done. I am hoping the Health Protection Agency team will tell us more."

"Enough Miss Beaufort," replied Pelham in a steely voice.

"Sir, we knew about this bacterium three months ago. We have waited far too long. If we don't take action now we could be facing an epidemic in the camps. We isolated the camps fairly quickly but we still need a program of vaccination for those poor souls in the camps. What on God's name are we doing forcing more people into the camps? We could be sending them to their deaths."

"I said enough!" Pelham shouted, finally losing his patience and banging his fist on the table. However, Beaufort had made her point. In the heavy silence that followed, the ministers stared at their tablets, shocked at the graphic images of the victims of this mysterious disease. Pelham continued, calmer but authoritative. "Miss Beaufort, we have a program of reform that you and I both know cannot be derailed. This image is provocative and alarmist. As you so rightly pointed out we don't know enough about this disease to draw any firm conclusions. We have to continue to work within our mandate, one that you and the rest of the Cabinet endorsed and supported. This image must be placed in context. It's clearly an isolated incident. It is not representative of what is happening in the camps."

"How do we know that? The camps are sealed off and we have no information coming out of the camps," Beaufort countered.

Pelham stood up and slammed his glass on the table. "Do not push me, Miss Beaufort. You made your point." He picked up his tablet. "We're done here." He swept out of the room and his bodyguards stirred from their inert poses and raced after him.

When Chamberlain entered the Drawing Room at 10 Downing Street for his weekly post-Cabinet strategy meeting with Pelham later that day, he expected to find the Prime Minister apoplectic with fury. His tactic of storming out of the room when he was challenged or losing an argument was an all-too familiar sight amongst the Party faithful, although it was becoming less common for his politicians to have the courage to openly disagree with him. When the Deputy Prime Minister arrived, however, Pelham had a relaxed grin and offered him a sherry. Their meeting was one of the few times when the P.M. did not have two PIA guards lurking in the corner of the room. The paranoia that had gripped Pelham did not extend to mistrust of his Deputy.

"She's a feisty one isn't she," Pelham said smiling as he handed Chamberlain the glass. "She has more balls than the rest of the spineless cowards put together. It's a shame she isn't ten years younger."

Chamberlain nodded in agreement. He could sense the magnetic sexual attraction Pelham had to her that explained why he failed to persecute her to the same extent as the other Cabinet members. "I agree Lance, but be careful. She senses you are more receptive to her, and the other Cabinet members sense it too. They may use her as an emissary for their own ideas. She also has a history of challenging her superiors. That's a rare quality amongst this timid bunch, as long as she does not try to humiliate you."

"Where did she get the photo?"

"I don't know but I intend to find out. We need something in reserve in case she starts digging around. If she does she has the potential to hurt you. I suggest we monitor her closely. She's a very ambitious lady and clean as a whistle, as morally upright and sincere as you can get for a politician. But she is streetwise enough to know that even with the current media restrictions a scandal could damage her career. Something compromising would encourage her to pipe down a little. She is a very talented person to have in the Cabinet, quite apart from being the lone female. I am sure there is a lot we can do to ensure her loyalty."

Pelham sipped his drink and paced gently around the warm décor of the Drawing Room. "I'm surprised you haven't done that already Giles. But yes, go ahead; we need to hedge our bets." He peered out of the bulletproof glass installed in all the windows at No 10 since the assassination attempt, as if he were surveying his kingdom.

"I have some other good news for you," continued Chamberlain, briefly glancing at his tablet. "Griffiths thinks he has found Harry Clarke."

# REUTERS EDITORIAL OCTOBER 17

The Conservative Party has been in power for just over five months and in that time the nation has experienced a radical shift in the political and social landscape. The only true opposition to this authoritarian regime has gone missing. There is no true opponent on the other side of the House berating the government's policies and verbally attacking its leadership in the time honoured fashion of a democracy. There has rarely been any robust debate in Parliament since Pelham took power. The only resistance lies in the shadows of burnt out, crumbling buildings, insurgents desperately fighting for survival, hunted by a network of well equipped military and paramilitary forces, paid for by in part by a stinging round of tax hikes announced in the recent budget by the Chancellor of the Exchequer, Baron Edward Young. The rebels have been branded as terrorists for having the audacity to resist the ruling regime. Indeed as the sectarian violence grows and attacks become more frequent and intense, the stakes have become higher and the line between terrorism and resistance ever more blurred.

The major turning point in Pelham's regime occurred following the attack on the compound in Kent in early July, which the government hailed as a moral victory against terrorism. Although the garrison itself was relatively small, it was the hub of a network of cells, including that from which would-be assassin Faisal Khorasani had been drawn. The annihilation of this network was a key military victory for Pelham, and while sectarian violence has continued, the separatist forces suffer from lack of cohesion and leadership. With little political opposition, Pelham has established a formidable network of authoritarian forces.

The organizations tasked with maintaining order and consolidating Pelham's grip on power are wide ranging. This network of forces has effectively emasculated any free speech, and his control of all branches of the media, social, TV and radio, as well as suppression of the Internet has made it difficult for the wider population to fully appreciate just how the nation has changed. Instead they've been fed a diet of propaganda which has indoctrinated them into a false sense that the nation is making progress, while in their localities people are surrounded by chaos, bloodshed and fear.

The most feared and reviled of these forces is undoubtedly the People's Independent Army (PIA), the successor to FREE, the Fight to Return England to the English. The Prime Minister used FREE members to form his own unit of bodyguards following the attempt on his life in June. Supported by Central Government funding, they quickly assumed mainstream status as the PIA, gaining official recognition when they were unveiled as the government's 'Defence Corps.' Known for its ruthless and brutal tactics, the PIA has steadily grown in power, a vilified street force in the front line of the war of attrition against separatist insurgents. As administrators of the deportation camps, they have effectively sealed them off from the outside world, especially since the mysterious pandemic sweeping through the camps, and stories of the PIA's cruelty have filtered through to the media.

Aligned with the rise of the PIA has been the meteoric political rise of their leader Adam Griffiths, often described in the media as a white supremacist, a title he has consistently refuted, preferring to describe himself as a 'committed nationalist.' His influence has grown immensely since Pelham took power, part of his inner circle, a trusted confidante despite his lack of political experience.

Griffiths is also in charge of the interrogation and investigation arm of the PIA, the despised State Secret Police. The SSP investigate acts of treason, espionage, sabotage, terrorism and criminal attacks against Party members. This includes one of the most recent and frequently prosecuted crimes of harbouring immigrants. This crime is considered an indictable offence and therefore worthy on conviction of a stiff custodial sentence to act as a deterrent against this 'anti-social' behaviour. The people most commonly indicted for this type of crime are British people in mixed marriages. There are no exemptions for married couples and their children under the *Minorities Registration Act*, the seemingly innocuous title of the law which has so far displaced several million immigrants. The result is that many families have been torn apart, a cruel irony given Pelham's assertion in his election campaign that family stood at the heart of his Party's policies. More alarmingly, thanks to some clever political and legal manoeuvring by Pelham during the summer, the actions of the SSP are no longer subject to judicial oversight and they cannot be sued in the civil court. This means they can enter and search a property without a warrant, and have often done so. This in turn has raised the question of whether the evidence obtained by the SSP is admissible in court. A high profile case in the Appeal Court determined that it was not, but the Lord Chief Justice, in his role as the Head of the Judiciary, directed that the search was legal and so the evidence obtained could be used to support the prosecution case.

A directive of this nature overturning case law had rarely come from the Lord Chief Justice's office, preferring instead to let the courts decide, if necessary up to the House of Lords where the senior Law Lords would decide where matters of public policy were at stake. This prompted the senior judiciary and the Circuit Judges Association to rebel and for a two-week period during late summer, the judges went on strike and the already over-burdened court system ground to a shuddering halt. Pelham was forced to call a meeting with senior judges to discuss concessions. However during the middle of the summit one of the most senior rebel judges, Sir McKenzie Pemberton, a vociferous opponent of the new regime, was tragically found floating face down in the pool of his luxurious mansion near Swiss Cottage. Toxicology tests later found that he had died from a heart attack caused by extreme amounts of alcohol in his bloodstream.

The summit was halted and the judges quickly returned to work with the Lord Chief Justice's directive intact. As a result the SSP and its members enjoy an unprecedented immunity from criminal or civil prosecution. They have quickly gained a notorious reputation, fuelled by their sinister black ski masks and fabled interrogation rooms. Their targets are mainly political criminals, although this has often been construed widely, and there is sometimes an overlap with the State Security Service, the SSS.

The SSS is an intelligence agency that consists of a few hundred full time agents and several thousand informants, their task to locate and neutralize enemies of the State. The agency frequently works closely with the SSP, although in reality they often pursue the same people with a resulting turf war, particularly for high profile targets. The two agencies exist in a curious détente as they both vie for political credibility.

The key difference is the reporting structure. Whereas the SSP is an offshoot of the People's Independent Army and ultimately reports to Adam Griffiths, the SSS is affiliated to the national police force, the Order Police. They are an amalgamation of municipal, rural and local police, which Pelham abolished shortly after taking power. One of his manifesto promises was to get police back on the streets following many years in which they had retreated from the urban battleground. It is certainly one promise he has kept, although perhaps not in the way his constituents intended. They are better equipped and armed than ever, but the pendulum has swung firmly in favour of protecting the State not the individual. They are there to keep order as their name suggests, and to prosecute the lesser range of offences, but a complaint by a citizen of a crime by another citizen is far too often likely to be ignored.

The other branch of the police structure is the National Criminal Police Service or Cripo for short, which is the main federal body that holds and prosecutes serious offenders, often delivered to them by the Order Police or the SSS for prosecution at trial. They also have their own investigative and prosecution powers and are usually called in for cases such as homicide and gun crime. However, people could also be arrested for such crimes as sedition against the State, say by distributing literature which attacks the government, if the SSS has not reached them first, and so offenders may become political or non-political prisoners. The Order Police, SSS, and Cripo all report to the Head of the Police Service, Sir Robin Duncan, who in turn reports to the Home Office Minister for Homeland Security, Angus Shaw.

However, the front line in the war against armed insurgents is the Operational High Command, the military forces encompassing the Armed Forces, the Navy and the Royal Air Force. This is led by the Chief of the Defence Staff, Sir Terence Harding, a thirty-year Army veteran but a recent appointment following the removal of General Sir Huntington-Smythe. A hard-line right-wing Conservative, he has been highly supportive of the government's strategy on the war against insurgents. With Harding in place, the conflict is likely to continue for the foreseeable future.

It all adds up to a bewildering array of authoritarian forces aimed at protecting the State. The pervasive State sponsored media broadcasts have continually boasted that crime figures have dropped significantly in the five months the Conservatives have been in power, and the statistics are irrefutable. Less clear is the number of crimes that have gone unreported. Those critics still brave enough to be heard complain that Pelham is using taxpayers' money to beat the taxpayer round the head. For example, under the emergency provisions enacted under martial law in the immediate aftermath of the assassination attempt on Pelham, the authorities have the power to seize and detain a person without charge for a period of up to two years without formal charges being laid. This is an effective tool to stifle dissent, and it is unlikely that criticism of Pelham's regime will continue for long as those same critics are undoubtedly on the target list of one of the organizations described in this editorial.

Although Pelham's grip on power has never been in doubt, the many problems facing his administration are complex and multifarious. An undercurrent of violence and simmering revolution lurks behind closed doors and in dark corners of the nation's towns and cities despite the highly visible military and police presence on the streets. Although the deportation camps are already full to bursting, and receiving new inmates every day, there has been no sign of any actual deportations to other countries. This presents a major problem for the regime, as there are still many millions of 'ethnic minorities' that are yet to be apprehended and imprisoned. These people are fuelling the resistance, but it is apparent that opposition to the government is not confined to those groups, with many English people also reputedly engaged in guerrilla style warfare against Pelham's regime.

One issue the administration cannot gloss over is the deteriorating conditions in the deportation camps. The flood of immigrants sent to the camps remained undiminished throughout the summer, despite the outbreak of the mysterious pathogen with anthrax-like symptoms. The camps have been effectively sealed off; open only for the reception of new inmates as they wait to be deported. The Deputy P.M., Giles Chamberlain, recently explained that the mysterious outbreak was part of the reason why the deportation program had stalled, as they did not wish to transport immigrants to other countries if there was a risk of the disease spreading, and in any event it would be unlikely that the countries would accept their citizens back until they had received a clean bill of health. Although the camps all possess hastily assembled wooden barracks and shelters, these are vastly overcrowded as the influx continues, and the enforced intimacy of the camp residents is likely to accelerate the spread of the disease, particularly as none of the camps have running water.

To ease the confinement of the inmates as they wait, seemingly forever, to be expelled from the country, most able-bodied men and a number of women, particularly those without children have been assigned work in closely supervised conditions close to the deportation camp. They are usually assigned in work units on different projects, for example working on the roads to dig out and repair the many potholes infesting the highways. Nearby roads are usually closed and diversions created for a considerable distance, so that these gangs of workers are not immediately visible to passing cars, although they cannot be completely hidden. The work is often menial and repetitive at best and much of it is physically challenging. Of greater concern to human rights activists is the fact that the chain gang is not a euphemism. After an attempted breakout by inmates at the Felixstowe camp, the administrators of that camp decided to issue aluminium shackles and chains to restrain the workers from attempting to flee, and the practice has spread to other camps. Although the chains are nothing like the barbaric iron tools that weighed down prisoners in the early part of last century, they do evoke the legacy of the penal chain gangs of the American Deep South. It is difficult to remember that these workers are not convicted criminals – their only crime is to belong to a different ethnic group to the indigenous population.

As Pelham's vision takes shape and his policies become clearer, many are questioning the motives of the man, a politician with a mysterious past that adds to his intrigue. Remarkably no one has attempted to investigate his early years and Pelham has consistently refused to answer questions about it, even though it may provide some direction on what makes the Prime Minister tick.

# CHAPTER 6

"Don't move a muscle or I'll blow your head off." The deep baritone drawl was muffled but Harry recognized the unmistakable Cockney accent. He froze to the spot, hardly daring to breathe, until his assailant stepped back, the small pistol firmly pointed at him. He turned slowly and his heart sank as he peered at the black ski mask, the notorious guise of the SSP. Crystalline, hard eyes stared coldly at him from behind the mask, and they burned with thinly veiled contempt. The nearby bushes rustled and out of the gloom emerged six more black-clad masked figures with polished, knee length jackboots. The athletic, intimidating figures stood in a semi-circle around Harry, waiting expectantly.

The cold-eyed assailant holstered his pistol, safe that Harry was no threat against seven of them. He leaned toward Harry so that his face was barely inches away. "How about you tell me what you're doing living in the woods?"

Harry couldn't hide the quiver in his voice. "I'm homeless so I set up here. I haven't done anything wrong."

No sooner had he uttered the words when he doubled up under the weight of a sharp but heavy punch to his abdomen. He fell to the ground, gasping for breath as the SSP agent stood menacingly over him. "We'll decide whether you've done anything wrong or not. You've been plotting against the State haven't you? Where are your collaborators?"

Harry tried to get up but a firm leather boot on his shoulder pressed him down. "What are you talking about? I don't know anyone. I'm just trying to survive," he gasped.

"I don't believe you." The SSP agent stepped back and allowed Harry to stagger to his feet, but as soon as Harry was upright, the agent felled him again with a vicious blow to his chin. Harry collapsed again, feeling as if his jaw exploded. The SSP agent took off his black leather gloves and rubbed his palm with his other hand. Harry spotted the metal knuckle duster as he hit the rain soaked dirt, tasting blood in his mouth.

"Careful Bruce," said one of the other agents. "If you mess his face up the scanner is less reliable. There will be plenty of time for that later." Harry lay on the ground, rubbing furiously at his throbbing jaw. This time he was given no opportunity to stand up. Two of the agents circled him and pulled his arms behind his back, while a third snapped on a pair of steel handcuffs. He was hauled to his feet and dragged out of the forest clearing.

Nearby a black unmarked van idled on the small rutted track that led out of the forest, waiting for the agents. Harry was dumped unceremoniously into the back of the van and fell on his already painful chin onto the harsh metal floor. The handcuffs bit into his wrists and he lay forward on his stomach, unable to move as the agents climbed in behind him and sat on the Spartan benches that lined each side of the rear. The van jolted forward and bounced around crazily over the rutted forest track. Even the agents had to hold on and Harry, lying on the floor was unable to steady himself, incapacitated as he was by his manacles. He was jolted up and down until a few of the agents used him as a footrest. Their heavy steel capped boots kept him immobile but their heels dug painfully into his back.

The stench of dried sweat filled the interior, and his face was pressed against the grimy, pitted metal floor. The vehicle had just one window at the back, and it was so tiny and covered in wire mesh that no light filtered in. Through the blur of pain he saw flecks of red streaked across the van walls. He tasted blood in his mouth, and one of his teeth felt as if it had been loosened. He knew his pain was only a foretaste of what was to come. As soon as they recognized him as a wanted criminal his only prospect was a long and torturous death.

The bumping and jolting of the van soon passed and Harry guessed they had left the forest. The SSP agents kept their ski masks on but chatted excitedly amongst themselves, sometimes taunting Harry.

"Boss, how shall we kill this one? Shall we string him up and slit his throat until he squeals like a pig?"

"No, no, let's hang him over a bridge and use him for target practice," interjected another. They all laughed at this, like a pack of schoolboys innocently deciding on which game to play on a summer afternoon.

Harry guessed from the voices that they were probably not much older than adolescents, but then this generation grew up so much quicker than his own had; they were exposed to cruelty and violence much earlier in life, at an impressionable age when their intellects were still being shaped and they were indoctrinated to believe that violence was the social norm, the natural order of the society they lived in. Many commentators had blamed the surge in violent crimes among the young on various factors; back in the eighties it was 'video nasties.' Early in this century it was more the influence of video games that depicted and glorified brutal scenes which were so realistic in their imagery that they profoundly affected young impressionable minds.

His young tormentors were clearly no strangers to violence; they revelled in it. Harry surmised that they were the archetypal playground bully, the type who beat up opposition fans at soccer matches and hurled racist slurs at the other team's players. Now they had graduated to another level, one that had the tacit approval of the authorities. He could expect no clemency from these faceless thugs. At least they had not taken their masks off yet. He had heard rumours circulating that if an SSP agent took off his mask then the prisoner was as good as dead, because the agent had no concerns about being identified later.

Harry felt the van slow down and come to a gentle stop. The chatter between the agents stopped and immediately two of them grabbed Harry, one on each arm, and hauled him onto the long wooden bench on one side of the interior. Another grabbed him by his long straggly hair, and tugged hard, forcing Harry to hold his head steady. He recognized the cold ice-blue eyes of his first attacker, whom one agent had referred to as Bruce, as the agent cocked his head inches from Harry's. As he did so, Bruce produced a long, ornately decorated Bowie knife from a sheath next to the holster on his belt. The glassy eyes peered at Harry intently as he freed the blade from its fur cover and gently rubbed the long silver blade against the flat of his palm. The blade tapered to a fine point at its tip so that it was perfect for stabbing as well as slicing and it looked ominously sharp to Harry. The ski mask creased as if the agent were grinning behind it and the blade was raised close to Harry's face, so the tip was level with his eyes.

His Cockney accent carried a tremor of anticipation. "This Bowie knife has been in my family for generations. I sharpen and polish it every day, just waiting for moments like this."

Harry's eyes flicked down to the knife, the distinct carvings on the redwood handle suggesting that it was old and handmade. "Are you sure there isn't anything you want to tell me, like who you are?" He gently flicked the blade around close to Harry's eyes.

Harry fixed his gaze on the blade. "I told you I'm nobody. I'm just trying to survive."

"Well mate, your survival chances just got a lot slimmer." There was a hint of suppressed amusement in his gruff voice, and as the other agents crowded round, Harry's head was pushed back and the blade spun in the agent's hand. Powerless, Harry snapped his eyes shut as the blade sliced neatly through, but Harry felt no pain. As he opened his eyes, he saw a clump of hair in Bruce's hand. The agent threw it to the floor and continued to hack away at his beard and then at his hair, his accomplice pulling the hair straight so the blade could slice through cleanly. Within a minute Harry's beard had been reduced to untidy, grey flecked stubble, and his hair was shorter than at any time in the last few months. It felt almost liberating. Bruce nodded to his fellow agent. "OK Ethan, let's see who this tosser really is?"

His colleague Ethan, a tall, brawny figure with intense brown eyes peering out from behind his mask, reached into the deep pockets of his charcoal combat pants. He took out a small device no larger than a cell phone with a small screen and a laser in the centre. He held it a few inches from Harry's face and the arrow-like red laser played over his face, scanning the contours and analyzing the shape of his face. The gently buzzing laser was blinding and Harry pressed his eyes shut, the intense light seared onto his eyeballs so that he still visualized the beam even with his eyes shut tight.

When the scanning was finished, the machine was silent and the agent waited for a few seconds before it produced the result. Harry waited anxiously, knowing that as soon as the centralized database had downloaded his information onto the portable scanner, he was finished. As the agent stared at the machine, Harry saw the reflection in his eyes as the screen lit up. Harry watched the eyes carefully, but surprisingly they did not even flicker.

"We've got a 99% match on a name, Harry Clarke." Ethan looked up at his fellow agents. Harry could only see their eyes but could imagine the blank stares behind the mask. A couple of them shook their heads. Jesus, thought Harry; they did not recognize his name!

"Wait, the profile is being downloaded now." He looked again at Harry, his eyes registering cruel anticipation. "Let's see who you really are Harry Clarke. Then we can decide the severity of your punishment."

The machine buzzed and Ethan shook it in frustration. "Damn, the connection has been severed." He shook it and banged the flat of his palm against the small device like a frustrated viewer slapping an ancient cathode-ray tube television in days gone by. "This crappy machine is always playing up," he cursed in exasperation.

Bruce sat to one side, listening intently to a tiny hand device pressed against his ear. He nodded as if he was taking instructions and then he stood up. His deep voice carried a hint of anger. "We don't have time for this. We've had reports of rebel gunfire in East Harnham. The army is closing in but they want us on the ground to identify any known insurgents. He's just a rotten vagrant. We need to catch the big fish."

"So what do we do with him now?" asked Ethan, still checking the machine. "Can we string him up?"

In answer, Bruce turned to Harry and raised the Bowie knife so the sharp point pricked the bottom of Harry's chin. The others crowded round in anticipation at their leader's next move. "You, mate, got lucky today." His voice was loud for the benefit of his companions. "Your next trip is to the deportation camp." His piercing blue eyes glinted with cruel amusement. "From the stories I've heard about the diseases there, you might soon wish we had finished you off today." Bruce returned the long blade to its sheath and he spoke through the small grille to the van's driver. "Message the Salisbury Camp and tell them we have a prisoner for them to pick up, and quickly. We need to get moving."

The van continued on its way and Harry was ignored as the SSP agents checked their weapons and chattered excitedly amongst themselves, knowing they were headed into conflict. It seemed to excite and animate them. Within five minutes, however, the van was stationary again, and their attention once more turned to Harry. Several agents grabbed him by each arm and dragged him out of the truck. They shoved him unceremoniously onto the muddy road and Harry fell awkwardly, unable to balance with the cuffs still digging into his wrists. He rolled over, uninjured. The sky was inky blue now, and he saw the dim shadows of trees gently rustling in the stiff autumn breeze. The rain had stopped but it was bitterly cold.

He heard harsh voices shouting at him and the solid beam of a flashlight shone in his face. He blinked hard, temporarily blinded. "Get up!" the voice demanded. As his vision refocused, he saw he was at an army checkpoint, surrounded by several soldiers in combat fatigues. Harry struggled to get up, unable to use his hands, and the soldiers made no move to help, amused by his efforts. Determined to avoid humiliation, he forced himself onto his knees where he was able to raise himself to a standing position.

The SSP leader rebuked the soldiers. "Enough. We're short of time." He spun Harry round and surprisingly unlocked the handcuffs. Harry rubbed his wrists, sore and blistered from the steel restraints.

Ethan pulled out his facial recognition scanner and checked it one last time without success. He squared up to Harry, the mask inches from his face. "You're lucky," the SSP agent whispered harshly. "If it was up to me you'd be dead by now."

The SSP agents jumped into the rear of the van and the vehicle roared off into the distance, quickly swallowed up in the dark woods as it rounded a bend. He was now in the custody of the soldiers, and two of them guarded him, waiting in the deepening gloom.

# CHAPTER 7

Presently the laboured drone of a large truck resounded in the chill air, and a large set of headlights pierced the gloom. The truck pulled up to the checkpoint barrier and the driver spoke to one of the soldiers, who pointed in the direction of Harry and his captors. The occupant gave a nod and the soldier pointed to the rear of the truck. As Harry's eyes adjusted to the dark he noticed the large steel cage that occupied the back. Gaunt, hollow faces stared at him blankly as the soldiers herded him onto the truck. They lifted down the tailgate and pushed him into the crowd of people squashed into the narrow cage. As the metal door clanged shut, the crowd swelled around him, like a crowded subway squeezing in a lone passenger. Despite the warmth of bodies pressed tightly against him, Harry shivered with apprehension. An aura of exhaustion and dejection hung over the throng. He estimated that there were at least thirty people squashed into the cage like cattle, but only the wailing of a few babies in the arms of their mothers broke the crowd's silence. The chill air was pungent with the aroma of stale body odour and dried vomit.

The truck shuddered forward and as it bounced over a pothole the crowd swayed in unison, staggering to keep their balance. Several grabbed at the rusted metal grid-like fencing and hung on. Harry had no idea how long they had been crammed in this cage, forced to stand, but their weary, resigned expressions suggested a long time. Mercifully, the cage did not have a roof, but the bitter breeze seemed to weave itself amongst the crowd, many of whom wore only light clothing, as if they had been plucked from their homes without warning.

The crowd quickly lost interest in the latest prisoner, and as he tried to strike up a conversation with an old man pressed close against him, the diminutive pensioner grimaced, revealing a row of broken, decaying teeth. His fleshy chin moved up and down as he chewed on his jaw, lips smacking together, and he turned his back on Harry. An attractive black lady in a headscarf stood nursing her tiny infant child and stared vacantly through him. His forced smile elicited no reaction.

As the truck bounced along in the dark, each bump forcing the cage's occupants to press and sway together, a group of people walking along the roadside were caught in the glow of the vehicle's headlights. The truck blasted its horn and as they passed, Harry could see they were chained together, accompanied by several men in uniform, toting what appeared to be large rifles and white breathing masks. This miserable rag-tag bunch barely looked up as the truck passed, as they concentrated on keeping a rhythm to avoid tripping on their shackles. Harry heard the uniformed men yelling at the group, which numbered about twenty, predominantly women. He had caught rumours of these chain gangs but of course they had been strenuously denied by the government and their existence suppressed in the state-controlled media. He felt sickened at the sight of these poor scapegoats of a sadistic and intolerant regime, whose power base was so consummate that these abuses would continue to go unchecked for the foreseeable future.

A mile or so further on, they ascended a steep hill, the engine revving hard as it strained against the incline, hampered by the weight of its human cargo. From there Harry had a good view of the Salisbury deportation camp. He remembered sitting in his car on the same hill looking down on the camp during his last ill-fated attempt to rescue his family. At that time the camp was no more than a chaotic collection of tents and razor wire. As Harry peered over the bodies pressed close to him through the metal grids of the cage, he saw that the camp was illuminated by an array of powerful arc lamps placed around the perimeter. They bathed the grounds in a soft yellow glow, revealing a line of long, narrow huts with flat roofs. The squat buildings reminded Harry of army barracks, but placed closer together to make as much use of the available space as physically possible. Harry counted at least twenty of these long huts lined together, and behind them another similar line. Another set of barracks appeared to be under construction. Clearly the camp was planning to accommodate a large expansion of inmates. No light emanated from these barracks, and there was little movement around them. Harry spotted other buildings where various figures were milling around.

The truck, its gears grinding, descended the hill and curved around the winding road. The caustic whiff of diesel fumes mixed with sweat and body odour made Harry feel claustrophobic amongst the sea of bodies pressing against him. He fought to keep his breathing regular as he sucked in the clammy air. They soon reached level ground and as they rounded another curve in the dark, pitted road, passed through a heavily protected army checkpoint before the lights of the camp entrance greeted them. The large, scruffy sign above the barricaded gate informed them of their arrival at Salisbury deportation camp. The truck slowed to a stop, its brakes squealing as it idled toward the entrance, waiting for the barrier, a long steel pole, to rise up and let the vehicle through.

When Harry had left Julianne back in July, his plan was to break in to the camp and rescue his former wife Tamara and their son Byron. Now he was here, three months later than planned, and as he grasped how well guarded and secure the facility had become, he realized how incredibly optimistic and naive he had been. "At least I will get to see them," he murmured to himself.

"No you won't," retorted a tired voice. A stocky, balding figure squeezed in next to Harry. The middle-aged man removed his spectacles and peered up at Harry, who was six inches taller. In the reflected light from the arc lamps by the camp entrance, Harry could see the dark circles around his bloodshot eyes. "They keep families apart. It is easier for the camp authorities to keep order. You'll never get to see them." His accent was exotic, of Persian origin. He dabbed his brow with a grubby handkerchief. Harry saw that he wore a suit, but his white shirt was heavily stained and his jacket crumpled.

"How do you know that?"

A thin smile traced across his cracked lips. "Because when they took my wife Leila away they told me I would never see her in the camp. They assured me they'd come back for me when they had the paperwork and they kept their promise. I doubt I will get to see my wife again." Tears glistened in his eyes but he quickly wiped them away and replaced his spectacles.

"I'm sorry. The name's Harry."

The man nodded and took Harry's extended hand. "Omar," he

replied. His hands were hard, slightly calloused. "You look terrible, even compared to us," he chided gently. "I was an Islamic banker before they came, but I always knew it was a matter of time. I had hoped they were wrong about seeing my wife but now I know they meant it. It's been two months since they took Leila away. They give no information. I don't even know if she's still alive." The thought of this set him off again and he blew his nose with the handkerchief.

Harry thought of his own family. They had been in the camp much longer and he too had to face the prospect that they might have perished in the disease ridden camp. Before he could reply the cage was surrounded by a dozen heavily built men in dark jackets and heavy boots, toting high powered rifles and bandoliers of ammunition. They unlocked the cage and swung the doors open.

"Come on, move it," one of them grunted at the occupants. They were still waiting behind the barrier but it appeared to Harry that they would be entering the camp on foot. He heard one of the camp guards instructing another on the delivery of new inmates. At that moment the ground was rocked with the percussive boom of an explosion that sent the truck crashing on its side.

The SSP van was just outside East Hamham when the message came through. The SSP agents had taken off their masks as they rode in the van, still sitting in the back, and Bruce saw the greenish tint of the facial recognition device light up his comrade Ethan's angular face. Ethan was in his early twenties, and his ash-blond hair and lithe, athletic body could easily have qualified him as a male model. However, his extreme political views and his loathing for the foreign merchants he blamed for his father's business failure and subsequent suicide made him an obsessive and competent disciple of the State Secret Police. It was important in this job, Bruce reflected, that you learned to suppress your emotions, because there was no room for that in this job. Emotions meant compassion, a dangerous trait that would draw the derision of your peers and the disapproval of your bosses. The SSP was founded on discipline and allowed no room for benevolence. Everyone had a reason to be part of this elite organization, but Ethan was one of the best.

Bruce waited for Ethan to convey the message, but as soon as he saw the expression on his face he knew it was not good news. Ethan's caramel eyes were wide with horror and he looked up at the group assembled around him. "We have an identity match on Harry Clarke." Ethan fought to keep the tremor from his voice. "It's accompanied by a personal message from Adam Griffiths himself congratulating us on capturing one of the most wanted men in Britain, accused of the murder of a prominent government minister. He has already informed the Prime Minister that we're holding him and he is to be brought to London immediately."

Bruce felt the blood drain from his face and suddenly the interior of the van was too hot and claustrophobic, the sides pressing in on him. He felt many pairs of eyes staring, waiting for his direction. Without warning he banged hard on the grille that separated them from the cab.

"Turn round, quickly!" he yelled at the driver. "We have to take Harry Clarke back before he reaches the deportation centre."

The driver complied and the van swung around in a sharp U-turn, tossing the men in the rear like rag-dolls. Bruce hung on and hardly noticed. He was preoccupied with the consequences if they did not catch up with Harry Clarke before he was quarantined in the deportation camp.

# CHAPTER 8

The truck keeled over with a tortured groan, a huge gaping hole in its undercarriage. The prisoners screamed in unison as they tumbled over each other, clutching and clawing at anything they could find. The cage crashed to the ground and the mass of bodies spilled out in a heap, the less fortunate ones crushed under the weight of others who fell on top of them like a huge rugby scrum. Several children were thrown clear and scrambled onto the dirt road, crying for their parents.

Harry felt a sense of vertigo as his world turned ninety degrees and flailing limbs struck him before he fell heavily, cushioned by the large, flabby bulk of a fellow prisoner who grunted breathlessly as Harry landed heavily on him. The weight of falling bodies pressed Harry down but with the tenacity and strength of a survivor, he managed to extricate himself from the tangled mass of flesh. He staggered to his feet, the noise and confusion of panic-stricken men, women and children shouting and clawing at the heap, searching for loved ones. More sinister were those people who made no noise at all, but lay motionless, crushed by the weight of their fellow prisoners. Harry had a fleeting view of a mother still clutching her small baby which squirmed in her immobile but protective arms. He could not tell if she was alive before he was propelled forward by the pressure of the crowd.

Those that could stand suddenly understood they were now free of the cage and several of them looked around wildly and sprinted off as fast as they could into the night. The camp guards were slow to react and there were few of them. The camp administrators had not expected such a brazen attack so close to the camp, and in the immediate aftermath it was unclear who had sabotaged the truck.

Harry looked around, feeling as if his body had been used as a punch bag, and swiftly considered his options. If he was going to rescue Tamara and Byron he could stay here and wait to be interred in the camp, but he considered Omar's words. As if on cue, a firm hand grasped his shoulder and he spun round to see the dark, frightened eyes of the banker.

"Come on," he urged Harry. "It's our only chance!" He dragged Harry forward with surprising strength and they stumbled away from the wreckage of fallen bodies. The engine of the truck was still revving and the upturned wheels spinning in air, and Harry saw the smoking hole torn from the chassis of the vehicle. The incendiary had been precisely placed to topple the vehicle but otherwise cause minimal damage. Harry guessed the bomb had been placed there earlier and detonated remotely.

He looked around and saw a detachment of black-uniformed men with machine guns swarm out of the entrance to the camp and race toward them. At that moment his decision was made for him. Escape was the only viable option, and he followed Omar, who was running away from the men as fast as his stubby legs would allow.

The camp searchlights swept across the perimeter of the fence and illuminated the confused crowd of people running aimlessly, providing targets for the security team who raised their weapons and fired a volley of shots into the crowd with a deafening crack. A number of people fell to the ground, and the collective panic escalated in intensity as the horde scattered to escape the carnage. Harry instinctively rolled over and as he got up, saw a dark van careening down the road, heading for the camp entrance.

The headlights blinded him as the van lurched forward and he instinctively raised his hands as a shield. The van headed straight for him, lurching over the bumpy dirt track, and for a second he was paralysed. A tiny part of his brain recognized it as the same vehicle the SSP had held him in, and he vaguely wondered why it was back. The thought caused him to hesitate a split second too long and the vehicle bore down on him, its engine revving noisily. It was about to strike him when his arm was pulled with such force it felt like it had been wrenched out of its socket. The motion sent him reeling to the ground, rolling inches away from the thick tyre on the driver's side.

"Come on get up!" urged Omar, his fleshy face a mask of determination. Harry staggered up and followed Omar, who moved with an agility that belied his bulk, heading for the blackness, anywhere away from the dark figures fanning out in military style formation. The air resounded with the burst of gunfire as they spotted fleeing targets. One of the perimeter lights illuminated the fugitive pair and immediately a volley of gunfire sputtered on the ground next to Harry and Omar, kicking up dirt dangerously close to their feet. They continued sprinting into the darkness with renewed vigour and as Harry cast a fleeting glance back, he spotted a new danger. The van had left the road and was barrelling straight for them, its lights bouncing crazily as the vehicle lurched drunkenly over the bumpy ground. It bounded over a lifeless body but the van hardly slowed as it careened toward them.

Harry's heart lurched and he gasped for breath. Despite the darkness and the chaos, they had somehow spotted him, and were making up ground extremely quickly.

In the van the SSP leader, now sitting in the cab of the vehicle, shouted frantic directions at the driver who was fighting to stay in control, gripping the steering wheel hard. They had scanned the area with the facial recognition long range scanner, and had found him amongst the sea of faces. The device continued to track the fugitive, and Bruce was convinced that even in the dark he would not escape. A sense of relief washed over him – he might just save his career after all. All they had to do was capture him alive before the morons from the PIA shot him dead.

"Christ Omar, move it! They're nearly on us!" Harry cried desperately. Immediately behind him he heard the banker wheezing and coughing, struggling to keep up with Harry, whose own legs were burning with effort. Harry heard the high pitched whistle of a bullet whizz past his ear, far too close for comfort. He dived onto the ground and as he did so, stole another quick glance at his pursuers. He saw the chasing van swerve in front of the armed figures so their line of sight was cut off, protecting the fugitives from further gunfire.

Harry had little time to process this confusing development, because the van's front grille was like a prize bull charging at them. The noise of the racing engine filled the air, and Harry saw the harsh yellow lights illuminate everything around him. Omar was only a few steps behind him but the van was just about to mow him down when he saw the ground fall away into a small gulley. It was too late for him to react and he skidded over the edge and tumbled on the hard, rocky ground. Omar followed close behind, also losing his balance and falling heavily down the gulley. The van followed and with a screech of tearing metal, the vehicle slewed over the lip of the gulley and bounced down it, the rocky outcrops tearing at the underside of the chassis. It came to rest with a crunch at the bottom of the gulley, which was less than ten feet deep, but enough to cave in the front of the vehicle. The engine coughed and cut out and despite the driver's attempts to turn over the engine, it failed to start.

Both Harry and Omar rolled painfully on the rocky bottom of the gulley and hauled their battered bodies up the other side. Harry was first and straining with effort he heaved Omar's bulky frame over the other side of the small rift. They staggered up and continued running hard, fuelled by adrenaline.

Omar pulled at Harry's sleeve. "They're persistent." His voice was calm but it was strained and breathless.

Harry glanced back and saw several figures in pursuit, the lights on their rifles bouncing crazily as they scrambled up the bank and sprinted toward them. The vehicle's demise had allowed the fugitives a precious hundred metres but Omar was visibly wilting, and Harry figured they would soon be in shooting range. In the darkness ahead they saw a line of deeper black running against the trees, and they heard the faint tinkle of running water.

"How the hell are they seeing us in the dark?" shouted Harry to Omar.

"Facial scanners," wheezed Omar. They used it on Leila. "They have a long range. It's like a GPS. They must have fixed on your face. Once they have a lock on you, they can track you anywhere as long as you are in range."

"What can we do?"

Omar's voice came in gasps. "There is only one way to counteract the device." Omar pointed into the distance as they ran and for a second Harry failed to understand. The sound of rushing water became louder, and then Harry understood. He nodded and they dashed toward the black line cut by the water. As they reached the edge, Harry hesitated and looked back. The small bobbing lights were closer and above the noise of the water he heard shouting.

"Hold it right there!" a harsh voice shouted. A warning shot struck the ground inches from Harry's foot and he traded glances with Omar. They had no choice.

"Keep your face in the water as much as possible so they can't track you."

Bracing themselves, they plunged into the black water. Harry felt as if he had been stabbed with a thousand sharp icy needles and the shock of the water enveloping him sapped his waning strength. He struggled to the surface, gasping for breath and instantly felt himself being swept along in the strong current. The current forced him under again and he felt his body begin to seize up, his core temperature falling rapidly. He broke the surface, gulping in the cool air and tried to move his arms to swim with the current. His arms were like blocks of stone and his body was swept along with relentless force completely outside his control. He vaguely heard frantic shouting from the river bank but then it was lost in the gurgling of the water. He went under again but only briefly this time, and saw the foamy tops of the white water reflected in the starlight. With a huge effort of will, he managed to spin round and turn so that he travelled feet first along the current. He was just in time as a large protruding rock barred his way and his feet scraped along the immovable object. He was fortunate it had not been his head, but his survival remained in doubt.

The cold seemed to envelop him like a shroud and an overwhelming tiredness swept over him. As the cold bit into his body, he lost all feeling in his limbs and his eyes became heavy with the inescapable urge to sleep. The white water continued to rage around but the sound became muffled, more distant, as if the sensation belonged to someone else, and he was an observer looking down.

For a bizarre second he felt almost warm, as if he were sitting with Tamara on the beautiful Persian rug on the hearth they used to curl up in beside a roaring log fire. It was where they had often made love in those wonderful, carefree days before it had all gone wrong. He smiled to himself at the memory before his vision faded to black and exhaustion finally overcame him.

# CHAPTER 9

On the shore Ethan cursed loudly, smacking his facial scanner in frustration. The tracking image for Harry Clarke had flickered, become intermittent and finally died. The device used thermal imaging and therefore relied on the body heat of the person being tracked. The scanner, having located the heat source, could scan the contours of the target's face and use algorithms to match the face against the image stored in its scanner. The problem was the heat source was gone, although when he saw the splashing of limbs in the water become more distant with each passing second, he understood why. The water was icy to the touch, and Ethan baulked at following the fugitives into the water. His comrades also stood at the edge, watching in fury as the two figures swept further away from their grasp.

Bruce watched the thrashing figures receding into the distance with impotent fury. The river was swollen from the recent rains, and the torrent of water swept through the valley away from the deportation camp. The nearest road bridge was several miles away and they would never reach them in time. Harry Clarke, one of the most wanted men in the country, a murderer and a traitor, had been within their grasp, and he had slipped away. The only comfort he could draw was that the bastard was likely to die of hypothermia if he didn't drown first. But the revered leader of the State Secret Police, Adam Griffiths himself, had personally ordered that Clarke be brought to London. He did not relish having to break the news to his ultimate boss. His mind raced with possibilities as to how he could assign blame for this ignominious failure. He was determined not to take the fall for Clarke's disappearance.

Omar dragged himself out of the dark water onto the muddy river bank, gasping with exhaustion. He pulled at a bank of reeds and hauled himself onto the soft earth, flopping onto his back and peering up at the starlit sky. A crescent moon was just starting to rise over the black shapes of the trees, illuminating them in a soft glow. His body shivered violently, and his extremities were numb and cold to the touch. His brain felt slow and lethargic, but he remembered his army training from all those years ago. The extreme cold weather training had been an essential part of their national service, and he struggled to picture his regimental commander, with his huge grey moustache and angry face, barking instructions at them.

He removed his clothing despite the chill air, stripping down to his tatty boxer shorts, so that his soaked clothes did not continue to freeze his bare skin. He dried his whole body, gently massaging his hands and feet until the circulation slowly began to return and he was able to gingerly wiggle his toes. The river ran slower as it approached the bend, and it had given him the opportunity to reach the bank as he fought to stay conscious.

Omar knew he was well clear of his pursuers. He fixed his gaze in the direction he had just travelled, and the crescent moon cast a ghostly pallor over the shimmering water. It was in those shadows that he saw the white shape, and he noted with alarm that it was motionless, bobbing gently at the mercy of the rippling current. Ignoring his own discomfort, he waded back into the water and stretched out to grab the body as it rode past on the current, like grabbing his case from the conveyor belt at the airport baggage reclaim.

He gently guided the body through the water and bent into the water up to his neck so that his shoulder was underneath. Gripping the back of the body's upper legs, he raised the limp mass on his shoulder and staggered to the bank, holding the body in a fireman's carry. He collapsed just as he reached the slimy ground and the heavy, soaking body rolled easily onto the mud.

Omar scrutinized his new friend and noted with concern the unhealthy pallor of his skin. He put his ear to his mouth and was relieved to detect him breathing shallowly. He placed his finger over the carotid artery in Harry's neck to check his pulse and found it slow but steady. Harry was unconscious and may have swallowed a lot of water, and urgently needed resuscitation. Omar gave him thirty chest compressions followed by a short sharp blow of two breaths into his mouth while he pinched his nose. He then repeated the exercise and had counted to eighteen on the chest compressions when Harry suddenly bolted awake, coughing violently. He turned over and spewed up a pool of water and then lay on the floor, shivering. Omar rolled him into the recovery position.

"Harry, if you can hear me, stay still. We're safe for now, but I need to get you warm as quickly as possible. You are suffering from mild hypothermia and I need to get your circulation back."

Omar quickly analyzed his friend. He was suffering from a level of extreme cold that the army medics described as immersion syndrome. His hands were blue and swollen from having been immersed in the cold water. Omar knew that he needed to get circulation to his friend's feet and hands as soon as possible or Harry was at risk of losing fingers and toes. He carefully removed Harry's boots and socks and dried off both feet. He then massaged them briskly until the bluish pallor began to turn a little pinker, visible even in the dim light. He worked on his hands immediately after, while Harry stayed put, conscious but groggy.

"Harry, try wiggling your fingers."

It took Harry a moment to respond, his brain slowed by the cold, but when he did the fingers were stiff but moved freely.

"Keep moving them," instructed Omar. "I have to remove your clothes and get you dry."

Harry, more alert now but still shivering violently, was able to assist Omar in his task, and before long they both sat on the bank stripped to their underwear. With slow and difficult movement, Harry crawled over to the base of a large oak tree under Omar's guidance and flopped down on the ground, his hands and feet still itchy and burning. He still could not feel or move his toes but as he lay there in the darkness, Omar worked feverishly to collect twigs and kindling into a pyramid-shaped pyre, and with the skilled use of two rocks as a flint, quickly got sparks going. After several unsuccessful attempts it finally took hold, bursting into flame. He added more sticks and blew into the rapidly expanding flames until the camp fire crackled and sizzled. Harry reached with his hands and feet toward the fire to burn away the cold but Omar cautioned him.

"Let the warmth come gradually. If you heat them up too quickly you may get tissue damage."

As the fire crackled and its warmth slowly brought feeling to his raw skin, Harry lay back on a bed of leaves and rested. Omar however, continued to collect sticks and also found several large boughs for shelter, and some blackberries from a mulberry tree. Harry watched him as he laboured with quiet efficiency, his rescuer praising Allah when he found an old discarded tin. He filled it with water from the river and boiled it on the fire, balancing the tin on a small flat rock placed in the middle of the blaze.

As the water boiled he set up their shelter and dug into the soft earth to create two hollow depressions by the fire. When Omar retrieved the smouldering round tin from the fire using a pair of large twigs pressed against it, they had to wait a while before the water was sufficiently cooled for them to drink. The sharp, sweet taste of the berries took away the residual earthy taste of the water, and when they had finished their survival meal, Omar directed them to the depressions where he piled the leaves and tree boughs around Harry and then did the same for his spot. Within seconds Harry had drifted off, his body still stiff but his circulation returning to normal.

Harry was in the middle of a bad dream, fighting a rising barrage of water, his chest heavy as he fought for breath, when he snapped instantly awake as a hand grasped his shoulder. Disoriented, he forgot where he was and stared vacantly at the dark figure silhouetted against the deep pink sky. The sun was just starting to peek over the treetops, and the first threads of daylight cast a soft glow onto the forested glade.

"Sorry I didn't mean to startle you," the voice said gently. The tone was low and accented, and everything came flooding back. "I made mulberry leaves tea for you. Drink it; it's full of vitamins and nutrients." Omar handed him the old tin and Harry took it gratefully, sipping at the warming liquid which tasted fruity and surprisingly good. He was still cold and shivery, and realized that he was absolutely famished, but at least he was alive thanks to Omar.

"How the hell did you learn all this stuff?" Harry glanced over Omar's shoulder and saw the camp fire roaring nearby. He could feel the welcome warmth radiating from it, and saw his damp clothes placed on a set of branches close to the fire, steam gently rising from them. He saw the softly spoken banker in a new light.

Omar smiled, revealing a large gap in his front teeth. "The Iraqi Army. I spent two years National Service and five years as a Reservist twenty years ago. They put us through absolute hell but the one good thing is that you never forget what you learned. We did plenty of cold weather training up in the Eastern Zagros Mountains near the Iran border. We learned how to close our bodies down to survive in extreme temperatures. You were lucky my friend. I doubt you would have lasted much longer in that freezing river."

Harry forced his stiffened body out of the temporary shelter that Omar had fashioned for them and crawled over to the crackling fire. His body relaxed with the sudden warmth that washed over him, as if it was thawing out, the pain of the last few days melting away. He cast his hands out toward the fire. Occasionally the breeze would change direction and the smoke would send him into bouts of coughing. Harry turned to Omar. "I owe you my life."

Omar gave a dismissive laugh. "Don't be ridiculous." His expression turned more serious. "I hate to spoil the party, but we will have to get going soon Harry. It's past first light and the fire may attract attention. They're sure to be on our trail before long."

They feasted on a breakfast of berries, watchful for any signs of movement in the trees. Omar had built the camp fire in the wooded glade set back from the river bank. The trees provided excellent cover from the nearby road that cut through the fields, but Omar knew an alert patrol could easily spot the camp fire or the rising smoke.

Harry stared into the coals of the fire, enjoying its warmth. However he had little time for reflection and reluctantly put on his damp clothes, feeling rested and stronger. He glanced at Omar, regarding the short, stocky banker with huge respect. He looked exhausted, the dark circles around his eyes thicker, and Harry noticed he had lost his spectacles. It seemed to matter little to him, and Harry was happy to take his lead when they extinguished the camp fire and ventured out toward the road. It had been a long time since he had felt the glow of companionship, and Omar with his skills would undoubtedly prove a valuable ally in their flight. They reached the road that bisected the rolling fields, the spires of distant churches gleaming in the steadily rising sun. In the north, a pall of smoke drifted into the cool early morning air. It was a sign of the times, reflected Harry ruefully. The peaceful rural scene before them reflected an England that had been lost many years ago, and the smoke that blackened that tiny corner of the pale sky was the new reality, a nation under siege.

"We need transport and quickly," said Omar. "The river was swollen and flowing fast. I think we floated at least five miles, well away from the area around the camp and the checkpoints. They would not know where we had reached shore so they may be combing the area closer to the camp and working outwards. They may not even be looking for us at all, probably assuming that we had drowned, although somehow I doubt it. My guess is that they will reach this area fairly soon. We need to put some distance between them."

The pair discussed their plan and then trudged along the road in silence for a while, both of them lost in their own thoughts but alert to any signs of their pursuers. They kept close to the straggly hedge that bordered the road, keeping low. The hedge provided natural cover, but the road curved upwards into a small hill, and anyone observing the sweeping fields of the valley from the crest would probably see them.

The distant sound of an engine snapped them out of their reverie. Omar listened intently and grinned. "Time for action." Harry nodded and lay motionless in the middle of the road. As the car moved closer, Omar ran out into the road in a state of panic. He knew he was taking a huge risk. There were very few Good Samaritans left and many drivers, confronted by this situation, would likely speed up. The lone driver, seeing the stocky figure in a scruffy, heavily creased suit running wildly toward him, began to slow down. Even so, he almost hit the agitated figure who stepped directly in front of the vehicle and he had to slam his brakes to avoid a collision. His BMW screeched to a halt and the driver instinctively reached for his gun in the glove compartment.

The figure banged on his window, his weary, lined face a mask of panic, his dark eyes wide with fright. The driver wound down his window and the figure gestured into the road. "Sir you have to help me," he cried. "The Army shot my brother. He needs urgent help. Please." He tugged gently at the door.

"All right, all right," said the driver. He stepped out of the car, his gun firmly in hand, and followed the short figure to where his companion lay. He knelt down and took his eye off the man for just a moment. It was all that Omar needed. With a swift devastating chop to the neck, he felled the driver who grunted sharply and collapsed to the ground next to Harry, who instantly got up. They quickly hauled the unconscious body into the bottom of the bush running alongside the road and relieved him of his keys and gun.

They got in and Harry took the wheel. "Don't worry," assured Omar. "He will be up and about in a few hours, dazed and with a sore neck but otherwise okay." He grinned. "It's been a while since I did that. I'm starting to enjoy myself."

Harry stared at him with undisguised admiration, relieved that unlike the last time he commandeered a vehicle, the driver would be fine.

"Yes, yes another Iraqi Army trick," continued Omar, in answer to an unspoken question. "Also," he continued, grinning from ear to ear, "the vast majority of people faced with the prospect of hitting someone who jumps out on them would slam on the brakes, even today. I played the numbers game." He looked in the back seat and grabbed the satchel lying there and rifled through it. "Praise Allah, this is definitely our lucky day. Sandwiches, fruit, cheese and chocolate." He let out a contented sigh. "And two bottles of beer. Mohammed has been kind to us today."

The thought of eating properly for the first time since he could remember excited Harry, but they needed to get some miles under their belt. Last night he had nearly died; he was starving hungry and his stiff, cold body ached painfully from his ordeal in the water; he was a wanted fugitive who risked being caught any moment; yet perversely he felt uplifted, his spirits vibrant. It had been far too long since he had felt like that.

They continued driving, chatting away like old friends on a carefree fishing trip, enjoying the warmth of the pale sun on their faces through the windshield. If the government had not been in complete control of the airwaves, they would have probably put on a music channel and sung along. Harry sat back, enjoying the feel of driving again, knowing that at least for now they were safe.

# CHAPTER 10

Dr. Hilary Warnecki sat in her makeshift 'office' in the main ward of Camp Salisbury hospital and rubbed her attractive but tired face, pulling back her straggly blond hair from around her almond shaped face and azure eyes. Those eyes continually sparkled with humour and empathy, a quality that quickly endeared the dedicated medic to her many patients; but recently those eyes had been dulled by fatigue and a sense of despair that had settled over her like a black cloud.

Dr. Hilary, as she had always been known, was a twenty year veteran in the medical profession, specializing in emergency multi-casualty situations. Her first such posting had been as part of a European disaster relief task force that had travelled to Banda Aceh in Sumatra to treat injured victims of the massive tsunami that had engulfed the Indian Ocean coast in 2004. As a naive twenty-three year old, she had witnessed first-hand the trauma of a catastrophe that at the time had been the worst natural disaster in human history. The suffering and anguish of her patients had enveloped her, not just because of their injuries, but because of the pain of losing so many loved ones in one disaster. Whole families had been wiped out; the cruel irony was that many other families had just one or two survivors consumed by grief for their lost relatives.

At the time the media had called it an 'Act of God' and it had shaken her faith to its very foundations. If the carnage and misery she had suffered was an Act of God, then it was a cruel and merciless deity that had taken fathers, mothers, sons and daughters randomly and without mercy. However, she knew she had found her calling. It was no longer sufficient to provide on-site emergency medical care. She took the role of a grief counsellor, a positive force and motivator to the poor souls who saw little point in continuing this unforgiving existence. In particular she was drawn to children, partly because she had been told as a teenager that she was infertile due to a genetic ovarian disorder; but more so because the tragedies she witnessed always involved children, who were far too young to lose everything, as they often did in these disasters.

With little prospect of raising a family of her own, she had devoted herself to a career saving children, and had spent her entire medical career working for Médecins Sans Frontières. Her work for this humanitarian non-governmental secular organization had taken her around the world, to places such as Haiti after the earthquake in 2010, the Syrian civil war in 2013 and the cholera epidemic in Bangladesh following the devastating floods in 2018.

Some of her work had involved remote locations, and there were often supply problems that resulted in the shortage of necessary medical resources. Her experience taught her that the lack of immediately available medical equipment and medicines was the largest contributor to preventable deaths, but most often this was a logistical rather than a political issue. This time, however, the issue was firmly political. It was not as if the Salisbury camp was located in a remote hillside like the Kashmir earthquake that struck in 2005 when supply trucks had to battle almost impenetrable high mountain passes with significant snowfall and landslides that blocked a number of key roads.

The supply requisition she put through here was never met in full, and sometimes only a third of the equipment she ordered was provided. There was never any explanation, just an implied suggestion to make do and feel lucky with what she had. When supplies were scarce, tough decisions had to be made and she was making those daily. She had prioritized the children first, but that hardly made it easier.

She rubbed her knotted brow, pressing her temple with her thumb and forefinger. It was one of her many habits in times of stress. Another one had been chain-smoking, but mercifully there were few cigarettes to be found in this desolate place. She would kill for a cigarette now, however. She smiled at the irony of such a thought coming from a medical doctor. Her acute stress was not due to the death and suffering that surrounded her; she had grown accustomed to that after so many years in the field. It was the sense of utter futility fuelled by the apparent indifference of the camp authorities to the plight of the rapidly increasing numbers of people contracting this mysterious pathogen. Already the infirmary, set up like a field army hospital with a tented roof and makeshift camp beds totally unsuitable for ill patients, was overflowing. There was a macabre waiting list whereby the deceased made room for new cases, and the turnover of beds was increasing daily.

In most disasters she had seen a glimmer of hope in the chaos, but here even that was absent. She perceived this whole humanitarian crisis unfolding before her as unnecessary, and that added to her unusual degree of despondency. This was not a spectacular natural disaster with scores of casualties needing immediate attention where broken limbs, burns or lacerations predominated; it was not a war zone where bullet wounds and shrapnel injuries from landmines or bomb blasts were the most frequent injuries. This was less apparent, more subtle, and that's what made it so much more dangerous. This was a slow, insidious illness with a long incubation period that in many ways was even worse than a natural disaster such as an earthquake.

Until recently Britain was one of the richest nations on earth, a country that was the last place Hilary would have expected a new disease to originate from. Yet it was here in Camp Salisbury that she was forced to confront the limits of her own abilities. None of the usual remedies or drugs had worked and she had no tools to fight it and nothing to stop it spreading.

Hilary took the ear-piece from her stethoscope, folded it and laid it on her desk. She leaned back in her ratty plastic chair, her shift over for now. The hospital had eight nurses only, all deportees, and four of them were on shift. Her head was throbbing and she needed to sleep, but that was a luxury she could barely afford over the last few weeks. It was often a case of snatching an hour or two where she could, much like her meals.

She picked up the pile of notes she had made on each patient, skimming through them. Even such supplies as paper were in rare supply here, and she'd had to beg the camp administration for that. A tablet or a computer was out of the question, and no external communication was permitted except through the central office at the farmhouse, under the strict supervision of a camp administrator. It had been impossible for her to research the disease or indeed to communicate with or seek advice from other physicians. She had no idea how prevalent the disease was outside the camp. It developed and mutated in a way unlike any pathogen she had ever seen, and she was desperate for information, something that would help her understand how it was transmitted and more importantly how it could be combated.

She made a hasty list of supplies and resolved to talk to the Chief Camp Administrator in the morning. It was unlikely she would get far with that callous bastard Sullivan but she had to try. She owed it to her patients to attempt to obtain the medicines they so desperately needed. There had been rumours of a vaccination program but they were quickly dispelled by the camp hierarchy. There was no vaccine, they said, although they had been assured that Whitehall was working around the clock to search for one. The usual antibiotics and penicillin had little impact on the disease, merely to slow its rate of cell destruction. She could buy time, hoping that a cure might miraculously present itself, but there were not enough antibiotics to go around, hence the inevitable choices.

It was no good. Tiredness swept over her like a tidal wave, and she staggered over to her mattress in the corner, flopped down and pulled the thin blankets over her athletic but thinning body. As she drifted off quickly she mentally chastised herself, promising that she would eat better.

Hilary was drawn from her vivid dreams by the soft voice of one of her nurses gently rousing her. "Dr. Hilary, you wanted to know if the boy asked for you."

"Huh?" Dazed and confused, she slowly cleared the fog in her brain and gawped at the nurse with blurry eyes. Her mind vaguely registered that it was still dark, and she glanced at her watch. Five a.m. She had been asleep for just over four hours. The dim lights in her office hummed gently, a constant background noise, and she felt a chill as she stumbled out of bed, still in her clothes. She put her faded white lab coat on and checked herself in the mirror. Her flowing blond hair was a mess, but no one really cared here. She attached her breathing mask and followed the nurse into the main ward, a huge tented area with nothing more than a tarpaulin for a floor.

There was little activity, and the ward was fairly quiet, punctuated only by the low moans of some patients and the gentle snoring of others. However the stench of dried vomit and blood pervaded the air. In the low light, she saw at the far end of the row of camp beds the boy perched on the bed next to his mother, cooling her brow and uttering softly to her as he had done for the last eight days. She lay still, barely conscious, but her eyes were open. As Hilary approached, those glassy eyes appeared to stare right through her, as if they were peering out onto some distant horizon. Although her once beautiful face was a light bronze, Hilary could see the tell-tale patches of pale yellow skin, the jaundice that revealed the breaking down of her liver and its failure to detoxify her blood. Her eye whites, the conjunctiva, were also yellowed, indicating increased levels of bilirubin in her blood, which would usually be excreted by a healthy liver. The internal war raging within her had left her weak, and her breath came in shallow, wheezy gasps, a sure sign her lungs were headed the same way as her liver.

However, it was the skin lesions on these patients that alarmed Hilary the most. The purple bruising around affected areas, often broken skin from which blood and pus oozed out slowly, in some cases as a bubble like that of stab victims she had treated. The boy's mother had several around her face and neck, and they had grown steadily worse in the eight days she had been in the hospital. Hilary had compiled personal records of survival rates and the period between first infection and death. The range was three days to over a month but the average was around nine days, and the outward signs indicated that the boy's mother was a typical case.

Yet the boy, apparently unaffected and not even wearing a mask, sat by his mother's bed in tireless devotion. The nurses had practically adopted him, sharing their modest food supplies so the boy did not go hungry. Hilary looked at him. His young pre-adolescent features were only a shade lighter than his mother, but his rounded face and keen, intelligent eyes mirrored his mother's striking features. His face was streaked with tears, and he looked up at the doctor imploringly.

"She doesn't have long does she?" he said to her earnestly.

Hilary checked the patient's pulse, respiration and blood pressure; as if it really mattered. She could not lie to the boy; he was far too astute to allow that. Her voice was muffled through the mask as she spoke, a little guilty as she looked at the boy's unprotected face.

"We're doing everything we can Byron," she said soothingly. "She's in good hands. I know how proud she is of you." She took her stethoscope and placed it on his chest below his ragged shirt. "Mmm. You have a heartbeat as strong as an ox. You really should wear a mask Byron."

"I don't need one!" he snapped petulantly. "I'm alright. I don't care about myself. It's my Mum I care about."

Hilary shrank back, but understood his response. He had arrived with his mother over five months ago, one of the longest serving inmates in the camp. No doubt he had grown tougher and wiser in that time, but the boy was about to be orphaned in one of the most desolate God-forsaken places she had ever worked in, a place devoid of basic dignity. What hope was there for a twelve year-old boy without a family in this awful place?

A bony hand suddenly grasped her wrist with brittle strength and Byron's mother Tamara opened her yellow eyes wide, her intense gaze like a feline. She struggled to rise in her bed but the effort was too much and Hilary allowed Tamara to draw her down to the bed so she could whisper in her ear.

"Promise me you will get him out of here," she croaked, her hoarse voice punctuated by bouts of wheezing. She suddenly burst into a spasm of coughing and Hilary quickly grabbed the stained commode by her bed, which acted as the repository for the bodily fluids at all ends. Her raking cough was punctuated by deep retching and she brought up little more than a thin reddish mixture of blood and water, her stomach contents having been expelled long before.

Tamara stopped coughing and Byron wiped her mouth, but her breath had grown more shallow and Hilary recognized it instantly; the death-rattle. Before the doctor could respond to her entreaty, Tamara's eyes rolled back and she began convulsing. Her body jerked like a marionette and she threw off her thin covers. The skin on her emaciated body was almost translucent but the energy that sparked through her body sent her limbs flailing wildly.

"Nurses, she's having a seizure," cried the doctor. Several nurses came running and held her down firmly. One of them guided the howling boy away with soothing words. As they battled to save her, Hilary glanced back at Byron's tear-streaked face as he was led outside. This would end only one way, she thought ruefully.

# CHAPTER 11

The nurses had already sprayed the bed sparingly with the precious disinfectant in readiness for the next sick patient in line when Hilary left the hospital several hours later. She marched past the line of barracks that housed most of the camp residents. They were no more than hastily assembled breeze block structures with corrugated roofs. They had no electricity and no heating, and the blocks were often cracked or badly sealed, providing little insulation against the cold, especially at night. The air carried a sharpness that hinted at colder weather to come. Hilary feared that the camp and its occupants were ill-equipped to survive the bitter winters that had plagued the country in the last five years.

The dormitory occupants, however, were much better off than the newer entrants, who were forced to live in tents until the overcrowded barracks had room to house them. It was the unofficial hierarchy that existed within the camp. Although more breeze block structures were being hastily erected, it was never fast enough. At last it seemed, however that inmates were now leaving the camp, suggesting that the paperwork involved in their deportation was complete and they were on their way back to their original country. She could only guess at this, however as it was virtually impossible to obtain any independent news here.

She passed through a line of tents near the edge of the camp where a small group of ragged black children were kicking around a small plastic football in their bare feet. A white boy tried to join in but they pushed him away, calling him names. She shook her head sadly, afraid for the future when even children showed intolerance just because of skin colour. In darker moments of introspection, she considered herself lucky she was not bringing up her own children in this world.

Near the tents squeezed close to the razor wire perimeter at the edge of the camp, the deceased inmates were dumped in a pile ready to be burnt in a funeral pyre every other day, and as Hilary marched toward the farmhouse she glanced over at the large black sheet that covered the bodies gently flapping in the late October breeze. Somewhere in that macabre pile lay a deceased mother who had spent the last hour of her life comforting her son. Her bitter tears blurred her vision, and she angrily wiped them away. The boy had been incredibly brave, but his future was uncertain. She was glad he was going back to the barracks, because the hospital was the epicentre of the pathogen, and he was amazed that Byron had not contracted the disease yet, although the incubation period was long and he might yet become infected.

In the grounds of the farmhouse, the huge steel cages that new arrivals were funnelled into was brimming with exhausted, ragged people. Some of them stared through the bars at the doctor with hollow, listless eyes as she passed by. They were waiting to be processed and at the far opening of the cage was a huddle of administrators who registered the new arrivals in a tortuously slow process, issuing tents and basic supplies.

As usual the double doors to the farmhouse were closely guarded by two PIA goons and they towered over Hilary's diminutive five foot four frame. They made no attempt to move aside.

"I have an appointment with Mr. Sullivan."

"Name?" one of them said brusquely.

"Dr. Hilary Warnecki, the hospital in-charge."

They exchanged worried glances and quickly moved aside, adjusting their masks as they did so. Neither of them wanted to be near anyone in contact with the diseased hordes by the hospital. One of them ran and announced that Sullivan would see her immediately and they sighed with relief as she disappeared out of their sight into the farmhouse.

She reached Sullivan's office, formerly the house's study, and faced the Chief Administrator. For a man possessing a widespread reputation for his ruthless nature, he looked quite insubstantial, mused Hilary. His balding pate and thick rimmed spectacles would not look out of place in an accountant's office, and his thin, owlish face and air of twitchiness was incongruous with the power he yielded as the head of the camp. He did not get up, but if he had, she knew he would have stood barely an inch taller than her. The only indication that he had not spent all his life behind a desk was the huge purple scar that ran in a jagged line from the base of his nose under his jawline and down his neck. His attempt to cloak the scar through a close cropped salt and pepper beard was ineffective. It was the most obvious feature on an otherwise unimpressive face.

"Dr. Hilary, an unexpected pleasure. Please, take a seat." He motioned to a rickety wooden chair placed at right angles to his antique oak desk.

She detested the way he never met her eyes when he spoke. At least he had the good grace not to reach for his mask like his moronic oafs. He knew that even if she was infected she would have to cough all over him or spit at him so he inhaled her spores, or her saliva was absorbed by his skin. "Thank you, but I prefer to stand," she replied tersely.

"Please yourself. Make it quick. I'm busy."

"Do you have any idea what we're facing in the hospital? This is a pandemic that could wipe out the entire camp."

"I'm aware of that Doctor," Sullivan replied in a disinterested voice, still tapping away at his tablet.

Her pent-up fury suddenly unleashed itself. She swept her hand across his table and the tablet went clattering to the wooden floor. This time he looked directly at her. The two administrators lurking in the corner moved toward her but with a flick of his wrist he sent them back. "Do you know where I have been you callous prick? I've spent the last hour comforting a little boy, one of the bravest children I have ever met, who early this morning lost his mother after spending eight days by her bedside hoping and praying she would survive. No child should ever suffer like that."

Sullivan bent over to pick up his tablet, but he had the sense not to continue writing. " I'm sorry to hear that but I am sure that when he's deported his new country will make appropriate arrangements for his welfare." His tone was matter-of-fact, dismissive, and this irritated Hilary even further.

"How the hell do you know that?" she spat. "You couldn't care less whether all the people die in there!"

Sullivan leaned back in his chair, calmly accepting her onslaught.

She found it frustrating that the Chief never seemed to change his mood no matter what the provocation. It was impossible to ruffle that calm exterior, but it was not a quality to admire. He appeared to be devoid of all emotion, which probably made him an ideal person to run this hellhole.

"Whether I care or not is irrelevant. This disease is not of our making." He glanced at the tiny crucifix around her neck. "Perhaps you should ask your deity," he said with a trace of mockery. "Considering the chaos you've witnessed all over this planet, I am amazed that you still wear that thing."

"This has nothing to do with my faith. It is not his doing that we are denied basic supplies and resources to fight this disease. That is squarely down to you."

Sullivan scratched at his beard in mild irritation. It was about the most expressive she had seen him. "Doctor, you overestimate my importance in this project. I am an administrator. I have no military title and no political influence. I am expected to run this camp with the resources at my disposal to the best of my ability and that is what I am doing. I cannot demand resources, I can only communicate the conditions that we are facing to my superiors and let them make the decision."

"People are dying, Sullivan, and you won't even provide me with a computer so I can research and document the disease. I can't communicate with anyone outside the camp to seek advice or get some answers. What you are allowing to happen is inhumane and you are accountable." Her voice cracked with impotent fury.

"Look, I have had to deal with a serious emergency. Last night one of our transports was attacked by the camp entrance. These madmen are intent on killing innocent people. They don't care about the people in the camps. How can we get medical supplies when terrorists are lurking outside ready to blow them up? I have strict instructions. As far as I understand the government scientists are working around the clock to fight this disease and I can assure you that as soon as they have a cure or an effective vaccine you will be one of the first to know. I am just following my orders."

The doctor's voice was thick with contempt. "Yeah, that's always the way with people like you. Blame it on your superiors, never take responsibility yourself. History is full of people like you Sullivan. That's what the camp commanders said at Dachau and Auschwitz."

Sullivan's face twitched and he peered up at her. His steely grey eyes were hard. "I don't need a history lesson from you Doctor," he growled. "Surely your time is better spent trying to save your patients - which you don't seem to be able to do terribly well at the moment - than standing here castigating me."

"But we need more medicines," she said desperately.

"I will see what I can do. This meeting is over." His dismissive tone left Hilary in no doubt that he would do absolutely nothing. She saw his eyes under his thick spectacles flick to the corner of the room and his two colleagues adjusted their masks and moved toward her. One of them grabbed her by the arm and she angrily shook it off. "Don't worry I'm going," she said, deliberately coughing in his direction. The man moved hastily away, checking his mask.

Hilary stormed out of the farmhouse back into the chill air. She cursed herself for becoming too emotionally involved. Once again Sullivan had stonewalled her. Their battle of wills was exhausting and she felt all the positive enthusiasm that had carried her through so many catastrophic zones in the past waning under the weight of indifferent bureaucracy.

Sullivan watched her barge past his men, her shapely bottom cheeks moving in a mesmerizing rhythm. He felt a pang of guilt but hastily dismissed it. He allowed her visits only because he desired her, but his superiors had told him categorically there was no more room for medical supplies in the already stretched camp budget. In fact, Sullivan reflected, if she knew the whole truth she would probably have stabbed him with one of the few syringes she had been permitted.

# REUTERS EDITORIAL OCTOBER 18

As the disease ravaging the camps continues to spread, the government propaganda machine is in full flow. The TV screens, both in the home and on the vast screens overlooking town centres, and the social media continually show images of how the regime is trying to alleviate suffering in the camps and to stamp out the disease. Interviews with internees testifying how camp guards have sought to keep families together and done everything to improve conditions in the camp have been carefully circulated on all networks. This has been interspersed with images of medical personnel arriving in ambulances at the perimeter of the camps and unloading boxes of medical supplies, and medical workers treating supposedly ill people with great care and attention. Overlaid is a commentary detailing the resources that government-affiliated medical bodies are employing to address this mysterious disease of unknown origin.

These are the only images the government is allowing to circulate beyond its shores. The tight media control has made it difficult for international observers to accurately assess what is really happening in the country. This control has many precedents from previous administrations, a recent example being the Iran political elections, and the government is fully aware that media propaganda is a crucial battleground. Despite its military strength and the fear it has created in the populace as a deterrent to challenge, this regime still views the information flowing through media networks as a vital element in its strategy.

The inevitable effect of the propaganda war has been the steady isolation of this once open and transparent island. Many embassies have already closed down their operations. Tourism, once a key source of revenue for the U.K. economy, has virtually dried up. The only tourists allowed in are those who have submitted themselves to the most rigorous and intrusive background checks, and once inside the country are only allowed to go on closely supervised tours. No tourist is allowed to wander the country alone and they are denied Internet access while in the country. All photographs are carefully vetted before the tourist leaves the country.

The Home Office Minister for Homeland Security, Angus Shaw, states that these restrictive measures are necessary to protect foreign tourists against rebel forces, which they claim could kidnap and use hostages as bargaining tools. The argument actually has some relevance; however it has served to make the country so insular that its closed society has been compared to the communist state of North Korea. The Global Transparency Index issued by Transparency International rates Britain as the most closed nation in Europe, a far cry from the days when it was considered a bastion of democracy.

Isolated rebel attacks have continued, solitary expressions of rage with little sense or strategy. Nevertheless they continue to be a thorn in the regime's side; frequent sweeps of purported rebel strongholds in suburban areas, tenement blocks and high rise apartment buildings have yielded very little, despite their strong-arm tactics. Indeed, in order to save face, the authorities have occasionally taken into custody the person who gave the tip-off along with his or her family. The government has taken to condemning the attacks as the work of extremists trying to derail its legitimate aim to rebuild the country, and the rhetoric has been suitably aggressive. Pelham's Deputy and media spokesman Giles Chamberlain has promised, in his usual ebullient style, to crush insurgents with an iron fist. The arbitrary detentions and arrests, often on spurious anti-terrorism charges, have continued unabated with little respect for the rule of law, and it is difficult to estimate the numbers of political prisoners, because many of them are considered eligible for deportation.

The battle to suppress the rebellion against Conservative rule is far from complete, despite the regime's overwhelming military superiority. Enemy combatants are lurking in the shadows, the element of surprise the only real tactical advantage they have. Added to the regime's problems are the threats of economic sanctions imposed by the United Nations, supported by Europe, America and China. These sanctions could spiral the country into an economic tailspin. The relative scarcity of key goods and services is already noticeable as the country's isolated stance has severely curtailed the supply chain. There is talk of austerity measures that promise to be more stringent than the recent Great Recession, which remains all too vivid in people's memories. Travel in and out of the country is now only for the chosen few, and Heathrow, for so long the epicentre of global air routes, as much for its geographical location as its ability to absorb huge volumes of air traffic, has been usurped. Most flights have now switched to Frankfurt, Paris or Dublin. Landing on any part of the British mainland is considered too hazardous by cautious airline executives. Sea traffic has also declined, with few ferries leaving port, and the Eurotunnel train terminal has been closed until further notice.

Surprisingly the one area where travel was expected, the

deportation boats, has experienced little activity. Despite the *'Sonderzüge'* trains (a nickname derived from the Nazi holocaust trains that has persisted despite the government's media campaign) and the caged trucks arriving at several ports around the country such as Felixstowe and Pembroke, the fate of Britain's deportees is unknown. The ports are closed off to the public and so once the transports reach their destination, one can only speculate what is happening. Since the imposition of martial law, and even since it was lifted, the entry of journalists has been severely restricted. Even local reporters have been forced into disclaimers under threat of reprisals so that news from the front line has been sanitized and neutered.

Nevertheless there have been reported sightings of boats leaving the harbour at several ports, but what has become of them afterwards remains a mystery. No European government has claimed to have received a warning to expect an influx of refugees and no country has reported any boatloads of deportees entering their waters. It is one further mystery that this increasingly secretive regime has conceived.

# CHAPTER 12

The constant *drip-drip* of the water from the ceiling was the only sound to break the otherwise heavy silence inside the cell. It pinged onto the metal floor from a concealed pipe in the ceiling with a hollow tinny sound that drove Sean Kelly crazy. It seemed to grow louder and louder until it reverberated around the hollow metal six by four. After all the abuse he had suffered, it was the isolation and the maddening ping of the water that really affected him. It was strange how the mind played tricks when a person was imprisoned in an isolation cell as long as he had been. The mind could become your friend or your enemy. He had heard that some people could retreat deep into their private world, taking comfort in the memory of happier days. The isolation could also magnify your senses so that something as innocuous as dripping water became a torture in itself. He could not even move his chair or bed underneath the drip because, like the latrine and tiny sink in the corner, they were bolted to the floor. There had to be a way to get rid of the noise, but his brain was too lethargic to think of a solution.

He had no idea how long he had been in the cell. The only link to the outside world was a small metal grille at eye level, which occasionally opened for the delivery of food and water on the small shelf immediately below it. Without daylight and stripped of his watch, time moved so slowly, it felt like years. He guessed it was no more than a week since he had last seen another human being. The prison officer claimed she was a woman but in Sean's opinion she bore only a passing resemblance to one. She had the physique of a shot putter, huge but muscular, and her shoulders were as broad as any man. The furrowed skin on her face was marked with several warts from which sprouted small but tough hairs, which complemented the wiry stubble on her upper lip and double chin. Her deep, throaty voice matched her physique. Although Belmarsh was a maximum security all-male prison, Officer Marcia Sutcliffe held a position as one of the chief warders, and enjoyed a fearsome reputation.

Even as he thought of the old sow, he felt a need for human contact, even one as repugnant as hers. Seeing another person was a mixed blessing, however. It often meant another torture session, although they were becoming less common these days. When the soldiers had shot him in the thigh they had hauled him into the assault tank and taken him prisoner as they continued to destroy the farmhouse that served as the cell's base of operations. They were ruthless, and most of his compatriots had died on that calamitous day. The one person he had wanted to die, however, appeared to have survived. He last saw Harry running hard for the perimeter of the compound, hand in hand with Julianne, just before the burning shot that felt as if his leg had been ripped from its socket. He had gone down, spurting blood and they had hastily patched him up. He had spent a day in a field hospital before they took him for interrogation at the local police station.

The authorities quickly discovered that they had ensnared the putative leader of the movement, not through any disclosure of his, but from their surveillance and inside knowledge, which probably came from a spy in their camp. It was an unexpected bonus to capture the leader alive and they had transferred him to Belmarsh Prison for more specialist interrogation.

The high-walled maximum security prison was one of the newest prisons in the country, less than forty years old, considerably younger than some of the crumbling, overcrowded Victorian institutions such as HM Prison Manchester, formerly known as Strangeways. Located in Woolwich on the site of the former Royal Arsenal, it was linked to the Woolwich Crown Court by an underground passage that meant it was useful for high profile cases and those involving national security. Indeed it was the usual location for terrorist trials, and Sean remembered with a shudder that Faisal, the cell's failed suicide bomber, had been executed here. He had only seen the gallows yard once, but it was enough. It stood there silent and brooding, the noose swaying gently in the gust that whipped around the courtyard, kicking up swirls of grey dust.

The prison had a history of trouble, including several riots, and staff at Belmarsh had a reputation for intimidation, part of the policy to keep prisoners in line. It was rumoured that there was a whole section situated underground, used mainly for political prisoners. On his few forays in the prison yard, he had heard prisoners refer to it as 'the Dungeon.' However, the prison had been modernized extensively in the past ten years and the wing that Sean occupied was modern and clinical, more like an asylum with its utilitarian metal and harsh fluorescent lighting.

Since his initial interrogation he had been in relative isolation in this windowless, soulless, high-tech steel impound. He had only seen other inmates and daylight perhaps five or six times since he had arrived here, and his view of the sky from the prison yard was pierced with twisted razor wire. In those early days they had bled him dry, extracting the information slowly and carefully, knowing they had plenty of time to get what they needed from him.

The first few days had been the worst. They had handcuffed him to a chair and two interrogators had entered, one short, stocky and aggressive with crew-cut hair, the other taller, ascetic looking. The short one bristled like a caged fighter until the taller one, quite clearly the leader, let him loose. The shorter one took great pleasure in punching his face on cue from a short nod by the taller man until it was puffy and swollen, his features bloody, bruised and unrecognizable, eyes closed up like two slits. Then the short man worked on his body like a boxer, with a perverse ability to target his kidney and spleen with gruelling force. All the time the taller man sat back, scratching at his hooked nose impatiently, reeling off incessant questions, appealing to Sean's common sense; that it would end much quicker if he cooperated.

Then they abruptly disappeared and he never saw them again. The physical punishment was over but they were not finished with him. The next stage was the psychological torture, to gradually break him down, destroy his spirit and depersonalize him. They were not necessarily crude; they did not leave any visible scars. Instead they induced a state of helplessness in him, whereby he lost any control over his environment. The questions continued endlessly. They promised him that if he cooperated he would be allowed to sleep or go to the toilet or eat. When these basic necessities were denied for long periods, the effect on his ability to resist their questioning was startling. That in turn made him weaker and prone to suggestion, further eroding his self-image, breaking him down progressively.

Apart from relentless questioning under the stress of starvation or sleep deprivation, they had depersonalized him by other less direct methods. They had used sensory deprivation techniques such as chaining him up and placing a hood over his head, or taking his clothes and lowering the cell temperature to marginally above freezing so that he stood all night naked and shivering. They had also used sensory assault by blasting his cell with death metal music, the fierce charging beats assaulting his brain until he wanted to tear his ears off to escape the clamour. Then it would be replaced with a hideously melodious German ditty from the middle of last century that was repeated over and over again for hours on end, so that the irritatingly cheerful tune seared into his brain, becoming so hard-wired that it blocked out every other thought.

This constant sensory assault and interrogation sessions occurred randomly during the day or night. Throughout this perpetual barrage of questions they stripped him down, indoctrinated him and sought to reconstruct his personality until he had regressed to the point that he truly believed their lies until they were lies no longer. He really was a terrorist as they suggested, and he deserved the punishment they meted out to him. He truly was the monster they claimed him to be, but they were trying to help him. They had driven him to the edge of insanity, and squeezed him like an orange until every piece of information he had about the associated terrorist cells had been extracted from him. He could hardly remember what he had told them, but it was surely enough to implicate nearly everyone of importance in the network and dismantle its rebellion against the government. He had even told them things he thought they wanted to hear, if only to get them to stop.

They relayed in graphic detail how he had been betrayed by Julianne, that while she appeared to be supporting his cause, she was plotting to undermine him with her lover, the traitor Harry Clarke. They had escaped and left him to rot, his tormentors reminded him, and they suggested to him constantly, almost with empathy, how that betrayal must have left him burning with hate toward them. They had stoked his anger until it had obsessed and consumed him. After the first intensive interrogation sessions, they had eased off and left him in isolation, sometimes for weeks on end, his only company the old witch Marcia Sutcliffe when she made her infrequent meal visits.

The interminable *drip-drip* reverberated like a jackhammer in his brain, but it was presently accompanied by a new sound; the click of a lock releasing and the whirring of the electronic door sliding back. The fearsome bulk that filled the door was a familiar sight, and he felt almost glad to see her.

"Prisoner 4567 Kelly," she barked at him. "You know the drill you lowlife scum. Turn around and face the wall, hands behind your back or I'll spit in your food again."

Sean smiled sardonically. "You've lost none of your charm, Marcia. I've missed our little trysts."

"Did I say you could speak?" she raged. "You shut your fat mouth until I say otherwise and it's Officer Sutcliffe to you."

"Yes Marcia," he replied, still smiling, knowing he had got to her. It was a tiny moment of pleasure, a minor victory that was all he could hope for in this malignant institution.

As Sean faced the wall, the prison officer wrenched his arms around his back a little harder than necessary with her powerful, meaty hands and he let out a yelp of pain. Satisfied, she frogmarched him out of the isolation cell through the grey corridor, bathed in a harsh white light by bright fluorescent lights overhead, and lined with the heavy steel doors of other isolation cells. They passed through three more sets of electronic doors, all opened remotely, tiny security cameras tracking them as they passed through.

They arrived in a small holding area to another door. This one was not electronic, but Sutcliffe opened it with a set of keys that jangled on her waistband. The room was bathed in the same harsh light, the only furniture a table and chairs either side, all bolted to the floor. On one wall was a large mirror which Sean guessed was an observation window. He recognized the room, one of the several interrogation rooms they used to torture him. He looked rough, he knew, too gaunt and thin, his chin raw and angry-looking from the blunt razor they had given him to shave with. The lines around his eyes were deeper, and his skin was blotchy and pale from the poor diet and lack of sunlight. Even the spidery veins that laced his cheeks were darker, even though he had not had a drink in nearly four months. Christ, what he wouldn't give for a pint of Guinness now.

He mentally braced himself for whatever might come next. He had told them everything and a few lies for good measure. Any more torture was surely now for their recreation?

The prison officer hauled Sean into the room and dumped him in one of the metal chairs and retreated to the corner of the room, her huge arms folded across her ample chest. "You've got some visitors Kelly, though Jesus knows who would want to visit a sorry lowlife like you."

"You mean this is not another interrogation session?"

"You heard me," Sutcliffe growled.

Sean sat there, intrigued, but he did not have to wait long. His face fell when he saw the two tough-looking SSP officers in their charcoal black uniforms. Clearly this was going to be more of the same. They settled into the two chairs opposite Sean, their athletic frames comfortably filling the narrow steel chairs. They were both quite young, one in his mid to late twenties, the other one hardly out of his teens. They both had that raw, feral appearance of FREE boot boys, the short, spiky hair and the angular faces creased in a permanent frown as if they had been born angry. The older one had blond hair with dark roots and cold blue eyes that bore into him like small icebergs. Those eyes glowered with barely disguised hostility.

"Prisoner Sean Kelly," he began. How would you like to get out of here?"

# CHAPTER 13

The Cockney drawl of the SSP officer sounded arrogant and condescending to Sean, but he was sure he had heard him right. Were they offering a way out?

"You look like crap," continued the officer. "Is the food not agreeing with you or is it the company?" He leaned forward conspiratorially and nodded in the general direction of the guard skulking in the corner, her bulk casting huge shadows in the harsh fluorescent light. "Is that the only woman you've seen in the last four months? I guess you could use a little female company." His colleague leaned back and smirked, and Sean would have liked to have smashed his fist into that baby face if it were not for the handcuffs.

"Why are you here?"

The SSP officer produced a plain manila file and flicked through it. "Seems like you and I have something - or someone - in common. A mutual enemy so to speak."

"What are you talking about?"

The agent pulled a large photograph from the file. When he saw it he felt that familiar rage shudder through him. He had seen the photograph of Harry Clarke before, when they had interrogated him and suggested all the grotesque things he had done with Julianne while he languished in isolation. They had stoked the fires of hatred, taunting him for hours before leaving him alone to reflect on that hatred for Clarke, until it became an obsession.

"Like you, Kelly, my comrade Ethan and I have some unfinished business with Harry Clarke. Don't we Ethan?"

Ethan spoke for the first time. His voice was cultured, as if he had a decent middle class upbringing. It reminded him of Andrew the stockbroker at the compound. "That's right Bruce," he nodded in agreement. "He needs to suffer." His chiseled features twisted into a cruel grimace.

"I couldn't agree more. If you catch up with him make sure he suffers a particularly nasty death."

"That's the problem," replied Bruce. He cracked his knuckles in a frustrated gesture. "We had him, but we didn't know who he was and so we gave him to a deportation camp transport. The truck got ambushed and Clarke escaped. He dived into the river that runs past the Salisbury deportation camp and we were convinced he would never survive that. This morning we received a report from a driver who had been ambushed and his description fits Clarke. He was with another fugitive identified as Omar Hussain. Have you heard of him?"

Sean shrugged and shook his head.

"Your friend Clarke has caused us a lot of trouble. We let one of the most wanted criminals in the country slip through our fingers. We've been told to find him and bring him back, and left in no doubt about the consequences if we fail." Bruce glanced at Ethan, who nodded in agreement, a flicker of fear crossing his pale, sinewy features.

"Good luck. Put a bullet in his brain from me when you see him. What has this to do with me?"

"Failure is not an option, Kelly. We need your help. You have quite a reputation, building a whole cell network like that. Even Griffiths admires your skills. You could be a useful asset for us. In any event you're the only person who really knows him."

Sean leaned forward, the metal chair hard on his back and his bound wrists aching. "What's in it for me if I help you?"

Bruce and Ethan exchanged conspiratorial glances and the older agent chuckled ironically. "You're not really in much of a position to negotiate. However since you asked, we still carry a lot of influence, although that might not last much longer if we don't find Clarke. You realize that there is still a huge array of charges pending against you." He licked his index finger and flicked through the file. "Too many charges to mention, most of them under the Prevention of Terrorism Act; and a number of charges related to sedition and plotting against the State. Technically you are still on remand. I am sure our beloved Prime Minister will love a show trial and make an example of you to deter his enemies. He's just waiting for the right moment. I hardly need to remind you what happened to the young Muslim boy. He was part of your cell wasn't he? But you were the leader. Hanging would be too good. They might reintroduce the electric chair especially for you. Did you know it can take up to twelve minutes to die in Old Sparky? Can you imagine two and a half thousand volts surging through your body, frying your insides, your eyeballs sizzling until they pop, and all the while you are fully conscious, burning from the inside, biting your own tongue off, your pain responsive nerves one of the last things to go. They might even televise it live; at least you'll die famous."

Ethan grunted in obvious pleasure, picturing the scene that

boss had so vividly painted.

"I can offer a way out," continued Bruce. "If you cooperate with us, I can get you out of here, at least until we find him. After that, maybe the Crown Prosecution Service will drop some of the charges; maybe even reduce your sentence to a couple of years. You'll still be relatively young when you get out. If you are really lucky you might even get to sleep with Julianne again. If we find her too we can offer her as a prize for you." His ice cold eyes bored into Sean. "Come on, Kelly, this is a no-brainer. I'm offering you a chance to get revenge, and for a while at least you get out of this rat infested hole. You can hunt him down with us. Think of it as a little holiday." He paused, and added for effect. "Remember he scarpered with your girl and left you to face the music."

Sean scowled, just the memory of it burning at him. The months of interrogation and indoctrination had fused into him a reflex action when he thought of Harry Clarke. He would never have believed he could hate someone so much, even when he was plotting his attacks against this despotic regime. "Okay, but I want to be the one who sends him to the next world when he's begging for mercy."

Bruce's bloodless lips turned up, the first hint of a smile. "That's the spirit, although that won't be possible. Personally I would like to slice his balls off and feed them to him, but our orders from the top – Griffiths no less – are to capture him alive. Apart from being a terrorist in your little band, he murdered a Cabinet minister. Therefore he is an even greater prize than you. Perhaps they will reserve the electric chair for him instead."

"Then I want to be the one that pulls the lever."

Bruce laughed. "You hate him badly don't you? They did a good job on you! What is it to be? I can have you processed and out of here in twelve hour." He waved a brawny arm in Marcia's direction. "Unless you want her delightful company for the rest of your short life."

It took Sean a nanosecond to decide. Even another half day in this place was like a stretch of eternity. "I'm in."

Bruce sat back, his smile growing broader, a veneer of malice lying underneath. "A few ground rules. If you try to escape we will find you and send you straight back here, and what you have suffered up to now will be nothing compared to what you will endure. You'll be begging us to put you in the Chair when we are done. Just a friendly warning. Understood?"

Sean nodded. "You won't get any trouble from me. I plan to stick around until Harry's neck is under my boot."

"Great, I thought so. Pack up your belongings; we'll see you tonight. Oh I forgot; they confiscated all your gear didn't they?" Bruce clicked his fingers at Marcia who scowled and muttered an obscenity under her breath as Bruce and Ethan left the interrogation room.

Sean did not even mind when Marcia bundled him roughly back into his cell. All he could think about was exacting revenge on Harry Clarke.

# CHAPTER 14

The BMW encountered little traffic as they drove west, heading toward Wales. As Harry drove, Omar remained vigilant but there appeared to be no sign that they were being followed. They were fortunate the electric hybrid vehicle was fully charged with a full fuel tank. With gasoline so expensive and in short supply, there were fewer stations than ten years ago, and people generally filled up, not knowing when they might find the next station.

"You realize we only have a few hours before the car is reported stolen and patrols are on the lookout," Omar had cautioned. "We have to get away as far as possible from Salisbury."

Harry had protested but Omar's logic could not be faulted. Harry was ambivalent about leaving the vicinity of the camp – he still harboured some vague hope that he could somehow rescue Tamara and Byron. "Think with your head not with your heart, man," chided Omar, tapping his temple. "That place is a fortress. Once you are in you're never coming out. How is that going to help your family? We need cold hard logic not emotion if we are going to survive."

Harry could not argue, but when they swapped the driving duties, he lapsed into a reflective silence before turning on the radio. There were few music stations left, the surviving music bland and military in nature. The government controlled stations had stifled all creativity from a country that only a year before had a vibrant, progressive music scene. He flicked to a news station and the female newscaster's voice was appropriately sombre.

'The strange disease that has afflicted a number of deportation camps is a source of deep concern for the government. Scientists are working around the clock to understand the illness and produce a suitable vaccine, and are confident of a breakthrough soon. The Secretary of State for Health, Eleanor Beaufort, stated that reports of the disease were alarmist and had been greatly exaggerated, and whilst there had been some casualties, the numbers were only a handful. She assured the public that there is no risk outside the camps, and the disease is not infectious, except through close bodily contact. Even so, Prime Minister Pelham has taken a personal interest in the plight of those affected by the disease at the camps, and has promised detainees that his administration will double its efforts to find a solution. Once again the respected leader of our country has demonstrated his extraordinary compassion despite his time spent dealing with the terrorist problem in the country. The Opposition BNP Leader, Jane Forster, expressed her admiration for the work of the Prime Minister and offered her Party's support to address the situation in any way they could. Rarely has a leader engendered such widespread and universal acclaim.'

Harry flicked the digital radio off in disgust. "Jesus, now I know the world has gone mad. That's the voice of Susan Hartley, one of the most respected and balanced journalists before Pelham came to power. I knew her briefly when we covered the Parliamentary Standing Committees together for different newspapers. I'm surprised she didn't vomit when she was saying that. Has everyone sold out?" He let out a depressed sigh.

Omar turned to him, scratching at his bulbous nose. "Remember Harry, people are no longer living by the normal rules. They have to do whatever it takes to survive, and sometimes that may mean having to sacrifice your principles. The choice between that and death, or maybe a long time in prison, is not a difficult one to make for most people. Fear is the driving force in Pelham's revolution; fear of being caught, fear of being ratted out by your neighbour or even someone you thought was a friend. It leads to a lack of trust, to suspicion and paranoia. That is precisely what Pelham wants. The more fear he invokes in others the more control he has. People are incredibly destructive in this type of situation. Could you have possibly imagined that we would see the country like this before Pelham came to power? He has not done this alone, but people are afraid of his hierarchy and they follow his orders. Don't be too hard on her. For all we know she has been forced to say that because one of Pelham's cronies has a knife against her throat. I think most of us would do the same in her situation."

"I guess you're right," Harry conceded.

As they drove on, keeping a careful eye on other traffic, they spotted more chain gangs shuffling along in the distance. "Pelham's idea of full employment," Harry remarked scathingly.

They sped past, knowing that SSP officers were likely to be close by. There was little they could do to help these people and as they talked, they formulated a plan. Staying on these shores would be suicidal. The regime would hunt them down eventually. They needed to make it across to Ireland somehow. At least there they would no longer be hunted fugitives, and they could publicize what was really going on in Britain. The regime had such close control of the social media and news outlets that it was hard to imagine that people in other countries, even in this Internet age, fully understood what was really going on in the United Kingdom.

The drive was uneventful, although along the way they saw several isolated corpses on the roadside, some of them decomposed and being picked at by carrion scavengers, others newly deceased, a strong reminder that even in the apparently peaceful rural parts of Britain, murder and bloodshed lurked unseen, ready to strike. They programmed the car's built-in global positioning system to avoid the major roads and the drive took them past peaceful, rolling green fields. Harry knew these bucolic fields were riddled with malice. At any moment they could be hijacked or attacked, and the longer they stayed in the BMW, the greater the risk of being spotted. He had no doubt that the Police or PIA patrols were out in force looking for them, but they would have had no idea of the direction that he and Omar had taken. They had to keep moving.

On their drive, Omar talked about his family, and at times his voice faltered. "When I was taken, the soldiers raided our apartment block knowing it was occupied entirely by our Muslim brothers. This was their second run at the block. I told you they took Leila away two months before when I was away on business. People knew they would be back but what could they do? It was their home. They came in and beat down the door and forced all those inside to get out. They waved pieces of paper in front of our faces and made all the adults sign it. The paper was an undertaking that they would freely and without duress relinquish all rights to the property they occupied and furthermore, that they fully accepted the legality and fairness of the action taken and had not been mistreated in any way. One man refused to sign the paper. He threw it on the floor and tried to walk away but they pushed him to the floor and shot him in the leg. The next gun was aimed at his head but he signed it then."

Eyes glistening, Omar wiped away a tear as he continued. "Another family tried to hide their baby in a closet, trusting its survival to fate rather than in the deportation camp. That's how desperate people were. But the baby cried and a soldier heard it. I saw him throw the baby over the balcony like a rugby ball to one of his comrades to catch, while the parents howled in grief, restrained by other soldiers. The baby survived, but what evil could have possessed them to behave like that?

"When they finished clearing out the whole apartment block they lined everyone up in the courtyard, men, women and children. There were large plastic bins laid out, and the soldiers went up and down the line and ripped off every piece of jewellery they could find, including watches and ear-rings and threw them in the bins. It was a cold day and people had coats but most were forced to hand them over. They stood shivering like that for hours before the caged trucks took them away. All the while they insulted us and called us animals. They were the animals that day. One of the soldiers touched a woman on her breasts. Her husband stepped forward and smacked his hand away. Instantly a group of soldiers surrounded him like rabid dogs and beat him senseless. We all stood there, eyes to the floor, none of us daring to intervene. It sickens me to think I didn't help that poor man. I'm a fighter for God's sake."

The tears rolled down Omar's face and Harry laid a comforting hand on his arm. "If you had Omar, you would not be alive to look for your wife."

Harry listened intently as Omar patiently explained how Islam was more than just a religion, but a peaceful, willing submission to the code of conduct ordained by God. Its followers came from all corners of the globe, a way of life meant for all people regardless of race, nationality or culture. The Quran stated that God had placed mankind on the earth to test him with certain responsibilities and that Man lived to earn the approval of the Creator. The scripture was the same today as that revealed to the Prophet Muhammad over 1400 years ago. Its accuracy had been unchanged or untainted over the centuries and this made the purity of the teachings irrefutable. He asserted that while it was true that Islam rejected many of the permissive teachings of the secular society that existed in most western societies today, and encouraged self-discipline though regular prayer and fasting, the Islamic faith was fundamentally about tolerance and peace.

"Contrary to what many journalists feed the public, Islam specifically prohibits terrorism," he said. "Yes there are extremists, just as there are in any religion, but the media trying to define Islam through the acts and attitudes of the jihadists is like saying that all Christians support the Crusades. I fear for the future of this country, but more so for the Muslims. The fact that Pelham's attempted assassin was a Muslim has irreparably destroyed any chances of integration here."

In deference to his religion, Omar stopped every few hours to pray, kneeling on the ground, his hands raised in the air in supplication. These breaks presented an opportunity to swap the driving.

Progress was slow because of the condition of the back roads, most of which suffered from huge potholes. At one point they had to cross a large stream where the road bridge had completely collapsed, and they lost a vital hour negotiating the torrent of water, which was mercifully shallow enough not to let water in the engine. Harry found he was becoming more anxious as time wore on, even though they had not encountered any trouble, but when dusk settled, they had reached the northern outskirts of Bristol. The journey had taken over eight hours, a journey which on major roads in light traffic was less than two hours. The radio reported violent confrontations in Bristol, confined mainly to the town centre and some nearby suburbs. They had no need to travel near the trouble but as dusk fell, cloaking the countryside in a grey mist, they spotted the checkpoint only when they were close to it. There were no lights or other signs, just a white pole glowing faintly in the dim light. Harry was driving and he knew he was exhausted, still recovering from the trauma of the night before.

"Harry stop now!" shouted Omar urgently.

Harry snapped alert, spotting the dim outlines of soldiers milling around the pole. They saw the laser-like pinpricks of glowing red cigarette ends moving about as if disembodied, and Harry counted at least six soldiers. With a faint screech of tyres, he spun the BMW around, and they headed back the way they had come. A car behind them blasted its horn angrily and the occupant gestured at Harry and Omar as the cars passed in opposite directions. They quickly headed down the road, Omar anxiously glancing behind to see if they had alerted the checkpoint guards, and darted into a nearby side road. They kept driving in the darkness, headlights bouncing off the grass verge and occasionally picking out the glassy, frightened eyes of a fox or a rodent. They had no idea where they were going, and the GPS, set for the Severn Bridge, warned them in a flat robotic voice that they had taken a wrong turn. Harry glanced in the rear-view mirror and just saw a line of black, when without warning a pair of piercing yellow lights appeared over the horizon far behind them.

They glanced nervously at each other and Harry increased his speed, but the headlights kept a steady distance behind them, its bright lights like two laser beams, solid and unwavering. Omar recognized the distinctive circular lights of a military jeep, the lamps placed closer together than civilian vehicles. Harry accelerated past a lone vehicle in front and soon left it behind them, and presently they saw the headlights following them do the same, maintaining its steady distance. Harry was moving fast and steady, his lassitude temporarily forgotten, but he had to keep a sharp eye for potholes or obstructions, with little reaction time if they spotted one. He reached a junction ahead with a mass of signposts and was forced to slow down.

"Which way?" he asked, his voice quickening.

"Follow the motorway," said Omar, pointing at the distinctive blue sign that indicated the M32. Harry took the turn and they were soon on the motorway, joining and merging with other traffic which they hoped would help them to shake off their pursuer. The motorway was no longer lit, but they followed the tail lights of the vehicle in front. The lights of Bristol twinkled before them as they descended into the Avon valley toward the city. They saw the flickering orange glow of intermittent fires burning in the town. Within minutes they had reached the outer suburbs. The faint smell of burning reached them, drifting through the radiator grille and the horizon glowed orange. Behind them the distinctive headlights continued to track them, weaving in and out of traffic and gaining on them in outright pursuit.

"Pull off the motorway," instructed Omar, pointing to the exit sign that glowed in their headlights. Harry steered the car purposefully up the ramp and the sign indicated that they were heading toward the St. Paul's area, an outer suburb of Bristol notorious for its social unrest in the past few decades. Omar glanced back and their pursuers also exited. "Harry, it's definitely a military jeep. They must have seen us turn at the checkpoint."

Some of the buildings they passed looked blackened and cratered in the weak street lights, garbage and rocks strewn across the streets. Strangely there was no traffic at all even though they had reached one of the major suburbs of the city. Harry drove skillfully to avoid the debris as he weaved the car between the graffiti-ridden buildings. Their only company was the jeep gaining on them, the steady glow of the headlights now so close it illuminated the inside of their car.

"Harry I don't like the look of this," warned Omar.

"There's no other way," protested Harry, glancing anxiously in his wing mirror.

They heard the faint sound of a crowd roaring and shouting and as they turned the corner they saw them. The street opened up into a wide boulevard, City Road, the main retail area of St. Paul's. Harry had to brake hard to avoid running into the crowd that spread across the road, marching forward toward them.

"Harry turn around quick!" cried Omar.

Harry crunched the gears into reverse and spun the car around but it was too late. The angry mob quickly descended upon them, surrounding the car. They pounded on the windows, beating at the chassis, distorted faces twisted into malevolent, raging expressions. Before the crowd swarmed around them, cutting off their escape, Harry saw the black shapes and transparent shields of a cordon of riot police marching purposefully toward the mob. They had driven into the middle of a war zone.

# CHAPTER 15

D.C. Kendrick had languished in his own private purgatory in the months since the attack. He knew he had failed everyone in the farmhouse when the army attacked that fateful day in early July. His role as a detective constable in the police force had been to seek intelligence from the inside and feed that back to the resistance cell, but he had failed them at the key moment. While he visited the compound only sporadically, as much due to his heavy workload as to avoid suspicion, he had been swept up in the passion and energy of the group. As small and as poorly resourced as they were, they represented the only resistance against the tide of right-wing fascism that had asserted an iron grip on the country.

He felt a sense of deep guilt that he had not been there when the attack took place, even though his logical mind told him that he would have perished with the rest of them. Just when he was sinking to his lowest ebb, taking solace in the bottle as so many police officers had done before him, he had received the message on his tablet a few days before. It was cryptic and from an undisclosed address, but he knew exactly what it meant and who it was from. It had given him hope; a new sense of purpose, and partly assuaged his guilt.

Kendrick smoothed the creases in his rumpled suit. He had not worn the suit in months, which, like so many other parts of his life, had lain neglected. His boss, Detective Inspector Grayson, sat back in his tatty office recliner and puffed on his favourite Havana cigar, his piercing eyes narrowed in suspicion.

"I don't think you are up to it," he stated blandly in his gruff Yorkshire accent. It was expressed as a challenge to Kendrick, an invitation to convince him otherwise. It was typical of Grayson's approach. Everything about the man was abrasive, his speech, his scratchy polyester suit, and the way he glared rather than looked at people. His dark-rimmed eyes were like small boreholes. "Why are you so interested in this case, anyway?"

"Because he got away on my watch, sir. I want to see Harry Clarke taken down now that he has suddenly resurfaced." Kendrick circled his thumb and index finger close together. "I was this close to nailing the bastard, and he squirmed out of my grasp. It's not every day you get to arrest the alleged murderer of a government minister."

"Alleged?" countered Grayson, blowing blue smoke up in the stale air. "Nothing alleged about it. We had him bang to rights. No other suspects and a clear motive. We catch him and it will be quite a coup for our department." He let out a resigned sigh and the deep lines on his face darkened. "We don't stand a chance of copping him. You know the State Security Police have claimed jurisdiction, pronouncing him as a political dissident. Griffiths wants to present Clarke's head on a silver platter to our glorious P.M. It will make him look good."

"Then we have no time to waste. We can get to him first."

Grayson's cheeks hollowed as he puffed thoughtfully. "How the hell do you propose to do that?"

"I don't know yet. But at least let me try."

Grayson pondered a moment. "Well you've been a liability to this department since we lost the Irish boy," he said, referring to the riot in which Kendrick's younger detective partner, Donoghue, had been killed in the riot at Tower Hamlets in May.

Kendrick grimaced. Grayson was renowned for being brutally candid. He had turned over the events in his mind through countless insomniac nights, wondering if he could have done any more. He had spent several days in hospital after the riot but his injuries were fairly minor, and he had been back at work within a couple of weeks. His sense of failure, however, had been compounded by the attack on the farmhouse. It was enough to turn anyone to the bottle and he could not dispute Grayson's blunt assertion. "So give me a chance to redeem myself," he said.

"Okay, okay," agreed Grayson. "This is not an official police investigation. If anyone asks me whether we are pursuing Clarke, I will deny all knowledge. If I get any serious heat from the SSP for encroaching on their turf, I will personally see that you are burned and your carcass handed to them for target practice. As far as I am concerned you're a renegade. You're no good to me here so you might as well go out in the field. If you bring him back alive, only then will I be involved, mainly to take the credit. Is that understood?"

"Deal," said Kendrick. He felt like smiling for the first time in ages.

"Now get out of my office and do what you need to. Sign out one of the pool cars."

"Thank you sir," said Kendrick, hastily retreating before Grayson changed his mind. "And I want the car back!" Grayson shouted after him as the detective galloped out of the office.

Grayson watched Kendrick leave, breaking into a mild coughing fit as he did so. Jesus he had to stop these cigars, but why break the habit of a lifetime, he thought. He was impressed with the man's enthusiasm; he had not seen him so fired up since before he had partnered him with the Irish kid. Kendrick was one of his most senior detectives, a field veteran. There didn't appear to be any downside. If Kendrick found him and brought him back, it would be a massive coup for him personally. The invitation to the Temperance Club, the local Masonic lodge, whose members included the great and the good in the politico world, would be waiting in the wings. He allowed himself another long, satisfied drag on his cigar before he burst out coughing again.

When Kendrick arrived home to his bare, functional apartment, he placed his tablet on the table and tapped in the coordinates he knew so well. He had to be careful, and their messages were infrequent, used only when necessary. He admired her resilience in having laid low for so long, working behind the scenes, as restless and energetic as ever. Kendrick was not certain if she was a target of the SSP or the People's Independent Army, or even Cripo, the National Criminal Police Service. These matters were outside his knowledge. His employers, the Order Police, were not after her, he knew that. Even if she was a political dissident she had committed no offence that would attract his employers, and she had stayed off the grid so long, that if anyone was looking for her the trail had long since grown cold. Did the government even know she had escaped, or the high profile role she had held in the 'terrorist' cell?

His tablet chimed softly, indicating that a connection had been made. "J," he began, afraid to use her full name from a sense of paranoia that hung like a black cloud over society since the Tories regained power. "I think I know where he is."

At the other end, Julianne knew exactly who Kendrick was referring to. "I'll meet you under the Clock Tower in one hour."

# CHAPTER 16

The glass exploded inwards and Harry shielded his face from the shards, feeling the sting of broken glass that lacerated his skin. The sharp smell of petroleum and burning rubble assaulted his nostrils. Probing hands reached inside the car and clawed at him. Then someone forced open the door to the BMW and Harry's last line of protection was gone. His cries went unheard in the tumultuous clamour, but as he was pulled out and fell on the hard tarmac he saw the police line moving forward relentlessly, a sea of black marching purposefully toward the mob. Omar was hauled out from the passenger side and he heard his friend's cries as they dragged him around the side of the car and pushed him to the ground next to Harry. He looked up at the twisted anger and hatred on the faces of the mob. They were in a frenzied state, attacking anything, their rage and frustration evident in the raw savagery of battle.

Most of them had weapons, wooden stakes, broken bottles, and stones that they hurled at the tide of black. One acrobatic youth, his face covered by a large patterned headscarf, brandished a samurai sword, its blade gleaming in the reflected light of burning rubble. Many shops in the long Victorian terrace were boarded up, but other retailers with less foresight had their plate glass windows smashed to pieces, the contents of their store long since looted.

A blow from a wooden club landed heavily on the fleshy part

of Harry's thigh, avoiding his bone, but causing excruciating pain. He looked up at the soulless black eyes of his attacker, who swung the bat high over his head, ready for another swing. As his arm curved around, Omar, with surprising agility, staggered to his feet and pounced on the man. Omar continued pummelling him and the rioter staggered backward. Harry screamed at Omar to stop but his voice was lost in the uproar and confusion. The crowd was in an ugly mood and they turned rapidly on Omar. He was pushed off balance by another rioter, and angry hands grabbed at him while the man with the club, his face a mask of fury at the humiliation, lurched toward Omar and laid a sickening blow to his torso that sent Omar crashing back to the ground. Omar grunted in agony as the blows came raining down on his back and Harry heard a sound like the snapping of a twig, distinct against the noise of the turmoil around him. Harry tried to grapple free with all his strength to help Omar, but he was held back by strong hands and forced to witness his friend twitching with each blow. Then a solid blow struck Omar's head and his friend lay still, blood pooling around his head.

Harry let out an anguished scream. He had known Omar for just over a day, yet in that short time the Muslim ex-soldier had been a greater friend to him than anyone he could remember. Omar had saved his life, and made the ultimate sacrifice in protecting him. It was a blow as crushing as the weight of bodies pressed against him.

The people moved like a fluid mass, and Omar's attacker and his blood-stained club was swallowed up in the crowd. The people around Harry pushed and jostled, occasional fists flying amongst them, as the crowd surged backwards, forced back by the approaching line of police. Harry pressed himself against the car's chassis to avoid being crushed.

The flares of Molotov cocktails flying through the air lit up the darkness and the crowd picked up whatever missiles they could to throw at the police. Harry saw a placard bobbing up and down in the crowd, protesting about a breach of human rights. Near the centre of the crowd a burning effigy of Pelham was carried along on long metal poles by a small group, the grotesque rubber face melting as the flames consumed it. The solid black line was relentless, however, and they beat their batons menacingly against their riot shields. From within their ranks came the high-pitched whizz of rubber bullets, and several rioters dropped to the ground. The crowd began to retreat under the police onslaught, still throwing missiles but running back as they did so.

Harry felt himself being dragged away from the chassis of the car, his back scraping painfully against the hard road. Someone threw a flaming torch onto the passenger seat and the car was rapidly engulfed in flames, the searing heat clawing at Harry's skin. He curled himself into a ball to escape the heat and the boots trampling all over him, fearful that this time he could not escape being crushed. However the mob lost interest in him as they continued to retreat, and Harry lay on the ground, bruised and battered but otherwise unharmed.

The gap between opposing sides now closed, the line of police suddenly broke ranks and charged toward the rioters, who rapidly retreated under an onslaught of blows from the batons. Some of the rioters were not fast enough and groups of riot police descended on them like a pack of wild dogs moving in for the kill, the batons moving up and down rhythmically against the person pinned to the ground. Others he saw incapacitated by crackling Tasers, the familiar small blue arc shooting out, the victim jerking like a marionette.

He was suddenly hauled to his feet by two police officers. Through his transparent plastic visor, one of the officers snarled angrily and raised his baton. The other policeman grabbed his arm and shook his head. "No, no," he shouted. "This guy was in the car. He's not one of them." The other officer dropped his baton and Harry found himself being led away from the conflict.

To Harry's surprise the officer who restrained his colleague studied Harry. "Are you alright, sir?" he said, seeing Harry's face smeared with blood from several cuts. Harry nodded silently, appreciating this unexpected gesture of humanity.

They led him toward a police car waiting further down the road, away from the fighting. He heard the rhythmic thrumming of a distant helicopter which rapidly turned into a chopping roar that drowned out the noise of the conflict. As he looked back he saw the helicopter, a black silhouette against the night sky. It hovered about forty feet above the crowd, the wind from its blades fanning the many fires burning in the street.

A number of canisters were hurled from the helicopter and as they hit the ground, they exploded in a dense white cloud that briefly obscured everything around it. Harry did not need to guess the contents of those missiles. Even from a safe distance, he felt a mild stinging in his eyes. The chemical lacrimator, commonly known as tear gas, had been used as an effective dispersant against combative crowds for over a century, and it had an immediate effect. The crowd scattered, running around in confusion, rubbing at their eyes, no longer interested in attacking the police. They retreated en masse, but the officers stayed in pursuit, now firmly in control and flinging rioters in the back of the many police vans that had now arrived on the scene.

He was guided to the police jeep, its blue lights blazing, and ushered into the rear of the vehicle. "Stay here for now. You'll be safe. I will take a statement from you later." Harry just nodded dumbly and sat in the comfortable leather seat while the officer briefly talked to the driver out of earshot. The jeep had no restraining grille separating front and back, and he could see the driver clearly. The driver acknowledged Harry and peered at his passenger in his rear-view mirror, while Harry pondered the irony of his being 'safe' in the back of a police car.

The police driver scratched at his patchy white stubble that hung like tiny icicles on his sallow features and regarded Harry curiously. Had he recognized Harry already? He glanced over at the rear passenger door. It was unlocked if he needed to make a break for it. However, the driver just let out a bored sigh. "Rough night out there," he said casually. His door was open to allow the smoke from his cigarette drift into the cool night air, adding to the stench of burning.

"Yeah, looks like it," replied Harry in a non-committal tone. He could see the policeman's hooded eyes scrutinizing him. An awkward silence followed and they both looked out at the chaos further up the street. The police were in firm control, and most of the crowd had fled, the occasional few still throwing missiles before fleeing. A number of rioters in handcuffs were being manhandled into police vans, getting a cuff from a baton to add to the beating they had received when they were apprehended.

"The bloody PIA starts the whole thing and expects us to clear up the mess," continued the driver. "You know what they did? They have a list of Muslims that they want to round up for the camps and they go into a damned mosque, *with their shoes on*, and try to detain them. We told them to wait until they left the mosque but did they listen? I swear those guys did it for the hell of it, but when it all hits the fan they're nowhere to be seen. Luckily this little uprising wasn't as organized as some of them. It could have been a lot worse but this was more than just a load of Muslim kids angry about their mosque being desecrated, although I can't say I blame them. I'm a Catholic and I wouldn't want those thugs breaking into my Church.

"Good thing now, at least is that we're better prepared than ever against these protests. We've had the best riot training money can buy. Look at our lads." He pointed at the street, which was quieter; most of the protestors arrested or disappeared. "A year ago we would have been running scared, but now we're better equipped than ever. Thank God for the great British taxpayer." He laughed at his own comment, revealing yellowed, crooked teeth. His awry smile was quickly replaced by a confused frown. "Haven't I seen you before? You look familiar, I just can't think why."

The driver reached into his glove compartment. "Anyway we will soon find out. My sarge says I need to take your facial scan." He rummaged in the drawer, head buried low and away from Harry. "Where is that damn thing?" he said, frustrated. Harry, in a moment of blind panic, reacted quickly. The officer, engaged as he was, did not see his passenger reach forward in the wide gap between the seats. Harry shoved the officer as hard as he could and the officer, already unbalanced, tumbled out of the vehicle. Harry leaped forward quickly and slammed the driver door shut before the officer could react. The officer's face was pressed against the window in a mask of fury and he banged at the window, cursing as he tried to force open the door. Harry hit the ignition button and the engine burst into life.

As Harry slammed the car into gear the officer, beating the window furiously and shouting threats, was forced to jump aside to avoid being mowed down. Harry sped away, smoke billowing from the racing wheels. He glanced in the mirror to see the officer retreating into the distance, still waving and gesticulating wildly.

As Harry flew down the main street in a bid to escape, he passed an army truck parked by the roadside in the shadow of a large stone built Baptist Church. Its lone occupant glanced at the police jeep but then turned away, unaware it had been stolen.

All other police vehicles were tied up with the rioters and it was soon apparent he had made a clean escape. He knew the driver would probably have alerted his colleagues already. He had perhaps a few minutes. The radio suddenly burst into life with a hiss of static, confirming the theft and urging a rapid response. With shaking hands, he keyed in the GPS coordinates for the Severn Bridge and was soon the only vehicle on a poorly lit road that led out of town.

Momentarily out of danger, he let out a deep cry and clung to the steering wheel, no longer able to contain the feeling that welled up like a volcano inside him. His eyes blurry with tears, but intent on driving, he let out a spate of choking, grief stricken sobs – grief for the friend he had lost; someone he had known just a short time but with whom he had shared so much; someone from a different culture, religion and background but who had become like a brother to him; someone who made the ultimate sacrifice in protecting him, the most utterly selfless act he had ever witnessed. Most ironic of all was that he had been killed by his own brothers in arms, fighting for survival against a common enemy. He also grieved, however, for the ruin of his beloved country, questioning how this once proud nation had ever come to this?

# CHAPTER 17

It was a bitterly cold night, and the first spots of rain began beating against the helicopter window, blurring the sprawl of lights that stretched into the distance a thousand feet below them. Sean did not mind. Seeing the world outside of the high concrete walls and razor wire for the first time in months was therapeutic, even if it was Bristol on a foul October night.

He adjusted his thick black headphones and peered out into the moonless sky as the helicopter banked and turned northwest of the city toward the Severn estuary. The first faint glimmers of dawn arose in the east, but the cloud cover above them was unbroken, and the pilot had to compensate for the gusts that every so often rocked the vehicle.

Sean shifted in his seat as they hit turbulence and he turned to his fellow passenger as the helicopter swooped lower, the lights of the Severn Bridge appearing over the horizon. "Where was he last seen?" Despite the mike on his headphones, he had to shout above the roar of the blades.

The distorted metallic voice in his ear sounded nothing like the gruff London accent of the SSP officer, whom he only knew as Bruce. "Over there," replied Bruce, pointing a gloved hand towards the horizon where the lights of the bridge were getting closer. "There is a small tributary just off the main river where he dumped the police jeep. He was clearly in a hurry. I understand it was easy to spot because the roof was visible above the waterline. We think he's probably on his way across the Bridge to Wales. We have the checkpoint at Severn Bridge on alert. They haven't found anything yet, but if he's on foot he can't be too far." Bruce glanced at his wrist. "He has over seven hours on us but on foot that's not much of an advantage. He'll need to rest and stop to eat. We'll find him," he said confidently.

Behind him his colleague Ethan nodded in agreement. There was something that Sean loathed about the young SSP agent. He had an aura of malevolence that seemed to pervade his whole be-ing, as if the very essence of his humanity had been poisoned by hatred and bigotry. Earlier as they boarded the helicopter Ethan had taken the opportunity to grab his arm and threaten him again, his dark eyes narrowed with hostility. He had been keen to keep Sean in handcuffs, but much to his chagrin, Bruce had refused. "No," he had said. "If we find Clarke we might need to move fast. Cuffing him will delay us."

The Severn River came into view and the bridge was now clearly visible, its lights twinkling against the grey river below it. The im-pressive steel structure rose into the sky, small yellow lights run-ning along the length of the steel cables and struts, clearly marking out the shape of the bridge. The helicopter banked to the east and its powerful searchlight picked out the small tributary snaking away from the main river. Within fifteen seconds it was hovering two hun-dred feet off the ground, and the searchlight illuminated a hive of activity, where a number of figures milled around at the water's edge. Sean saw the flashing blue lights of a string of police vehicles and a small crane pulling the jeep from the water.

"Let's get some intel from these guys," said Bruce. He instructed the pilot to land and the helicopter manoeuvred gently lower, the pilot looking for a flat area in the darkness. The searchlight picked out an adjacent field, and with hardly a bump the helicopter was on the ground. As they stepped out of the helicopter Ethan took the opportunity to dig Sean in the ribs with his small handgun. "Remember Kelly, I'm just itching to blow a hole in that Irish brain of yours. Don't give me a reason." Sean said nothing and with the pilot waiting, the trio jogged across the field toward the riverbank.

They had wasted no time in setting off for the West Country, and because it was dark they had to stay vigilant. Apart from the checkpoints and the curfew in place at night, Kendrick knew that driving along the crumbling M4 motorway was risky. The roads were badly in need of repair, and with no highway lighting any more, one could easily hit a pothole without time to react. Some of those monsters could swallow up the battered old Ford he had signed out from the police lot. There were also the gangs of criminals who hijacked cars, usually forcing them to stop by placing obstacles in the way and then attacking the vehicle. These incidents had become more frequent since Pelham came to power; it had turned into a sport that typified the undercurrent of violence that characterized Pelham's regime. When the mood of the country turned ugly, violence became a social norm, as if it had somehow gained some degree of eminence, justified in the current climate.

As a result there was little traffic on the roads, just the odd blinding light crossing the other way. The curfew also discouraged overnight travel, although for some it was a necessity to get to and from their jobs, and it was only really enforced at the army checkpoints.

The rain further reduced visibility, but the clouds had begun to drift away as the first light of day emerged. They were just past Bristol on the way to the Severn Bridge checkpoint. They had avoided any gangs and successfully negotiated the first two checkpoints encountered on their journey. His police badge had secured him passage despite having to field some awkward questions. More importantly, however, they had not conducted a search of the vehicle. On both occasions his passenger had to crouch down deep into the narrow gap behind the front seats covered in a blanket. In the dark she was like an amorphous mass, impossible to tell if there was anything under the crumpled blankets. They had waved him on and as he drove away, he realized he had been holding his breath.

Kendrick glanced over at her in the passenger seat. She was slouched down, her lithe body covered to her neck in a woollen blanket, and her flame coloured hair hung about her face. She was snoring softly, but her eyes fluttered. He gently tapped her arm, and she suddenly bolted awake, eyes staring wide and looking around frantically, momentarily confused.

"Julianne, I'm sorry. I didn't mean to startle you. We'll be reaching the next checkpoint soon."

"Oh, okay." She yawned heavily. "Where are we?"

"Not far from the Severn Bridge. We've made good progress." He glanced at his watch. "Just past seven in the morning and the sun will be up soon. You had better get under in case there are any stray patrols."

They pulled over and Julianne hid herself under the blanket. The Severn Bridge checkpoint was likely to be more stringent. The last two were just groups of bored and tired soldiers more intent on getting rid of him than doing any work. The Bridge checkpoint was more permanent in nature, and being the gateway to Wales, was more likely to use facial recognition scanners and subject them to a random search. As far as Harry knew Julianne was not on any 'Wanted' list, but he could not be certain that Sean hadn't betrayed her. It was not a risk worth taking, although smuggling her across the checkpoints carried its own dangers.

He followed the road as it curved toward the crossing and presently joined the small line of traffic that filtered into three lanes of pitted tarmac approaching the bridge. The checkpoints here were constructed like border crossings, so that for each direction the barriers were at the end of the bridge. On the other side drivers were being stopped and questioned, and Kendrick watched anxiously as the Ford crawled slowly forward. Soon he was in the middle of the bridge and the huge expanse of the Severn River glittered in the glowing early morning light of the pale sun. Above him the thick steel suspension cable curved upwards in a huge arc to the huge white perpendicular support struts. He could feel an imperceptibly gentle sway in the bridge as he followed the line of traffic. It was a long wait despite the small volume of cars, and he saw a number of cars being turned back. His heart raced as he neared the large red and white pole running across the road, flanked on both sides by a number of army vehicles. Soldiers in combats and heavy black boots, sporting semi-automatic rifles, milled around the barrier, some of them searching cars that had been forced to pull over.

He had seen on the television recently that someone had tried to break through this checkpoint and escape but the soldiers had shot them down mercilessly and without hesitation. They had riddled the car with bullets. It had veered off the road and crashed into a nearby ditch, and as the wounded occupants staggered outside the vehicle the soldiers had finished them off. The State run news broadcast had shown the mutilated bodies in glorious close up not just on the TV but also on the huge media screens overlooking city centres, cautioning that it served as a warning to those who challenged the legitimate authority of the army checkpoints.

He heard Julianne stirring in the back. "Nearly there," he hissed. "Stay still." The car in front was allowed through after some time and the soldier at the gate waved Kendrick forward. He pulled up alongside the gate and a bored looking soldier cocked his thumb in a command to step out of the vehicle. He complied without hesitation and the soldier waved an electronic wand over him. He stopped short, scowling, and waved a couple of other soldiers over who cocked their machine guns, ready for trouble.

Kendrick smiled weakly. "It's okay, I'm a cop. I have a gun." He slowly inside his jacket and the two armed soldiers raised their guns, primed and ready, pointed at Kendrick's head. "Slowly, mate, or I'll use you for target practice," growled one soldier. Kendrick produced his Glock compact pistol and police card. The first soldier snatched the card, reviewed it and handed it back. He waved the others away and they skulked off, weapons still raised.

"So you're a cop are you?" he said, a touch of contempt in his voice. He reached into his pocket for his smartphone, clicked it and showed the screen to Kendrick. "You're not after this guy by any chance?"

Kendrick swallowed hard before he could compose himself. The picture was a grainy library shot of Harry Clarke. "Never seen him," he said casually. "Who is he?"

"Apparently one of the most wanted men in the country. He was last seen heading this way. He stole a police car. I thought you might know that, being a copper 'n all."

"No, they sent me from London."

The soldier's bored expression returned and he glanced into the car. His gaze lingered on the interior just a touch too long, and Kendrick felt an icy tremor stab through his body. "What's with the blankets?" asked the soldier curiously.

"Like I said I came from London. It's a long journey these days. I had to sleep in the car."

The soldier paused, thinking it over, but his interest in Kendrick had waned. He handed back Kendrick's ID card and quickly scouted around the underside of the vehicle with his wand, going through the motions. His thin lips cracked into a half smile. "No bombs today. You can go."

Kendrick got in quickly and drove off with a heavy sigh of relief. After a few miles he pulled over on a deserted rural road in the rolling South Wales countryside.

"Whoa that was close. You can come out now."

Julianne emerged from the blankets, her red hair plastered to her forehead. "Thank God, I was suffocating under there."

"He's here, Julianne. They showed me a picture of him. They are looking for him. He might already be in Wales. We have to find him before they do."

# CHAPTER 18

Harry had even less idea where he was than his pursuers, and as he struggled for breath in the severely cramped trunk of the car, he was beginning to think his ingenious plan to cross into Wales was about to horribly backfire in a slow, torturous death by asphyxiation. Having hurriedly abandoned the jeep in the river, he had managed to reach the bridge under cover of the night. A patrol helicopter had flashed by, and its powerful searchlight had nearly picked him out before he sought the cover of the thickets that skirted the riverbank. He had no idea how he would cross the Severn Bridge checkpoint, but as he reached the road that led directly to the bridge, he found inspiration. The car was parked in a bay by the roadside and the lone driver had his head buried in the hood, checking the engine. Harry quietly darted to the rear of the vehicle, a Ford Taurus, and found the trunk unlocked. With the driver still engrossed at the front of the car, Harry pressed the button and the trunk bounced open, and he climbed in stealthily. It was a large trunk for a sedan but still cramped and uncomfortable, and his knees were pressed against his chest as he curled his body into the tight space. He managed to gently close the trunk, and was enveloped in darkness.

Fortunately, the lone driver had not checked his trunk, and more importantly, neither had the soldiers, and he had crossed the checkpoint successfully. Harry heard the muffled voices and the probing questions of the soldiers, but they had not inspected the vehicle, and within minutes the driver had negotiated the barrier and was on his way. That was several hours ago, and Harry had lost the feeling in his legs some time before. Worse still, he was rapidly running out of air. There was a small hole where the bodywork had rusted and he had managed to claw at the rust to increase the size. The pockets of air that circulated smelt of diesel, better than the alternative, but now he was light-headed and close to losing consciousness. If he did so he might never wake up. Harry had hoped the driver would stop earlier but now he had no choice. From his cramped position he could hardly get any leverage, but he banged with all his strength on the tinny roof of the trunk. He kept banging to no avail; the car did not slow. He tried again, mustering all his force, and presently the car began to slow to a halt.

Harry could not open the trunk from the inside but he heard the driver jangling a set of keys before he flipped open the trunk and daylight flooded in, momentarily blinding Harry. It was no use making a run for it. His limbs were far too rigid. He could barely raise himself out of the trunk, his muscles screaming in protest.

The driver stepped back in bewilderment. "How the hell did you get in my car?" he exclaimed with great agitation. Harry stuck out a placating hand, still blinking furiously from the sudden influx of daylight. He tried to get out but could not. "Thanks for the ride. I needed to get across the bridge. Do you have any water?" The driver was a slight figure, and apart from a pronounced paunch, had the physique of a stick insect. Harry thought he could probably snap him in half if he hadn't been so weak from hunger and exhaustion. The man's grubby white shirt seemed to hang off his bony shoulders and stretched tight over his distended stomach, buttons straining and the tails flapping in the light breeze. His slender neck was taut and his eyes bulged with anxiety from their deep set sockets. He reached into the waistband of his jeans, pulled out a small handgun and pointed it at Harry. His hands were visibly shaking. "Get out of the vehicle...slowly," he said, fighting to keep the gun steady.

After everything Harry had been through, the driver did not alarm him, but the man's fear made him unpredictable. Harry, struggling out of the trunk, watched him closely. "I couldn't move fast if I tried," he said casually. His knees nearly buckled as he stood upright, and the driver waved him away from the vehicle.

"Who are you?" said the driver.

"The name's Ha- Andrew," he said. "I need to get to Pembroke Dock. Listen, I'm no threat, I am just trying to get a ferry out of here like everyone else. I'm just a nobody who lost his family. Do you have any water? I nearly passed out in there."

The driver relaxed, evidently deciding that his stowaway held no threat. He lowered the gun and waved at the back seat. "There's a flask in there. Help yourself. I'm heading for the Docks myself after I take care of some business in Ammanford so I can take you most of the way, but I would rather arrive at the Docks alone. You never know who's watching. Oh, and don't try anything funny. I keep my gun close by."

Harry shrugged, grateful for the driver's generosity, and before long they were on their way. Harry had not thought through his next move, and he was so famished that he found thinking difficult. The driver, who introduced himself as Les, was taciturn and had no food supplies. It had been over twenty-four hours since Harry and Omar had shared the bonus fare in the BMW. As he thought of Omar, a deep gloom settled over him, and he lapsed into a deep, reflective silence. For long stretches of the journey the only audible sound was the throb of the car engine.

After a while they pulled off the M4 motorway, which had degraded badly, heading north-west on rural side roads with little traffic. The quality of the roads in Wales was even poorer than England, as if the years of neglect became more pronounced the further one travelled from London. Les gritted his teeth in concentration, intent on avoiding the potholes and debris on the road, while Harry lapsed in and out of much needed sleep. His companion did not bother him, but when he awoke from one slumber, deeper than he had thought, the car was on the side of the road and Les was nowhere to be seen. He looked around startled. The sun was low in the sky, a bank of dark clouds rolling across it, and the light was subdued. He tried to get out of the car to stretch his stiff, aching limbs, but when he tried the lock it would not move. He looked out of the passenger window across a small field with a hedgerow, and peering into the distance he saw the flapping shirt tails of the driver crouched behind the bush. He was talking intently on his phone and Harry just knew. He looked around frantically for something to smash the window. Nothing. He reached over to the glove compartment and inside was a heavy Maglite flashlight. He quickly clambered to the rear passenger seats and swung the flashlight with all his remaining strength. The glass shattered and the cool air rushed in. He used the implement to sweep away broken glass before he rolled out of the back window and onto the trunk. He felt several sharp scratches through his trousers and blood trickled down his leg as he scrambled onto the ground, his legs almost buckling beneath him.

The driver, alerted by the sound of smashing glass, hastily slipped his phone in his pocket and yelled at Harry. "Hey, come back!"

Harry saw Les racing toward him as he ran up the gently rising road, his legs heavy, as if he was being pulled back by an invisible force. Harry felt so frail the driver would almost certainly catch him. Harry glanced back and inexplicably the driver had stopped, but his handgun was out and he took careful aim. Harry zigzagged, his legs screaming with the effort, and the ground exploded in a cloud of dust at his feet. The shot was inches from his foot, and Les began loping toward him, gun raised. Harry, teeth gritted and sweat streaming down his face despite the cool air, reached a large copse and fled off the road into the shelter of the undergrowth. Shielded by the thick barks of oak trees, he felt safer, but another shot whizzed by, gouging a hole in the bark close to his head. He staggered on, tripping over vines and bush, the light fading as he dived deeper into the forest. He briefly stopped, heart pounding and breath coming in short, shallow gasps. He hid in a small natural depression covered in undergrowth, and waited for the rustle of leaves. Nothing came. He waited for ten minutes, the only sounds the rustling of the canopy in the stiff breeze that whipped around the treetops, and the occasional high-pitched twittering of a tree-creeper bird. He gingerly ventured out onto the forest floor, alert for a white shirt amongst the trees, but saw nothing. It appeared he was no longer being pursued. He needed to eat quickly; he was already dizzy from lack of food.

He began jogging through the large copse until he came to a steep embankment, the other side of which he guessed was the vast plain of the Brecon Beacons National Park opening in front of him. In the distance, framed by a ridge of iron-grey peaks, stood a bank of isolated cottages, and further still black smoke rose from a clump of buildings that appeared to be a small town or settlement on the edge of the expansive park. He stood on the edge of the embankment considering his limited options when a searing pain shot through his right leg and he fell forward, tumbling down the steep slope, branches and undergrowth tearing and clawing at his clothes but slowing his fall. He landed heavily at the edge of the creek that cut through the woods, barely conscious, the skin on his thigh ripped up and pumping blood where the bullet had grazed it.

When he looked at the ragged skin and freely flowing blood on his thigh, he felt like vomiting, but there was nothing left in his stomach. He retched as he ripped the sleeve from his soiled, tatty shirt and wrapped it several times in layers tightly around his thigh. Curiously, it was not painful, but there was a numb feeling around the thigh, and Harry was aware enough to know that was a bad sign. If he did not stop the blood flow quickly, in his weakened state he would succumb, even though it was merely a flesh injury. The tourniquet rapidly turned crimson, but it appeared to be working. Harry had no idea where his pursuer was. The shot had come from nowhere, but he ceased to care as he lay back on the cool grass, shivering with the cold. He heard the distant hum of a helicopter before his consciousness finally deserted him.

# CHAPTER 19

Kendrick and Julianne had checked into an obscure, run-down motel on the western outskirts of Newport. The detective had gracefully offered to sleep on the floor with the spare blankets from the closet, so that Julianne had the bed all to herself. As they settled in, they formulated a plan of action. Other than confirmation that Harry had crossed the Severn Bridge, they had no idea where he might be headed. Kendrick was faced with the realization that without any definite leads, the chances of finding Harry before the State Secret Police were fairly remote. It was a typical needle in a haystack, a futile, hopeless mission.

Kendrick glanced out of the thin, tatty curtains at the parking lot, lost in thought. It was cold outside, and at this time of night no one was around. Somewhere out there was his quarry. He turned to Julianne, who was stretched out on a faded flower-patterned armchair reading a magazine.

"Why did he cross the border? Where is he heading?" he asked.

Julianne put down her magazine and ran a delicate hand through her lustrous curls. "All he told me was that he wanted to rescue his family. He was determined to go to Salisbury camp to try and rescue Tamara and Byron. I guess he never made it."

"So what's his plan now? What would you do if you were being hunted by the SSP?" Kendrick paced the length of the tiny room on the threadbare carpet, scratching at the wiry stubble round his chin.

Julianne looked up from her magazine. "I don't know but we need to find him. Our movement needs someone like him. I need him too."

Kendrick smiled inwardly. He had sensed her attraction to Harry at the farmhouse before he knew they were ex-lovers. "Tell me about this movement."

Julianne put down the magazine and shifted uncomfortably. "I can't say too much. I have my instructions. I have to be careful."

"Understood. I won't ask again."

Julianne gave a thin smile, her full red lips curling upward. "For God's sake sit down. You're making me edgy. It's not that I don't trust you...well it's hard to know who to trust any more. You are a police officer after all. Once we have Harry on board I promise I will tell you everything."

Kendrick stopped pacing the threadbare carpet and flopped into a ratty old wicker chair by the door. "Police officer or not, you know where my allegiance lies."

She hesitated, uncertain of how to express herself. "You weren't there Kendrick...when they invaded the compound I mean. You were our inside man, our intelligence but when we were attacked we had no warning and you were nowhere to be seen."

Kendrick sighed heavily. "Yes and there's not a day goes by I don't regret that. I was kept out of the loop. I'm only a detective. The operation was planned by the army and the Home Guard. My conscience is clean, but it still hurts and I will prove to you that I can be trusted. You must still have some faith in me or you wouldn't be taking this road trip."

"How do I know you won't turn Harry in when we find him? Get all the glory."

"If I wanted Harry turned in I would sit back and let the SSP do their job. We're on a race against time Julianne. We have to reach him first or God knows what his fate will be. I'm risking everything for this." He leaned back in the chair and rubbed his tired face. "If they ever found out what I was really doing I would lose more than my pension."

A heavy silence passed between them, the slightest aura of mistrust between two allies fighting the same cause. That's what this regime did to you, thought Kendrick bitterly. It made you mistrust your friend, your neighbour, your colleague, God even your family, not that he had much family left anymore. Julianne broke the silence.

"He's leaving the country."

"What?"

"It's obvious. We were missing it all along. He knows he can't get near the Salisbury camp and he is one of the most wanted men in Britain. He's going to try and get himself on a ferry to Ireland."

Kendrick frowned, the lines in his brow growing deeper. "How the hell is he going to do that? Are there still any ferries left running to Ireland?"

"It used to be a regular crossing before the Tories closed the borders. There used to be several ports on the Welsh coast that operated sea ferries. I doubt there are many crossing ports left."

Kendrick pulled out his tablet and began tapping furiously at the touch screen, a bluish glow illuminating his face in the gloomy half-light of a small corner lamp. "Here it is. Fishguard and Holyhead ceased operating ferries a while back. Pembroke only stopped running ferries at the end of September. It is one of the key focal points for the deportation transports and so has now been closed to the public. Harry may be heading to Pembroke believing they still operate."

He tapped again and brought up a map of Wales. "It makes sense – we follow the M4 and the 'A' roads all the way to the coast and arrive in Pembroke. We have to pray our intuition is correct and that he makes it all the way there without the SSP reaching him first. If he does arrive in Pembroke he could fall right into their hands. We have to get there first."

Julianne pursed her ruby lips in concern. "I know it's a long shot Kendrick but we mustn't fail him."

"Okay," replied Kendrick. "Get some sleep. It could be a while before we get another chance. We'll head out first thing in the morning."


When Harry drifted back into consciousness the gibbous moon was high in the sky and bathed the wooded area in a ghostly pallor. The severe throbbing pain in his thigh jerked him fully awake, and he looked down at his leg. In the faint light, he could see a patch of darker grass around his leg, but the tourniquet was still on tight and appeared to have stemmed the blood flow. His next sensation was the cold, biting him down to his very bones. His body ached all over, the pain of his leg coursing through his body combined with the chilly air. He had to find shelter or he would freeze out here. His skin was sore too, scratched and broken from the fall down the slope through the bushes and brambles. There was no sound except the gentle tinkling of the stream close to where he had landed, and more importantly no sign of his pursuer. He struggled to get up, but the slightest weight on his right leg caused him to collapse on the ground again. He crawled to the stream and reached down to take a gulp of water. It was fresh and invigorating and he felt more alert after drinking. He tore off a piece of his clothing and soaked it in the water. He carefully removed the tourniquet and gently dabbed at the wound to clean it, gritting his teeth from the pain. He tied the tourniquet back up and hopped across the shallow stream and hauled his body slowly up the other side, his arms aching from the intense effort.

Hopping through the wood before it opened out onto the vast plain, he spotted two large, solid branches lying in the undergrowth. They were white in the moonlight, the residue of a nearby fallen silver birch tree. He wrapped his arms around them to create an improvised crutch and hobbled forward, stumbling at first before he found his rhythm. The air was sharp and his breath came in short bursts, curling up and drifting away like a smoke signal. It was tiring work and as he exited the line of trees onto the hard stony ground that bordered the vast plain of the Brecon Beacons, his body screamed in protest, the pain and exhaustion threatening to overwhelm him. He sweated profusely despite the cold.

Harry looked across the plain and spotted the outline of several large cottages he had seen earlier when peering out over the vast moor. They were at least a mile distant, but the stony path he was on wound down an incline and appeared to curve around past the cottages like a ribbon of light under the Moon's glow. The sky was cloudless and the stars shone with pinpoint intensity, and the cold seemed to envelop and paralyse him. The cottages had no lights on, but he knew his only salvation was to reach them for food and shelter. He would surely die out here, and as he hobbled forward, each step took more effort than the last, as if his energy was draining away, only the cold and the pain driving him forward. He continued on, his body ready to collapse and rest on the stony ground. The pain sucked at his energy, rising in intensity as the sanctuary of the cottages grew closer.

It was a feat of endurance, but he eventually reached the front gate of the first cottage. It opened with a squeak and he hobbled to the solid wooden door. All he wanted to do was sleep, and a wave of nausea passed over him. Passing out now would surely be deadly. With his remaining strength, he hammered with the branch on the door, the sound resonant in the stillness of the night. Once again he banged hard, and the sound seemed to echo across the plain that stretched out to the hills beyond.

There was no response. It was over. In his weakened state, with severe blood loss turning him colder on an already freezing night, his body starved, he wondered whether, after all he had been through he would die a lonely death in the raw, peaceful beauty of the Brecon Beacons. He dropped to the floor in exhaustion, his eyelids fluttering, his consciousness drifting, when he heard the sharp click of a bolt being turned back.

The cottage door opened and a figure stooped over him, talking, but the words were unintelligible to Harry. A second figure emerged, and soon he felt the warmth of a blanket being draped over him. With that comforting warmth his mind drifted into a temperate, faraway trance. He did not resist when he felt strong hands under his arms pulling him inside the cottage.

# CHAPTER 20

The service station motel off the M4 ramp near Port Talbot was a ramshackle wreck and the hotel room was about as dingy and miserable as they come. Sean did not appreciate being handcuffed to the long metal lampshade in the corner. It had been Ethan's idea, convincing Bruce that he was a flight risk, especially as they ventured further into Wales where he could easily lose them. Bruce probably appreciated how easy that was, because the fugitive Harry Clarke appeared to have done the same thing. He had completely disappeared, apparently without a trace.

It was nearly three in the morning but the two SSP agents stood around a scratched and worn writing bureau, huddled over an old style paper map which they folded out and studied assiduously. Their voices were low and Sean, imprisoned in the corner, struggled to hear them. They had dispensed with the helicopter for now and commandeered a black SUV, but the trail had gone cold. He had heard Bruce take a call and his tone had been submissive, nodding into his cellphone like a scolded schoolboy, uttering "Yes sir" and "Of course, sir." The pressure was etched on their faces, revealing worried frowns and agitated discussions.

As Ethan bent over the map with his back to Sean, the Irishman saw the tattoo peeking out from under his shirt collar at the base of his neck – the Nazi swastika, etched in black on his fair white skin. He stood up straight and turned to Sean.

"So where is he headed?"

Sean gave a non-committal shrug. "How do I know?"

Ethan, infuriated, strode over to Sean so that their faces were inches apart. The wiry blond stubble on the agent's face accentuated his coarse features. "You're a waste of space. We should never have brought you." He turned toward his comrade. "Bruce, can I borrow your Bowie knife? Maybe I could do a little artwork before I slice him up?"

"Jesus Ethan, leave him alone. You're being stupid."

Ethan, wounded by the admonishment, made as if to head butt Sean who visibly flinched, raising a twisted smile in Ethan before he skulked away. Bruce's tablet chimed and he grabbed the device and studied the message intently.

"We've got a tip-off from a driver in an area just off the Brecon Beacons." He scowled and gripped the tablet hard in his powerful hands. "Damn, he called the tip in to the cops' yesterday evening, and those idiots have only just told us." He threw the tablet in his holdall and checked the scope on his Winchester sniper rifle.

"Come on, there's no time to lose. We're moving out."

Harry slept for longer than he had done for several months and when he awoke he felt refreshed and ravenous. He was in a proper bed with a pillow, and the soft mattress and warm duvet felt unfamiliar but luxurious. For a few seconds he could not recall how he had got there, but as the sun came streaming in through the pastel curtains gently fluttering in the light breeze, his memory flooded back. His leg was still throbbing but not with the same intensity and when he cautiously touched his wounded thigh he felt a large, thick bandage. The wound had been expertly dressed. Next to him on a white bedside was a large glass of water. He reached over and drained its contents. The water tasted sweet and pure. He lay back, enjoying the cosy, soft mattress. After so long sleeping on hard ground, it felt like the clean sheets and duvet were gently massaging his skin, bringing it back to life.

He looked around, and on a wooden rocking chair at one end was draped a set of clean clothes, which included a woollen polo neck sweater. He shivered as he thought of the biting cold from last night, his clothes scant protection because they were little more than rags, his shirt ripped up to treat his leg. Harry heard movement around the cottage and then he heard a polite knock on the door. Confused, all he could think of to say was "Come in."

An old lady of at least eighty tottered in, holding a tray of cereal and steaming hot coffee. The aroma was heavenly and she placed it on the bedside table. Her back was hunched and her small frame looked frail, but despite the deep wrinkles in her face, her expression was assertive, framed with clear, animated eyes. She was immediately followed in by a tall man of a similar age. His white hair tapered off into a balding pate, and he sported a neatly trimmed white beard around his weathered but tanned face. Despite his obvious age, he looked lean and fit, with hardly an ounce of body fat. He regarded Harry curiously from under his half-moon specs and when he spoke his voice was strong, a Polish twang underlying his Welsh accent. "Good, good, you're awake. How are you feeling?"

"Like I'm living again, thank you," Harry replied in a croaky voice.

"Good, so eat up. You're skin and bone. I'm Joszef and this is Martha."

Harry sat up and as he did so he winced in pain.

"That's going to hurt for a while," said Martha. "It's a flesh wound and it's ugly but it didn't damage the muscle and the bullet passed through. I disinfected and bandaged the wound while you were asleep. I used to be a nurse. You never forget."

"Royal Gwent Hospital's finest!" beamed Joszef proudly.

Harry wolfed down the cereal, and Martha hurried to bring him more.

In between mouthfuls, Harry spoke. "I must apologize. It has been a long time since I ate properly. Thank you for your hospitality. I didn't introduce myself. I'm-"

"We know who you are," interrupted Joszef. "Harry Clarke, political correspondent now fugitive framed for the murder of former Cabinet Minister Graham Matheson." His head rolled back as he let out a hearty laugh. "They are warning the public not to approach you. Armed and dangerous, they said on the TV and the social media. You don't look either to me, but then it wouldn't be the first or last time this government twisted the truth. Now eat up and get your strength back. We'll leave you in peace for now." He pointed to a small silver bell by the table lamp. "Ring if you need anything."

With that he ushered his wife out of the room and they departed.

# CHAPTER 21

Harry must have drifted off again because when he awoke the shadows in the room had shifted. He glanced at the wall clock; just after two o'clock. They had left him some toiletries and he felt strong enough to hobble to the nearby bathroom for a bath, careful to keep his dressing dry. He also had a shave, and it was heavenly. The smoothness of his chin after shaving off his beard was pure joy. He dressed himself in the warm sweater and thick brown corduroy pants they had left on a small wooden chair in the corner. They fitted well, a little long, as Joszef was a few inches taller than Harry. His dressing made his right leg tight but it was no longer agony when he put weight on it.

He stepped out into a long corridor with bright, subtle green walls that had a number of framed photographs hanging in a line. Most of them were grainy old sepia coloured photographs; he presumed they were of relatives. One photograph grabbed his attention. It was a group of emaciated men posing for the camera, all looking decidedly miserable and staring with hollow vacant eyes. They were dressed in identical striped black and white pyjamas, standing on snowy ground, and behind them a huge chimney stack belched smoke into the grey sky.

A voice behind startled him. "My father at Treblinka in October 1943 just before they closed the camp and tried to destroy all evidence it ever existed. It's the only picture I have of him. It's ironic that it was about thirty minutes before they put him and the others in the gas chambers. The Nazis loved to make the poor Jews pose like some family portrait before they executed them, the only real evidence that they were ever there. I was three at the time. I don't remember much – my mother told me that she and her family somehow escaped the purge in occupied Warsaw and fled to safety, but Marek my father was not so lucky."

Joszef stood there, his dark eyes pensive as he studied the picture. "My mother told me stories of how bad it was but it seemed a distant memory, like it happened to someone else. I guess I was shielded from most of it. My mother told me that people thought of her as a survivor of the Holocaust, but she said there were no real survivors. Sure, people were alive in body, but their spirit, the very essence of their soul, was irredeemably damaged such that they were never the same person they had been before the War. I used to see it in the vacant, hollow look in my mother's eyes. I never thought I would see anything like it again in my lifetime. Surely the world had learned from the horrors of the Holocaust. People couldn't make the same mistake again surely? Yet here we are in Britain in the 2020's and I see so many parallels. It's happening all over again."

He turned to face Harry and his lined face beamed into a friendly smile, showing even but yellowing teeth. "Come come, you're looking much better and Martha has a goulash waiting for you."

He guided Harry to a large country kitchen with a broad oak table as its centrepiece, and the aroma of cooked meat made Harry feel almost giddy. Martha beamed at him as he hobbled onto a solid dining chair. "How's the leg?" she asked. "I'll change that dressing later."

She served him up a large plate of steaming goulash and the three of them sat down and ate. Harry relayed his tale to them, feeling a warmth and comfort in this elderly couple not unlike surrogate parents. He ravenously demolished several platefuls. "It's good to see a man other than Joszef appreciate my food," she smiled. As she did so, she quickly reached for her handkerchief and turned away. Her frail body shook with a series of wheezing coughs. Joszef looked concerned as he went over to gently pat her back.

"Harry," began Joszef. "You know that it won't be long before they catch up with you. Maybe a day at the most. The TV said they suspected you were somewhere on the edge of the Brecon Beacons. They will probably carry out a house to house search. We can hide you but it may be too risky."

"Why are you helping me? You're putting yourselves in danger."

Martha glanced at her husband and he smiled ruefully. "There is nothing here for us. It's only a matter of time. We have already been forced to register. Any day they could come knocking on our door. It's helpful that we are so remote but it's only a stay of execution. You, my friend, have a future; maybe you can make a difference so long as they don't catch you." Joszef gave a pensive sigh. "Let me take you down to the basement. I want to show you something."

Harry finished his meal and hobbled after his host, accompanied by another bout of coughing from Martha as she cleared up the plates. They descended down a narrow set of steps into a dark cellar area. Joszef flicked a switch and the area was flooded with cold white fluorescent lighting. Harry saw a working laboratory, several workstations loaded with test tubes, petri dishes, spatulas, cylindrical glass jars, microscopes, syringes and more. It was an impressive array of equipment.

Joszef smiled at Harry's confused expression. "I used to be a biochemist specializing in genomes," he explained. "I still am, really, only an unpaid one. Martha always accused me of taking my work home so I thought I would make it official. I want to show you something."

Joszef donned a mask and pulled on a pair of elasticated gloves, and handed the same to Harry. He stood at a workbench where marked petri dishes were lined up along one end. He carefully opened one sealed dish and placed it under a powerful electron microscope, so that the culture inside was directly under the lens. He peered through the lens and then moved aside for Harry.

Harry looked through the lens and observed the microscopic rod-shaped cultures rushing around in chaotic fashion. They were red and angry looking and appeared to be propelled by small tails that snaked along behind them.

"What is it?" asked Harry, his voice muffled under the mask.

Joszef gave a tired sigh. "This is a swab I took from Martha's mouth last night when she was sleeping." He suddenly laughed. "Damn woman makes it easy for me when she is snoring and her jaws hang open. She's in the first stages of this mysterious illness that is sweeping through the deportation camps. Don't worry; it's not easily contagious unless you ingest her blood or saliva." He smiled thinly. "Don't let her cough in your face. However as a precaution I suggest you continue to wear the mask around us."

"What about you?" asked Harry, concerned.

"Martha's dying, Harry, and if she dies I have nothing to live for. There's a reason we live in such a remote place. I stopped believing in the human race many years ago. I am tired of Man's propensity for evil, not just through the greed and corruption of governments and corporations; but also in the petty selfishness of ordinary people, all clambering over each other to get ahead, with no sense of community or support. Is this what civilization has come to? If so I don't want any part of it. Martha is my sole reminder that there are some good people around, despite this sick regime. When she goes I will truly stop believing. I have seen too much suffering in my life Harry, and most of it was needless and senseless, born of barbaric hatred and intolerance. When I saw this-" he pointed to the microscope – "I knew that it was happening all over again, the mistakes of history repeating itself."

"What do you mean?"

"Look again through the microscope."

As Harry did so, Joszef continued. "Although it looks chaotic, there is a certain order to their movement." That order is different to natural micro-organisms which move even more chaotically. Let me show you." He carefully replaced the slide in its petri dish and placed another slide under the microscope. "This culture is a variant of the anthrax pathogen which usually attacks and spreads through the lymphatic system, but it is entirely natural. Look at this one."

Harry viewed the second slide. The bacillus strain was faster, more fluid, and apparently more random in its movement, but it was hard to tell for a layman. Joszef carefully put the slide back. "It's difficult to tell I know, but the properties are different. The natural pathogen does not have the same level of organization as the man-made pathogen.

"Scientists have been engineering genetic sequences for decades. Using synthetic biology, they have been able to recreate bacterial pathogens like smallpox and anthrax for many years. Synthetic pathogens are man-made infectious agents that are produced either from the manufacture or adaptation of DNA, cells and other biological structures using specialized genomes. Governments have been producing biological weapons for decades, but this is one of the most sophisticated I have ever seen. It's a highly effective killer, yet its conditions for transmission can be controlled so that it is not highly contagious except where people are usually in close proximity and more likely to ingest or be exposed to bodily fluids. Places such as deportation camps."

A cold shiver ran down Harry's spine as he realized the implications. His immediate thought was of Tamara and Byron.

Joszef nodded in answer to Harry's horrified expression. "Yes Harry. The Nazis had the gas chambers, the Rwandans had their Hutu death squads and Pelham's regime has this anthrax-like disease. The man is not just a dictator, he is genocidal."

# CHAPTER 22

As they ascended the narrow steps back into the brightly lit kitchen, Harry pondered over the government's *Five Year Plan*, the document which had led to his current troubles. He recalled an oblique reference to a controlled depopulation of the immigrant community by medical means, but he could not quite remember what it was, and at the time he had not paid much attention to it. The document had been too inflammatory and provocative for public consumption, yet it had clearly not fully set out just how far Pelham was prepared to go, even to his own Cabinet. There were some things that were just too atrocious to be committed to writing.

Martha was still coughing and Harry realized self-consciously that he still wore his mask, while Joszef had removed his.

"It's alright," Joszef assured him. "Martha knows. Keep the mask on. She won't be offended."

Harry, however, ripped off the mask and said. "No, I'll take my chances."

Martha smiled and then bent over again, facing away from them and coughing into her white cotton handkerchief. The first spots of red appeared and she glanced at Joszef. She looked scared. Joszef put his arm around her and guided her to a chair. "Relax old girl;

you've got plenty of time," he said with forced cheerfulness.

Harry turned to Martha. "How did you get infected living out here?"

"We had to register," wheezed Martha. "We were told to report to the Camarthen deportation camp last week. You don't ignore those demands. We went there and it was total chaos. They were trying to herd people into trucks, apparently to take them onto boats to God knows where. I have never seen such a miserable, hopeless bunch of people. Apparently these were people who had lived in the camp for a while. The camp guards kept pushing them to steer them onto trucks lined up near the camp perimeter." She paused and wheezed while Joszef gently rubbed her back, the concern in his eyes evident.

"The rest of us, the new entrants, were forced to wait in huge lines in the camp's main yard, surrounded by armed guards with nasty, barking Rottweilers straining on their leash, until it was our turn to be processed for living in the camp. We saw everything. There was a lot of pushing and shoving and people were shouting and protesting. They were not moving fast enough because of all of a sudden one of the guards began hitting a woman with children. He just picked on her randomly and began hitting her on the back with his baton. She was unfortunate to be on the edge of the crowd and easy to reach. Her young children began wailing, clutching at her as if they could fend off his blows. It was horrible but what happened next was worse."

She paused again, and Harry saw her eyes cloud over and tears roll down her sallow cheeks as she recalled the scene. The strength of character he had first glimpsed in her had diminished and her voice was stretched. "Her husband broke from the crowd and charged at the guard, knocking him over, his fists pumping into the man's face. Other guards swarmed around him and quickly pulled him off. They hit him with their batons until he lay like a limp rag doll on the floor. Then they dragged him to a patch of open ground and made him kneel down with his hands on his head. They all had their guns out now and waved them at the crowd to discourage them from intervening. They blindfolded him."

Her tears turned into choking sobs and Joszef soothed her. "We were yards away but we couldn't get to him. The guards held us back but we all watched, not believing what we were seeing. I couldn't turn away. The guard that the man had defended his wife against pulled out a small revolver and waved it around like a trophy. He stood behind the kneeling man and….and…" Martha could barely get the words out. "He shot him in the back of the head, in cold blood, in front of his wife and screaming children. I remember seeing the killer as he turned toward us, a satisfied smile on his face. His dark eyes were empty, devoid of all emotion, like he had no soul." Her words were slurred from sobbing and Joszef consoled her with a hug.

"Come on old girl," he said soothingly, rubbing her back. "Don't upset yourself."

Her chest shuddered as she cried. "God, have these people not got mothers and fathers, people they care about? We were all shocked, couldn't believe what we saw, but the crowd followed orders after that. How could they have become such savages? We always thought Britain was safe, a haven from a hostile world where killings like that happened every day in the war-torn countries. Not this country, surely?"

Her sobbing subsided and she calmed down and gulped at a

glass of water before spluttering into a coughing fit again. Joszef held her until she was calmer.

"How did you escape?" asked Harry.

Joszef took up the story. "They realized there were too many for them to cope with so they sent a group of us away. It was purely random and they told us they would serve papers on us later. We're still waiting for those papers but they're so disorganized it will probably be a while. All the guards had masks on but as we lined up to leave they brought out patients from the camp hospital. They marched these poor wretched souls across the yard right past us. Some of them could hardly stand yet they made them walk to the trucks. One man staggered and fell on the muddy ground. He was bone thin and his hollow eyes reminded me of the Holocaust pictures that mother showed me lest I forget. Martha, brave soul that she is, broke from our group and tried to help him. The dogs began barking and the guards came to remove her as she knelt down beside him, but she shouted back at them that she was a nurse and they held off.

"There was not much Martha could do. She had no equipment but she could never see a man suffer like that. Do you know what that man did? He spat in her face. I guess if you are treated like an animal then eventually you become one. I know he was dying but poor Martha was trying to help him. I was worried because we had heard that this mystery illness was rife in the camps, and he had come from the camp hospital. When Martha began coughing yesterday I somehow knew. I had to be certain, hence the tests, but I understand from media reports that the disease has an incubation period of about a week, and it's been eight days since we were in Carmarthen." Joszef's shoulders sagged and he wiped a solitary tear that rolled down his ruddy cheek. "We don't have long."

# CHAPTER 23

Rachel Thomas pushed her long blond hair back on the pillow and stared at the beautifully manicured stucco ceiling in the bedroom chambers at 10 Downing Street. Next to her the Prime Minister slept on his side on the luxurious King size bed, snoring contentedly. It was he who had a reputation in the media as a notorious insomniac. He constantly boasted to the Press how he got by on just four hours a night, carrying it like a badge of honour. That was probably true when the debates in the House dragged on until the early hours, but after their energetic love-making he always slept soundly, and tonight it was Rachel who had trouble sleeping.

It was only in the last few weeks that Pelham had taken to inviting her into the marital bed he shared with Helen. Previously their trysts had taken place at Rachel's Kensington apartment or a prearranged hotel in Knightsbridge with tight security, but recently Helen's overnight 'charity ventures' had become more frequent and the affair between Rachel and Pelham had developed into an open secret within the Party. No-one spoke openly of it, of course; to do so would lose them more than their job. For Rachel it was the surreptitious glances she received from his security staff, or from the chauffeur who would take her back to her apartment through the rat-infested streets of London at three o'clock in the morning. Pelham, however, had become less and less interested in what his staff thought and the security situation in recent weeks had made their meetings impossible other than directly at No. 10.

Rachel could not deny that her relationship as Pelham's mistress had brought spectacular career benefits. It was what she had seen today that rendered her sleepless. He had confided in her, his natural reticence when asked about his past replaced by an open, frank approach. She probably knew more about him than anyone, including his wife, and his disclosures put into context what she had seen today. It made him a dangerous man, and she shuddered at what might happen if he ever tired of her.

As his personal assistant, she accompanied him everywhere and today they had visited a large government laboratory secretly placed in the basement of a nondescript building in an industrial zone on the outskirts of Watford. The building was huge, like an aircraft hangar, and even the basement area was wide and expansive with corridors trailing off into various different directions, as well as multiple floors. Their delegation was made up of the P.M and his Deputy, Giles Chamberlain, Rachel, a couple of corporate sponsors who refused to reveal where they were from, and various security personnel. They were greeted by the sycophantic Head of Research, Dr. Raymond Heath. He was tall and gangly with an aquiline nose from the end of which balanced a pair of half-moon spectacles. He treated Pelham with the reverence of royalty and insisted on calling him Sir, constantly bleating about how honoured he was that Pelham had bestowed them with a visit.

His white laboratory coat was crisp and neatly pressed and he had a habit of bouncing on the balls of his feet which made everyone uncomfortable. Rachel took an instant dislike to the man, the more so because of the obvious pride he took in his work. As he walked them through the facility, he thanked the corporate sponsors for their generosity in funding this 'ground-breaking project.' The walls were bare brick and being underground had no windows. The subdued lighting from the recessed wall lights did little to dispel the gloomy, depressing feel of the place.

"I believe we are pushing the boundaries of genetic engineering and cognitive research further and further. Few scientists in history have had the opportunity to experiment on live subjects like we have," the doctor proclaimed. Rachel did not understand until they had moved deeper into the bowels of the building, through dark, narrow corridors that seemed to drive so far into the heart of this shadowy place that even if she turned and ran, she could not be confident of finding her way back.

It was then, with a sick feeling that levitated through her very soul, she realized what this laboratory truly was and fervently wished the P.M. had not brought her here. "Ladies and Gentlemen," announced Dr. Heath proudly. "I give you the Aryan Project."

The dark gloomy corridors were suddenly bathed in light, revealing a long row of glass fronted steel cells lit by harsh yellow fluorescent lights that buzzed like a swarm of flics. Each cell was clean and functional, but the harsh light and grey walls rendered them sterile and soulless. The most shocking aspect, however, was the occupants of the cells. At first Rachel turned away in horror, but after the initial wave of nausea, she became transfixed, much to her guilt and shame.

As they passed each cell, Dr. Heath smugly commented on the medical experiments they were performing on the poor unfortunate inhabitants. They were wretched creatures, some of them chained to the metallic beds and others wired up to large boxes of equipment and monitors. Some of them were grossly disfigured, twisted bones sticking out at odd angles, and one poor unfortunate soul was strapped to the bed with wires from a small electronic box feeding directly into his brain, the top of his skull having been removed so the grey brain matter was exposed and pulsing. The doctor explained that he was being subjected to various brain stimuli, and it was easier to observe and record without the top of the skull obstructing the equipment. Rachel fought the urge to vomit when she saw this destitute creature.

Many had suffered limb amputations and one distressed creature looked as if he had been skinned alive. His cries of pain and anguish failed to reach the assembled group through the thickened, soundproof glass, but Rachel could see his red mouth moving, and his eyes wide in their sockets. Yet some of the experiments they had embarked upon did not involve physical brutality. The doctor explained that psychological tests were an important part of their mission. He explained that one patient who sat with a black box that completely surrounded his head was the subject of a long term sensory deprivation project. He was unable to see or hear, smell or taste, as he was fed intravenously and his brain patterns were monitored regularly to test the effects. He casually mentioned that eventually the subject would become insane, but part of the study was to establish how long that would take.

As he led the group through the bizarre sideshow, he boasted that the laboratory was the most sophisticated biotechnology unit in the country. He summarized the experiments the laboratory was conducting, falling under two main areas, genetic engineering and cognitive therapy. The purpose of the experiments was to follow the ideological concept of transhumanism, which was designed to fundamentally transform the human condition by developing technologies to enhance human intellectual, physical, and psychological capacities.

"Our studies will help us identify and neutralize genes that cause hereditary conditions and genetic disorders. We will be able to predict and eventually eliminate Alzheimer's disease, cystic fibrosis, Down syndrome. On the other side we will be able to tap into the neurons and fibres of the brain to develop ways to enhance its capacity and to fulfil its huge potential. We all have the ability to become prodigies!" He waved his hands in the air like the archetypal mad scientist. "We truly will become the Master Race!"

They were no longer constrained by onerous ethical considerations, he continued. He pointed out one subject strapped to a gurney and attached to a machine like an electrocardiograph, with a range of tubes and electrodes running around his body. He explained that the patient was a good example of the type of work they undertook.

The subject had been injected with genetically modified DNA cells designed to enhance the immune system, following which a series of diseases, pathogens and biological agents were injected through the lymphatic system, first ranging from mild pathogens such as influenza and progressing in intensity to the most lethal diseases known to man. The subject's ability to fight the pathogens and the effects on his physiological state were closely monitored. Early signs were encouraging but inevitably the subject would die as more virulent diseases were introduced; however the data retrieved would inform further development in the laboratory. As part of the same experiment, some subjects were tested for the effect of chemical agents such as Sarin nerve gas, or potent poisons such as Ricin, a naturally occurring protein, a few grains of which were lethal.

They were also undertaking genetic enhancement work, whereby experiments were conducted to test modification or alteration of a human beings' appearance, adaptability, intelligence, character or behaviour. Examples of these included the creation of muscle building hormones that would decrease the loss of the mechano-growth factor hormone. This hormone regulated another naturally occurring hormone produced after exercise that stimulates muscle production. As people aged, the levels of this hormone fell, leading to loss of muscle mass. This experiment if successful would effectively delay the ageing process, and lead to a stronger and fitter breed of people.

Their work however was not just confined to creating a physically stronger race. They were also conducting a range of psychological experiments. For example they were testing what he termed as 'cognitive reprogramming' which consisted of various stimuli and suggestions that could be used to manipulate and control individuals. The purpose of this was to voluntarily subjugate a person's individuality to the concept of collectivism and dependence on the State. Other areas included cognitive behaviour therapy to modify a subject's psyche. Tests conducted under this area included the study of psychosis and criminal behaviour, and a subject's mental endurance. He proudly described a situation where a subject had been placed under the most extreme psychological stress to the point where he developed severe schizophrenia and killed himself, after which his brain was dissected, yielding important results.

Rachel found it all so factual and impassive. It was hard to believe the good doctor was discussing humans but then he had never described them as such, merely regarding them as 'subjects' in the same way one would describe laboratory rats. Perhaps that was how he appeased his conscience, if he had one, thought Rachel.

The Aryan Project was probably the most closely guarded secret in Pelham's whole regime. He had not even revealed the existence of this facility to the Cabinet; only Rachel and Chamberlain within his inner circle knew about this monstrous project, but rather than empowering Rachel, it petrified her, a secret that weighed so heavily it threatened to engulf her. The project was not a government initiative. It had been funded by a number of corporate sponsors, the representatives of whom were in the assembled party, corporations which either stood to benefit from the human vivisection they saw, or which had already received significant advantages in return for their financial patronage. Pelham, ever the capitalist, saw this as a natural trade, one which fitted his philosophy of corporatism.

She had patiently listened to his political lectures, and encouraged by her academic interest, something his wife eschewed, he had revealed his philosophies to her. Corporatism was the key to harmony amongst the social classes, and would reduce opposition and reward political loyalty. The association of people into corporate groups, headed by a strong leader was the way of the future, he had asserted. Only through corporatism and fascism could this country truly become great again. Rachel had smiled at the irony of Pelham's own naked self-interest which contradicted this philosophy. Rachel suspected he had personally received millions in corporate sponsorship, although he would never reveal that, not even to her.

She pictured herself again in the bowels of that malignant building, anxious to escape the suffocating air and the stench of atrocity. She had glanced furtively at Chamberlain and seen the revulsion in his face. Their eyes had locked, just for the merest moment, but it was enough, and then Rachel knew what she had to do.

# CHAPTER 24

The Black SUV took the road north from the village of Glyn-neath less than a mile south of the Brecon Beacons, the expansive iron grey hills flecked by the wispy mists that drifted across the dull late afternoon sky. Bruce was exhausted, but he remained focused on the road ahead. They had been on the road since three that morning, negotiating the crumbling rural roads, taking several hours to reach the area. They had spent the day conducting house to house searches in the village. Their presence had been intimidating to the villagers and they were met with barely disguised hostility, although that did not prevent the villagers from cooperating. Their fear of the State Secret Police and its reputation far outweighed their antipathy toward the trio and while their questions were met with curt replies, no householder was foolhardy enough to prevent him, Ethan and Sean from searching their property.

However, the search had yielded nothing until Bruce received a cryptic message on his tablet suggesting Harry was still in the vicinity, but not in the village. There was a group of secluded cottages that formed their own tiny hamlet on the edge of the vast desolate moor just north of the village and the message suggested they should concentrate their search in that area.

Ethan looked at his GPS. "Over there," he instructed Bruce, pointing to a small lane that forked off the main road. The lane was gravelly and potholed, the recent downpour creating puddles in the holes which masked their depth. Even the SUV was vulnerable and as Bruce spun the robust vehicle onto the lane, careful to avoid the deceptive puddles, the wheels spun slightly as they gained traction, the crunch of gravel loud in the cab. Although Bruce fought to control his fatigue, the pursuit of Harry had become more like an obsession to him, and he had an instinct they were close. He could smell his blood, and as they emerged from a dense canopy of trees the road opened up and he spotted a number of cottages and farmhouses dotted along the lane.

Bruce turned to Sean, who was manacled to the seat rest. "Well hotshot, any ideas? You're supposed to be our tracker. I agree with Ethan. You've been worse than useless. Here's a chance to redeem yourself."

Sean had no more idea than the two SSP agents but he tried to sound confident. "We ditch the SUV and go on foot. If he's here he'll be alerted by the SUV so we should keep the search low profile. I guess our informer is one of the cottage residents? Do we know which one?"

Bruce and Ethan glanced at each other. "No we don't," replied Bruce. "But I agree we lose the SUV. Let's park up." They pulled into a small clearing surrounded by dense undergrowth just before the woodland surrendered to the stubby, coarse grass of the moorland. While Ethan unchained Sean, Bruce took the sniper rifle from his holdall in the trunk. Looking through the scope he could see the cottages much more clearly. The Winchester had a range that could take out a person with precision in any of the cottages, even from his remote position. There was no movement in any of the buildings, however, and he had to remind himself that his instructions were explicit; to bring back Harry Clarke alive. That was inconvenient, but the rifle was precise enough to wound without being lethal. The short hairs on his muscular neck bristled with anticipation. His quarry was near, he could feel it.

After they had eaten Joszef drove into Glynneath and Harry had a chance to talk to Martha, who remained busy and industrious in the kitchen. Every now and then she would burst into a violent coughing fit, but resisted any attempts at Harry to intervene. "Stay away Harry, don't risk yourself," she urged him, her arm outstretched to prevent him getting closer.

Despite her own troubles, she attended to Harry's leg with consummate skill, examining the wound carefully, cleaning it and replacing the dressing. Although it looked ugly, and Harry had to turn away when she disinfected the wound, Martha declared that the wound was healing nicely. She confirmed that she found no sign of the bullet, suggesting it had grazed his thigh rather than penetrated it. When she told him that he would probably have a nice permanent scar, he touched his collar bone, recalling the bullet from Sean that had rasped his shoulder as he fled the attack on the compound with Julianne back in July.

Harry felt safe and relaxed, as if the trauma of the last few days had been no more than a terrible nightmare. He knew it was a temporary respite, but somehow the cottage felt secure, its remoteness a shield that would buy him time against his pursuers.

Sipping at a large mug of coffee, Harry told Martha about his family, and his struggles to reach Tamara and Byron, interred in the

Salisbury deportation camp.

"The camps are heavily guarded now," said Martha. "They were totally disorganized at first. The government had no clue what it was doing. Now they're almost impossible to escape from. I saw that when we had to go to Carmarthen. They are frightful places. I can only imagine what you must be going through."

Harry tentatively asked if she and Joszef had children, and she gave a doleful sigh. "No, we never could. Joszef and I met long after the war but we had the memories of the Holocaust and what it did to our families as a common bond. Only for me it wasn't just a memory. Of course we tried and went to counselling and did the usual tests. Joszef was fine, so they put it down to the trauma of my childhood, which they suggested had caused a psychological block to getting pregnant, only it wasn't that. I spent time in a concentration camp as a toddler. I don't remember what they did; only that it hurt terribly. I dreaded telling him in case he left me, but whatever they did to me had left me infertile. It took me decades to summon up the courage to tell him, long after we stopped trying, but he just comforted me and scolded me for keeping such a terrible secret to myself for so many years. I should have known he would understand. That's the type of man he is, a good, kind man in a world of evil. It's probably just as well we couldn't have children, looking at the way the world is today."

Harry told Martha about his family and his foolishness at having lost them. He berated himself for having failed to rescue them, but Martha squeezed his hand in empathy. "There was nothing you could do. The best thing you can do for them is stay alive. At least you'll have a chance."

"The worst thing," said Harry pensively, "is that I never even got a chance to speak to them. When I broke into the camp shortly after it opened I saw Tamara and Byron but the soldiers kicked me out, without even a chance to say goodbye. Before they were taken I was just getting to know my son again."

Martha said nothing, but the mere presence of this dear old lady was comforting to him. He had not spoken about his family so openly to anyone for so long, not even to Omar. He found it therapeutic, but it also made him realize how lonely he was. The thought of Omar brought fresh pain, but Martha continued to listen attentively as he talked falteringly about his friend and his cruel demise. "The irony is that, in the eyes of Pelham's regime, people like Omar are the enemy, but in the short time I knew him he was the greatest friend I could ever have wished for. He saved my life and then made the ultimate sacrifice to protect me. God, if only we hadn't gone to St. Paul's he might still be alive."

"Harry, I know you must be carrying a lot of guilt, but it's not you who should feel guilty. It's every man and woman who supports this evil regime – they're the guilty ones. Who gave this government the mandate to choose who we can and cannot be friends with? It was not the people. Friendship is not bound by colour, culture or religion. How dare they tell us otherwise!" she concluded indignantly. Her agitation caused her to cough and splutter again and she turned away and lurched for the sink. As she did so Harry could see tiny spots of blood spray onto the ivory worktop. He was about to rush to her aid when Joszef came storming through the door, almost taking it off its hinges.

His expression registered serious concern, but it was Harry he was looking at. "Harry, I made some enquiries in the village. The SSP have been making house to house searches and I was told they had been directed to this area. Further up the lane I spotted a black SUV parked amongst the bushes, like someone made a poor attempt to hide it. They must already be in the area. There aren't too many cottages here. It won't be long before they're knocking on our door. You'd better go."

He turned to Martha. "Pack him what you can from the refrigerator. The boy needs supplies." She nodded and hastily gathered together a number of Tupperware dishes full of food and packed it into a large backpack.

As she did so, Joszef said "Come with me." Harry followed him into the garage at the rear of the building, where a battered Yamaha motorbike stood on a kickstand. It still radiated heat. The chassis was electric blue, and the chrome trim was scratched and faded but its sleek body still looked as if it could carry some speed. Joszef tossed the keys to Harry. "Your getaway vehicle," he smiled.

Harry gasped. "I couldn't possibly-"

"Yes you could," interrupted Joszef. "You don't have much choice. They will be here any moment and you need a quick escape. I take it you can ride a motorbike?"

"Of course," beamed Harry, running his fingers lightly over the hot metal of the chassis.

"Good, because this thing moves fast; you have to respect it though. It has a 1300cc straight four engine, so don't go crazy and it might just save your life, but we have to hurry."

Joszef handed Harry a thick brown fleece-lined jacket. The wool felt soft and warm when he put it on. Martha shuffled in with the backpack and Harry slung it over his shoulder. "I wish I could give you a weapon, but as a point of principle we never keep such things in the house," said Joszef. However, he slipped a small case containing a pair of field glasses in the pocket of the jacket. "These might come in handy to spot them before they spot you."

Harry hugged Martha, his eyes glistening and Joszef gripped his hand in a firm handshake. "Godspeed son," he said simply. Harry straddled the bike, donned the helmet and fired up the engine, which gave a throaty roar and settled into a purr that held the promise of great power. "Thank you for everything. I will return the bike, whatever it takes."

"Don't worry, son, I have a feeling I'm not going to need it."

Harry kicked away the stand and the bike shot out of the open garage and up the lane. The noise of the engine resonated in the still air, sending a flock of birds perched on a nearby tree fluttering into the dreary sky. The lane curved upwards and he passed the wooded area that separated the lane from the main road. He glanced into the clearing and saw the SUV partly concealed in the undergrowth. He braked hard and stopped in the clearing, propping the motorbike on its stand. From his sheltered position he had a clear view of the three figures striding purposefully toward Joszef and Martha's cottage. This was no social call. He reached for the field glasses in his pocket and found a wad of cash stuffed in the carry-case. He smiled at the couple's generosity, but the smile disappeared when he peered at the trio. They were dressed all in black, the usual attire of the SSP but they were not masked. He did not recognize the first two, but the third figure, when he turned into view, confused and unnerved him. It looked uncannily like his nemesis in the compound, Sean Kelly.

# CHAPTER 25

It had not taken them long to explore the area, because the person who had called in the tip came stomping out to greet them. He moved as fast as his walking stick would allow, and shouted at them, beckoning wildly.

"Jesus," cried Bruce. "He's going to alert the whole neighbourhood. Get him inside." They quickened their pace and gestured to the man to go inside and they followed him into his cottage. The man's face was tanned and weathered, his skin so leathery that it was hard at first glance to tell his age. His iron coloured, straggly hair was combed over a huge bald spot, and the hair flapped about as he hurried back inside the cottage. "I know where he is," he said in an excited tone, as the trio followed him into the large but untidy kitchen. As he spoke he wiped his nose with the back of a liver-spotted hand, and his breath was wheezy like wind whistling through a pipe.

"It's the Jews hiding him," he said. "I always thought there was something funny about them. I knew they were trouble, coming in here buying up our land. This land is for decent British folk like me; not those greedy Jewish bastards." The man continued to rant and waved his cane in the air for effect. "Damn foreigners. Pelham got my vote. It's about time someone stood up to 'em."

Bruce's face creased with impatience. He grabbed the lapels of the man's winter coat. "Tell me which cottage," he said.

The man hesitated and his blotchy eyes widened in surprise at the SSP officer's aggression. "Over there," he said, pointing outside the kitchen window. "The last cottage in the lane."

Bruce let go and picked up his rifle from the counter. "Okay, let's move it," he commanded Ethan and Sean.

The owner brushed down his dusty old coat and jabbed his finger at them in protest. "Hey, what about my money?" he complained indignantly. "The hotline said there was a big reward for his arrest."

Bruce turned around and faced the owner, who shrank back as his muscular physique towered above the man's stringy, gaunt frame. With a sweeping motion, Bruce casually brought the long rifle crashing down on the owner's head. A deep gash opened on his forehead where the sharp metal had abraded the skin and the man collapsed to the floor, yelping like a wounded animal.

"Your reward is doing your duty for your country," taunted Bruce. The man let out a stream of obscenities but they were left unanswered as Bruce led Ethan and Sean out of the cottage. Just as they did the roar of a motorcycle engine shattered the relative peace and they watched as a motorcycle tore up the lane and disappeared around the curve on the way to the main road, the sound of the engine fading. They strode across the cold, damp ground to the far cottage, checking their weapons as they did so. Ethan glanced up the lane, curious about the motorcyclist. He caught Bruce's eye and his boss nodded in understanding. They hurried to the end cottage, anxious to close in on their target but fearful that he might have slipped away.

From his crouched position, Harry watched the three figures move toward Joszef and Martha's cottage. Their movement was way too confident for a random house to house search. His heart pounding, he realized they *knew* he had been there. The couple came out to greet them on the front lawn of the cottage, and the five of them stood there as Harry watched helplessly. Joszef seemed to be waving his arms as if he was trying to make a point. It looked like the couple were being shouted at, because Joszef put his hands forward, palms flat in a calming gesture. Harry could feel the blood pumping in his ears as he watched anxiously. Then it all happened quickly. The lead antagonist raised the long rifle at his side and without warning shot Martha square in the chest. The shot resounded across the cool air, sending another flock of birds flapping away into the gloomy sky. Martha collapsed instantly to the ground, twitched once and lay still. Joszef stood there impassively and Harry knew it was inevitable. The assassin raised the rifle again and from point blank range, shot the old man stone dead.

Harry cried out in anguish, unable to mentally process the cold-blooded execution he had just witnessed. In a haze of impotent anger, he pulled a carving knife the couple had placed in his backpack and furiously slashed at the tyres of the SUV until they deflated with an angry hiss. It provided little catharsis for the horror, but it would buy Harry some time. Scarcely concerned whether they saw him or not, he clipped on the helmet, fired up the bike's engine and roared away as fast as the bike would allow.

# CHAPTER 26

When Julianne and Kendrick had arrived in Pembroke the day before, they were greeted by chaotic scenes. They considered it fortunate to have encountered no more checkpoints on the road to the port, only long lines of unmanned concrete blocks that prevented cars gaining access to the dock area on the mouth of the estuary. They had left the car and walked unmolested toward the dockyard, where the ferries left port. When they observed the masses of people and the soldiers aggressively keeping them in line, it was not difficult to see why they had not been stopped. Manning a checkpoint appeared to be the lowest priority as the authorities had their hands full. For a government so intent on appearances, however, it was a surprising omission. Any civilian could walk into Pembroke Docks without being harassed and witness the truth of the government's activities.

They did not venture any further although Julianne had been tempted to charge in and try to help in some misguided way. Kendrick had convinced her it would be foolish to do so, and she had listened reluctantly. Instead they returned to the outskirts of town and were now holed up in a dilapidated room in a shabby motel that Kendrick found near Pembroke Castle. It was one of the few motels still operating in the area. Perhaps, reflected Julianne ironically as she stared at the soiled, peeling walls, they no longer needed a checkpoint here. No sane person would come to this place of their own free will. She began to doubt her own sanity in venturing out this far on what was rapidly turning into a hopeless mission and getting harder by the hour. Even if her intuition was right, and Harry was desperate enough to attempt a crossing to Ireland, they would never find him in the mayhem.

It was late and Julianne gazed pensively from between the thin curtains. As she watched, an old Hispanic woman was dragged screaming from one of the nearby rooms by a group of four masked men dressed all in black. She was thrown recklessly into the back of a SUV, which sped off into the night. It was becoming a familiar scene across the country. The dreaded knock on the door late at night had symbolized the rule of the military junta in Argentina back in the 1970s, when so many political dissidents had joined the ranks of the 'disappeared.' They had called it the Dirty War, but it was no less dirty than the tyranny being perpetrated across Britain fifty years on. Her studies of that regime in her political history degree had been a major factor in the shaping of her ideology. She had been sickened by the state sponsored terrorism and guerrilla warfare carried out by right wing militias. They had targeted anyone they perceived to be left wing or leaning toward socialism, including trade unionists, students, journalists and Marxists, most of whom simply disappeared, much like the current regime. Her studies had equipped her with enough political insight to be aware that even while the Labour government held power, the seeds of a new right wing dynasty were already being sown. She had thrown her energies into political rallies and marches in an effort to make her voice heard.

With a heavy sense of guilt and frustration, she stepped away from the curtain, powerless to prevent another savage blow to democracy every time a person was forcibly taken from their home and family. She briefly wondered why the woman was in the motel. Perhaps she too was hopeful of escaping across the water to a better land.

"What would Harry do in this situation?" asked Kendrick, interrupting her thoughts.

"I know one thing he would do," she replied, suddenly fired up. "He would get out his old Nikon and he would photograph the atrocities being carried out in the government's name. He would refuse to be silenced." She turned away from the curtain, her face a mask of determination.

"We have to be cautious, Julianne. You know the approach of the PIA to anyone trying to photograph their activities. They don't just grab your camera and smash it on the floor now. We mustn't draw attention to ourselves."

Julianne glared at Kendrick. "It's our moral duty to expose these criminals," she snapped, the irritation in her voice obvious.

She heard Kendrick breath hard, leaning back in the worn out old chair, shifting uncomfortably as if the springs stuck in his back. "I understand how you feel," he began in a tone of genuine empathy, "But remember why we are here. Our mission is to find Harry. Getting ourselves arrested and ending up at the bottom of a mass grave will be the only outcome."

"How can we just sit idly by and let this happen?" she exclaimed.

"Because we need to stick to the plan. There is nothing that you or I can do for these poor people and if we draw attention to ourselves then we'll suffer the same fate. You can be too idealistic. I know you want to help them, but the best way is to find Harry. We'll go near the docks and make some more enquiries tomorrow, but I'm not hopeful. This really is a needle in a haystack."

Julianne nodded sullenly, unable to refute his logic, and flopped on the bed, deeply troubled.

Harry rode the motorbike like a demon, eating up the miles as the cold air rushed past, sucking the heat from his body and funnelling around his helmet. Tears of anger and sorrow blurred his vision but spurred him on. He had a considerable gain on his pursuers, at least for now, but he had to flee the country or risk arrest or worse. It was clear the secret police were prepared to kill in their obsessive pursuit of him. Soon a cloak of darkness enveloped him and a biting wind picked up, forcing him to slow down. The narrow country road was empty but there was always the risk of hitting a pothole that could materialize in his headlights before he could avoid it. The holes filled with water were the most dangerous, because it was impossible to guess their depth.

Harry's swirling thoughts returned to his sighting of the three SSP officers who had executed Joszef and Martha. He felt deeply troubled. He had assumed that Sean had perished along with many others in the attack on the cell's base in Kent, yet he was convinced it was Sean. If he had changed allegiance, could it be possible that Julianne had too? As he remembered his former lover a deep pang of melancholy arose in him. In addition to losing his family to the camps, he had suffered the grief of losing Omar and the Jewish couple who had survived the Holocaust only to be shot like dogs on their front lawn. He had also lost Julianne, he reflected sombrely, and the thought that maybe she had followed Sean in supporting this insane regime was troubling. He refused to believe it but could not dismiss the insane notion from his mind.

Depressed and weary, having been on the road for two hours, he passed by an old public house set back from the main road just east of Pembroke. It loomed black and silent against the faint light of the night sky, and in the glow of the motorbike's headlights, Harry could see the structure was abandoned. The brick construction was generally intact but heavily pockmarked, and the windows had been boarded up. He parked the bike in a small alcove around the back of the building, out of sight to any casual visitor, and entered by the front door, which swung open lazily as he stepped in. He heard the sound of unknown creatures scurrying and the faint squeal of a rodent. Cobwebs brushed his face but he was too tired to care.

He trudged upstairs, his footsteps creaking on the bare wooden boards and found some torn old blankets in a linen closet on the landing. Despite its ramshackle state, the interior felt solid, and, too exhausted to contemplate the possibility that his pursuers might catch up with him, curled up in the blankets in one of the bedrooms and quickly fell into a dreamless but fitful sleep.

# CHAPTER 27

The following morning was grey and dank, and the murky daylight struggled to dispel the gloom inside the house. There was no electricity but when Harry turned on the rusty taps, there was a tinny rattle before water spluttered out, and he was able to enjoy a thorough wash. His leg was aching, and his stomach churned with hunger, as if his first proper food in months had reawakened his appetite. He munched through some of the supplies Martha had packed for him, but rationed them, not knowing when his next meal would arrive. Apart from one large spider, the rats and other creatures that had taken over the house remained hidden, only faint scratching sounds welling up through the air vents marking their presence. Perhaps the owners had been sent to a deportation camp, Harry thought. The uprooting of immigrant families into the camps had created a number of empty buildings throughout the country, which gradually fell into disrepair and became derelict. This huge disruption to the property market had caused a severe decline in house prices, not that anyone really cared anymore.

Feeling more refreshed, and encouraged that the motorbike was still there, he was soon on his way. As he passed Pembroke Road on the way to the dockyard, the traffic began to build up. However as he rode closer to the docks he saw that the cars were being diverted away and he eventually arrived at a number of hastily erected concrete blocks that obstructed the road toward the dockyard area. The cars were forced to turn back as the ring of concrete blocks circling the area stretched as far as the eye could see. The blocks were not high, only about five feet tall, and they were spaced unevenly so that as he rode alongside the blocks, he soon found a gap that was just large enough for him to squeeze the bike through. With no military personnel on patrol, he was able to cross the barrier unchallenged. As he rode closer to the port area past a row of abandoned terraced stone houses, the sharp, salty aroma of the sea pervaded the air. Up above in the leaden sky a group of squawking seagulls swooped up and down, looking for rich pickings from the garbage that humans inevitably left. A low buzz of chattering voices, as if from a distant crowd, carried through the air.

The smell and the noise became more pronounced as he followed signs toward the car ferry terminal. They were rusted and decrepit, a white boat on a wavy line with a blue background. The only vehicles other than the green military jeeps and Hummers were the rusting hulks of burnt out cars, victims of the street violence that had spread throughout Britain like a cancer. The military vehicles stood silent, devoid of activity, although Harry remained vigilant as he passed them. He turned up London Road on the approach to the terminal and saw the crowd. He instinctively slowed down, but even from a distance he could see the excited, fluid movement of the crowd. They were surrounded by the black clad soldiers of the People's Independent Army who were pushing, shoving and striking people as they herded them toward a large waiting area. In the past this area was used for cars to park prior to boarding the ferries. It now appeared to be a holding area for deportees before they were put on the boats.

Occasional high pitched screams pierced the general buzz of the crowd and as he slowed and observed the gathering, he saw that many of them were imprisoned in open steel cages similar to the one he had been transported in on the way to Salisbury. Around the trucks a number of large Alsatian dogs strained at their leashes, slavering and baring their teeth in an intimidating display of fury at the cowering people. Harry recalled the claustrophobic cages all too well and he rode further in to get a closer look, wary of the black-suited soldiers and their dogs, who had yet to notice or react to his presence. There appeared to be some order in the chaos, because he distinctively saw a number of children being separated from their parents and funnelled into another line where they were immediately led away, most of them crying, straining to see their mothers and fathers who were pushed quickly out of sight in the general confusion. Harry saw one young woman holding a toddler tight, clinging onto the child with all her strength, as a soldier barged forward and briefly tussled with her to wrench the child from her arms. Her howls of anguish rose above the general clamour as the soldier carried the kicking, screaming child under his arm and dumped the toddler on the hard ground amongst a group of other children away from the main crowd. Harry saw the young mother cover her face before the crowd closed in around her. He felt a wave of sympathy as he wondered whether they would ever be reunited.

The line of people snaked away from the ferry terminal as far as Harry could see. He estimated that there were at least twenty thousand people. They heavily outnumbered the black figures that stood on the outer edge of the crowd, but the soldiers were heavily armed and continued to shove and prod the throng like a herd of cattle toward the old parking lot that now served as the main holding area.

Harry took the crumbling road north-east toward the Pembroke Dock rail station. The graceful Victorian building was now dwarfed by a monstrous prefabricated metal hangar which had been hastily constructed in the huge yard used mainly for housing old rail stock. Being the end of the line, the yard also housed an ancient engine turntable, a relic of bygone days. The yard and hangar were fenced off but Harry skirted the fence on his motorbike and could see the activity clearly through the wire. A large box train stood motionless in the siding, and behind the large engine stood at least forty carriages made of dark wood clearly designed for freight containers and cattle. Only it wasn't freight or cattle that streamed out of the carriage when the shutters were drawn back. Desperate, dishevelled people spilled out onto the dusty ground of the yard, several at the front being pushed to the ground by those behind desperate to escape the dark, squalid confines. Harry could only guess how long they had been in there and what it was like inside, but he gasped at the number of bodies that poured out of a carriage smaller than his scruffy apartment in Kings Cross.

The process was repeated along the length of the train, each carriage in turn being opened to release their human cargo. The crowd that literally fell out of each carriage was made up of men, women and children, young and old alike, some clearly having fallen ill from their journey. The misery that poured from the carriages was almost palpable, like a cloud of foul malevolence that hung in the cold, damp air. He saw several old people collapse to the ground, exhausted after being forced to stand in the squashed confines of the dark, airless carriage for who knows how long. They received no respite however. The soldiers that surrounded each grimy carriage were immediately onto them, pulling old people to their feet, dragging and hitting them to force the crowd into obedience. Plaintive, despairing cries resounded along the carriages, especially amongst the children, who could not understand the cruelty inflicted upon them.

Once the soldiers had carved the crowd into a formation that suited them, they forced them to march forward, and those who did not keep up were struck with batons or large rifles carried by many of the soldiers. They were herded into the huge hangar, no doubt to join the huge throng by the ferry terminal that was already being processed in readiness for the boat that would carry them to exile.

As Harry watched appalled, his thoughts turned to Tamara and Byron, and a surge of impotent rage welled up inside him as he thought of the indignity and suffering they would have to face on this box train from hell. Perhaps they had already taken this train. He had no way of knowing. In this age of instant global communications, the regime had taken the nation back half a century. Knowledge was power, and the regime controlled its flow, so that people could no longer reach out to each other as they had in the recent past. Keeping people isolated reinforced the regime's power, and made the government less accountable.

Not far from the fence that separated Harry from the vast rail yard, a boy broke free from the large group streaming out of a box carriage, and with the agility of youth avoided a baton that swung at him in an attempt to bring him down.

"He has a phone!" Harry heard the soldier cry.

The boy sprinted toward the fence and Harry watched in fascinated horror as the soldier the boy had evaded raised his rifle and paused, waiting for the right shot. As he did so a man barged him and the shot fired wildly into the air with a sharp crack, sending convulsions of panic through the crowd. The boy kept running and in less than a minute had reached the fence. He hastily skirted the perimeter, looking back quickly for his pursuer, and found a small gap in the bottom of the fence which he wriggled under and squeezed his lithe body through. With the speed of desperation, he pulled himself up on the other side as a soldier sprinted toward him, rifle in hand. The soldier stopped and raised his rifle, taking careful aim before letting loose a volley of gunfire, while the crowd behind screamed in terror.

The boy however, seemed to have a sixth sense and dived to the ground just as the gunfire ripped through the steel fence and tore up the tarmac on the road not far from his head. The boy immediately jumped to his feet and ran hard toward Harry, who snapped out of his reverie when he saw the pleading look in the boy's dirty tear-streaked face and the soldier reloading his weapon behind him. Harry spun the bike around, engine racing, and the boy leaped athletically onto the back seat and grabbed Harry's midriff tight as the bike hurtled away. Harry looked back briefly and saw the soldier's face twisted in impotent rage. As they sped off the boy gave a nonchalant wave and Harry had to suppress a smile. With the soldiers on the other side of the fence, and the only exit from the huge yard half a mile away, they were safe for the moment as they rode fast through the clammy mist that was descending like a cloak to mask the horrors of what they had seen.

# CHAPTER 28

The only vehicles that Harry and his companion encountered as they rode away from the station were military jeeps and the black SUVs commonly used by the People's Independent Army. Harry was especially anxious to avoid the latter as his pursuers had probably fixed the SUV he sabotaged in Glynneath. They heard the occasional sound of gunfire and as they raced past, one unit even shot half-heartedly in their direction, more for sport than in genuine pursuit. Where possible he avoided them by taking narrow streets and back alleys. The sight of a motorbike here would arouse suspicion, but even more so if the army units were made aware that one had just helped a deportee make an audacious escape.

They reached a bombed out church just inside the wall of concrete blocks that marked the perimeter of the restricted zone around Pembroke. Although the front of the ruined building was a mess of fallen masonry and rubble, enough of the construction was intact to provide sufficient shelter and some degree of cover from random patrols. Harry parked the motorbike in the damaged vestry and they reached a small private chapel that was still intact at the rear of the building. Even the heavy wooden door was in place and they barricaded it from inside with a small set of pews. They sat on a narrow bench and Harry shared most of the remainder of his supplies, spreading them out on an oak table which held a communion chalice and a thurible of incense, as if in preparation for a service that now would never happen.

The boy wolfed down the supplies, cramming food into his mouth with an intensity that Harry recalled from his own experience of being famished. The boy had caramel skin, and his front teeth protruded from thin lips above which hung a wispy thin moustache. His hollow cheeks and pointed nose and ears lent his face an angular quality, and his slender frame matched his willowy features. On his head was a dirty, but tightly wound turban worn by Sikhs. Behind his wire rimmed spectacles, one lens of which was badly cracked, the Sikh boy's dark-rimmed eyes looked pensive.

Harry watched him curiously as the boy stuffed food into his mouth. "So what's your name?" he enquired casually.

"Amir," he said between mouthfuls. A heavy silence followed, the only sound coming from his chewing and the cooing of birds perched high up on the partly collapsed roof of the main church. There were so many questions that Harry wanted to ask, but he waited patiently until the boy had finished eating. When he was done he was suddenly talkative, his accent strong. "We came from Kashmir to escape the fighting two years ago, and we had just got settled here when they took us away."

"Who did?"

"The cruel men dressed in black. They beat down our door and came for us in the night. We had no time to even dress and they loaded us all on the truck and drove us to a deportation camp. We were there for three months. My grandparents are still there but Grandpa doesn't have long – he has that horrible coughing disease. Lots of people started to get sick and then two days ago they took a group of us away. My parents protested because they didn't want to leave Nana and Grandpa, but the men just laughed and spat at us. They said we had no choice and threatened us if we did not go with them. They crammed us into those cattle trucks you saw. It was standing room only and they stank. There was no air inside and with just a tiny shutter at the top it was pitch black. It was hot and stuffy in there but freezing cold at night. It took us two days to get to this place, and I'm sure some people died on the way. Where are we anyway?"

"We're in Pembroke in Wales," replied Harry.

"Wales? Where are they taking us?"

A scraping sound disturbed them and Harry put his finger to his lips for silence. The scraping continued, ever closer, and then from under a hole in the wall a rat squeezed through and scurried across the floor. Amir stood up and aimed at a kick at the vermin which squealed as it ran away.

"Dirty, disgusting creatures," he said, his sharp nose wrinkling in distaste.

"Which camp did you come from?"

"We lived in Blackburn. They took us to a camp in the country but not far away."

"What happened to your parents?"

Amir's face fell. He took off his spectacles and wiped away tears with the back of his hand. "They were put on another carriage with my little sister," he replied, his voice thick with emotion. "I have to find them."

Harry felt a huge wave of sympathy for the boy, who was probably no more than fifteen, only a few years older than Byron. "Amir, you will never find them amongst these crowds. It will be impossible."

Amir's eyes flashed. "Don't say that!" he responded angrily. "I will find them! What else do I do? The soldiers will hurt them!"

Harry had to acknowledge the boy's courage, but then what choice did Amir have? He would be caught eventually and rounded up with all the other immigrants. It was only a matter of time. At least there was some chance, however small, of being reunited with his parents, and whatever fate awaited them, they could face it together.

Amir studiously inspected the crack on his glasses and looked up at Harry. "Where will you go?"

"I'm wanted for murder."

A brief flash of fear surfaced in the boy's angular features and he edged back along the bench, knocking the chalice off the table and sending it clattering to the stone floor.

Harry smiled reassuringly. "Don't worry, I haven't killed anyone. This government has me in their sights as much as any so-called immigrant. I'm a fugitive and I have some nasty people after me. Somehow in this chaos I have to get on one of those boats and escape the country. My plan is to get a ferry to Ireland but it doesn't matter where as long as it is away from Britain."

Amir was silent for a while, and his bushy eyebrows knitted together as if in concentration. Then he reached into the folds of his turban and like a magic trick pulled out a tiny smartphone, small enough to fit comfortably in his small palm. Harry preferred the older, larger style phones, but the trend for newer smartphones had been towards miniaturization. The 'nanophone' as it was styled was one of the smallest devices on the market, and more popular with kids because their smaller, more dexterous fingers were better equipped to handle the tiny touchscreen. It was ironic that most young people in the country had smartphones, but not nearly as many kids had enough food for a proper nutritious diet.

The boy thrust the miniature phone at Harry. "Here, take it. When they were not looking on the train I would take film. They searched us when we got on the train but they never looked here." He tapped his turban proudly. "They are ignorant savages. There is nearly thirty minutes of film here. We need to tell the world what is happening. It is the only way."

Harry put up his hands. "No, Amir, I can't take this. The phone belongs to you."

Amir was impatient. "It's not about the phone!" he cried. "I have to find my family. If they find the phone they will kill me. You must take it!"

Harry let out a deep sigh and took the tiny phone and slipped it into a small compartment on the inside of the fleece-lined jacket Joszef gave him. He felt a keen sense of Déjà vu; he had accepted the ancient compact disc from Graham Matheson and that been the prelude to all his troubles. Still, it could hardly get worse. He had no idea whether Amir's film would ever see the light of day.

Amir explained in detail what he had seen, and the film he had secretly taken. The boy did so articulately and with a maturity beyond his tender years. No doubt he had been forced to grow up quickly, exposed as he was to the horrors of the deportation camp and the Holocaust-style trains. Harry could not help but admire the boy's spirit. Most men would have been broken if they had witnessed the events that Amir explained eloquently and factually. Only occasionally did his voice falter with emotion, when he referred to his family. He was also astute enough to know that his shelter with Harry was a temporary reprieve. "They'll find me soon enough," he said casually.

Amir described the horrors of the camp. At first, he said, the regular Army soldiers had been administering the camp and while they had been highly disorganized, they had shown at least had some semblance of humanity. They had treated the camp internees with diffidence rather than hostility. A number of important dignitaries, including diplomats and influential businessmen who had been sent to the camp were able to bribe the Army officers to get safe passage on the Army transport flights out of the country. It did not matter where, because those people were the ones who had seen the signs of the coming storm. In those potentially life or death situations, people either became endowed with legendary courage or they reverted to cowards, intent on saving themselves at whatever cost with hardly a backward glance for the masses left behind.

Amir's family, despite only having been in England for two years, had reasonable funds and his father was a businessman in the export and import trade who had strong contacts in Pakistan and India. Just before the soldiers had come for them they had tried to call many influential people overseas without success. Even after they arrived in the camp his father continued to call until they confiscated all mobile phones, which was when Amir hid his in his turban. Rumours circulated throughout the camp that the United Nations would come charging in like the cavalry and rescue the people imprisoned there, but it was more hope than expectation. Some of the people, like his father, were highly educated and astute, and they were more realistic. In these cases, they said, the UN kept a watching brief and was unlikely to intervene in the affairs of one of its founding members.

Time went by with little sign of intervention. Hope, the one thing that kept people going for so long, began to fade. The conditions were terrible, as the only shelter they had were leaky tents issued one per family on a muddy field. There was no running water or adequate sanitary facilities and very soon many people began to sicken, especially older people. The army continued to build long rows of wooden huts that would provide decent shelter, but progress was so slow that many stronger prisoners, including his father, offered to help them build the huts in the hope of completing them more quickly. This was despite the fact that no-one was given sufficient food to eat, and the camp administrators continued to blame 'supply problems.' There was also no sign of when people would be deported, yet every week came a new influx of trucks with cages full of people, adding to the stress of an already overcrowded camp.

Then, Amir explained, two things happened around the same time several months ago. Firstly the army pulled out, soon after they had completed the huts. They were replaced by new camp administrators from the People's Independent Army. The PIA began enforcing rules which turned the camp into a prison system, and anyone disobeying them was met with harsh retribution. Their intent was to spread fear and hatred throughout the camp. The food rations were cut still further, and they barely treated the prisoners as humans.

Camp inmates, both men and women, were forced to suffer the humiliation and exhausting physical labour of the chain gangs, digging up and resurfacing roads. Amir himself was put to work on one of the chain gangs, but only for a short time before they were sent away on the train.

Even more distressing than the chain gangs, however, was the 'coughing' disease that swept through the camp. Its origin was unknown, but its appearance coincided with the arrival of fresh medical supplies. The PIA to set up a working field hospital which rapidly became full. A number of patients fell ill after receiving antibiotics for dysentery or vaccinations against cholera. His father told him that the poorly trained medical staff had no understanding of the disease and the illness was transmitted rapidly, turning the already overflowing hospital into a no-go area. Only last week his grandfather had fallen ill with the disease and he visibly wilted before their eyes. They left him behind because he was too weak to travel. He would surely have died in the overcrowded, airless carriage. His grandmother stayed and he knew that when they left them with hardly time to say goodbye before they were herded onto the transports, it would be the last time he saw them.

"That's why you need to show this film," Amir urged Harry.

Harry nodded in acknowledgement, disturbed but not surprised by Amir's harrowing story. He knew that whatever happened he must not fail him.

# REUTERS EDITORIAL OCTOBER 22

The government's policy of deporting immigrants is now in full flow, with reports of the *Sonderzüge* trains arriving regularly at several ports throughout the country, all of which are sealed off once they arrive. Concrete barriers have been erected around most of the ports so it is impossible to get through with vehicles; however it appears that the military forces are stretched tight and some of the ports are inadequately guarded, allowing several journalists to slip into the restricted zone. These brave individuals have been limited to long range photos as it is clearly too dangerous to venture closer to the crowds of dishevelled refugees and thereby alert the attention of the authorities. One journalist, a former war correspondent in the Middle East and Afghanistan, apparently did so, and she has now been officially reported as 'missing.'

These photographs made their way into the House and prompted questions from the floor. Pelham was typically indifferent, dismissing the photographs as having been manipulated for sensationalist purposes by enemies of the government, whilst robustly defending the actions of the military authorities supervising the deportation process. Predictably, he was not given a difficult time by the Opposition Leader, Jane Forster the Head of the British National Party. Like the Cabinet, the Opposition, at least for now, is careful not to antagonize the Prime Minister.

Nevertheless, despite the regime's attempts to suppress the photographs, they have reached the international news media, causing a storm of protest. One photograph that has symbolized the crisis is a black and white still of a uniformed PIA soldier raising his baton as a woman cowers, holding her child. The picture

circulated worldwide and found its way into the offices of Ghan-
aian diplomat, Kobie Emosi, the Secretary-General of the United
Nations, a man vilified for his failure to take proactive measures
in the face of the growing crisis, preferring instead to work with
the British government in a 'productive dialogue.'

It is unclear just what dialogue has taken place, productive
or otherwise, but the photograph prompted Emosi to at last take
action. He contacted Pelham to negotiate a small UN monitoring and peacekeeping force but was firmly rebuffed, resulting in
a tense political stand-off. It seems that Pelham was able to stare
the UN leader down, because the next step in the negotiation was
for the UN to propose a delegation of diplomats to speak with Pelham and aim for some degree of independent oversight over the
deportation program. Once again, however, such overtures were
firmly resisted by Pelham, leaving the UN with no alternative but
to vote in favour of imposing economic sanctions that will further
damage a nation marginalized and isolated in the international
community.

As the nation's increasing isolation bites, with food and medical supplies running short, the government has been forced to
raid some of its stockpiles of provisions. However, there have
been reports of nepotism and corruption in the distribution of
those supplies and while the Party cronies continue to enjoy a high
standard of living, the average British man on the street is feeling
the pinch. Inflation is running at over 40%, unthinkable even in
recent times, and there appears to be a thriving black market in
perishable goods and necessities, driving up prices even further.
It appears the sacrifices Pelham has urged the British people to

endure for the long term benefit of the country do not extend to his own Party faithful. The rumblings of discontent among his English constituents, the only people he is interested in, has been muted for fear of reprisals from the Order Police or worse still, the People's Independent Army. Even so, those protests erupted into another full scale riot in the St. Paul's area of Bristol several nights ago, as police and army units struggled to contain a vociferous crowd intent on destruction.

Unconfirmed reports suggested that many English people stood shoulder to shoulder with the predominantly Muslim crowd who attacked the authorities, and this will surely be considered an unwelcome development for the Prime Minister as his policies continue to face a rising tide of discontent on the streets. This protest riot was the latest in a long line of attacks against government policies, and once again the authorities faced accusations of being heavy-handed in their response to such protests. During Prime Minister's question time, Pelham dismissed such accusations as 'baseless,' further inflaming the antipathy between both sides.

Near Waterloo Station artists have created a Wall of Remembrance reminiscent of a similar Wall in Syria during the wretched Assad years. The colourful graffiti depicts the names and faces of many dissidents and opponents of the State who have simply disappeared under the regime, their fate unknown. They are possibly being held as political prisoners; or may be dead. No one truly knows, except that people such as Bernard Maxwell, former editor of the now defunct *British Guardian,* depicted puffing on his trademark cigar, have been arrested or abducted and never heard from again. The unknown artists have promised to collect the name of every dissident taken and eventually place them on the Wall, although this will present a significant challenge as the list is growing daily.

Meanwhile the mystery of the deportation boats continues to deepen, with the government remaining tight-lipped about the fate of those immigrants who have apparently fallen into a black hole. Those journalists who managed to breach the security perimeter reported that boats were leaving the harbour, but there is no record of them having reached any other destination. There are rumours that the PIA, charged with administering the deportation of all non-indigenous people, have maintained detailed passenger manifests and records of each boat leaving port. If these records truly exist, then they are not being offered up and as yet the Prime Minister has not faced any tough questioning in the House about it. All that can be verified at present is eye witness accounts of overcrowded trains reaching coastal ports in preparation for deportation.

Some experienced political commentators are claiming to see the signs. They fear that the United Kingdom is on the brink of a huge humanitarian crisis, while the world looks on, bound by UN resolutions to continue dialogue, while every day that passes the crisis deepens.

# CHAPTER 29

It had been one of the most depressing days Julianne could remember in this whole war. That was how she regarded it; a war. It was a war on every person who could not satisfy the stringent requirements of the *Minorities Registration Act*. It was impossible to categorize these people, but the general media referred to them collectively as 'immigrants.' It was purely for want of a better term, because many of the people being displaced had been born in this country, and knew no other home.

She recalled Harry's grief that his son, Byron, who had been born in London, had been sent to a deportation camp along with his mother because of the provisions in the Act. As she tossed and turned on the thin mattress in her motel room, unable to sleep, her thoughts settled on Harry. They had spent the day looking for him but the scale of the task had been impossible, and although they had managed to get closer, taking a number of photographs, the sheer scale of the operation and the crowds made searching for one person hopeless. She had initially been optimistic and assured herself she would see Harry again. However, as time passed and she witnessed the huge crowds being displaced, her optimism faded, a severe reality check. Even if her intuition about Harry heading for a ferry to Pembroke was correct, how did they expect to find him in these crowds? Indeed, she began to seriously doubt her instincts. He could be anywhere now, that is if he was still alive.

They had spent the last few days searching aimlessly for Harry, but it was dangerous to approach too near the crowds and she and Kendrick had to remain vigilant because, although the military appeared to be fully occupied, the two of them were trespassers inside the perimeter zone. Julianne had been restricted to taking long range photographs which failed to convey the true misery of the tide of people being herded toward the ferry terminal for one of the deportation boats. The terminal itself was impossible to reach, and Julianne had no idea how many boats were waiting to take the hordes of deportees. Judging by the number of people, they would need a fleet.

The day had been much like the day before, cold and grey, with a dank fog drifting off the sea and hanging like a suffocating cloud over the masses, all of whom had no protection from the chilly drizzle that intermittently soaked them. It was a truly depressing scene and both she and Kendrick were bereft of ideas on how they would find Harry. Worse still, as they made their way back toward the concrete perimeter near to where Kendrick's car was parked, a lone soldier jumped out of a small jeep that had appeared deserted. The soldier was no more than eighteen, but his acne-ridden face held the wild-eyed expression of zeal she had seen so many times. He was bent on destruction and as he shouted he began running toward them. Fortunately they had kept a safe distance from any military vehicles and were far enough away to escape. However that did not stop the soldier aiming a speculative shot in their direction and as she ran Julianne felt the whoosh of a bullet as it flew inches from her torso and kicked up the wet tarmac close by.

Kendrick scurried away with an intensity that belied his age, and they soon reached the concrete barriers. The soldier fired twice more, but the shots were random, fired more as a warning and to her relief he did not chase them any further once they had cleared the perimeter. Even so, Kendrick cautioned that the soldier might call for back up, so they fled to the detective's car and he drove them back to the motel on the outskirts of town as fast as he could.

The thought of the soldier dismayed Julianne to the very depths of her soul. He epitomized everything that was wrong with this country, the mindless indoctrination to the cause of hatred and intolerance. It was almost as if the policies and propaganda that Pelham espoused had created a mind-shift, not just amongst the Party faithful but in the average person, who regarded their neighbours with suspicion and looked down upon them if they even suspected they could be deported.

Although the government's deportation program was now firmly established, the sheer numbers of people subject to displacement meant there were still millions of people that the regime had not yet caught up with. Those people lived in abject fear, petrified of any knock on the door, yet looked down upon as second class citizens like an unofficial apartheid. The daily diatribe spouted by the regime's propaganda machine, the TV, social media and the vast intrusive media screens placed on street corners of every town fortified this attitude.

Pelham's war was not on any particular race or creed; it was on everyone who did not fit his ideology, although his vitriol was aimed mainly at the Muslim population, particularly since the suicide bombing attempt on his life. Julianne's cell had been close to achieving the assassination that would have prevented the crisis she was now witnessing here in Pembroke, and which was being repeated in nearly every coastal port in the country.

Deep in thought and still unable to sleep, she heard the soft chiming of Kendrick's tablet before he did. He was gently snoring on the small camp bed, oblivious to the world. As she debated whether to answer it, he jerked awake, quickly rubbed his eyes and reached for the tablet. Grey light began to filter through the thin curtains, marking the start of another dreary day.

As he tapped the screen to answer the call he gave a tired but quizzical glance at Julianne, who was now sitting up in her bed. He slotted in his earpiece and said "Hello?" and then listened. All Julianne heard was Kendrick saying "Yes sir.....understood sir..... Thank you sir."

When he had finished the call he turned to Julianne, and his grizzled features broke into a smile. "We have a lead from the most unlikely of places."

"What do you mean?" asked Julianne, genuinely puzzled.

"It seems I misjudged that crusty old bugger. My boss Grayson has been hacking into the PIA communications network. He's taking a huge risk, but he passed me some valuable intelligence. I never thought he would help; he told me I was on my own on this case. There have been reports of a man on a black motorbike seen around the huge yard behind Pembroke railway station, which as you know is well inside the restricted zone. They shot at him but he escaped. Apparently there is a SSP pursuit team assigned to track down Harry, and they are convinced the man on the motorbike is one and the same. They nearly caught up with Harry but he escaped on the bike. It seems your intuition was right Julianne. There won't be any bikers beyond the perimeter unless they have a good reason for being there. Maybe he's trying to get on one of the deportation boats, if they even exist."

Julianne nodded sombrely, refusing to contemplate the rumours that boats leaving English shores never arrived at any foreign port. "So what next?"

"Even with this lead it won't be easy. Grayson will continue to monitor the PIA network and has promised to keep me informed of any more sightings. So, we go back, risk getting shot at again, and find him before he boards one of the boats." He flicked the curtain back and the diffuse light filtered into the room. "Let's get ready and go."

# CHAPTER 30

Harry dozed off as he battled to stay awake in a vain attempt to keep guard, but when the soft daylight permeated the upper windows of the chapel, he awoke suddenly, instantly alert. He was relieved to note that the boy slept peacefully, undisturbed, and outside it was quiet. He gently roused the boy, who sat up, rubbing his eyes and yawning. The low rumble of a jeep passing by briefly disturbed the relative peace.

"How are you feeling Amir?"

He glanced at Harry with tired eyes, but managed a thin smile. "It's my first sleep for many nights. I feel strong!"

They shared the last of the modest provisions in Harry's backpack and got ready to leave. "Why don't you come with me Amir, you will be safer."

Amir's face was set firm and he shook his head dismissively. "No I have to find my family. I have already lost some of them."

Outside the air was cold and damp, and the light mist rolling in off the sea drifted around the town, making visibility limited. Harry rode cautiously toward the ferry area, alert for military vehicles, several of which were parked on the side of the road adjacent to bombed out retail shops and buildings, its residents having been driven away long before. Harry passed by a crumbling wall which carried in large white letters 'STAND DOWN PELHAM.' He could only guess at the fate of the authors of the message. As he arrived closer to the dockyard, the low buzz of the crowds reached him again and there were a number of military vehicles moving around and patrolling the area.

It became too dangerous to ride openly, and Amir tapped him on the shoulder. Harry pulled into a side street and Harry parked the motorbike behind an old dumpster which was overflowing with stinking garbage. They scouted the area on foot, alert for military patrols, and found an old grocer's shop with its windows smashed in. They stepped through the broken glass and the stench of rotting fruit and vegetables was overpowering. However, they managed to find a few packs of non-perishable items such as tinned meat loaf and cookies. It was hardly a balanced meal but they ate what they could and Harry filled his backpack, uncertain when this opportunity would present itself again. He thought longingly of Martha's sumptuous meal and quickly dismissed the thought. Amir galloped through the aisles stuffing his pockets and chomping on chocolate bars till he felt dizzy from the unfamiliar sugar rush. Then they saw a pair of rats peek out from one of the broken chiller cabinets, their snouts sniffing the air and their tiny pink eyes fixing on them as if they were the intruders.

When they saw the rats it was time to go and they hid out for a few hours with their booty until the gloom of late afternoon had descended and they were less likely to be spotted, preferring the safety of the shadows and semi-darkness.

In the distance the huge line of people shuffled along in the direction of the ferry terminal. Harry planned to stowaway to exile on any ship he could, a refugee just like the crowds of displaced people in the distance, many torn from the only home they had ever known. The pair cautiously headed toward the crowds, darting into the shadows when they saw the sinister black uniform of the PIA soldiers patrolling the area. The soldiers carried heavy assault rifles, and unlike the regular army which also had a strong presence in town, were protected by the anonymity of their ski masks. These soldiers carried out their brutality with total impunity, never likely to be recognized. When questions were asked at trial, as Harry believed they surely would in time, these soldiers could deny they were ever there.

Harry felt a rising surge of impotent anger as one soldier swaggered past, whistling, as if they were on a day out at the beach. He passed by, and then Amir tugged Harry's shoulder. "It's time for me to go now," he said.

"Are you sure you won't stay with me?"

Amir shook his head again in that assured, assertive manner he possessed, and stuck out a bony hand. "No, I have to find my family. They'll be worried about me. You have the phone?"

Harry nodded and took Amir's hand, impressed by his bravery. The boy was mature beyond his years, but Harry was not hopeful of the boy finding his parents. He had to admire his optimism, but he feared for Amir. "Good luck Amir. I hope you find your parents," he said, a lump forming in his throat.

Amir saluted him and replied, "Thank you my friend." Before Harry could respond, Amir darted off and was quickly lost in the gloom. Harry thought of Byron and suddenly felt very alone.

# CHAPTER 31

Albert had been working these docks for nigh on forty years and seen everything, or so he thought. When he started out as a fresh faced nineteen year-old back in the mid-eighties he had spent his first day on the job on strike, his union showing solidarity with the National Union of Miners in their fight against Thatcher's program of savage cuts. The characters that had played out that drama were now a distant, faded memory, most of them dead by now, but he had seen plenty of drama in the intervening years.

He had seen his fair share of strife in this job. Hell, he had suffered enough of his own to last several lifetimes. The lowest point of all, however, had come a few years ago when his cherished son, damaged by the black despair of being unable to find a job, had eventually given in to his feelings of frustration and uselessness. The bland government statistics about unemployment during the Labour years masked the true extent of the misery and despair that it brought to families, but not as much as the even bleaker figures of exploding suicide rates. When people lost hope, like Peter had, it was too late for them. Albert had always urged Peter to keep trying, that something would turn up soon, but even his words of encouragement sounded hollow to him. During the deep recession that gripped the country, he could see the lines of men outside Pembroke Docks waiting and hoping for a day's labour so they could feed their families that day. It was like the old movie newsreels he had seen of America in the thirties during the Great Depression.

Albert had been lucky, if he could call it that. He had managed to stay fully employed throughout all those years, even if he had carried out the same repetitive work during that time. At least he brought an honest wage home, something that was denied so many good and able-bodied men like Peter. His son had not even reached thirty when he took his own life in the attic rafters using a bunch of knotted sheets.

Albert and his wife still grieved over their loss; they would do so for the rest of their lives, he was certain. Not grieving felt wrong, as if it somehow sullied his memory. Peter had been their only child, and they had poured all the love they had on him. There were days when he hardly thought of Peter, and then at the end of the day he was faced with an overwhelming sense of guilt. His wife was a mere projection of herself, a hollowed out body with the soul ripped out. They both feared the long lonely years ahead without the prospect of grandchildren.

Then came the greatest irony of them all, this new job in which he was surrounded by children. Of all the things he had seen in his long service at the Docks, this was by far the most bizarre. A few weeks ago his usual employers had inexplicably disappeared and the usual cargo ships and passenger ferries finally ceased operations. The port had been in rapid decline since the new government had taken power, but it had survived the Great Recession and Albert was confident there would still be work. However, when the business dried up altogether and his employers disappeared, he feared the worst. He had a little bit put away but his pension, even if was honoured, would be pitiful. His previous bosses, however, were replaced by the military, both from the regular army and the new PIA, the latter which his colleague described disparagingly as 'Pelham's foot soldiers.' He knew little about the politics; London was so far away and he had never had any interest in politics, regarding all politicians as corrupt and self-serving. The army, however, set up barricades around a large area leading to the docks and assigned new tasks to the workers. Their entry through the barricades at the beginning and end of the day was closely controlled.

They were also told never to discuss their work, not even with their spouses, and each man was asked to sign a form with a ton of legal gibberish that the army officer told them was a confidentiality agreement.

Unlike a number of his colleagues, Albert had always had a habit of asking questions. He liked information, to know why he was doing something rather than to blindly follow directions. It helped him to assuage the anxiety he felt when he attempted something new or out of his comfort zone. Even as a child when his parents took him out for the day, he needed to know where they were going, how long the journey would take, how far they were travelling, and what time they would get home. His parents had tolerated it with good grace, and his employers had endured it, often becoming exasperated, but this this time the questions were met with barely suppressed hostility by his new supervisors. They made it clear that such questions were unwelcome and there was a suggestion that any persistent questioning would be met with reprisals that went beyond losing their job at the docks. An atmosphere of fear began to permeate amongst his colleagues, but this type of culture inevitably led to ugly rumours and snatched whispers about the real purpose of why they remained on the job.

When the crowds of dishevelled and exhausted deportees began to arrive, they were given brief instructions on their task. A large warehouse near the ferry terminal had been converted into a huge holding area, and as the crowds filtered through, the children were separated by the army and placed in front of people like Albert. This understandably led to some angry protests from the parents and guardians, but the army was in no mood for nonsense, and Albert saw them use force to tear the children away from their emotional parents a number of times. His heart went out to those parents, reminding him of his own deep-seated loss, but he assured himself that the separation would at best be temporary, a necessary act of administration.

Once separated, the children, ranging from three years old to sixteen (mercifully the youngest children were not separated) were brought before people like Albert who sat behind an old desk like a school principal, a huge departure from their role as dock workers. The former Dockers were given a tablet with a long questionnaire on its home screen. They were required to complete the question-naire for each child. They were instructed not to deviate from the questions, and the objective was to get through as many children as possible. Any empathy or conversation with the children was strong-ly discouraged.

As the procession of small, stick-thin children with sunken eyes were herded into long lines that stretched before each desk he mechanically went through the questions. At his shoulder was a doctor who carried out a cursory examination once Albert had finished with them. The doctor was broody and silent, his face inscrutable behind thick bifocals. His examinations were rough and intrusive, his thick sausage-like fingers probing and grabbing at the children with little sensitivity, even when one or two squealed in pain. Albert wanted to talk to the children, many of whom cried silently, to comfort them and assure them that it would be okay. The army supervisors patrolling the huge hangar made it impossible, and in any event he could not be certain that it would be okay for these children. He had no idea when they would see their parents again, and with his obsessive need for information, he could feel his old anxiety attacks coming on again. He took his medication to calm his nerves, but before the end of the day he was emotionally exhausted. He had to know what happened to the children after they had been vetted and examined and led out of the holding area.

They were allowed a fifteen minute smoking break, and he excused himself and slipped out of the back of the huge metallic structure through a corrugated metal door. In the chill air, the mist descended in tiny droplets that clung to his thinning hair and dripped onto his nose. He thought of the large groups of people who had been outside, exposed to the harsh autumn weather for the last few days. The crowds never seemed to disperse, and more people seemed to be joining the throng, closely supervised by the soldiers. He shuddered and slipped past a group of soldiers huddled together, smoke rising from their cigarettes, their conversation punctuated by raucous laughter. He was invisible to them, which was how he liked it. He walked to the other end of the huge building, thinking about the nasty rumours that his colleague had whispered to them at the last break that morning. "Cut out their organs and sell 'em on the street," he confided, as if he really knew. Another replied that they were being taken away for experiments. "Pelham doesn't need lab rats anymore. He's got the children."

Albert refused to believe it, but all this loose talk added to his anxiety. He wished they would stop talking in that way without knowing the facts. He walked on until a tall metal fence topped with razor wire barred his way. He peered through the slats in the fence and he saw an enclosed area adjacent to the rear of the hangar he worked in. The children were being led like the Pied Piper into a procession of caged trucks much like those he had seen transporting immigrants to the deportation camps. Clearly after they were questioned and examined, they were led to this place and loaded onto these trucks, out of sight of any of the people working in the building. Where they were being taken he could only speculate. It was certainly not to be reunited with their parents, he thought bleakly. Most of the children were quiet and compliant, but then one boy, an Asian lad of about fifteen, a stained white turban on his head, struggled against the fierce grip of two soldiers either side. "Let me go!" he protested. "I need to find my parents!"

"Shut your mouth boy and get in the truck!" screamed one of them in his face. The boy continued to struggle as he was hauled up the tailgate of the truck and pushed through the small cage door. He tried to break out but the soldier quelled him with a sharp blow to the head. The other children in the truck sat immobile, their eyes to the floor. The boy stopped dead, stunned, holding his head. The soldier immediately shut the cage door, and gave a signal. The truck roared off and Albert peered after it, shocked not only by what he had seen but by his own imagination.

Saddened, he turned to go when a firm, meaty hand clapped its heavy weight on his shoulder. He turned around and a soldier, six inches taller, glared down at him, his face blank except for the serious look in his cold, steely eyes, which conveyed the impression that Albert's transgression would not be without repercussions. When he spoke it was in a drawl. "You shouldn't be here," he said threateningly.

# CHAPTER 32

As Harry headed closer to the crowds the patrols increased, and he was relieved that the darkening late afternoon sky provided him some protection. The units were situated primarily along the main approach roads to Pembroke Dock, and so Harry flitted through alleyways and side streets, many of them between buildings that had been reduced to crumbling ruins, its occupants long since fled. On one street corner, he spotted several amorphous figures which upon closer inspection revealed three corpses heaped in a pile. The topmost corpse stared up at the sky with glassy eyes, a ragged red bullet-hole through his forehead, the features frozen in the terror of imminent death. Harry suspected his fate could be similar if he was not careful, and while the level of security around the terminal suggested a degree of complacency, he realized with increased urgency that he had to avoid detection.

Alert and watchful, Harry moved as close as he could to the ferry parking lot where the grim crowd stood waiting in the cold, clammy mist, surrounded by PIA soldiers. The crowd was at least a kilometre away, but he expected to see the outline of at least one of the huge white car ferries on which he had crossed to Ireland several times as a young man. He recalled the white behemoths that dominated the skyline when they were docked in the harbour. Despite the gloom and mist he expected the ship to be clearly visible, towering over the dockyard. But there appeared to be nothing beyond the crowds and small port buildings except grey seas and dank, rolling mist. However the dockyard area extended for several miles further up the estuary past the now disused power station, the top of the two redundant towers lost in the low lying mist. It reached the old cargo port, where the crude oil tankers used to be loaded in the deep water until the Great Recession caused the cargo port to fall into decline.

He could see in the distance the vast oil drums, a row of redundant and rusting cylinders of various sizes, a legacy of more prosperous economic times. A large portion of the crowd was sectioned off and herded by their captors along the road that snaked toward the oil drums. Harry decided to follow them as they shuffled along the cracked tarmac. He maintained cover by using the empty dockyard warehouses on the other side of the open waste-ground as a shield. This whole area, he reflected ruefully, was once a thriving industrial area, but was now a barren, deserted economic wasteland. Despite the crowd that trudged wearily along the muddy road under the close supervision of the PIA thugs, the place appeared soulless and lonely. Harry felt a weight of depression as he watched this human tragedy in progress. The rain began to fall lightly as if to mirror his feeling of despair and he shuddered with the cold, grateful for the thick fleece jacket that Joszef had gifted him. It was a luxury that many in the crowd, including women and children, did not possess. Many barely had coats, dressed only in thin shirts and pants, and he could only guess at how cold they must be, exposed to the chilling rain that felt like drops of ice when they fell on his head.

Behind the vast oil drums, which blocked any view of the dark, rolling sea, the woodland had been cleared and there was an army of large container trucks parked at the base of the drums. Positioned around each drum were large hydraulic cranes that stretched upward toward the low-lying clouds. He saw one crane lift a large metal industrial container and place it skilfully onto one of the large trucks. A number of workers scrambled around the truck, securing the container before the truck rumbled away down the dirt road. The road was flanked on both sides by steep hedges and Harry surmised that it led to the jetties, where the boats would be waiting to take their human cargo overseas. Whatever their fate, he surmised, it was probably a mercy for them to be rid of this country. He was a little confused at the containers however, and curiously he noticed that the tide of people was being directed not around the oil drums but *inside* them. As he drew closer he saw the staircase that coiled around the side of each drum appeared to be manned. There were black shapes high up on the stairs, the height of the drums making them look like large insects clinging to the side.

The crowd was sectioned off and funnelled into different drums through large doorways that had been cut into the structures, which, no longer required as storage, was no more than a vast empty hangar. As Harry peered over the parapet of a damaged brick wall from his concealed vantage point, he saw several hundred people filing into each drum, closely supervised by armed soldiers. They were probably grateful to be out of the cold, damp conditions, but Harry could not figure out why they were being herded inside the drums. The crowd dissipated as the many groups trudged slowly into their respective drums until everyone had been accounted for, and the large steel doors closed behind them. A number of black suits guarded the outside of the drums, and then just before it began Harry realized what was about to happen. The biting cold was nothing to the chill that struck at the very depths of his soul.

# CHAPTER 33

The rain beat against the dark windows in a rhythmic tapping, and the ornate chandelier was fully lit, casting a diffuse glow over the assembled Cabinet. As usual, Pelham sat at one end of the long polished table, his chair raised high, peering down at his ministers, enjoying the subtle psychological edge it gave him. He enjoyed the fact that they feared him. His two bodyguards stood immobile in the corner of the room, impassive behind their mirror sunglasses. Chamberlain could not help thinking they looked faintly ridiculous wearing those things when there had not been a hint of sun for many days.

The miserable weather seemed to sum up the mood of the country, and the Deputy Prime Minister perceived a tension in the room that had always been there, but had somehow escalated to another level of barely disguised hostility toward Pelham. During their pre-brief, he had warned the P.M. that this could be a difficult session, but Pelham, with his usual arrogance, had dismissed it out of hand. "They don't have the balls to challenge me," he had declared haughtily. Chamberlain was uncertain how much more the Cabinet was prepared to accept. This emergency Cabinet meeting had been called by several ministers appalled at the crisis that gripped the country, and under the Cabinet protocol that Pelham had authorized himself, he was forced to attend.

The main protagonist for this emergency evening meeting was Eleanor Beaufort, the Secretary of State for Health, and she stood up as she addressed Pelham, sweeping back her greying blond hair and peering at Pelham over her half-moon spectacles like a headmistress scolding a pupil. She was ten years Pelham's senior and Chamberlain sensed she was unlikely to be as compliant as she had been only a week before. "Mr. Prime Minister," she began stiffly. "This country is in a crisis as bad as anything we have faced since the War. What do you propose to do about it?"

There was a subdued murmur of assent from around the table but when Pelham glared at a number of the ministers they quickly shut up and buried their heads in their tablet. Only yesterday during the weekly conference with his deputy, Pelham had dismissed them as spineless fools, lacking vision and any concept of what he was seeking to achieve. They were merely administrators, he said, ensuring that their respective areas of responsibility followed the policies of the government, but without the courage to make the hard decisions necessary.

Beaufort continued, "I have just had a difficult call with the Secretary General's office at the United Nations. The SG is furious that we are not allowing them access to inspect the deportation camps and transports. We cannot afford to alienate the UN as well. They have been allies up to now. If we lose the support of the UN we will be truly isolated. The only reason that the Americans haven't completely washed their hands of us is that we allowed their citizens to leave on mercy flights. Let them in Lawrence and show them we have nothing to hide."

There were muted whispers of agreement around the table but no one was prepared to speak openly in support until Pelham had his say. The P.M. sat back, looking pensive. Chamberlain knew how much Pelham resented the interference of the UN. He had recently confided to Chamberlain that as far as he was concerned they had compromised their mandate years ago. Too many times, he had explained, they had sat idly by in their ivory towers, unable to agree on a firm resolution while warring nations tore each other to shreds and perpetrated atrocities. The UN had too much blood on their hands. Pelham was determined not to bow to pressure, but Chamberlain sensed the subtle change in the mood of the Cabinet in the last week. As weak as they were, their unquestioning support was waning, and while Chamberlain suspected that Pelham's real power base lay in his corporate sponsorship, he could not ignore their enmity. If they knew the truth, they would understand that he had everything to hide.

"Miss Beaufort," he began with a condescending smile to the Health Minister. "Are you the unofficial spokesperson for the rest of the Cabinet?" He swept his arm to indicate the rest of the group. The smile quickly faded. "You should be concentrating on getting this disease under control. I am told that we are facing an epidemic that could quickly spread outside of the deportation camps if we do not contain it quickly. What I want to hear from you are solutions not criticism."

Chamberlain observed the dialogue with great interest. He recognized the warning in Pelham's tone but surprisingly the Health Minister did not back down. "Enough is enough Lawrence," she countered. "This goes beyond the disease. We want answers to our questions. We need transparency. Not only are the UN and the Americans on our back, but have you seen the latest report from Amnesty International?" She waved a small folder in her hand in Pelham's direction.

"They are alleging human rights abuses that compare us to Nazi Germany. We have a number of embassies at bursting point with their own countrymen seeking refuge there, afraid of deportation. It's the only reason why many countries don't close their embassies and move out. We have students boycotting campuses, some going on hunger strike and sewing up their mouths in protest. The war on the insurgents has merely resulted in more arrests and detention until our prisons are bursting, yet every dissident the authorities arrest brings two more attacks. There are ugly rumours that children are being separated from their parents and that the deportation boats are not reaching their destination, yet the PIA is not prepared to release passenger manifests to address the rumours. The country is on its knees Lawrence. I am not sure how much more the people can stand. I think it is about time for a U-turn. We have to accept that our policies are not working."

Pelham's face was a mask of restrained fury. He stood up and glared at his adversary, who remained standing so that they were like two prize fighters sizing up each other. Chamberlain glanced at one of the PIA bodyguards and saw his face twitch ever so slightly.

"These are ugly, false rumours being bandied about by left-wing socialists. Can't you see that they are trying to derail us by scaremongering? It won't work. Even so I am duty bound to remind you, *Ms.* Beaufort, that you were a signatory to the five year plan? You knew that we had to reverse the tide of immigration before we could take our great nation forward. As I recall your father was a staunch advocate of the picket lines at British Leyland in Cowley, imploring us to buy British. I warned you all there would be tough times ahead, that we had to be strong to see it through. We have been in power less than six months and you have the audacity to suggest to me that we should abandon our policies? We have made significant progress, but we knew there would be opposition. We will wipe out all enemies because anyone that opposes the policies of the government is considered a traitor. And that goes for all of you. Do I make myself clear?"

Eleanor Beaufort returned to her seat but Pelham was not finished. "I need your skills Eleanor while we tackle this epidemic but consider this a warning. I will not abandon my position and do not suggest to me that I should do so. The next time I will not be so tolerant, and remember you are expendable."

The implied threat was left hanging in the air. Chamberlain had to admire Pelham's ambiguous choice of words. The Health Minister could not be certain whether it meant she was expendable in her position or whether she was expendable generally. Pelham had rendered her a great deal of latitude, but he appeared to have finally lost patience. She would be unwise to push it any further, although he had to admit she was remarkably resilient. If she continued to antagonize the P.M. it was unclear how Pelham would react.

Chamberlain was closer to Pelham than any other politician, his only political confidante to the true nature of Pelham's policies, and even that was born out of necessity, thought Chamberlain. He had observed the change in Pelham since his rise to power. The Cabinet was unaware that the real power brokers in this regime were the fascist and extreme right-wing movements and figures both within the corporate sphere and outside it. Pelham had allied himself to them, and they in turn had tacitly supported the barbaric actions of government affiliates such as the People's Independent Army. These power brokers were largely unknown even to Chamberlain, but he was determined to find out who they were one way or another.

Pelham had become more volatile and capricious, particularly since the assassination attempt, which he often used to justify his actions, and increasingly during his tenure, which was still in its infancy, he cut an increasingly isolated figure. He would bring them all down with him, standing in the dock at the International Criminal Court in The Hague. Which was why, Chamberlain knew, he needed to make his move soon.

# CHAPTER 34

The vast Parliamentary chambers stood silent and empty this time of night, save for the security guards that prowled the shadowy corners. The vaulted ceilings echoed with the ghosts of the great figures who had graced these halls through the last few centuries. Those characters had shaped a glorious empire followed by a slow and terminal decline that seemed to have accelerated over the last few decades like a cancer that had taken hold and spread rapidly. The days of fractious debates that extended long into the night were over, for these types of debates, often used as a platform for political egos, suggested a democratic process that no longer existed. At three o'clock in the morning there was nothing left to discuss, and the politicians were nowhere to be seen - which was precisely why Chamberlain had to be so careful.

Unlike Pelham, the Deputy Prime Minister had refused to be assigned a legion of bodyguards who tracked his every movement. Although he received death threats daily, he paid little attention to them. They were often rambling, incoherent expressions of vitriol, desperate cries of hate from people with no opportunity to carry out their threats. He hardly bothered to read them now. His fear was not from the mob, but from those of real influence who could ask awkward questions such as what was he doing skulking around the corridors of power at this unearthly hour?

He checked his gold Rolex, and in the dimly lit passage its dial glowed at five past the hour. She was late, but just as he felt the first stab of anger for keeping him waiting he heard the sharp click of stilettos tapping on the hard wooden floor. She emerged from the shadows, her ash-blond hair pulled back, accentuating the high cheekbones and soft, flawless skin that had captivated his boss. He had to admit she was quite alluring. Dressed in a red power suit, she was tall and athletic, and walked with a confidence borne of constant attention wherever she went. As she reached him, she took off her glasses and he observed suspicion in her aquamarine eyes.

"Rachel," he smiled reassuringly. "I am so glad you came. We have a lot to discuss. Follow me." She did not respond, and hesitated. "Come, there's nothing to fear. We're quite alone." She followed him into one of the windowless committee rooms, its dark wood panelling gloomy and cheerless in the subdued light.

Chamberlain shut the heavy mahogany door and sat in one of the high backed leather chairs and motioned for her to sit opposite. As she crossed her toned legs in front of him he had to admit that Pelham's choice of mistress was admirable, even if it had meant a lot of extra work for the Deputy in keeping their liaisons out of the social media.

"How's our mutual friend?" he began.

"Snoring like a baby," she replied, a faint smile playing across her rouge lips.

He smiled back in affirmation. Considering she had just come from another frisky session in the bedroom with the nation's despotic leader, her make-up was perfect.

"Before we start, I want you to know that I appreciate the risk you're taking – that we are *both* taking – by being here. I will do whatever I can to protect you but we must remain vigilant."

Rachel squirmed uncomfortably, as though this was the last place she wanted to be. "Don't make promises you can't keep, Giles."

"I know you think that you're betraying him, but believe me you are not. He has led this country down a path to ruin. When we swept to power the people were fully behind us, and there was real hope he could turn things around. In the six months since, I have seen him visibly change before my eyes. I don't recognize him anymore, and I know you feel the same."

A single tear rolled down her cheek and she hastily brushed it away. "I'm scared Giles. The Aryan Project was the last straw. When I met him he was the liveliest, most charismatic and intelligent man I had ever met. I hear the rumours going around Parliament; I'm a gold digger and only after him to further my career, but he made all the running, although I have to admit he really blew the other men I had met out of the water. Yes he is powerful, but at first he was really charming too. Guys my own age can be so immature, even the successful ones, but I was besotted with him. As callous as it may seem, I hardly gave a second thought to his wife."

"Helen will survive. So why did you agree to speak to me?"

Rachel rubbed her temple. "Because I cannot go on like this, living a lie, making love to someone I am beginning to regard as a monster. I need your help. I heard about the conditions in the deportation camps and saw the pictures from the Health Protection Agency's report on the disease. However, it's when you see it for yourself that it really has impact. I saw your expression at the lab–you were as sickened by those experiments as I was. He's asked me to be his liaison with the facility. We need to tell the Cabinet about this dreadful project."

Chamberlain's tone was condescending. "Rachel, it's not that easy. You should know by now that the Cabinet has no real power to oppose him. Their authority is derived from government to implement Pelham's wishes, not to mount a challenge. Pelham is in control of the military and they are fiercely loyal to him. But even more worrying is the sponsorship and support he has received from the corporate world. Even I have no idea to what extent, but I suspect it is extremely powerful. There is only one way I can think of to remove him, and even that is likely to fail."

"What can we do?"

He looked around conspiratorially before answering. "Pelham has not yet dismantled the Parliamentary Constitution completely. It has not been used for so long that even a quarter century ago the Joint Committee considered that the procedure could probably be considered obsolete."

Rachel gave a confused frown, and Chamberlain enjoyed the feeling of lecturing her like one of his former students at law school. "Impeachment," he continued.

"Impeachment?" she echoed. "How?"

"Like I said, it will probably fail. Technically, however, the House of Commons holds the power of initiating an impeachment. In order to do so, an M.P. has to move that he be impeached by referring to the crimes that the Prime Minister has committed and supporting that with evidence. The Commons can then draw up the charges and create articles of impeachment. Technically it also has to go through an approval process with the House of Lords. They still exist, barely, even though they have been essentially emasculated. The last time anyone attempted to use it was over twenty years ago back in '04 to attack Tony Blair for Britain's role in the invasion of Iraq. Needless to say it was struck down. However, if we build enough evidence it might be sufficient to convince the Cabinet to take it forward to the judiciary. There are still some judges left who still believe in the concept of an independent judiciary, that are not in the pockets of the Prime Minister. However, it needs an M.P. with the guts to support the petition and see it through, someone that has more strength of character than the rest of *her* colleagues put together."

"You mean Eleanor Beaufort?"

"Who could be better?"

"I agree, but where do I come in."

Chamberlain paused and gave an ironic smile. "You need to keep doing what you are doing. Sleep with him and make sure he continues to confide in you. Listen to everything he says and pass it to me to build a case. Rachel, you are the key to assembling the evidence against him. He tells you more than any government minister, including me. You're the one person he is vulnerable around. You need to exploit it. I know I'm asking a lot Rachel, and it could be dangerous. Can I rely on you?"

Rachel looked troubled, and her eyes welled with tears, smudging the mascara lines around her blue eyes. She was a pawn in a high powered chess game between two formidable adversaries. "I'll do it, but am I doing this for my country or for you?"

Chamberlain flashed the rugged, handsome smile that had preceded so many news conferences. "For your country of course."

"So who would take over if he was impeached?"

His smile broadened. "That's obvious. It will be me."

# CHAPTER 35

Events were moving quickly for Kendrick and Julianne. Grayson had been true to his promise and delivered some interesting news for them. The black motorcycle the SSP pursuit team was convinced belonged to Harry had been found abandoned on the road leading to the docks, well inside the restricted zone. Julianne was now certain that Harry was attempting to board a boat. She had a sense that he was close by, but there were obvious dangers searching for him inside the perimeter. They had no choice but to search on foot inside the zone, but even this option was denied them when they suddenly found the presence of soldiers guarding the perimeter had increased dramatically.

"Something is going down," Kendrick said pensively as they sat in a long line of cars diverted around the barriers. Even now people were trying to conduct their usual business, as if the country still retained some degree of normality. There were no warning signs and the cars had to find their own way around the obstruction.

They wasted several frustrating hours travelling the entire perimeter of the restricted zone looking for a way in, but unlike the day before when they had passed through a narrow access point into the zone with little difficulty, the perimeter was heavily patrolled.

There were also a number of military vehicles positioned outside the zone, and one SUV began to track and follow them, its intimidating presence forcing Kendrick to abandon his reconnaissance of the barriers. There was no opening in any event, and he drove away from the restricted zone for several miles along rural roads deep into the countryside in no particular direction until Pembroke was left far behind. Eventually the SUV lost interest and veered off.

Kendrick pulled over and slammed his fists on the steering wheel in frustration. Julianne did not react, but her face was a mask of conflicting emotions. They would never reach Harry now. As they contemplated their narrowing set of options, Kendrick's tablet chimed. It was Grayson again. Kendrick listened and nodded, saying little, and when he put the tablet down he looked gravely at Julianne, who peered at him expectantly.

"We have to move," he said. "I'll explain on the way."

They headed west along the peninsula. The light was failing and the mist swirled around the car like ephemeral ghosts, reducing visibility even further. The only light came from their headlamps, and the mist reflected it back. The road quickly became little better than a dirt path and in places the rain had carved out deep ruts so that the old Ford slid and lurched drunkenly at times, completely unsuited for this type of terrain. They soldiered on, however, at times no more than crawling speed, the suspension rattling at each bump, but Julianne could see by Kendrick's intense expression and the way he gripped the steering wheel that he was fighting against a deadline. She stayed silent, preferring to let him talk when ready.

Finally he spoke, his eyes still fixed on the swirling darkness ahead. "There are boats leaving," he said simply.

The car slipped and veered to the left, the high bushes flanking the track slapping against the window. He fought to regain control and slowed down.

"There is? So maybe Harry got on a boat and is safe.

"You don't understand."

"What do you mean? Where are the boats going?"

"They aren't going anywhere." Julianne frowned at Kendrick. He was making no sense.

Then he turned to her, his features creased into a grave expression. "If Harry is on one of those boats, he is done for. Grayson told me that they intend to blow them up once they're clear of the estuary and in deeper water."

"What? For God's sake why?" The tremor in Julianne's voice betrayed her fear. She knew how resourceful Harry was. He had probably reached one of the boats.

"Grayson doesn't know. All he could find out was that the ships were large container vessels, and the cargo was scheduled for destruction. Grayson found no reference to what the cargo was, but whatever it is they are going to great lengths to get rid of it."

# CHAPTER 36

Initially he thought his senses had betrayed him. He refused to believe that even this regime could stoop to such a level of barbarity, but when the second round of gunfire ripped through the darkening sky, he knew the terrible truth. The metal walls of the oil drums muffled but failed to mute the rattle of the gunfire, but it was the collective high pitched screams of scores of people dying that shredded Harry's senses. He knew it was a sound that would haunt him for the rest of his life.

Harry collapsed to the wet ground, leaned his back to the wall and cried softly. The guns ceased and the cranes immediately sprung into life. Mercifully he was spared the carnage inside the oil drums, but the cranes presently hauled a number of containers onto the waiting trucks, which rumbled down the dirt road to the jetties.

In the deepening gloom, a succession of powerful Klieg lights snapped on, bathing the whole grisly operation in a powerful glow. The area around the drums was a hive of activity as the containers were loaded onto the trucks and Harry took advantage of the fading daylight to skirt around the area until he reached the road that led to the jetty. The steep hedges bordering the road allowed no cover, but in the gloom he was able to wedge himself against the bush, curled into a ball so that he would only be seen if a passing driver was specifically looking at him.

He waited for a truck to rumble past. The rutted, bumpy road was slippery from the drizzle and the truck moved slowly. Even so, he had to run behind the truck as fast as his injured thigh would allow. He saw that the metal container did not extend the full length of the truck's flatbed, leaving a small gap barely two feet in length at the rear. Harry had to time his jump perfectly or the motion of the truck would cause him to slip off onto the road. He had little time to think so he sprung forward and landed awkwardly, banging his knees against the container, but hung on grimly to the edge of the chassis. It was impossible for the driver to see him as the container blocked his view, even with its wide wing mirrors.

The metal of the truck's chassis was slick from the mist and drizzle and it was difficult to get a firm grip. The bumpy track caused the truck to bounce and lurch, almost flinging Harry off the vehicle. Fortunately the journey was relatively short and as the truck rounded a corner he saw a large container ship moored alongside the large jetty. The bustling activity was again lit like a floodlit football match from a further array of Klieg lamps.

The ship was stacked high with containers and the crew buzzed around on the deck of the ship whilst stevedores attached steel rope fittings from a huge gantry crane, which then expertly lifted each container off the stationary truck and gently placed it on the stack of containers on the ship. More stevedores stood on a catwalk running through the middle of the container stack on the ship, and they released the fittings and began lashing the container down to secure it. The now empty truck drove away, followed by the next truck in line, and the process was repeated. Harry's truck slowed down, brakes squealing like a wounded animal as it headed toward the unloading area, which shimmered in the bank of lights flooding the area. Harry glanced around the container which hid him from view and he saw several dock workers dressed in overalls and hard hats, directing the truck to the unloading area.

If Harry waited on the truck any longer he would be seen, so he braced himself and jumped off the back of the truck. He misjudged the speed of the truck and landed heavily, rolling painfully on the soft but rutted ground, and a stabbing pain shot through his damaged right thigh. He gasped with the pain and fought to recover his composure. He quickly looked around, relieved that no-one had spotted him. He rested a moment before getting up and found he was able to put a little weight on his leg. Now dirty and wet, he stumbled forward. Although it had turned completely dark, the residual glare from the lights in the distance was enough for Harry to find his way. A narrow path diverged from the main road down to the docks and disappeared into a bank of trees, and Harry followed the path, which headed toward the water's edge. The trees gradually fell away and he could see gentle ripples in the black water. The ground became quite marshy and as he stepped down his feet got sucked in and it took an effort to release his shoe from the cloying mud.

The jetty was several hundred yards further up the estuary, and in between was a field of tall straw-like grass. He stepped through the field, having to push the thick grass aside to get through, feet squelching on the wet ground. However, the grass provided perfect cover as it was taller than him. When he emerged on the other side he noticed the gangplank onto the ship was unoccupied. The jetty, however, was exposed and it was the only way to reach the gang-plank. He had to get onto the boat and document the truth of what he had seen. He patted the inside pocket of his fleece jacket where Amir's mobile phone was hidden.

He waited, crouched in the grass, the sodden ground bitterly cold, even through his clothes. However, his indirect route had taken him behind the bank of lights, where the bustling activity was centred on the unloading area. The jetty was set further back and outside the range of the Klieg lights and poorly lit. Harry waited his moment, and then, heart pounding, ran up the jetty alongside the huge hull of the container ship, which towered above him. Ahead was the steel gangplank, swaying rhythmically as the ship rocked gently in the swell of the water. He had no way of knowing if anyone was inside the entrance to the ship. If they were, it would be all over; he would never evade them. However he had to take that chance.

He was twenty yards from the gangplank when a dark figure emerged from the boat and Harry stopped dead, convinced he had been seen. The figure, however, turned and walked in the opposite direction further up the jetty. Harry spotted a narrow steel safety ladder on the side of the hull. However, with the curve of the hull, it was a five foot jump from the edge of the jetty. Spotting the figure coming back in his direction, he acted without thinking and leaped onto the ladder and grabbed it with both hands. One hand slipped but his left arm gripped firmly even as he swung around, twisting his grip as he scrambled to plant his feet on a rung. He swung back and found a better grip and clambered up the ladder to the deck. He cautiously stuck his head over the parapet, and all being clear, hauled himself onto the empty deck.

As soon as he was on the deck, however, he heard voices moving closer. Two crew members were in animated conversation and their voices carried in the still air. Looking around frantically, he saw several lifeboats tethered to the parapet of the deck, their covers on. He quickly darted under one of the covers, hardly daring to breathe, listening to the two crewmen as they passed by.

"Last container Chief Officer Wainwright and we're ready to go."

"About bloody time! This has taken far too long. As soon as the container is loaded let's get out of here. I want to finish this quickly and forget it ever happened."

"We're all with you on that one sir."

The second, older voice continued. "I can smell death all around us. I wish they hadn't told us what was in those containers. It's the most macabre cargo I will ever carry."

"It won't be for long, sir," the younger man replied. "We are going to dump it in the sea as soon as we get past Chapel Bay. The detonators are in place and we are nearly ready to leave."

The older man let out a sigh. "Why dump them at sea anyway?"

"Because they don't want mass graves on land like those found in Syria after Assad was deposed ten years ago. This is cleaner."

Their voices faded as they walked by, boots clattering on the metal deck, and Harry sat in the darkness, a large void in the pit of his stomach. Their meaning was all too clear to him. He pulled the covers back and crept out onto the deck, alert for signs of anyone else. Apart from the narrow but tall navigation bridge, towering several stories high so that it overlooked the cargo, the deck was filled with containers. It was quite gloomy, the only light coming from the diffuse glow of the masthead lights way above him.

The narrow walkway around the perimeter of the ship, where the lifeboats were placed, was the only space available to walk, and so he was taking a great risk, with nowhere to go if he was seen. He had to confirm the truth, however, and he soon stood at the base of the consignment of containers that stretched above him. They had been stacked carelessly and several had not been secured properly, so there was a gap between the double doors of the container at the front of the rectangular box. It looked like they had been sealed in a hurry. The only object holding the doors together was a long, thin metal rod placed between the gaps in the door handles so that it stretched across both doors, securing them. The rod itself was lashed against the doors for additional security. The narrow gap between the container doors was too dark to see anything but the smell emanating from the large box caught in Harry's throat. It was exactly as the crew member had described; the smell of death, but also mixed with terror and the stench of freshly spilt blood.

Harry's first instinct was to get away from there as fast as possible, to shut his eyes and ears to the enormity of what he was witnessing. It was almost too much to take in, but he needed confirmation, as vile as that would be. He looked around and spotted near the parapet a life-jacket and an orange life preserver ring. Next to it in a sealed glass box was a fire extinguisher and a small but pristine looking axe. He kicked in the glass box with a high pitched tinkle of splintering glass. He crouched behind a lifeboat, waiting for the inevitable crew member coming to investigate, but after several minutes no one had arrived. He emerged from his hiding place and grabbed the axe. It felt solid in his hands, and the silver head felt sharp to the touch.

He positioned the axe over the rod securing the doors of the nearest container and took a practice swing. He then stepped back and brought the axe down in a wide arc, snapping the rod instantly and sending the broken halves clattering to the floor. No longer sealed, the two container doors swung slowly outwards from the weight of the cargo inside, and as it did so, Harry stepped back and felt a tide of nausea rise up within him. A pile of bodies, their skin already ashen but awash with blood, spilt out onto the deck floor. Several still had their eyes open, faces frozen in a mask of terror at the instant of death. The bodies included women and even a few children, but it was the smell that Harry could no longer bear. The truth swept through him like a tidal wave and he slumped to the floor and emptied the contents of his stomach onto the deck. It barely helped his nausea, and his vision was swimming, the taste of vomit in his mouth. He staggered away from the grisly scene to the edge of the deck where he sought sanctuary in the darkness underneath the covers of a lifeboat. It scarcely seemed to help, and the vision of the bodies stayed in his mind like a horror movie burned into his retinas so he could not escape it no matter how tightly he squeezed his eyes shut.

He took deep breaths, fighting hard not to hyperventilate. Eventually he calmed down enough to think more clearly as the initial nausea subsided. He remembered the cellphone Amir had given to him and took it out from his jacket pocket. As he turned it on it cast a comforting greenish glow in the darkness. He turned it over in his hands, thankful that the battery was still intact. He had to record the horrible truth and ensure that the horror of Pelham's regime, even more profound than that revealed in the five-year plan that Harry had acquired, was exposed to the world. He stepped back onto the deck, alert for crew members, and took several pictures and a short video recording, careful not to engage the flash.

Harry felt a slight lurch, and heard a gentle thrum of the ship's engines rising in intensity. He could feel the motion of the ship as it left port. His thoughts raced, chaotic and unstructured, and then a crazy idea surfaced. He still remembered her cellphone number; in fact it was imprinted on his brain. It was a random chance, highly unlikely that she would answer. He had no idea if she was still alive, but he had to try anyway. The phone beeped as he pressed the eleven digits of a number he had once known so well. He heard the reassuring click of a connection being made and the line rang. It kept ringing but there was no answer. He felt a peculiar sense of dejection, even though he knew it would be a miracle if she answered. He needed to share what he had seen with someone quickly, if only for some sense of catharsis, so he would not go mad, but a looming sense of loneliness and despondency soon settled over him again.

# CHAPTER 37

It was a miracle that Kendrick's police-issued Ford was still intact, but despite being jolted like a bumper car, the old jalopy had shown its versatility, and soon the track improved until it became a solid tarmac road again. The darkness surrounded them like a shroud, and Julianne saw the dark shadows of overhanging trees hugging the road and joining together to create a sealed canopy overhead. Presently however, a set of lights flickered through the gap in the forest, and they headed toward it, curious, but also comforted by some vestige of civilization. They reached a small cottage, set in the grounds of a large church lit by spotlights dug into the soil that lit the impressive stone building in a phosphorescent glow.

The cottage was run down but brightly lit, and a large sign, illuminated by their headlights, indicated that they had arrived at the Church of Saint Mary in Angle. Across the road stood more houses and even a pub, but they were dark and several appeared to be derelict. They pulled up outside the cottage and hesitantly rapped on the large brass knocker on the door. Julianne saw a pair of curtains twitch in the window and presently the sound of a number of bolts being drawn back. The door opened a crack, still secured by a chain, and they found themselves at the end of the stout barrel of a large handgun. Its owner, a slender, balding man thrust his sallow face in the gap.

"Who are you? What do you want?" He scowled at them, his narrow eyes darting from Julianne to Kendrick, alert for trouble. "Are you military?"

Kendrick thrust his identification in the gap. "I am D.C. Kendrick with the London Police and this is my friend Julianne. Don't worry. I'm off duty. We need your help."

The man studied Kendrick's card and looked past them to satisfy himself that they had no back-up in the shadows. As he stretched his lean neck Julianne noticed he wore the white dog collar of the Church. Satisfied the visitors represented no threat, he holstered his gun, unlocked the chain and let them in. "Come in." He paused, eyeing them carefully. "You're a long way from home." He ushered them into the simple living room where a log fire was burning, casting a comforting glow around the sparsely furnished room.

"As you can imagine we don't get many visitors here, even less since the troubles. Sorry about the gun. Can't be too careful these days with military sniffing around. They have no respect for the Church and ransacked my vestibule, but I am not surprised given the government's policies. They've already plundered most of the village for supplies. Most of us have left; only the brave or stupid ones like me remain." He touched his dog collar. "I'm preaching to empty pulpits these days."

The man introduced himself as Pastor Ewan Evans. His face looked windswept, as if he had spent far too long outdoors in the turbulent sea air. Julianne estimated him to be at least mid-fifties. Even so he moved around his cottage with almost supine agility and quick bird-like movements. His frame looked lean and fit, as if his head had been supplanted onto a younger body. She imagined him stepping out regularly for long walks on the moor.

Pastor Evans offered them tea, but Kendrick shook his head. "Thank you but we have no time to waste. We have to get to the headland. There are some ships moving up the estuary and we have reason to believe they are going to be deliberately sunk. We think one of our friends is on the boat and we have to somehow warn him. Do you have a large flashlight?"

Evans pondered for a moment. "Yes, in the store room. He hurried out of the room and emerged seconds later with a powerful electric torch. He turned it on to test it and the beam was blinding in the enclosed space. "I use it for church services when there is a power outage, which is fairly common these days."

"That's perfect," replied Kendrick. "Can you direct us to the headland? We need to be positioned so we can signal the boat."

The Pastor peered out of the window. "I can do better than that. I will take you there. Your car is not going to make it over the stony ground and it's highly dangerous in the dark for someone who doesn't know the land. Follow me." He grabbed a set of keys and a heavy overcoat and scurried out of the cottage, as if he was suddenly energized by the prospect of adventure, a welcome break from his lonely routine in this remote outpost. Kendrick, carrying the large lamp, and Julianne raced to keep up as the Pastor beeped a large Range Rover, its headlights flashing. They got in, Kendrick in the front passenger seat.

They traversed the road and followed a dirt track that seemed to run into oblivion, even the powerful headlights of the Range Rover unable to penetrate beyond the track. The vehicle bounced and jolted, but its suspension was much softer than Kendrick's Ford and they rode out the troughs in the ground with comfort. As they travelled closer to the edge, the mist began to disperse, and a stiff breeze ruffled the long grass either side of the vehicle. Pastor Evans, clearly enjoying the escapade, beamed at Kendrick. "If our Lord in heaven needed a vehicle, I think he would choose a Range Rover," he said smiling. "These things can get past anything."

Julianne fervently hoped that the Lord was guiding them, because they were heading aimlessly toward the black sea. Any second the land could drop away beneath them. She found herself involuntarily gripping her seat tight.

As if he had read her thoughts, Pastor Evans continued chatting amiably. "It's a good thing I'm here. This land is treacherous at night if you're not familiar with it. This track goes right off the cliff and it's a forty foot drop to the rocks below."

He continued driving for several minutes before slowing down, moving cautiously. "I know the landmarks here. We're close to the edge so I'll pull up here, but watch your step." Julianne could not see anything except featureless grass in the headlights, but she felt a sense of relief when the Range Rover juddered to a halt.

As they got out, Evans took the lamp from Kendrick and set it on the ground. He switched it on and its powerful beam cut through the darkness until it was lost somewhere in the black water. "Don't go past the lamp," he warned them. "It is close to the edge of the cliff." As he spoke his breath condensed in the chilly air. Julianne shivered, knowing that all they could do now was wait and reflect on how hopeless their mission really was. She picked up her small tablet from the inside pocket of her thick Cashmere coat and turned it over, anxious to stay occupied. The screen cast an eerie blue glow over her face, and the device beeped softly. Intrigued, she checked it and saw that she had received a missed call from an unfamiliar number. Curious and with nothing to do but wait, she flicked the call back facility on the tablet and the line immediately began to ring. It continued to ring for a while and she was just about to hang up when an excited voice answered. At that very moment the hulking presence of a large container ship drifted into view as it cleared the bend in the estuary. Julianne stared at the tablet phone, uncomprehending, tears rolling down her face.

Holed up under the covers of a lifeboat, shivering not just with the cold but with the intensity of what he had witnessed, Harry tried but failed to comprehend the enormity of the crimes he had witnessed. His sense of burning outrage did not come even close to conveying the monumental weight of emotion bearing down on him. He hardly even cared when he heard movement close by, followed by a number of harsh, whispered voices. Outside, on the deck, it sounded to Harry as if the entire crew had assembled just a few feet from where he hid in the darkness.

He heard covers being pulled back and lifeboats drawn up on the pulleys and lowered into the sea. The voices were close now, and he would be a sitting duck if they took the covers on his lifeboat.

Directly above him, he heard a hoarse voice yell out. "What about this boat, Captain?" Harry held his breath, bracing himself to spring forward, hoping the element of surprise might help him escape.

A voice from further away yelled back. "Leave it Morrison, we have enough. Come on, move it. We have less than five minutes." He heard several boats splash in the water and the voices dispersed until the only sound was the deep rumble of the engines from within the bowels of the ship and the roar of displaced water as the hull sliced through the unfathomable depths of the estuary.

He emerged onto the deck and ran to the parapet. In the black water, he saw a small fleet of eight lifeboats moving slowly and rhythmically away from the ship. The container vessel, however, continued its forward motion, apparently now rudderless and devoid of crew, like a modern *Marie Celeste*.

At the edge of his field of vision, Harry noticed several blinking lights positioned along the railing by the containers. With a sense of foreboding he raced to one of the blinking lights. Strapped tightly around the railing were several large explosive charges sealed together by a wax-like substance and surrounded by wires. The largest depth charge contained an LED counter, and when he looked at the timer he knew he was in trouble. For a second he was struck rigid, frozen in the face of imminent danger. He recalled the life-jacket and the orange life preserver ring and raced along the deck to retrieve them. Focused on this task, he did not immediately hear the phone in his jacket pocket buzzing. He found the equipment scattered on the deck where he had left it and hastily slipped on the life-jacket. He became aware of the phone and grabbed it. When he heard the voice on the other line he could not contain his surprise.

"Julianne. I can't believe it's you!" he cried. "I may need to call you back. I have a situation here."

Julianne was stricken with emotion. "You have to get off the boat Harry. It's about to blow!"

"Tell me about it. The crew have already left." He looked at the timer. Oh God, he would never make it clear of the boat in time.

On the edge of the cliff overlooking the estuary, Julianne watched the container vessel as it continued to plough forward through the black water. The Pastor trained his powerful beam across the water toward the distant ship. "Harry," she urged him. *"Get out now!"* She fought to wipe away her tears.

"I don't think I have enough.....

The line went dead, just a hiss of static. Almost instantaneously, the boat exploded in a huge rippling fireball that briefly lit up the entire estuary.

# CHAPTER 38

Anxious and unable to sleep following her meeting with Chamberlain, Rachel lay in bed in the sanctuary of her Kensington apartment staring at the ceiling. She studied the elegant cornice that divided the ceiling and walls, but was unable to escape the dizzying array of thoughts that spun wildly through her brain. She was caught between the two most powerful men in the country, unsure of whether to trust either of them. After her meeting with Chamberlain, she felt a lingering sense of betrayal as she drove through the rubble-filled streets to her apartment. She was not convinced by Chamberlain but she had little choice other than to take his lead. Whilst she disliked the Deputy, allied with a slight degree of repugnance she couldn't quite define, he represented her only chance to do the right thing.

Even so, she was deeply afraid of Pelham. In the bedroom he was like a playful puppy, and more energetic than most men half his age, but she had seen flashes of temper in his dealings with very senior public policy figures, and she had occasionally received the brunt of it. However, it was not his temper that scared her, but his firm, lucid conviction that the atrocities he oversaw were genuinely for the good of the country.

Admitting defeat in her attempts to sleep, Rachel got up and

showered, trying to erase the last lingering scent of cologne. She
went to her study and in the light of her small desk lamp switched
on her tablet. The faint glow lit up her features and as they did so
she caught her reflection in the wall mirror opposite. She looked
tired and drawn, her usually flawless skin blotchy and dry. Her bright,
liquid eyes looked dull, as if the colour had been drained from them.
The strain of the last few weeks had taken their toll.

She entered the log-in details for the newspaper archive portal.
It was a website that had once been available to the public worldwide, but since the government had tightened its noose around
liberal website access, the site was restricted to selected politicians
and public sector employees only. It was another example of how
Pelham's regime had asserted its power by taking control over social media, closing down websites it regarded as seditious, a term
used in the widest possible sense to eliminate sites which the regime
judged to be subversive or anti-establishment. The government was
in control of the propaganda war, and only those on the inside knew
the true extent of the regime's activities, such as the experimental
research laboratory in Watford. She thought of the tiny SD card
locked securely away that contained film of the facility she had taken
at great risk.

Rachel was certain Pelham had other darker secrets that he had
not even revealed to her. While Chamberlain had suggested that Pelham confided in Rachel more than anyone, she was not convinced
the Prime Minister was totally candid. Several passing comments he
had made confused her, and she wondered what was really going on
in that brilliant, twisted mind of his. He had recently confided to
her that some people had judged him crazy, although they had not

been foolish enough to openly state that to him. Playing her role of supportive mistress, she had vehemently dismissed those people as failing to understand him, that he was a visionary leader. Privately however, she feared it was true, and she had increasingly begun to wonder who he really was, and why he behaved like he did. The clue was surely in his past, something he protected fiercely, and that was why she was now in the portal, looking for evidence about his past.

She knew her use of the archive could be monitored but she was willing to take the risk. Once in the portal, the site showed up like a 3D library, its impressive graphics folding out like a simulated print version of the article retrieved. It had a search facility, and she entered in various searches based on information she had collected about Pelham. Very little was known by the public about his childhood, although it was widely understood that the death of his aristocratic parents had left him an orphan as a young boy. The earliest reference to his existence was his emergence as a public school prefect at Eton, followed by his appearances as a President of the Oxford Union Debating Society. Rachel found this somewhat ironic, as the Society enjoyed a global reputation founded upon the principles of free speech and open debate.

Despite her fatigue, she spent the next several hours in dogged pursuit of any references to Pelham, particularly his childhood. She occasionally dozed off in front of her tablet, but reawakened with a tenacity born of an anxiety to find the truth, to understand the man who held such sway over her. Despite Rachel trying every search parameter she could think of, the portal yielded virtually nothing. Then, half-asleep, she came across a grainy Polaroid photo from thirty-six years ago and instantly snapped awake.

Pelham had previously mentioned that his natural father had been a biologist, but he had refused to elaborate, putting up his usual wall of silence when she probed him. She knew that the memory of his father somehow caused him pain. Something had happened to Pelham that he refused to discuss, as if wishing to obliterate it from his memory. Rachel had searched a list of biologists in the news but nothing had linked them to Pelham until she came across the photo. It was of a statuesque, proud looking man whose intelligence and forceful nature exuded from the screen, despite the poor quality of the photo, its colours smudged and runny. His grey-tinged wavy hair suggested that he was middle-aged, although he was lean and sinewy. Next to him stood a shy looking boy in school uniform, clearly the man's son. The boy looked happy to have his father's strong arm around his shoulder. It was the boy who sent a shudder down Rachel's spine. There was no doubt of his identity. Even at that tender age he showed a glimmer of the rugged handsomeness that had seduced a nation. It was the smile, however, that convinced Rachel. The slight, almost imperceptible twist of the mouth on one side gave him away. She had never seen any pictures of Lance as a boy, until now.

The headline was alarming; '*Human Biologist's secret life as a white supremacist exposed.*' She read the introduction:

*'Renowned physicist Duncan Cavendish was today sentenced to twenty five years in prison for a series of shocking...'*

That was as far as the article went. The rest had been deleted, the electronic equivalent of tearing out the page so it could not be read. Perhaps this was why Pelham had never talked about his father, but it still raised more questions than answers. What had his father done to warrant such a hefty tariff? If he was indeed Pelham's father, as Rachel was convinced he was, why did they hold different names? She looked for more search references for Duncan Cavendish, but curiously, any articles referencing him had been partly deleted as well. Someone had gone to great lengths to ensure that the curious surfer did not find out the truth about Duncan Cavendish.

Rachel paused, deep in thought. The growl of early morning traffic had already begun and London was waking to another day of oppression. A police siren sounded in the distance. Her head hurt as she agonized what to do with this information. She considered going straight to Chamberlain with these revelations, but something deep in her subconscious urged caution. She could not articulate her feeling, knowing it was not rational, but it didn't matter. This would remain her secret, at least for now.

# CHAPTER 39

Julianne stared vacantly at the phone, uncomprehending at first, but as the gravity of what she had just heard became clear, she choked back tears of anguish. Kendrick caught her as she slumped forward. He wrapped his arms around her as she shook uncontrollably, a deep well of emotion rising through her body in choking sobs. They had found Harry at last, only for him to be taken in such a cruel fashion. It was in the desperate throes of grief that Julianne realized just how she felt about him. She had dismissed it as infatuation, even when she longed for him while they were apart, but had deluded herself. She had never told Harry that she loved him, and now it was too late.

The raging fireball which seconds before had been a huge container ship lit the estuary in an eerie glow, casting shadows that danced on the water. Despite the distance, a warm rush of air breezed past them, and a harsh cracking sound was clearly audible. Julianne buried her face in Kendrick's chest, inconsolable. Kendrick glanced back at the devastation and then looked at Evans. The Pastor suddenly became animated, waving his arms frenetically as he looked out over the dark ocean, where the burning hulk of the huge vessel was listing badly in the water.

He turned to them, his cornflower blue eyes bright and wide in the reflected glow from the burning wreckage. "Look, over there!" He pointed frantically at a spot in the water, its rippling surface reflecting the orange glow of the flaming carcass of the ship. Kendrick followed his pointed finger, but struggled to understand. Then he saw it, a regular but intermittent flashing in the midst of the orange glow. Dark against the orange glow was the unmistakable shape of a man clinging to a life ring.

Evans quickly darted off and with renewed hope Julianne and Kendrick followed the fleet-footed Pastor as he skirted the cliff edge. "Be careful," he called back. "It's very steep and some of the boulders are loose." He tossed a spare flashlight from his overcoat to Kendrick and scrambled over the edge, picking his way carefully down the steep incline. Kendrick followed, slowly threading his way down the steep rocky path. Julianne wiped her tear-streaked face with the back of her hand and stood at the edge of the steep, dark path, ready to scramble down.

"No," Kendrick called to her. "You stay here. It's too dangerous without a flashlight."

She nodded her assent and stood at the top, her eyes fixed on the blinking light still perilously close to the flaming wreckage. Doubts began to creep into her mind. What was to say that the figure was Harry, and even if it was, that he was conscious or even still alive? A chill swept through her and she hugged herself to keep warm. It was a bitter night. All she could do was wait and hope.

Harry gained consciousness by choking on acidic, salty sea water. He coughed violently and thrashed about, expelling the sea water. Behind him the huge container ship was listing badly on its port side, and the entire hull on that side was now submerged. As it slowly began to sink, a hiss could be heard as burning metal hit the water and a strange deep gurgling emerged, like the death throes of a giant Kraken. The sinking boat created a huge swell and Harry bobbed up and down violently, grabbing his life ring tightly as the waves battered his cold, aching body.

It was hard to believe he was still alive. In moments of high stress, staring death in the face, people do irrational things. Harry did not understand why he had lost valuable seconds in answering the phone but he was glad he had. However as soon as he jumped from the vessel into the icy cold water the ship had exploded in a vast fireball. The impact had sent a huge concussion that reverberated through the water, pushing him down into the depths with terrifying force. He had immediately lost consciousness and would surely have drowned but for the life-jacket and ring.

As he drifted aimlessly, he found himself surrounded by twisted pieces of wood and metal wreckage. His body was cold from the chill water, and his clothes torn and soaked, but he had apparently escaped serious injury. He was well aware from his time interviewing war veterans that the most devastating injuries in explosions resulted from shrapnel that literally sliced through the bodies of anyone in the blast zone. He had already hit the water before the ship blew, substantially lessening the impact of the blast, although that was no guarantee against severe injury. He considered himself miraculously fortunate but as the next swell buffeted him, he recognized that he was far from being out of danger.

The flotsam on the surface of the water rose and fell on the waves, lit up by the burning wreckage behind him. With a gasp of horror, he noticed that it was not just wood and metal floating. The cold touch of a disembodied hand, black and heavily burnt, brushed against him. With a cry of terror he grabbed the hand and quickly flung it away where it landed with a plop in the rippling water. A wave of nausea gripped him, and with rising panic he tried to escape the mass of body parts that bobbed rhythmically in the water like a child's sailboat. He kicked his legs out as fast as his battered, aching body would allow in an attempt to escape the mass of charred human flesh that seemed to crowd in on him like some zombie horror B-movie. As he thrashed forward with rasping breath he bumped into a large soft object. He turned and was confronted by the torso of a small child, its glassy, lifeless eyes staring beyond him into the darkness. It was then that he could no longer contain his bile, his stomach retching heavily. As his throat convulsed, he recalled the poor mother who had clung to her toddler before it had been wrenched away by the soldiers. He had seen some children who had not been separated, and their parents had clung to them in relief. The irony was that those families would have died together, but the toddler, unlike its mother, was probably alive, at least for now.

Exhausted, he pushed on, heading for the dark outline of land which felt too distant to reach. The icy water pulled at his body, draining the last of his energy, his spirit crushed from what he had witnessed and the horror that surrounded him. He hardly cared if he lived, because life was so cheap in this country anyway. Another part of him clung on, admonishing him for his negative thoughts and urging him to survive. He felt the shape of the phone in the sodden breast pocket of his jacket and vaguely hoped that Amir had made it. He owed it to him to survive and tell his story. Also, he wanted to see Julianne again, but more importantly he longed to see Tamara and Byron. As he considered the possibility of never seeing his son again, however, his energy finally seeped away, and even the sight of a regularly flashing light from the shore was not enough to prevent him from losing his battle to stay conscious.

# CHAPTER 40

"There!" cried Kendrick excitedly. Pastor Evans steered the vessel, no larger than a rowing boat fitted with a small outboard motor, in the direction of Kendrick's outstretched hand. The light still flashed but became intermittently lost as it bobbed up and down in the increasing swell of the water. The motorboat was buffeted by the waves, its engine spluttering, and a sick feeling grew in the pit of Kendrick's stomach. He was relieved to reach the motionless shape sprawled over the life ring. It was only when they reached the barely conscious figure that he could tell beyond doubt it was Harry. He hardly recognized him. His face was bloated and he was shivering and mumbling incoherently. His skin was a ghastly grey pallor, with a touch of blue around the tips of his ears and fingertips.

"Jesus he looks in bad shape," said Kendrick.

The Pastor shot him an admonishing look and helped Kendrick heave the prostrate figure into the boat. Harry was as limp as a rag doll and the heaviness of his soaked clothes made it difficult to pull him over the hull. He landed with a soft thump on the floor of the boat and Evans immediately turned the craft in a tight circle and headed back to shore. Kendrick grabbed a blanket from one of the wooden seats and draped it over Harry. Within a few minutes they had reached the base of the cliff and Harry stirred and groaned.

Grasping the rudder to gently steer the boat onto the sandy beach, Evans said, "We'll never get him up the path by ourselves. We need to revive him." He reached below the wooden slats which served as seats. "This might help," he said, producing a dark bottle of brandy. Kendrick gave him a questioning look and the Pastor felt compelled to explain. "I used to teach survival training on the moors. Medicinal brandy acts as a cardiac stimulant and also against severe cold." He smiled and added, "Plus it's a damn good drink."

They got out and pushed the boat further up the beach and Evans tied it to a small wooden post. Together they hauled Harry onto the sand, gasping with effort, his inert frame a solid weight.

They laid Harry on his back and Kendrick checked his airway. He was breathing shallowly but Kendrick carried out a series of chest compressions to clear any residual water from his lungs. Within seconds Harry snapped awake, gasping and coughing, spitting out the acrid sea water. Evans immediately brought the brandy bottle to Harry's lips, and he gulped it down, resulting in further spasms of coughing as the warmth spread through his body.

"Easy, easy," chided the Pastor, gently taking the bottle back. "We need you sober for our little climb." He turned to Kendrick, pointing at the dark rocks they had climbed down. "It may be difficult getting him up there but there is no other way. In my experience of severe cold, it is critical to raise the core body temperature quickly. If he stays out here he will surely die. We need to get him back to the cottage as soon as we can."

Harry did not remember the climb up the steep rocky path. He was so exhausted he just wanted to sleep but strong arms supported him, pushing him forward, and encouraging voices urged him on. He vaguely recalled Julianne, her face beaming, embracing him tightly, but dismissed it as a dream or a vision spurred on by his wish to see her again. He fell into a big car and his next recollection was sitting in a hot bath in a warm, inviting cottage. He laid back, eyes closed, the water lapping invitingly around his body, and when he opened them, he saw Julianne again. The extreme cold of the water had dulled his senses, but he snapped alert, and as Julianne sat on the edge of the bath, her graceful features glowing, his memory came flooding back.

"You're not in my dream. It's really you isn't it?"

Her red hair glowed in the soft light of the bathroom. "Of course. We've taken a lot of trouble to find you. I thought I had lost you for good, but I forgot you have nine lives."

"Well I've probably used eight of them in the last few days." His voice was strained from exhaustion, but the warmth of the water had a reviving quality.

She shot a flirtatious glance at his body, naked except for the fresh strapping on his injured leg. "Jesus Harry you're a bag of bones. You're not as buff as I remember you," she chided gently, giggling girlishly.

"Yes well fine dining has not been high on my list of priorities recently."

Julianne turned more serious. "It must have been hell for you out there," she said.

Harry grew more pensive, running a hand through his tangled, matted hair. "Not as much as it was for those poor souls I saw forced to march to their death, shot like animals in those old oil drums. The sound of those guns will haunt me to my dying day." He looked up at Julianne, eyes glistening with tears. "I was stupid and naive Julianne. I should have realized that Pelham is far more dangerous and ruthless than even we suspected. Beneath that veneer of respectability and patriotic fervour beats the heart of a cold blooded genocidal maniac. Just because he is not prepared to get his hands dirty, he is more culpable than anyone else in this despicable regime. Under his watch he has allowed organizations like FREE to run wild, to create the chaos that we see every day in our towns and cities. For every citizen shot dead and dumped like animals in those stinking containers, or the thousands dying in deportation camps, their blood is on his hands. Somehow we have to hold him accountable. We have to do something."

"What brought you to Pembroke Harry?"

"I had to get out of the country. I still have a price on my head and the Secret Police nearly caught up with me."

"And what about Tamara and Byron?" Julianne did not mean to sound accusatory, but she saw Harry wince and cast his eyes downwards, turning away so she could not see the guilt written over his features.

"I couldn't reach them. Lord knows I tried but I would be no use to them if I was dead. I had to get away. It probably sounds cowardly but I had no other option."

Julianne laid a soft hand on his. "I'm not judging you Harry. I know you would have done what you could. There is no way off this island now. We have to stand up and fight." Her hazel eyes flicked to the bathroom door and she got up and gently closed it. "I have a proposal for you."

Without waiting for his answer she continued. "When the compound was destroyed there were few survivors other than us. But Chen was one of them. When you left I was in a haze of depression. I didn't know what to do. But several weeks later Chen found me; Lord knows how but I'm glad he did. I felt my life no longer had any purpose. I had lost Sean, but I didn't care about that. More importantly I had lost you, and any hope that I could do anything to carry on the fight. I thought it was just a matter of time before I would be imprisoned and tortured. I could feel the net closing in but Chen found me and took me under his wing."

She gave a cursory glance to the bathroom door, as if expecting someone to barge in. "Sean had it all wrong. There is no hope in hell we could fight the military, not even as an insurgency. We were always likely to be crushed; it was just a matter of time. As far as I know none of our cells survived. Others like the Muslim Brotherhood have taken up the fight, but they are poorly equipped and too disparate to be any real threat. You just have to look up at Pelham's hideous media screens; tanks rolling through every large town and city, soldiers goose-stepping through the streets. They don't stand a chance. Eventually the government forces will root them out like they did to us, destroy their strongholds and declare victory against another terrorist threat."

Harry glanced up at Julianne, her delicate features and flowing red hair framed softly against the harsh yellow glare of the bathroom light. The energy and passion that had captivated him before radiated from her as she spoke.

"I was blinded by Sean's insistence that meeting violence with violence was the only solution. Chen was right but we didn't listen to him. There is another way. It takes subtlety and intellect, something that Sean and his savage sidekick Luka could barely understand, let alone possess. This government is built on the strength of Pelham's personality and its ability to control the media to force its propaganda on the people. Chen introduced me to an organization that works in the shadows to attack the government from the inside. We have no guns or soldiers but we have a weapon that is far superior; some brilliant minds and the complacency of a regime that believes it is in total control. We are working to undermine the government from the inside, to attack its infrastructure and destroy its credibility. Our attacks will be silent, unnoticed at first but devastating in their consequences. They will never even know who or where the attacks came from, and so they will never be able to anticipate them."

Julianne paused for breath, a hint of rouge around her cheeks. She spoke with a new sense of purpose.

"What does Kendrick think to this?"

Julianne sighed, and pursed her lips. "I haven't told Kendrick." She glanced at the closed bathroom door again and her voice was barely a whisper. "Can we really trust him? I have my doubts about him."

"But he took you all this way to find me?" Harry protested mildly.

"Yes, I accept that, and he has not betrayed me yet," Julianne conceded. "But I just can't be sure. Don't you think it was strange that when the compound was hit he was nowhere to be seen? He was supposed to be our warning signal for any attacks. Then there was the call he took from his boss. He told me he was a lone wolf; that he had been asked to track you down before the SSP reached you. He told me that he intended to find you but never hand you in, so why is he in contact with his boss? It doesn't make sense."

Harry grabbed a towel from the nearby shelf and stepped out of the bath, wrapping the towel around his lower body. His muscles were stiff and ached with every movement, but the hot bath was a rare luxury. "Yet you went with him to find me? Surely, if he had wanted, he could have turned you in at any time."

"It was a risk I had to take." She handed Harry a dry set of clothes that Pastor Evans had donated. "I weighed it up and felt it was worth it to find you. We need you – I need you." She paused, a pensive look in her eyes. "Maybe I have been unfair to him, I don't know. Or maybe he was just using me to get to you. Now we are together he can turn us both in and get the glory. We need to be vigilant Harry."

"So what makes me so important?"

"Chen always knew I was going to look for you. He liked you immensely. I was not strong enough to stop Sean. With him in control of the cell Chen told me that he saw only one outcome. The cell would be crushed eventually. With the assassination attempt on Pelham we had stuck our head above the parapet and invited the military to crush the resistance. We didn't stand a chance. Chen had always advocated non-violence but Sean and Luka despised him. Sean only tolerated Chen because of his undoubted technical skills. He used those skills to make contact with another underground cell, this one far better suited to his philosophy and way of working. This resistance cell has no conventional weapons. They are not interested in armed combat or engaging the enemy face to face. Their only tools are banks of computers and tablets."

"But what good will they do?" asked Harry. "It's impossible

to use the Internet without it being sanctioned by the government. Computers are useless if they can't communicate."

Julianne nodded in agreement. "That's what I thought. But Chen and his colleagues have developed a communications network that falls outside the Internet. I don't know the technical details; I will leave that to Chen to explain. What I do know is that it is sophisticated enough to be a thorn in the government's side and Chen says that they have not even fully explored the potential of the system. Like most societies worldwide, the nation's infrastructure is connected through the Internet, which makes it vulnerable to outside attack. Some installations are not even encrypted. The cell has been exploiting gateways and loopholes to hack into government systems. We have only scored modest victories so far, but if we can cause enough chaos to the country's infrastructure we can bring down this government."

Harry finished dressing and inspected his new clothes. The grey slacks were ill-fitting and the bulky turtleneck sweater seemed to hang off him. He grabbed the partly dried fleece jacket with its valuable contents. Julianne gave a playful grin. You look like you're about to head out to sea in your trawler," she laughed.

"Ha ha. So they are like cyber saboteurs?"

Julianne's smile turned to a frown. "Cyber warriors would be more accurate."

"But why me? The last resistance cell you recruited me for didn't end so well."

"We need someone to be the public face of what we are trying to do, someone who can talk to the people and help them to understand the atrocities that the regime they elected is perpetrating.

You've seen those atrocities first hand Harry. You were a political correspondent, and like it or not you are still one of the most wanted men in the country, so you have credibility." Julianne's cheeks flushed with excitement. "I can't promise you will be safe but I truly believe that with you we can make a difference. What do you say?"

Harry's voice was heavy with scorn. "If you think a bunch of computer geeks can stop this regime after what I saw today -"

Julianne's eyes flashed in anger, but before he could continue they were both startled by a heavy pounding on the front door of the cottage.

# CHAPTER 41

Kendrick burst into the bathroom, his expression revealing deep concern. At this time of night in such a remote village, it was clearly no social call. "Come on Harry," he whispered harshly. "Follow me."

Harry glanced at Julianne and then followed Kendrick down the steps to the ground floor, through a recessed doorway which led to another set of steps. These stone steps trailed off into the darkness of a cellar. Kendrick held a kerosene lamp and its pale, flickering light revealed a large area with a sizable storage bunker. He opened the top cover and motioned for Harry to get inside. Harry clambered in and the pungent smell of pure coal seemed to envelop him as he lay gingerly on the crystalline rock. It was highly uncomfortable but Kendrick closed the lid anyway.

Pastor Evans opened the front door on its chain, and he stepped back when he saw three powerfully built figures dressed in the black combat attire of the State Secret Police, complete with ski masks. As soon as he opened the door, the tallest figure raised his jackboot and kicked the door, which flung inwards, snapping the chain easily with a sharp crack. They marched into the living room and ripped off their masks.

"Good evening Pastor, or should I say good morning," said the leader with a touch of wry amusement. He smoothed his blond hair and his red-rimmed eyes bore into Evans, appraising him.

"This is an outrage. Get out. I didn't invite you in!" cried Evans.

The leader ignored him and exchanged glances with his two colleagues, who blocked the open doorway from which a chill breeze drifted in. "Why are your trousers so dirty? It's a bit late to be hiking near the cliffs on a night like this." Evans looked down at his tunic and noticed for the first time the streaks of mud splashed across his legs and abdomen. He looked sheepishly back at the leader but before he could respond the SSP agent whipped out a large Bowie knife and held the flat blade against the Pastor's throat, his muscular right arm grabbing his tunic just under the dog collar. His sheer physical presence was overpowering, and Evans let out a strangled sob.

"Easy Bruce, don't cut his vocal chords; we need him to talk," said one of his companions, a youthful SSP officer with keen eyes who looked to Evans like he could rip him apart with his bare hands.

"Shut up Ethan," admonished Bruce. He turned to Evans, pressing the knife close. "We haven't much time, so unless you want to meet the God you worship so much a little earlier than expected, you'll tell us everything."

Evans fought off rising panic. He had always possessed a strong faith, even in the current troubles, but confronted by the devil casting his foul breath on him, he was deeply afraid. "Tell you what exactly? I've just been out for a walk. It gets lonely here."

"Not that lonely," replied Bruce. "There are several sets of footprints in your doorway and they're not ours. "Where is he?" The serrated edge of the knife glinted as Bruce twisted it closer to the Pastor's neck.

His eyes fixed on the sharp blade of the knife, Evans felt a chill run through him. He had to force himself to be strong. He took a deep breath and closed his eyes meditatively. *"Yea though I walk through the valley of the shadow of death I will fear no evil....."*

Bruce silenced him with a sharp punch to the abdomen that knocked the breath out of the Pastor. He staggered to the floor, clutching his stomach. His two comrades hauled the Pastor to his feet and Bruce waved the long knife in front of his stricken face. "Start talking or it will be the knife, not my fist in your stomach next," he spat fiercely.

The door at the opposite end of the room suddenly clicked open and a figure emerged, stepping quickly forward, his pistol levelled at the trio.

"I wouldn't do that if I were you."

Startled, Bruce stepped back and his two companions released their grip on the Pastor, who took the opportunity to deftly push past them and scurry out of the room.

Bruce composed himself and gave a wry smile. "That's a compact Glock. It might be semi-automatic but it would never fire quick enough to take all three of us down."

"You want to take that chance?" The figure eyed Bruce's companions and grunted in surprise. "Sean, what brings you here? Did they cut you a sweet deal?"

Sean looked sheepish. "Come on Kendrick, we're not interested in you. It's Harry Clarke we want. Our intelligence confirmed he was on the container ship and you picked up someone from it didn't you?"

Kendrick gave a dismissive shake of the head. "Your intelligence is wrong. No-one could have survived the blast on that ship."

Sean reached inside his pocket and Kendrick aimed the Glock at him, keeping a close eye on Bruce and Ethan. "Slowly," cautioned Kendrick.

Sean pulled out a small tablet from his jacket and held it up. He touched the screen and it flickered to life. "I recorded this footage of a man jumping overboard just before it blew. Even with the zoom on full it was impossible to see who it was but you clearly went to a lot of trouble to find him. Hand him over and this all goes away."

Kendrick's hand stayed firm on the gun. "You're in no position to negotiate."

Another voice came from the hallway. "What makes you think we would ever hand him over to you Sean?" The female voice was familiar and as she strode into the room, Sean's face turned ashen. Grim-faced, Julianne pointed the Pastor's large handgun directly at his head. "You're a bloody traitor Sean Kelly. I should just spatter your brains over the wall now," she hissed, as her finger slowly began to squeeze the trigger.

Sean could feel the heat of Bruce and Ethan's gaze. The latter had a wry look of satisfaction on his face. "It's not how it seems." he stammered. He pointed at his companions. "They forced me into it. I'm with you. Put that away and we can-"

"Save it," she interrupted tersely. She turned to Kendrick. "Let's do what we need to and get out of here."

The SSP officers were forced to give up their weapons and tablets, kicking them out of harm's way where Evans gathered them up. Kendrick motioned with his gun and closely supervised the SSP officers as Evans led the way to the cellar. He brought the kerosene lamp and ushered them into the cold, damp underground room. Kendrick waved them into a dark, dusty corner and then tapped on the coal bunker where they sat. The lid opened outwards and Harry clambered out. "Thank God," he muttered. "That was the worst hiding place I've ever been in, and I've just had a bath!"

Bruce snarled angrily as he saw Harry emerge from the coal bunker in the dim light of the lamp.

"Quiet!" ordered Kendrick, his weapon still trained firmly on them. Evans handed the lamp to Harry, scampered up the stone steps and quickly emerged with a large plastic bottle of water that he flung into the corner at their captives. "Kendrick, I have nothing to tie them up with but the door is rock solid. They will never get out."

"Thank you Pastor." His voice was flat in the dank surroundings and somewhere in the recesses of the cellar a monotonous *drip-drip* could be heard. "You can stay here for a few days. We'll get a message to someone to open the door, but not before we're long gone. We've given you water so you'll survive but you'll be on a strict diet for a while, unless you like coal."

Bruce growled in rage and in the dim light he looked ready to charge like a bull at a matador. Only Kendrick's gun pointed directly at his head prevented him. "I'm going to find you and hunt you down whatever it takes," he spat.

"Save your breath, I don't frighten easily," replied Kendrick dismissively.

Julianne, her own weapon poised, suddenly beckoned to Sean. "I want to show you something," she said in a sultry voice. Kendrick looked at her strangely. Sean ambled over cautiously as her gun tracked his movement until he stood opposite her. He gave a baffled smile. "I knew you would understand, Julianne."

"Understand this." In a blur of movement, her hand shot up and delivered a stinging slap that sent him reeling backwards, clutching his cheek. "That's for all the times you hurt me, for all those bruises," she snapped. Harry, observing his shocked expression, almost felt a twinge of sympathy for his nemesis, but it quickly passed.

They climbed the narrow stairs to the cellar door and slammed it shut, leaving their cursing prisoners in darkness. Evans locked and bolted the door. "Don't worry," he said. They're going nowhere. That cellar is as secure as the Lord's forgiveness."

"Plenty of time for a getaway," said Harry, brushing the black coal dust from the slacks and sweater the Pastor had provided him.

Kendrick eyed Harry with concern. "Are you fit enough to travel? You were having a midnight swim in the estuary less than two hours ago."

"Yeah, I'm fine. Let's get out of here as soon as possible. Don't ask me to drive though. I need to sleep." They waited for the Pastor to gather up a few small personal effects in a duffel bag and he raided his refrigerator and handed Julianne a bag of food supplies. They walked out into the cold night air. The sky was a hazy black, dawn still several hours away and most stars obscured by low lying cloud. The Pastor tossed the keys for the Range Rover to Kendrick. "Let's swap cars. The Range Rover will come in more useful to you than me and they are more likely to be looking for your car at the checkpoints." Kendrick nodded thankfully and passed the keys to the battered old Ford to Evans. "Are you sure? What will you do now?"

The Pastor smiled. "My work in this parish is done. There are no God fearing people left. The only thing they fear is Whitehall and their angels of death. I have some relatives living in a remote part of North Wales. I think now is a good time to visit, at least until the insanity that has gripped the country is over."

"That could be a long wait, but thank you – for everything," replied Kendrick, gripping his hand firmly. The Pastor embraced Julianne and Harry and with a whispered "God be with you" departed into the night in the old Ford.

"Just one more thing to do," said Kendrick. The SUV was parked carelessly on a small, uneven patch of grass near the cottage. He raised his gun and smashed a window to get in, opened the bonnet and ripped out the ignition cables. He also shot out the communications console in the car, and the crack of the gunshot resounded in the still air. "That will slow them down," he grinned as he took the wheel of the large Range Rover. "Remind me to make an anonymous call to the SSP. It would be a shame if we forgot about them in that dark cellar."

Julianne and Harry climbed into the spacious vehicle and they bounced along the rutted path away from the remote cottage. Harry

lay back in the rear seats and within seconds he was fast asleep.

# REUTERS EDITORIAL OCTOBER 25

The United Nations Security Council today sat in emergency session at its headquarters in New York to discuss the growing humanitarian crisis unfolding in the United Kingdom. The question at hand was whether to impose UN Security Resolution Number 2817, which authorizes consideration of a close monitoring role and possible military solution to the current troubles in the U.K. Prior to the session, the U.K.'s representative at the UN was summoned to a private meeting with Kobie Emosi the Secretary-General, at which the SG allegedly accused Britain of 'waging war against its citizens.'

There are several complexities facing the UN in this case. Firstly there is the special relationship which Britain has with powerful allies such as the United States and India. These and many European countries have refused to consider the use of a military solution, not even as a last resort. The views on the Council, however, are deeply polarized, creating a political minefield. Russia, a permanent Council member, has advocated a firmer stance against Pelham, perhaps conscious of its own recent post-Communist history of dictatorial rule. Similarly the Middle Eastern and Asian nations, many of which have already closed U.K. embassies and expelled U.K. diplomatic staff from their land, have come out in open support of a military solution. This is not unexpected, given that most of the countries are predominantly Muslim, whose people are the largest group in Pelham's line of fire.

The second complication is the demographics of the nation. As Britain is an island, there is nowhere for refugees to go; they cannot escape the violence in a mass migration. Experts have predicted that if it was possible to do so, it would be the largest refugee exodus since the Syrian crisis over a decade ago, when over three million people spilled across local borders to escape the conflict. The people that the United Nations are trying to save are trapped in the country, with nowhere to go, and therefore potential hostages in any escalation of military force.

Another potential issue for the UN is the strength of the military forces in Britain. Despite its declining dominance as a world force, and the Great Recession that hit the middle classes so hard, defence spending has continued to rise significantly year on year; the U.K. has one of the largest, well trained and technologically sophisticated military forces in the Western world. If the UN attempted air strikes on military targets, it could potentially be repelled by the U.K.'s highly advanced air defence system. An aborted attempt would be a huge embarrassment for the United Nations, resulting in huge financial and reputation damage. Even if a force landed successfully, it could get dragged into the quagmire of the messy civil war already raging on the ground. The UN is walking a tightrope of credibility, under immense pressure to take strong action but concerned at the potential consequences. The failure of Pelham's regime to allow a UN inspection team on the mainland together with a terse refusal to allow a peacekeeping force to set foot on English soil has tested the Secretary General's patience to the limit.

Every day the UN fails to act is another day of bloodshed in the U.K. The economic sanctions imposed have so far failed to act as a deterrent, merely adding to the suffering of a people ravaged by the policies of their government. The nation's Conservative regime has openly criticized the use of sanctions, stating that it has achieved nothing except to hurt innocent people; and while it seems the government is doing precisely that, there is a certain credence to the assertion. The shortage of food and water has driven up prices in basic goods, and because the government has not only repelled the UN but also any non-governmental organizations (NGOs) such as the Red Cross, the distribution of scarce supplies is entirely in the hands of the military. The irony is that many aid agencies actually have their administrative offices in London.

It could be argued that economic sanctions have worked in the government's favour, as they are using the scarcity of supplies to 'smoke out' insurgents, essentially playing a waiting game. Nevertheless, the State forces are not idle, aggressively pursuing and crushing any pockets of resistance where they find it. The State Secret Police has issued a Kill List of known 'terrorists' and has made no secret of who is on it, projecting it onto the huge propaganda screens that dominate town centres, promising substantial rewards for anyone turning them in. It's a clever tactic to tempt the desperate hordes to betray their kinsmen as they struggle to survive any way they can in a hostile environment. The Kill List regards these so called 'terrorists' as legitimate targets for execution without trial, and authorizes military forces to shoot on sight. It is rumoured that the List has been personally sanctioned by Adam Griffiths, the Head of the State Secret Police and a man with a growing reputation for barbarity in his role as an enforcer within the government's brutal regime.

In desperation, rebel forces have taken to extreme tactics seen far too many times in the Middle Eastern conflict. This has included roadside bombs and suicide attacks, which, whilst aimed at military targets, are too indiscriminate to avoid civilian casualties. However, the rebel forces appear to regard these deaths as necessary collateral damage in the fight for freedom. None of the actors in this sectarian battle have covered themselves in glory. Another tactic of war, that of taking hostages to use as bargaining tools, has occasionally been used but with little success. The regime has shown little inclination to negotiate for the return of individuals kidnapped by rebel forces. Journalists and aid workers, a common target for hostage-takers, are noticeably absent, and key figures in the Party hierarchy are closely protected. As a result, there is little incentive to use this strategy.

With commercial flights currently suspended, and all ports effectively blockaded, there is virtually no movement in and out of the country. The only international transport is limited cargo and business traffic, and the occasional diplomatic flight as more embassies pull their delegates out of the country amidst rising tensions. Several people who escaped the country in this manner, interviewed by Reuters, have reported on the state of the nation, and it is a very different story to the information churning out from the State propaganda machine.

Highways are strewn with rotting corpses fed upon by legions of rats in the cold, damp conditions; long lines of internal refugees of all generations forced from their homes by lack of food and water or by escalating violence are trudging aimlessly from one town to another, a mass exodus to nowhere as there is no escape. It is a tide of human misery unprecedented in British history. For those able or brave enough to soldier on in their homes, the biggest issue is not so much the fear of violence or the threat of being blown up by a roadside bomb, it is the disruption to the routine of daily life. They tolerate the irritation of mains water being turned off regularly and long lines at water taps, the lack of clean water a particular problem, as well as the inconvenience of regular power cuts and scarcity of food in the shops. People trying to lead a normal, routine life are finding it increasingly difficult as the infrastructure continues to slowly disintegrate.

Amidst this increasingly anarchic background, the Prime Minister continues to spout his own brand of patriotism through the media, although it is some time since he has been seen in person. He continues to rage about the terrorists derailing a peaceful process, promising to root out the insurgents with an 'iron fist.' With the U.K. having become, to all intents and purposes, a closed country, the reliability of independent information and communications is a major issue.

Even so, the flow of information can never be totally blocked and reports filtering through suggest that despite the mysterious respiratory disease storming through the camps, the flow of trains transporting detainees to the barricaded coastal ports continues unabated, resulting in the displacement of many families. More sinister, however, is the fact that once the vast number of deportees arrive at the port ready to be loaded onto deportation boats, their fate is completely unknown. Still no country has claimed to receive British boats, and with the U.K. Navy jealously guarding its territorial waters, it is impossible to assess where the boats are heading.

Similarly, when the U.K.'s ministerial representative for the European Parliament was presented with testimony by many who had left the country that they strongly suspected the government had been guilty of perpetrating a number of atrocities related to the deportation camps across the country, he dismissed it as fantastical lies by people needing a good story to support their cowardly flight from the country.

A UN spokesperson, when questioned at this morning's Press conference, suggested that they were aware of 'one or two isolated acts of genocide,' to which one journalist retorted, "How many acts of genocide are needed before it becomes genocide?" It is indicative of the indecision that appears to have paralysed the UN as it grapples with the U.K. problem, but to which today's emergency meeting apparently yielded nothing new, with the possibility of air strikes or any other military intervention still seen as a last resort the UN is afraid to confront. Meanwhile, as the politicians continue to play political chess, a humanitarian catastrophe continues to unfold in front of a watching world.

# CHAPTER 42

It was one of those rare occasions when Pelham actually ventured outside the sanctuary of Whitehall and traversed the streets of London. The large SUV, with its heavily tinted windows, held no clues to the outside observer as to its occupants, but even so Chamberlain, sitting opposite Pelham in the spacious rear, knew the Prime Minister was taking a gamble. The convoy was deliberately light, at Pelham's instruction, to avoid attention being drawn to them. Although the unmarked vehicle with bulletproof windows was tailed discreetly by two other cars and had a car a hundred metres in front, the P.M. had too many enemies on the streets to feel safe. Chamberlain was well aware just how seriously his boss viewed matters on the ground.

The obligatory sentinel sat impassively in the corner, his heavily muscled frame spilling over his seat and his fleshy face inscrutable behind the mirror sunglasses. His driver was a highly skilled former police driver with thirty years' experience of car chases and lightning reflexes, employed after the assassination attempt in June. Even so, Chamberlain had reacted nervously when Pelham suggested a ride through the streets of London. In the gloomy light of a fresh late autumn day, they had crossed the rippling grey mass of the Thames across the Westminster Bridge and now headed south of the river through the Borough of Lambeth. Care was required crossing bridges as several had already been blown up by insurgents, and each major bridge was now manned by army checkpoints at both ends. They had to call ahead to obtain clearance and the reverential Corporal in charge allowed them through without any formalities, saluting stiffly as they passed by.

Pelham surveyed the panorama he had helped create, and Chamberlain observed a troubled look in his eyes. After his ebullience when he had been informed of the UN decision to suspend further action, this was a reality check for the P.M. A watery sun broke through the clouds, but it did little to dispel the gloom of the afternoon. There was traffic, but it was light, a fraction of the bustling activity that used to clog up every London street, even during the deepest part of the Great Recession. The roads were partly obstructed by the hulking shells of burnt out cars, steel skeletons abandoned to rot like dead animals picked at by carrion. On the sidewalks stood piles of steaming garbage, some of them scavenged by homeless people looking for anything to survive. The walls of the buildings lining the road were shabby, badly damaged and crumbling in places, pockmarked with bullet holes. The graffiti here was varied and colourful. One artistic rendition was a cruel parody of Pelham which exaggerated his angular features in a sinister fashion so that he looked like some hideous grimacing stick insect sporting a baton raised in anger. Chamberlain stifled a laugh as he saw the P.M. scowling at his parody. Next to the graffiti was a random splash of red, and Chamberlain realized that it was not red paint.

The streets were relatively quiet, apart from the odd distant *rat-a-tat-tat* of gunfire, but the threat of violence hung in the air. It was difficult to explain, because it could be neither seen nor heard, just perceived. Chamberlain felt it, and he muttered briefly to the driver through the glass dividing screen. It was the type of area where gangs could appear from a building or back alley in a split second and ambush the car, and the driver needed to stay alert. The driver just nodded, clearly irritated that the Deputy P.M. tried to tell him how to do a job he had done for thirty years with distinction.

They took a right turn along St. George's Road and headed toward the huge traffic circle of Elephant and Castle. The iconic red Elephant with a castle turret atop its back on a large plinth still towered over the surrounding roads, remarkably intact; however, its concrete hide was pockmarked with a succession of bullet holes, as if it had been used for target practice. The turret walls were crumbling too, a symbol of the decay of its surroundings. Near the monument was another plinth, and this one supported a huge television monitor, on which a government spokesman, his face twisted in rage, wagged his finger at his audience and spouted his propaganda to the proletariat.

They passed the entrance to the Elephant and Castle shopping centre, the vaulted glass entrance now a broken shell, barricaded with wooden boards where the glass lay shattered on the ground. There were still a few people milling around the entrance, picking their way through the broken glass to reach inside the mall, but Chamberlain knew that at this time of day, just before rush hour, this place would have been heaving with bodies a year or two before. The area had lost its vibrancy. A place that was in constant movement at any time of the day was now quiet, apart from the furious bleating from the overhead screen, but it held an undercurrent of malice. People moved furtively and with caution, afraid to be there. Their anxiety was compounded by the sight of PIA soldiers leisurely patrolling the streets, caressing their weapons. Suddenly from nowhere a small blast shook a nearby pub fifty yards up the road from their car. Glass from shattered windows sprayed onto the sidewalk and masonry was hurled onto the road. Everyone in the surrounding area instinctively dived to the ground, and a number of people struck by shrapnel from the small but powerful explosion fell and lay motionless on the floor. The shrill racket of a fire alarm rippled through the air, followed quickly by a police siren. The driver sped forward and swerved around the devastation. Pelham peered at the half dozen figures lying motionless on the red-stained road as they hurried past.

Chamberlain turned to Pelham. "Well Lance, have you seen enough?"

Pelham stroked his chin as he stared out the window, deep in thought. Chamberlain detected a few hints of grey in the day-old stubble, a far cry from his polished clean-cut public persona. Pelham turned to his Deputy. "I knew the UN would not have the balls to take action against us. It vindicates our approach Giles. We continue down this road. We have a clear run."

"But the UN could easily reverse their position," protested Chamberlain. "A number of the Muslim States are lobbying the Secretary-General to force another debate. We may have got a reprieve for now but for how long? They are already asking tough questions about the fate of the deportation boats."

Pelham's eyes narrowed in irritation. "Let them ask," he snapped. "There is absolutely no way we can allow these refugees to reach other shores and spread lies that will derail our project. Part of our invulnerability is to close the loop on the information flow." He adjusted the cuff-links on his neatly pressed Jermyn Street shirt with finely manicured fingers. "History will judge me, Giles. They will see that I did the right thing for this country."

As Pelham said this, his Deputy glanced out of the window where he saw a gaunt, elderly man dressed in rags rifling through a pile of garbage. As they passed by, he saw a gang of youths emerge from a side alley, and spotting the old man, immediately began to surround him. The car moved on and the scene was gone, like a fleeting image in a movie. Chamberlain turned to Pelham, and his voice was hesitant. "Lance, do you sometimes wonder if we have been too premature? Is the nation ready for this? According to our source, there were many English people standing toe to toe with immigrants during the Bristol riots a few days ago. Have we chosen a dangerous path for ourselves?"

Pelham's tone was faintly mocking but his eyes were cold. "Are you losing your nerve Giles? I have begun to doubt even you lately."

Chamberlain let out a tense laugh. "Of course not."

"Good, because if you are with me it has to be one hundred per cent."

"Lance, you know I will stand by you to the bitter end." The words felt sour to Chamberlain even as he said them.

"The end will not be bitter," countered Pelham. "It will be a glorious success. I admit as I look around now, it does not look that way, but we still have the old bulldog spirit that has won us every war we have fought. I left the people in no doubt that the road would be long and hard and full of sacrifice, and those that really matter in this country are still behind us. We have to look at the longer term, not just the five year plan but beyond that, even to the next generation. By then the disease will have rooted out the weak and Britain will be free of immigrants. The experiments we are conducting now will ensure that we have a beautifully crafted race that will be stronger, healthier and more pure than any race on this planet. It calls for patience but it also requires clear thinking and a firm resolve."

Chamberlain consulted his tablet, its blue light bathing his face in an effervescent glow, more pronounced as the gloomy sky began to darken. "There are still a number of liberal factions alive and well, and if they found out about our facility in Watford there would be further riots. We will eventually root them out and destroy all of them, but that process will take time."

Pelham snorted derisively. "It's the bloody liberals that have always acted as a ball and chain on progress. Medical research has been hampered by ethical considerations throughout time, but ask any of those liberals if they had children with cystic fibrosis or Down syndrome would they change their views? If we could cure those children do you really think the parents would care how? The liberals are nothing better than hypocrites impeding progress. They complain about using animals for experiments, but would they really care about a rhesus monkey or a gaggle of albino mice if their child was restored to health? Now we have better subjects than animals, and unhampered by the chains of ethical considerations and the lack of live human guinea pigs, we can make progress faster than ever before. The potential to achieve great advances is unlimited." He paused, and muttered almost to himself, "I can see my father's dream coming true."

Chamberlain shot him an odd glance. He could not recall Pelham ever having mentioned his father. He desperately wanted to follow up but Pelham had made it clear throughout their relationship that his family background was a closed book. Instead he decided to stroke his ego. "You're right Lance. It takes true genius to see it," he said sycophantically. "We stick to the path and never waver, whatever the pressure."

"Exactly," replied Pelham with a sharp grin. "Tell Griffiths to deliver me the Kill List within the next hour. I want to review it when we are back at Downing Street. Find out as well what happened with Harry Clarke. I understand Griffiths authorized a pursuit team when Clarke materialized in Salisbury. They surely must have found him by now, so why have I not been informed? I hope they have not killed him; he could be useful to us."

Chamberlain tapped away at his tablet. "I'll find out immediately Lance."

The driver tapped on the glass partition that separated the rear compartment, and Chamberlain pulled back the glass curtain. "What is it?" he said, his voice betraying irritation.

The driver's keen eyes showed concern. "I'm sorry to disturb you sir, but I've lost contact with the lead car. They're not responding to my instant messaging."

"When did you last hear from them?"

"Sir, we agreed to message every two minutes." He pointed to the road ahead which curved around a bend, flanked on either side by tall, close buildings. "They turned around the bend two minutes ago so they should have been in touch by now. George is pretty reliable. Something's wrong."

"Continue, but stay cautious," instructed Chamberlain.

"Yessir," replied the driver, who fiddled with his on-board tablet, still trying to reach the front car. They rounded the bend and the driver slammed on the brakes and expertly engaged the reverse gear. Facing them was an angry mob, and it was surging forward, a mass of seething humanity. The driver, trained to spot little details even in high stress situations, identified George's car flipped on its side, flames pouring out from the broken windows, the crowd weaving around it. The driver could not tell if George or his co-driver were in there, but even if they had escaped the wreckage he did not rate their chances. As the car spun around, the driver shouted over his shoulder, "Hold tight!"

The world outside spun like a crazy fairground ride and the three occupants in the rear pivoted in their seats, thankful for their seat-belts. From nowhere a heavy thud hit the chassis, followed by two more. "They've got guns, stay down!" screamed the driver. The mob was heading in the direction of the pub that had suffered the blast, and they were moving fast. A faint smell of burning tyres wafted into the interior as the driver expertly swung the car back in the direction it had come, but just as the car was positioned to escape the throbbing mass, Pelham screamed in panic. Another car, veering crazily out of control, slammed into the side of the SUV on the Prime Minister's side. It struck with such force that its front end crumpled forward and the driver sprang forward before his belt restrained him and he snapped back like a marionette, his head lolling crazily. The SUV's reinforced aluminium side impact bars absorbed the severe collision intact. However, the engine stalled and the government car was impeded by other traffic that, similar to the driver that hit them, was desperately trying to turn around in the face of the advancing human wall.

The driver turned the engine over but it failed to start. Suddenly the angry mob reached them and the inside of the car vibrated with the hammering and beating of hands and feet on the chassis. Although the SUV was sound-proofed, the muted roar of tempestuous voices penetrated the vehicle. The bodyguard pressed his bulky frame between Pelham and the near window, but Chamberlain spotted a look of abject fear on the Prime Minister's face. Only the tinted glass stood between them and the murderous sea of faces pressed against the car. Chamberlain shuddered at the thought of what they would do if they could see inside the car at its occupants.

The enraged face of a toothless old man with brown leathery skin, a straggly grey beard and a skull cap pressed against the window. He held up a piece of paper and gesticulated as if he could see them. On it was a photograph of a gallows and hanging limply from it was a figure with the face of the Prime Minister, his tongue lolling from a bloated face turned blue from the noose that cut into his neck. It was an expertly produced fake photograph, genuine enough to leave Pelham visibly shaken.

He had little time to recover his composure before an axe came crashing against the window. Its owner, however, was astonished that his wild swing had merely dented the glass and he took another frenzied swing. The window cracked but held firm.

"Get this bloody car moving!" screamed Chamberlain at the driver.

The driver, hands shaking, knew he had mere seconds before the crush of bodies would be too great for him to drive through. He turned the key again and this time the engine roared into life. He immediately engaged the forward gear and the car, its engine racing nudged forward through the bodies, pushing people aside who yelled and hammered on the vehicle. Every face was a mass of seething hatred, enraged that the vehicle was getting away. Some people tried to hang onto the vehicle, but fell away as they collided with other members of the mob pressing around the car. The SUV pushed through, revving noisily until the driver saw a gap in the crowd and he increased speed. A few brave or crazy people tried to impede the car in the thinning crowd but they were brushed aside, and Chamberlain heard the solid bump of metal against bone. The SUV jolted as it ran over something and Chamberlain glanced back through the rear windscreen to see a figure lying on the floor clutching his leg which protruded at an odd angle. The crowd dispersed further and the driver sped away, relieved to be clear of the hostile crowd. They immediately returned to Downing Street without stopping as darkness and the insidious threat that accompanied it closed in.

# CHAPTER 43

"I heard our glorious leader had a little scare tonight." Chamberlain detected a trace of amusement in Rachel's voice. She sat back on the deep pile cushions on her sofa, visibly more relaxed in her own apartment than in the shadowy corridors they had met in last time. Dressed in a casual lounge suit, her toned legs folded up on the sofa, she sipped at her gin and tonic, leaving faint smudge marks from her lipstick around the glass. In the gentle glow of the wall lights, Chamberlain could understand a little more why Pelham was so besotted with her. Rachel's refined features were soft and beguiling, a natural beauty that hinted at the fires within, an underlying passion and zest for life. She was gifted with an athletic body that had a subtle sexuality to it, even if it was understated in the loose fitting jumpsuit that failed to do justice to her curves. Perhaps, thought Chamberlain, he could take more than just his boss's position.

"I have something for you," continued Rachel.

Lost in his train of thought, Chamberlain felt a twinge of excitement and immediately dismissed it. Now was not the time. "What is it?" he said. It was she who had asked him to her apartment. He had to admit that meeting in the Parliamentary chambers was risky, even at this late hour, but a small part of him had wondered, had *hoped,* that it was to do more than just trade information.

Pelham had not summoned his mistress tonight, too disturbed by the events of the day to have any appetite even for Rachel's vivacious charms. He had called Rachel, explaining that Helen was back from one of her charitable ventures, and their little trysts would have to cease for a week. She had graciously accepted his call, secretly relieved. She had felt a creeping revulsion toward him but had no idea how to extricate herself from this toxic relationship. He was used to people bending to his will, particularly since he had assumed power. Rachel had the feeling that he would not take rejection well. He had the power to destroy her personally and professionally and she had worked too hard, made too many sacrifices to throw it all away.

She sat up straight and picked up her tablet with her long, delicate fingers. "Duncan Cavendish. What do you know about him?"

Chamberlain shrugged. "Never heard of him. Should I have?"

"A few things that Lance revealed to me set me thinking. His father was a biochemist but he refused to elaborate. Clearly he had been a successful one because we know that Lance went to the finest schools. I did some more research, clutching at straws really, looking at prominent biochemists between twenty-five and forty-five years older than Lance, a similar age to what I expect his father would be. It was a needle in a haystack, and I am sure investigative journalists tried to crack open his background back in the time before they were imprisoned or silenced. It was almost by chance that I came across this."

She patted the sofa next to her, inviting Chamberlain to sit beside her. As he settled next to her he could smell the delicate musky scent of her perfume. Her eyes seemed to glow in the light of the tablet and he followed her gaze at the small screen. On it was a picture of a tall, proud looking man in his forties with his arms around a thin but boyishly handsome lad no more than eleven or twelve. The man was unfamiliar to Chamberlain but when he saw the boy, he had to do a double take. Like Rachel, he knew instantly the identity of the boy. It was the headline that grabbed his attention.

"Whoa. Twenty-five years in prison." Chamberlain whistled in shock. "No wonder Lance never talks about him. Oddly enough he muttered a comment today almost to himself about his father's dreams coming true. I don't even think he meant me to hear it. A white supremacist no less. I wonder if he is still alive."

"I doubt we would be able to find out. Look at the rest of the article. Wherever I look for references to Duncan Cavendish - and there are quite a few - they are all deleted." Rachel deftly flicked through a few other articles that referenced Cavendish, screen shots of old newspapers from a time when they were printed, all of which had the same thick black lines scrawled through the text. "Even with my access privileges, I seem to have hit a brick wall. I need you to help me take this further."

Chamberlain sat back on the firm cushions, enjoying the subtle ambience of Rachel's lounge. He tapped his chin thoughtfully and turned to Rachel. "Leave it with me. I think I know who can help."

He turned and looked into her clear blue eyes. "We make a good team, you and I Rachel." His breathing was shorter and the rhythmic drumming of his heart beat in his ears.

She gave a short laugh. "Yes we certainly do."

He moved imperceptibly closer so that their thighs touched. "I think we want the same things," he said in a low whisper.

She let out another nervous laugh and turned away from his keen gaze. "Yes we need to impeach him as soon as possible."

"I don't mean that." She could feel his hot breath on her neck and she moved back slightly, uncomfortable at his physical proximity. Even in his suit she could tell that he was in good physical shape, and for a fleeting moment she thought how ruggedly handsome he was.

Chamberlain reached forward to kiss Rachel and his hand lightly brushed her breasts.

She pulled away and pushed at him. "No!" she cried. "What do you think you're doing?"

Chamberlain backed away and stood up, smoothing down his tie. He could feel the heat rising in his cheeks. "I thought you wanted the same," he hissed.

"You thought wrong Giles. This is a business arrangement!" She stood up and pointed to the door, her hand trembling. "I think you should leave."

With a sense of deep embarrassment, he strode out, suddenly anxious to leave as quickly as possible, but he turned back before he left. "This project is too important to jeopardize, Rachel. Forget this ever happened. I will be in touch."

She nodded, barely able to look at him, her own feelings in turmoil. "Okay. Just go."

As Chamberlain reached his car, he slapped the bonnet in frustration, and drove away fast with a screech of burning rubber, sending a pair of rats scurrying for the sewer. He was furious with himself, angry that he had misread the situation. As he drove he grew calmer, nursing his bruised ego. He was not used to rejection and a creeping sense of animosity began stirring within him. How dare she refuse his advances! He was the deputy Prime Minister, a powerful man who like his boss was used to getting what he wanted. Yes she was beautiful and yes he desired her, but she was little better than an intern made good. What made Pelham so much more attractive than him? What right did she have to turn him down? The project would continue and she would help him achieve his political goals, but she had also crossed him, and he never forgot...

# CHAPTER 44

Harry barely remembered the long drive back through the Welsh countryside. They only reached the checkpoint on the English border in the early afternoon and Harry had slept the whole way. It was a rehabilitating sleep, a chance to purge the toxic experiences of the recent past. Several times, however, he recalled waking up screaming, only for his exhausted body to drift back into another abyss that was either dreamless and cathartic, or filled with nightmarish visions as his mind sought to process all he had seen.

He became vaguely aware that Kendrick had taken a different route to cross the border into England, avoiding the heavily guarded Severn Bridge checkpoint. He later learned that they took a huge detour along the Severn River north-east toward Gloucester where they were able to cross the border without incident. It made their journey considerably longer, and Harry was deposited in the trunk of the Range Rover during an anxious pass through. Only Kendrick's status as a police officer could secure them safe passage and ensure that the soldiers on patrol, most of whom were young, bored and lazy, failed to take their job seriously and search the car.

The next stage of the drive was the long road to London. Whilst they were anxious to get there as soon as possible, Kendrick urged caution and they rested during the remainder of the daylight, hiding out in woodland near Gloucester. They continued their journey as night fell with Kendrick at the wheel, his face gritted in concentration as they drove through the night. With no lights either on the motorway or on any smaller roads, and Kendrick using only side lights to avoid attention, the drive was through an interminable blackness. It reminded Harry of a time many years before in his old life as a political correspondent, when he had driven in Cameroon from the coastal city of Douala to the capital Yaoundé on an international assignment to monitor the local election. It had that same claustrophobic, primitive feel, as if they were light years from any trace of civilization.

The inky black hid all manner of potential menace; huge potholes from poorly maintained roads were a constant threat; the wreckage of recent conflict strewn across the road, including the rotting corpses of casualties; and the fatal habit of gangs trying to hijack drivers by pushing the rusting carcasses of wrecked or abandoned cars in the middle of the road. All of this contrived to make progress painfully slow at night. Technically the emergency laws were still in force, which meant a curfew outside of daylight hours, and the prospect of encountering a roadside patrol. Despite travelling for most of the night without incident, they had only reached the outskirts of Oxford by daybreak, over twenty-four hours after they had begun their journey. Although they were less than sixty miles from Central London, the risk of encountering a patrol was greater as they skirted the commuter belt of the vast metropolitan area.

This became plainly obvious to them when, just as the sun was creeping over the horizon on a crisp but clear day, the travellers turned a bend in the road and were suddenly confronted by a convoy of four armoured personnel carriers trundling rapidly toward them. The wide, squat vehicles moved steadily along the middle of the road, completely blocking it. They were decorated in combat green and the chassis sat on huge wheels, lending them an imposing presence. Kendrick quickly concluded that there was no getting past them. The vehicles had mortar guns fixed on each side of the small turret. The weapons could destroy the car and its occupants so completely that there would be nothing left of them but a scorch mark on the ground. Kendrick immediately switched off all lights on the Range Rover and swerved off the road. They were adjacent to a field of corn and the robust vehicle bounced and jolted as it thrashed its way through the tall ears of corn until they emerged onto a narrow dirt track that ran along the opposite side of the field.

They stayed in the car, Julianne gingerly rubbing her elbow which she had whacked against the door handle, and waited. Harry could hear Kendrick's tense breathing as he stared at the convoy. With a low growl, the armoured vehicles pushed on forward relentlessly along the road as if the Range Rover and its occupants either had not been spotted or were of too little consequence to pursue. Kendrick heaved a huge sigh of relief. "It's far too dangerous to continue in daylight despite the curfew. We'll find a place here to shelter and continue tonight. The patrols are sure to increase as we get closer to the city."

They continued along the dirt track until they reached a small area of woodland that skirted a group of fields, and set up camp there. They still had water and a few supplies the Pastor had handed to Julianne, and shared some bread and jam, careful to conserve a little just in case, although they expected to reach their destination that night.

Kendrick looked around him. There was nothing but fields and woodland, and a derelict farmhouse in the distance. "I guess it won't hurt to have a small camp fire. I'm desperate for a cup of tea. I'll go and find some dry wood if there is any."

The police officer discreetly trudged off into the bush and within seconds he was lost amongst the trees. The ground was damp from the morning dew, and there was a carpet of brown leaves in the small clearing where Harry and Julianne sat together on a log. Julianne stared in the direction Kendrick had taken until she was certain he had gone. She then turned conspiratorially toward Harry, who was yawning and rubbing his injured leg.

"How is it?" she said, pointing to his thigh, which was enlarged by the bandages and strapping under his trousers.

"Very sore," he replied.

"We may not have much time. We never finished our conversation. I know you're sceptical Harry but keep an open mind. They're not just a bunch of computer geeks as you so eloquently phrased it. They can make a difference. *You* can make a difference."

The hoot of an owl sounded somewhere amongst the trees. The emerging day was chilly but there was a serenity about the place that provided a pleasant interlude from chaos. There was no sound of gunfire; no human voices raised in anger, in fact no trace of any other humans at all. In places like this it was hard to believe the country was in the grip of a sectarian war.

Julianne continued. "As I said back at the cottage, our victories have so far been modest, but we have managed to penetrate the military communications traffic a number of times. In the cases where we have been able to determine where units have been headed we have had an eighty per cent success rate with roadside bombs. That's an incredible statistic Harry. Usually this type of attack is random and its success is dependent on pure luck. If we know from the messages where they are headed then we can target them more effectively. It enables us to use our scarce weapon resources more effectively."

Harry brushed away a small spider that had emerged from a hollow in the log and was gently running up his leg. "A few roadside bombs will not hurt this regime. I have seen their raw power and the lengths they're prepared to go to."

"Yes, but look at the wider picture Harry. It may be a few roadside bombs now but what if we can make an effective hit on their infrastructure? This regime is the most reliant in history on technology, not just to keep the regime in power, but to run all the essential services. Transport, energy, hospitals, finance, communications and most importantly for them, their defence systems, are all dependent on automated cyber-based controls, most of which are online and vulnerable to attack. No one flicks switches anymore. Can you imagine if we were able to infiltrate these systems and knock them out, strike silently and efficiently with devastating effect when they least expect it? They would never know where and when the next attack was coming from. A continuous round of high profile attacks would weaken and undermine the government to such an extent that it would render it unsustainable, particularly if we could halt the military. We would probably have to bring the country to its knees but then it is not that far off in any event. No one wants anarchy, least of all this government. Maybe this could be the catalyst for the people to stand up and fight."

Harry glanced at Julianne. He saw the same raw passion; the sparkle in her hazel eyes that had first mesmerized him so long ago.

"You always made a convincing case Julianne. I can see you truly believe in this but I think this government is too powerful. I agree that this shadow organization of yours can score a few isolated victories but they will be precisely that; no more than an annoyance."

Julianne shook her head vigorously, her long red locks glinting in the early morning sun. "No you don't understand." Her tone was urgent, almost pleading. "This regime is complacent to cyber-attacks. Perhaps it reflects Pelham's arrogance to think that his power base is indestructible. This is our best opportunity. Talk to Chen and you will understand. We can strike from within; Pelham's biggest enemy will be literally on his doorstep."

Harry gave a weak smile. "Do I have a choice?"

Julianne sighed and put her hand on his. "Of course you do Harry, but let's face it your options are limited. You know that escaping the country is impossible, so how long will it be before they catch up with you? You had a SSP unit pursuing you. Don't you think they'll try again especially after you had the audacity to escape from them? We're all in the firing line now but you are a highly prized asset. They will find you."

She stroked his fingers and it felt comforting to Harry. His eyes were red and blotchy from constantly interrupted sleep, but she peered intently into them. "Harry you can be a great asset to us but it's not just about that. When Kendrick contacted me, I knew I had to find you. Despite the risks, Chen allowed me to go. He could hardly refuse. He understood precisely why I needed to go, not just for what you could do for us." She squeezed his fingers. "I need you too Harry." Julianne reached forward to kiss him but as their lips brushed he pulled back. She frowned and let go of his hand. An awkward silence passed between them, punctuated only by the shrill call of a starling high up in the trees.

"I'm sorry Julianne. I need more time. I still can't help thinking of Tamara and Byron."

Julianne could not disguise the hurt in her voice. "I know Harry, but the best thing you can do for them is to fight this evil regime. As remote as it is, it's your only chance of seeing them again. Please come with me."

"Where is this cyber cell of yours?"

"You'll see Harry. When I said that Pelham's biggest enemy was on his doorstep, I literally meant it."

They were interrupted by a crack of twigs under heavy boots and Kendrick emerged from the undergrowth. He had very little wood in his arms but his cellphone was pressed to his ear. He spoke a curt "Okay" into the phone and rang off, putting the phone in an inside pocket of his woollen coat. As he did so, his hand lingered there and he pulled out his Glock pistol. He turned it over in his hands, like he was cradling a toy, and then abruptly pointed it at his two companions.

# CHAPTER 45

The summons was not completely unexpected but as Bruce read the message, a cold shiver passed down his spine. It was from the very top and it had been signed off by Griffiths' Chief of Staff, an old bulldog named Ramsey. When they had been rescued after nearly two days from the dark, dank basement by their colleagues at the State Secret Police following an anonymous phone call, they had been flown back to headquarters in Whitehall to await debriefing. The flight in an old Chinook helicopter had been short but tense. There had been no suggestion that they were under arrest or in any trouble, but they had been closely supervised by six armed SSP operatives, which Bruce felt was complete overkill, quite apart from the fact that they were too weak from hunger to be any threat.

The trio had begun the debriefing together, but had been quickly separated. Bruce was searched and relieved of the one small knife he had managed to hide from Kendrick. They took him to a small interrogation room with metallic furniture and blindingly harsh overhead lights that cast stark shadows. He was questioned by two interrogators for nearly three hours. They were curt but civil, but never took off their ski masks. Bruce had to admit he found it intimidating, especially when they traded glances with each other. The questions came fast and the interrogators probed ceaselessly, extracting every small detail from him, each question like a trap, waiting for Bruce to contradict himself. He realized it looked bad, especially as he was the leader of the trio, and tried futilely to shift the blame onto Ethan. Bruce knew they were not convinced of his reasons for the failed mission, but when one of them consulted his tablet as it pinged, they abruptly left the room, leaving him alone in the clinical surroundings.

His own tablet gently chimed and it was then that he saw the Chief's message. He was to report immediately to the office of the leader himself, Adam Griffiths. His legs felt weak as he stepped out of the room, relieved to be free of the harsh glare, but both interrogators were waiting outside. It was difficult to place any characteristics on them when all he could see were their cold, expressionless eyes, but the taller one, the more aggressive interviewer, nodded briefly and in a gruff voice said simply, "Follow me." Bruce complied and the stocky, shorter interrogator walked behind the pair as they passed through the labyrinthine corridors until they reached an area that was plush and carpet-lined with paintings of old Masters on the wall, like the executive C-suite of a major corporation. They reached a set of sealed glass doors and were ushered in by the Chief of Staff who flicked a switch and the doors swung open. The outer office was spacious and luxurious, with several staff working quietly at their desks. Ramsey even had the saggy jowls of a bulldog, and as he led them through he scowled at them, revealing deep ingrained furrows in his brow from his perpetual habit. Legend had it that no one in the SSP had ever seen him smile, and now seeing him in person for the first time, Bruce could well believe it. He directed them to a plush sofa and they waited there until Ramsey received a signal and the grandiose mahogany doors to Griffiths' office gently opened inwards, as if gliding on air. The Chief of Staff led them through into the spacious inner sanctum.

Griffiths' office was a symbol of his precipitous rise through the political ranks. The Head of the People's Independent Army and the State Secret Police, he was as much a senior figure and confidante in Pelham's regime as any Cabinet Minister. Two sides of his corner office housed huge, expansive windows offering commanding views of the London skyline from its eighth story vantage point. On a large bureau table set to one side was a large photograph of Griffiths shaking hands warmly with the Prime Minister like old friends.

Bruce never had the honour to meet him before but his status and ruthless reputation were legendary amongst the SSP. Bruce had been a follower when Griffiths had been the head of the neo-Nazi FREE group, which before the election of the current government had been a fringe organization, considered a criminal group before it gained huge credibility in furthering the Prime Minister's agenda.

Griffiths was considered a faithful Lieutenant to Pelham, the type of ruthless and dogged enforcer that the government needed to push its immigration policies through. He was in full black combat uniform, as if he was just about to parade into the field with his loyal followers from the PIA or the SSP. He stood behind his huge mahogany desk, hands behind his back, peering out at the grey River Thames snaking through the City on a dreary, rain-swept day. Griffiths was wiry, not as lean as Bruce, but when he turned around his expression carried the arrogance of high office. His dark eyes appraised Bruce, and his inimical stare made the SSP officer deeply nervous. Bruce saluted stiffly and said "Sir!" loudly but Griffiths merely gave a curt nod. The two interrogators stood close behind Bruce and the dynamics of the situation made him feel weak with trepidation. Griffiths did not offer a chair, though there were several plush armchairs on the deep pile carpet.

Griffiths settled into the black leather chair behind his desk and with his black outfit merging into the seat, it almost gave the impression of a disembodied head. He picked up his tablet and briefly studied it before he steepled his fingers and sat back nonchalantly. "Bruce Campbell, senior intelligence operative, six years' service in the regular army including one year in Special Forces before a dishonourable discharge; former FREE operative, three years in prison following a conviction for grievous bodily harm to a Pakistani taxi driver. Highly skilled in unarmed combat, weapons training and pursuit techniques; considered a natural leader. All very impressive. You were the right person for the job, or so we thought." He left the sentence hanging threateningly and Bruce felt compelled to fill the uncomfortable void.

"Yes sir. Thank you."

Griffiths continued as if he hadn't heard Bruce. "Only you were not the right man for the job. You let Harry Clarke get away and now he has disappeared. He is one of the most high profile criminals on our target list. You were assigned to track him down and you failed."

Bruce felt the sweat trickling down his neck. "Sir I can explain-"

Griffiths held up his hand and his expression stopped Bruce in his tracks. "I wasn't asking for an explanation, Campbell. You've had the debriefing. I'm only interested in the bare facts. You were sent on a mission for the skills you were alleged to possess and you failed in that mission. I was asked personally by the Prime Minister himself to acquire Harry Clarke and I assured him that it would be done. I have had to call Mr. Pelham and explain that we failed to catch him. This was at deep personal embarrassment and loss of credibility. Mr. Pelham does not take failure well. There is only one person I know who hates failure more than he does." He left the statement hanging in the air for emphasis. "And that's me."

Bruce felt the walls closing in and the rush of cortisone through his body made his legs wobble. He didn't know whether to pour out a bunch of mitigating excuses or stay silent. His conflict was quickly resolved as Griffiths continued. "I asked a subordinate to research your background and it would appear that you should have registered as an immigrant under the Minorities Registration Act."

Bruce's blood ran cold. "W-What do you mean?" he stuttered.

"It's quite simple. Your maternal grandmother was born in Portugal but became a British citizen at age three. Under one of the Statutory Instruments passed in conjunction with the Act, we have the retroactive power to revoke the citizenship of any U.K. resident born outside of these shores. We found that the grounds for her citizenship were deficient by modern standards and therefore we invoked the power. She is no longer a British citizen. That means that your mother, whilst born in England, does not qualify under the lineage test as she is not the necessary two-thirds English lineage. Whilst the place of birth is a contributing factor, it is parentage that the law is most concerned with. Therefore as only one of your mother's parents under the test is English, that makes her subject to registration under the Act. Quod Erat Demonstrandum– If your mother cannot be considered as pure English lineage, then under the two-thirds test neither can you."

Bruce fought to suppress a rising panic. His throat was too constricted to speak.

Griffiths continued, his voice even and matter-of-fact. "I don't need to tell you what that means. We have sent a unit to collect your grandmother and mother and they will be transferred to the nearest deportation camp as soon as practical. I'm afraid that registered minorities are not eligible to serve in the State Secret Police for obvious reasons, and so I accept your resignation."

Bruce finally found his voice. "You can't do this!" he shouted in protest.

Griffiths gave the merest flick of his eyes beyond Bruce and the two SSP agents standing close behind him suddenly grabbed his arms and wrenched them behind his back. One held his arms in a vice-like grip while the other clapped on a pair of steel handcuffs.

"It's already done."

His body felt too numb to resist as he was dragged away and in a hoarse voice he shouted, "For God's sake, just take me, spare my family!"

However, the doors were already closing and his last glimpse of Griffiths was with a narcissistic grin on his face. Bruce knew all too well the implications of being sent to a deportation camp. He suddenly understood the primal fear of all the poor souls he had ruthlessly pursued and bullied in the name of the government.

# CHAPTER 46

Harry and Julianne sat on the log, stupefied, staring into the barrel of Kendrick's pistol. The older policeman looked pensive as he turned to Harry. "I could get decorated for bringing you in. There's a bounty on your head that makes you a highly prized asset. I've just come off a call with Grayson. He tells me I will have to be careful if I am to deliver you without the SSP getting in the way. There are lots of patrols and the checkpoints could present a problem. He told me the social media chatter suggests the secret police want you badly."

Harry eyed him cautiously but said nothing. He remembered Julianne's reservations about Kendrick, how she did not entirely trust him. From his peripheral vision he saw her stiffen and inch away. The tension in the air was palpable, but was unexpectedly broken by a throaty laugh from Kendrick.

"On no, no, no!" he bellowed. "It's not like that! Here." He handed the pistol to Harry who hesitantly accepted it, bemused by the turn of events. "I didn't mean to scare you, but I am a little disappointed that you thought so badly of me."

Harry stole a glance at Julianne. Her face was flushed deep red, but she said nothing. Kendrick continued. "It's okay, I'm not judging you. It's hard to know who to trust anymore. That is what this government has done. It has divided loyalties, and made families and friends suspicious of each other, wondering who will betray them." Kendrick rested his solid frame on the log and closed his eyes wearily. "You're going to need that gun Harry. I need you to shoot me in the shoulder."

"What on earth are you talking about?"

The detective shrugged pensively. "Grayson knows I got you this far. He is expecting me to deliver you to him later today. He even got up early to take my call. That callous bugger wants to bask in the glory of leading the operation to capture one of the most wanted men in Britain. Only I won't get the opportunity because you escape by trying to steal my gun and in the ensuing struggle you shoot me in the shoulder before making your escape."

"I can't possibly do that!"

"Harry, this is not a choice," urged Kendrick, taking back the gun for now. "As it is he will chew me up and spit me out. But if he even suspects that my loyalties are not one hundred percent on the job then I will be finished. He will turn me in as an enemy of the State and the only trace of me will be another name on the Remembrance Wall. You have to shoot me, just not yet. Let's get there first."

They waited until twilight to continue their journey and Harry was able to sleep fitfully, his slumber disrupted by disturbing dreams. Julianne stayed alert, observing Kendrick, still unconvinced despite his overtures. At intervals during the day, they heard the rumble of passing military convoys, and when they started out on the last leg of their journey Kendrick warned them this would be the most hazardous.

"There are parts of London that have become no-go areas. It's difficult to get much information through the social media, so we have to stay focused and alert for trouble, especially as we reach inner London. I can guarantee that we will get stopped, so we must be prepared for that. Grayson has told me to pass through the Shepherd's Bush checkpoint. He has issued a pass to us which the soldiers manning the checkpoint will have, so hopefully we should be able to cross without trouble. My biggest concern is if we are stopped by a random patrol." He let out a rueful laugh. "And, of course, there's also the risk of being hit by sniper fire or running into a blockade."

Despite Kendrick's warnings, the journey into London passed without incident. They passed only one patrol near the North Circular Road and saw it early so they were able to pull off the road and sit tight until the three jeeps passed by. Shortly before they arrived at the designated checkpoint well within the perimeter of the city, they stopped the car and Julianne was deposited in the trunk. Harry was manacled to the door handle so that he was immobilized. As they pulled up slowly to the large black pole set across the road, a soldier in the small wooden hut at the side of the barrier shone a blinding white light into the cab. Kendrick shielded his eyes from the dazzling glare of the powerful lamp as another soldier strode up to the car and tapped harshly on the window.

Kendrick wound it down and found a large rifle pointed in his face. The hollow-cheeked soldier was young, still a teenager, and Kendrick noticed his hands shaking. His deep set, bloodshot eyes sunk further as he gave a confused frown when he saw the other passenger handcuffed to the door. Kendrick quietly explained the situation and the boy nodded curtly and went off to verify the police officer's story.

"The lad looks petrified. I thought the only child soldiers were in the Congo," commented Kendrick quietly. Other young soldiers manned the checkpoint, staring balefully at the car and its two occupants. A few tense minutes later the first soldier came jogging back and his expression was not promising. He appraised Kendrick coolly. "Get out of the car!"

The detective exchanged a furtive glance with Harry and complied, and the soldier pushed him against the bonnet of the Range Rover and began to search him, his bony fingers digging into Kendrick's body. Two other soldiers stood close by, alert for trouble.

"Any weapons?" asked the soldier tersely.

"Just my police issue Glock," replied Kendrick. He briefly wondered if Grayson had set him up but abruptly the adolescent soldier stopped the search and casually said, "You're clear. You can move on."

Kendrick muttered a surprised "Thanks!" got in the car and quickly drove through as the barrier swung upwards. "That was easier than I thought," he whispered to Harry as they left the barrier behind in the darkness. "Grayson will be aware that we have crossed the checkpoint and expect us in an hour or so if we don't run into any trouble. That's a big if, of course."

They drove a little further until the barrier was out of sight and stopped by the side of the poorly lit road. Kendrick released Harry's cuffs and opened the trunk and helped Julianne, who was curled like a ball in one corner of the spacious trunk of the Range Rover, covered in a shapeless tarpaulin. She stretched her legs and gently jogged on the spot to get her circulation back. "Oh, at last," she said, arching her body backwards to stretch her back. "I was turning as stiff as a board in there. I thought I would never get out."

"Be thankful you didn't have to get out sooner," Kendrick countered.

They continued past Holland Park and Notting Hill Gate on the main road past the shops and businesses of this once thriving area. The potholed road was now littered along its route with the charred skeletons of cars and heaps of rubble which Kendrick negotiated skilfully. The once beautiful tree-lined avenues had lost their greenery, lending a stark, apocalyptic feel to the surroundings. Many retail outlets and businesses were boarded up along the route, the brickwork scarred and pitted, although a few brave business owners limped on, the lights from their premises a welcome relief from the shroud of darkness that cloaked the streets in menacing shadows.

"Stay alert," Kendrick warned them. "We are in breach of the curfew and there could be patrolling army units. Worse still, snipers could be lurking anywhere. They will see us long before we see them."

Harry spotted a large rat scamper across the road, its glassy eyes briefly caught in the Range Rover's headlights. Kendrick saw it too and swerved gently. They felt a satisfying bump as the heavy tyre squashed its body. It was a reminder to Harry that they were back in the city, where the rats were most prevalent.

As they travelled, the trio stayed vigilant. It had been nearly six months since Harry had last been in London and as he looked around him, the sense of devastation was palpable, even at night. The evidence of conflict was ubiquitous. On the skyline he could see several concrete tower blocks, lit sporadically by lights in individual apartments. Many of these high-rise blocks were slums even before the start of the conflict. He looked at a closer block about twenty storeys high. In the dim reflected light Harry could see that the concrete was crumbling and had fallen away in places, a large gaping wound in the front exposing apartments whose outer walls had been destroyed. It looked to Harry as if the tower block had been shelled or succumbed to rocket fire. He could see smoke billowing from an apartment about ten storeys up on one of the distant towers, and he heard the strident blare of fire engines racing through the night. The crack of distant gunfire resounded through the cold night air, and the acrid smell of burning drifted through the vents inside the Range Rover.

"Another night out on the town," said Kendrick sarcastically. "Some nights are peaceful but it is highly unpredictable. Although fighting could break out anywhere, the real danger zones are still in the primarily Muslim enclaves like Tower Hamlets. It reminds me of the devastation in Basra when I served in the Iraq War. I would love to take you for a tour of the Hamlets, but only someone with a death-wish would venture anywhere near places like that."

Harry peered out of the window, shocked at how the city he loved and spent many happy years in had collapsed into such a state of anarchy. They passed the junction with Ladbroke Grove with its beautiful tall white Georgian buildings, many now pitted and scarred with bullet holes. As he looked down the road he witnessed a brief flash of youths fighting before the car sped past. They reached the Bayswater Road and to their south stretched the vast parkland of Kensington Gardens. Harry expected to see a dark expanse beyond the border hedge as the park was traditionally closed at dusk, but instead he saw, in the reflected glow of small campfires dotted around the park, a huge cluster of tents with people moving about around them. The hedge itself was torn out in places and many of the trees that lined the road had fallen, a number of them now just blackened stumps.

It served to underline to Harry what the country had become. His mind wandered back to a happier time when he and Tamara had enjoyed long romantic walks in the park by Kensington, while he pushed the infant Byron in the pushchair, the little boy gurgling happily in the warm rays of the sun. The pleasant memory brought only melancholy, a sense that something precious had been lost, never to be found again.

Kendrick glanced at Harry. "Try and avoid the park if you can. You might never get out of that warren. It's become an ugly place full of undernourished children running around aimlessly in rags. The stench and the filth are unbelievable. There is no running water or proper sewage. I'm surprised that it has not been struck by the mysterious disease that has gripped the deportation camps. The place is full of registered minorities that have fled their homes rather than waiting for the dreaded knock on the door. They are hiding out here, but every so often the army or the secret police have a purge and round up groups of people quite indiscriminately. It doesn't happen much because they find the smell too overpowering. It's the people's only protection. It's not just the immigrant population that are here, though. There are a lot of British people too, displaced from their homes by unemployment, foreclosures or fighting. Did you know there are more abandoned houses in the country than at any other time, even during the height of the Great Recession?"

Kendrick's tablet beeped and he read the message quickly, one eye on the dark road ahead. "That was from Grayson. He's expecting us very shortly." He reached into his coat and handed the Glock pistol to Harry, who took it reluctantly. As they travelled up Constitution Hill and passed the grand facade of Buckingham Palace, bathed in a soft glow from spotlights set in the ground, Harry saw an encampment of protesters outside the imposing iron-black gates. The large throng of people held banners and candles while security guards monitored them closely from the edge of the group, riot shields at the ready. This time it was Julianne who explained to Harry. "After Pelham's speech at Wembley, a small group of protesters gathered at the gates in an attempt to lobby the King to support a petition to impeach the Prime Minister. Of course they have absolutely no clue about the political process. What can the King do? The petition must be moved by a member of the House of Commons, which is never going to happen in this regime. It was more an act of desperation, but the group seemed to get bigger day by day. I heard the King even came out and addressed them one day, probably in an attempt to get them to disperse. If someone was camped on my doorstep for months on end I would ask them to leave too."

They passed quickly by and Kendrick surveyed the area carefully before he pulled over. The majestic Georgian buildings on both sides of the road, with their grand facades and white Roman columns stood silent and unoccupied. They were mainly government offices, and the cold streets stood empty too. Kendrick turned off the engine. "New Scotland Yard is a just a few blocks away and Grayson is waiting impatiently. Now is the time."

Harry turned the gun over in his hands. "Jesus I can't do this."

Julianne reached forward from the back seat and gently touched him on the shoulder. "Kendrick's right. We have no other choice. The entrance to our operation is just over half a mile away. We will need to run but it's the right thing to do."

"Do I have to do this? Couldn't we just give you a black eye or something?" pleaded Harry.

Kendrick gave an ironic smile. "Hardly convincing. Let's get it over with." He stepped out of the car and Harry and Julianne followed. The street was quiet, although the sounds of a tumultuous city drifted to them in the bitterly cold air. Kendrick pointed to his shoulder. "Keep a steady hand Harry. Shoot me square in the shoulder right here – any higher and you will shatter my collar bone. Here it's just muscle and fat."

Harry stood back, and as he planted his feet firmly on the ground to position himself for the shot, he noticed that Kendrick was perspiring freely despite the cold. His own hands were clammy, and the gun was slippery in his trembling hands. He was less than five feet from Kendrick, the gun pointed exactly where Kendrick had shown him.

"Last chance -"

"For Christ's sake just do it!" Kendrick yelled.

With a deafening crack the gun fired and Kendrick collapsed to the ground, holding his left shoulder, which was oozing blood through his fingers. He let out a chilling scream and Harry ran to him, appalled by what he had done. "Go, go, I'll survive!" Kendrick gasped, stumbling back into the car. Before he could react, Julianne grabbed Harry's hand and hauled him away from the stricken detective. In a blur they were running through the dark streets as fast as his injured leg would allow.

# CHAPTER 47

Following its renovation and rebuilding in the latter part of the last century, Westminster Tube station had been hailed as a magnificent engineering achievement, a deep level station that serviced the modern Jubilee Line. The work involved an immense amount of excavation and complex planning. This included a system of huge steel tubes installed horizontally beneath Big Ben and injected with concrete grouting to protect the foundation and manage settlement in the sub-soil around the huge clock tower. The finished project had been six years in the making and resulted in a gleaming but austere new station that dropped thirty metres down into the earth, and which suited the strategic importance of the station, opening as it did onto Parliament Square. Less well known was the fact that the engineers and construction crews had carved out a number of service tunnels and platforms to support the underground building work and to place huge underpinning steel struts.

One of those spaces was a large chamber with interconnected passageways radiating from them like the legs of a spider. The passageways were set fifteen metres down into the earth, and therefore closer to the surface than the Tube station. They housed vast grid-like pipe systems and solid concrete buttresses, as well as the network of struts that provided the foundation for the heavy buildings above.

After the construction these tunnels and storage chambers had been effectively abandoned, having served their purpose, scheduled only for the odd maintenance visit that never happened. The result was a subterranean network that provided a home to the sewer rats and the occasional hobo who tired of life on the surface.

That was until two years ago, when a group of enterprising computer engineers had gradually turned the dark, claustrophobic man-made caves into an underground bunker that served as a secret facility. The derelict, abandoned network was now a thriving operations centre, manned by more than thirty people crouched over servers, computers, laptops and tablets, a tribute to the ingenuity and resourcefulness of the engineers who had developed this bunker.

Chen stood over the shoulder of one of the engineers who diligently worked a large touch screen in which a grainy image showed the inside of a small chapel on the surface. There was no movement but Chen waited patiently as the engineer continued to work a bank of controls, his fingers moving deftly over a small keyboard. He swore softly to himself, feeling the temptation for another cigarette. Since he had arrived at the underground base, he had been forced to virtually give up on his cherished habit. The leader of this small group had banned smoking in these caverns. The implications of even a small fire starting here was too awful to contemplate. Of course he fully respected and understood that, but giving them up did not make it any easier and he found himself getting easily irritated and tetchy. They should be here by now, he thought.

A movement on the image caught his eye and two blurred figures appeared at the corner of the screen, running toward the camera. "Nikolai, is it them?" he said excitedly to his seated colleague.

The engineer, a Romanian in his late twenties with long, greasy hair set in a ponytail fingered the bridge of his small round spectacles. He continued to tap away, his stubby fingers dancing, whilst he squinted at the screen. He did not answer for a second and then said, "Yes, yes, it is them."

Chen realized he had been holding his breath and exhaled deeply. The figures began to dominate the screen and he was now able to confirm Nikolai's analysis. It was indeed them, but just as importantly they were not being pursued. "Okay, release the grille," he instructed his colleague.

On the surface, Harry desperately tried to keep hold of Julianne's hand as she drove him forward. He felt his right thigh burning as the muscles and scar tissue screamed in protest at the unwelcome exertion. His breath came in short gasps, staccato like a steam train in the night air, but she pushed on relentlessly. "Come on!" she urged him. "Not too far now."

That was of little encouragement to Harry as he still had no idea where they were going. Skirting around a corner on the slick sidewalk, they spotted a small mob armed with baseball bats and axes which they smashed against a line of cars. One of the vehicles had already been torched and the faces of one of the mob reflected in the fierce glow as he stared down the street at them. Underneath the hoodie his face was heavily pitted but youthful, barely twenty, yet his eyes shone with an animal ferocity that stopped them short. He then gave a sinister grin which chilled Harry to the bone. They were less than fifty yards away and he saw the youth gesture to his friends.

"I don't think this is the way Julianne," Harry cautioned, his eyes fixed on the mob.

Julianne shrank back. "Yes, I see your point." She did a quick mental calculation and they backed away from the youths and shot up a dark side-alley. Harry was slower, gritting his teeth against the pain in his leg, with no choice but to follow.

"Come on Harry!" she hissed impatiently. "The police will be on our trail before long!"

They emerged out of the black alley onto a poorly lit side road and Harry saw the two Gothic towers of Westminster Abbey rising up behind nearer buildings a few blocks away. They headed toward the Parliament buildings, the seat of the enemy, but he was too breathless to question Julianne. He followed as fast as he could and they emerged onto Great George Street, next to Parliament Square. The whole square, its Winston Churchill statue standing forlorn, had been completely cordoned off by metal barriers, but there were still crowds of people squashed against them. Many carried placards, and many shouted in protest as people pushed and jostled against each other. Julianne and Harry quickly skirted past the buzz of activity, careful not to get sucked into the mob, especially with so many riot police waiting in the wings for the first sign of trouble.

Harry followed Julianne toward the Thames, the towering monolith of Big Ben now on his right and he thought for a moment they had to cross the river. Up ahead he could see a heavy Army checkpoint, several Hummers blocking the wide bridge. To Harry's relief Julianne abruptly turned and headed down another alleyway that was so narrow it was easy to overlook. It was barely shoulder-width, clearly a by-product of Victorian London when gaps between buildings were created purely for dumping garbage and stinking waste. The stench was overpowering and Harry gagged at the assault on his senses, and in the darkness the ground felt wet and squidgy. He barely had time to contemplate what he was treading on when the alleyway opened out into a small square. The concrete piazza supported a tiny old chapel lit up by a large spotlight set in the small surrounding grassy verge. It was an insignificant, pollution stained building dwarfed by the newer buildings around it. The ancient chapel looked forgotten, the yellow spotlight crudely exposing the crumbling, dusty brickwork.

Curiously, Julianne headed directly to the door of the old chapel and hauled its heavy iron door open as if she knew it wasn't locked. Harry followed her inside the small chapel. The reflected glow from the surrounding buildings cast a ghostly pallor. In the dim bluish light, Harry could see that the interior was in a worse state of repair than the outside, but it hardly seemed to matter. The chapel had clearly been abandoned, no doubt discarded and left to rot. It was astonishing that, sitting as it was on a prime piece of Westminster real estate, the chapel had not been torn down. More confused than ever, Harry observed Julianne move purposefully forward to the altar. He caught up with her as she paused over a metal grille set in the stone floor. Harry felt the faintest caress of a warm breeze from the grille. Oddly enough she gave a 'thumbs-up' sign at the grille and a tiny flash sparked from the metal surround.

"Help me with this Harry." They both grasped several rods in the metal grille and with a little effort were able to lift it. A ladder descended until it was lost in the darkness.

Julianne turned to Harry, smiling. "Does this not give you a sense of Déjà vu Harry? Following me into an underground abyss again?" She deftly swung round onto the ladder and looked up at Harry. "Follow me but make sure you replace the grille precisely. It's very important. If it's not on properly they cannot magnetize it."

Harry gave a bewildered nod followed her instructions and soon they were hanging onto the vertical ladder, descending deep into the bowels of a black shaft.

# CHAPTER 48

"Good morning, welcome to the Resistance." The accented voice sounded familiar and as Harry struggled into consciousness he opened his eyes gradually, blinking in the subdued light. Standing before him was the tall, gaunt figure of Yi Chen, and the Cantonese man gave him a broad smile. "It's good to see you Harry."

Harry sat up from the hard camp bed, swinging his legs over the side and shook Chen's extended hand. "Likewise. Julianne told me you had survived. It's amazing anyone did in that carnage," he said, referring to the attack on the cell's compound in Kent.

"You did, and I'm glad Julianne got you back. It was a dangerous mission but you know Julianne. When she sets her mind to something she usually does it. Sorry to wake you but we have a lot of work to do."

Harry felt groggy and he looked around at the spartan surroundings. Alongside his camp bed another dozen were lined up in dormitory style around the cramped chamber, all empty. The black walls were pitted and the small electric lamp offered a muted, cheerless glow.

"Julianne warned us you'd be exhausted after everything you'd been through. You've been asleep over fifteen hours." Chen pointed to a small alcove in one wall. "Through there is a bathroom. I'll wait for you."

Harry rubbed his stubbly face and was glad to freshen up before he followed Chen through a series of narrow passages. It reminded him of a submarine, and presently they reached the gloomy mess hall where Harry was able to satisfy his craving hunger. Chen merely nibbled at a plate of rice cakes. Considering they were underground, their food stores appeared well stocked, although it was mainly freeze-dried produce.

Chen responded to Harry's unspoken question as if he was telepathic. "I know, we do quite well here but it's still a daily battle for supplies. The food distribution system has all but broken down. Supermarkets are nearly empty and it seems only the Party faithful get access to the good stuff. It's no longer supply and demand. The irony is that for an extreme right-wing government it now seems to be running a communist style of governance. The privileged few get the best goods and the rest of the proletariat have to scrabble around in the dirt. Since things really deteriorated the UN have been dropping food aid, and the air defence systems have not intercepted them yet. I think Pelham realizes that at the moment it's a necessary evil. We have been quite effective in retrieving the sacks mainly because our systems allow us advance warning of when they are about to deliver. Even so, when we go above ground we risk mobs of desperate hungry people, all of whom want their share, not to mention random snipers in dark alleys and buildings. So far we have got by without any casualties."

The descent through the black shaft on the ladder had taken only a few minutes, but at the time, in the coal-black darkness, it had felt like forever as he felt his way down each rung, one faltering step at a time. Julianne had guided him with her voice until they reached firm, level ground. Julianne had used the faint light from her phone to lead the way, and as his eyes adjusted he saw a narrow but level passageway that tapered off and rounded a corner. He heard the slow but incessant drip of water, and when he stumbled and put his hand against the wall, it had felt slimy. Something brushed his leg, and as they turned the bend in the passage, it was both a relief and surprise to see a thick metal door. Although it was an obstruction, it was at least some sign of civilization, which Harry found oddly comforting even after such a short time in the suffocating subterranean darkness. Julianne had strode toward the door confidently and after a short moment, it swung open with a hydraulic hiss and they had reached their destination.

He felt much more refreshed after sleeping and eating, something which in the last few frantic weeks had been a luxury. His thoughts drifted back to Amir, and as he did so he patted the inside pocket of his fleece jacket draped over a chair. The boy's phone had survived everything he had been through since they had parted. He hardly dared contemplate where the boy was now, or even if he was still alive.

"Where's Julianne?"

"Oh, she's upstairs, as we like to call it. On another scavenge for supplies. She can't stay too long in the tunnels like some of us. She's our eyes and ears above ground. The rest of us just sit at our computers and tablets and try to think of ways to damage the government's infrastructure. That's the true nature of the resistance movement in these modern times. Unlike Sean's compound, we don't possess a cache of weapons, just a bank of computers, tablets and a touch of ingenuity."

Harry frowned. "Exactly what do you do here in this little rabbit warren?"

Chen's smile was tight. "Ever the diplomat Harry. I would use your words cautiously round here. Most of the people are proud of this place and what we've achieved. Come on, I want you to meet the man who started this 'rabbit warren' as you call it."

They stepped through another narrow passageway into a labyrinth of other shadowy corridors, which suggested to Harry that the place was considerably larger than he imagined when he first arrived. "Watch your step," cautioned Chen. "The floors are not that even; oh and if you come across a rat do us a favour and squash its head if you can. We've managed to get rid of most of them but they're persistent vermin."

Harry heard a muted rumble like the sound of distant thunder which grew louder until the rumble felt like it was immediately beneath their feet, shaking the foundations. The crescendo quickly died and the rumble receded. Chen laughed at Harry's look of consternation. "Jubilee Line, forty feet below us. It's still operating in spite of everything, although fortunately for us the trains are less frequent these days. This whole network is part of the construction chambers for Westminster Tube station. It's quite ironic that we are so close to the enemy."

They soon reached another steel door. It had a raised wheel like a submarine hatch and Chen turned it heavily anticlockwise. With an effort the heavy door creaked open. Harry saw that this room was more brightly lit than other areas, although it still had a subdued air to it. However, it was clearly the focal point of whatever this place was. The chamber was relatively large and there were at least twenty people, mostly young men, all hunched over a desktop computer or a tablet, arranged in three rough semi-circles around a central screen that currently projected a satellite image of the London urban sprawl. A few looked up curiously as he and Chen entered the room, but most of them focused on their tasks.

"Our operations centre," explained Chen. "This is the battle-ground for a new type of war. Follow me; there's someone I want you to meet." As Harry passed by, he saw that the men were fairly young, perhaps in their twenties. Several of them had long hair tied in ponytails and most had stubble of varying lengths, a few of which had graduated into small beards. Even in the bluish light he could tell their faces looked ghostly pale, even the four women that completed the group. It was hardly surprising given their subterranean existence. As he passed through the area, Chen took him to a glass partition behind which was situated in a small office. As they entered, the occupant, a suave black man with boyish features rose from behind his cluttered desk and greeted Harry with an iron grip of a handshake.

He looked vaguely familiar to Harry and his impeccable suit and tie offered a contrast to the scruffy slacks worn by the operatives in the control room. He flashed a broad smile, his even teeth pearly white. "Welcome Harry. We were relieved you got here in one piece. It was touch and go."

He ushered Harry to a seat and Chen excused himself.

"I've seen you before. I just can't place you," said Harry.

His host gave a sardonic smile. "My name here is a pseudonym. They call me the Czar and so that is the name I have adopted. I am alternatively known as Anatoly Kessler, the former Chief of Staff at the Joint Cyber Reserve Unit."

Harry sat up, more animated. "Yes, yes, I thought I recognized your face. But you drowned in a boating accident on the Solent. I remember the rumours; they suggested you jumped off your boat, committed suicide when the net closed in."

The Czar looked at him quizzically and flicked dust off his smart woollen suit. "I can assure you I feel fully alive. You're right. I did perish in the Solent according to media reports. I faked my own death, disappeared for a few years and followed my passion for sailing and lying on secluded beaches around the world. It didn't take long for the media to tire of looking for me, and I had covered my tracks pretty well, left no clues. That's the beauty of it when you don't have a family to worry about. No-one to come looking for you after the media has lost interest."

"So why did you fake your own death?"

"The position isn't one you can just resign from. Remember the Cyber Reserve Unit is a joint military and civil operation. Being based at GCHQ in Cheltenham, we were overloaded with bureaucracy. I had already signed the Official Secrets Act but that wasn't enough. I had long grown disillusioned with the lack of support for cyber security in this country. Our resources were limited and during the economic turmoil, the Labour government made drastic cutbacks. They buried their head in the sand while we lived under constant threat of valuable military and economic secrets being stolen from under our noses. I pleaded with them to give me the tools I asked for, but they turned a deaf ear. They made empty noises about diverting the money to where it was needed most. Just because the country had not suffered a direct cyber-terrorist attack, they considered our unit more expendable than others. It was our diligence that kept the country safe, not because the threat wasn't there. I talked about leaving and that was when I received the first death threat. It was difficult to know who was behind it but after the second one the message was loud and clear. I would not be leaving the job alive. So with a bit of forward planning and a few trusted friends I decided to die by my own hand and not theirs."

Harry glanced behind Kessler and the Czar spotted the movement in his eyes. He reached under his desk and spun round quickly in his swivel chair and swatted a small rodent scurrying against the wall. His swatter had an electric charge and it crackled with a blue bolt of light before the rat dropped dead, the smell of sizzled fur drifting from its smoking body. "Damn rats," he snarled. "Filthy creatures; they're a real nuisance here. They like to chew on the fibre-optic cables, and believe me we have a lot of cable."

"So what made you come back?" asked Harry.

"I enjoyed sailing and travelling but I couldn't do that forever. I missed the damn country, can you believe that? I have an I.Q. of one hundred and fifty-eight and am highly obsessive, and I had some unfinished business, a point to prove. But as the tide began to turn I realized that I would end up in a deportation camp like every other immigrant. By then the government was already restricting access and I left it too late to leave. I could not risk drawing attention to myself. The facial scanners would have recognized me in an instant and so I had to go underground." He smiled broadly, the perfect white teeth glinting. "And so here we are."

Harry nodded approvingly. "You've certainly built an impressive facility here."

Kessler put the swatter back in his desk and stood up. "Let me show you around, what little there is. This facility is a triumph in logistics. It was a difficult task, but we Estonians are the most gifted cyber-warriors in the world."

"You don't look Estonian," remarked Harry.

The Czar fixed his gaze on him with shrewd, appraising eyes. "And what does an Estonian look like? Blond and blue eyed, perhaps?"

Harry began to apologize but Kessler raised his smooth hand. "It's okay, I am teasing you," he said in a good-natured tone. "At least I won't go as pale as the rest of the geeks down here! My family came to Estonia in the mid-seventies during Communist rule and I'm a second generation Estonian. Of course we faced racism but my parents are still there and because we stood out we received plenty of attention, not all of it negative. When I showed a gift for applied maths at an early age we gained several scholarships, and I secured a position at the newly created NATO Cooperative Cyber Defence Centre of Excellence in Tallinn in 2008. A combination of hard work and brilliance on my part led me to become one of the country's leading experts on cyber defence before I was head hunted to the Cyber Reserve Unit here in the U.K. Now the gatekeeper has turned poacher."

Harry smiled at Kessler's conceit as he followed the Czar into the operations centre, which hummed with the low buzz of computer activity. Kessler quietly explained that the workforce of twenty-eight was composed of criminals, hackers and spammers, originally from China, Korea, Russia and the Baltic States, the heartland of the cyber war.

"We even have two Koreans from north and south of the border. Considering their nations have been at cyber-war with each other for the last quarter-century, they get on quite well," he joked. Kessler explained that each member had the same motivation, which was to take down the regime little by little through a series of co-ordinated attacks on the country's infrastructure, an extraordinary amount of which relied on computerized processes and therefore rendered itself vulnerable to a remote attack.

"It's still early days," Kessler continued. "We formed shortly after Pelham took power, but have only occupied this place for the last three months. Since then it has been a huge logistical exercise to get the right equipment down here and build our systems, but Chen is a brilliant engineer and together we designed most of what you see. We are only now beginning to realize the full potential of what we can achieve against this regime. We could strike silently from the shadows for ever, but we need a voice for the propaganda war, which is where you come in, Harry."

Kessler slapped a firm but friendly hand on Harry's shoulder. "Let me show you around the rest of the place. I'm afraid it's a little pokey in parts but think of it like you are on a tour of duty in a submarine. It might stop you going stir crazy because I should point out that for the foreseeable future you are not going anywhere..."

# CHAPTER 49

The underground was claustrophobic and stifling and Julianne relished her time on the surface. She had immediately volunteered to go out on another mission as soon as Harry had been safely delivered to Kessler and his group of computer scientists who collectively called themselves simply 'The Resistance.' The name offered no clue as to how they really acted, and that was maybe part of the plan. Julianne was convinced Kessler harboured some romantic notion that his underground unit was like the French Resistance in World War Two, operating in the shadows, attacking the government covertly before fleeing in readiness for the next opportunity. It was a *modus operandi* that had been used by countless insurgencies in countless nations since, most of them branded as terrorists for daring to challenge the ruling elite.

A bone-chilling November wind whistled through the small side-street, the energy from a blustery day funnelled down the dark lane running between buildings huddled close together. There were numerous tiny lanes like this in London and in better days a brave tourist venturing off the beaten track would find a treasure trove of hidden delights; maybe some quaint little junk store or a tiny coffee shop brimming with character, selling the best patisseries in London. The coffee shop she was heading for had no character at all. It was a drab, cheerless place with grimy windows and yellowed wallpaper. A faint smell of cigarette smoke clung to the walls and the owner was a fragile old woman with a truculent manner, but it was close to the

Parliament building and that's what counted.

She adjusted the brim of her wide hat so that any casual passer-by would never be able to see her face, and the collar of her Cashmere coat was turned up high, lending her a fashionable look. She was glad to escape the biting wind as she entered the shop. The old lady was mopping up and there was only one other customer, an old man with a wrinkled face who hugged his mug of coffee with fingerless gloves.

"Hello Hilda. It's been a while," she said as she entered the small room.

"Good 'eavens," said the old lady, putting down her mop. Her liver-spotted, skeletal hand grasped Julianne's with surprising strength. "Miss Julianne. Where ya been?"

"You'd be amazed," replied Julianne, resting her coat and hat on the back of a plastic chair.

Hilda fixed her a cup of instant coffee and resumed her mopping around the feet of the old man, who got the hint and departed into the blustery, uninviting street.

"Is your friend coming?" Hilda's scratchy voice was low, faintly conspiratorial.

Julianne glanced at her phone. "Yes, he'll be here soon."

Hilda laid another cup of coffee on the table and disappeared discreetly to the back. As if on cue, the door opened and the bell chimed. In walked a dark-clad, athletic figure. He was dressed in black jogging bottoms and a navy tank top, the hood drawn tightly over his head and the look completed by a pair of large sunglasses. A thin silk scarf covered his mouth and nose. Even so, his movements were twitchy and as he entered he continually glanced either side to ensure he had not been followed.

Julianne smiled at the figure and as he sauntered over she stood up and embraced him like a long-lost friend. She recalled how they had shared much more than that. He had found her when she was lost and infused her with new hope that Pelham's terrible rule could be challenged. She smiled to herself at the irony of it. Someone at the very heart of this atrocious regime had revealed himself to be human, vulnerable and committed to taking down the government from the inside. Of course he wasn't just anyone, which is why Julianne was convinced he had the power to do it.

"You're taking a risk coming here."

The man smiled under his sunglasses. "I could say the same to you. Yet here we are. I understand your mission was a success."

She sipped at her coffee, a little confused. She wondered whether the man wanted her for who she was or what she could offer him. Perhaps it was a combination of both. She let her hand rest on his and he didn't pull it away. "Harry is a good man. He's been through a lot but he can be our best advocate."

Finally the man took off his sunglasses and his handsome, chiseled face was earnest. "Do you still believe in me Julianne?"

She squeezed his hand. "Of course I do Giles."

Chamberlain thought of that blisteringly hot July day when he had found Julianne. For her it was a chance meeting, but his network of researchers had done their job well. They had prepared a detailed report on all the known escapees from the attack on the compound in Kent. He had been fascinated by Julianne's profile and ordered his network to find her. When the news arrived that she had been located, he insisted on collecting her personally, in order to reinforce the apparent coincidence of their meeting.

He had driven past in his limousine, its tinted windows and air-conditioning protecting against the fierce heat of the sun. Unlike Pelham, who since the assassination attempt the previous month had become ever more reclusive, Giles refused to be forced into hiding. He even rejected the services of a bodyguard from the PIA. The unmarked limousine was just him and the driver, although the town car had enough armoury to repel any attack from the street. Since then he had eschewed even the limo in favour of an unmarked car. Despite its protection, the limo was still too tempting a target.

Chamberlain noticed her flaming red hair first, glinting in the sun as she sat on a street corner begging barely two blocks away from the Parliament buildings. She looked so desolate, as if she had lost everything in the world. She would undoubtedly get moved on by the police very soon, and he ordered the driver to stop. He asked her to get in and she hesitated only briefly before doing so.

That was the start of a brief but passionate fling. She had mistrusted him at first but he had placed her in one of his several Knightsbridge apartments to keep her safe and she had gradually opened up to him. She even confided in him about her escape, not knowing that he was already fully aware. She had been living rough since then, locating to Westminster so she could join the hordes chanting their futile protests at an administration that would never listen.

Her time at the compound meant she knew Harry Clarke, although by then he had disappeared, but even more importantly she knew Chen. Chamberlain enjoyed unquestionable loyalty from his close network of trusted advisers and facilitators. There were far more people inside the administration disillusioned with Pelham and his policies than the Prime Minister suspected. The man was caught up in his own arrogance and supposed invincibility, and that made it easier for Chamberlain to keep his network under the radar. It was a fine balancing act, being the spokesperson for a regime with which he had become disenchanted, whilst working in the background on his true objectives. Most of the people outside of Westminster politics regarded Chamberlain as Pelham's right hand man and equally culpable for the atrocities this government had perpetrated. That included world leaders, and he often wondered whether his reputation was too tarnished to ever succeed Pelham. Only time would tell, even if the opportunity arose. Julianne's initial mistrust was a telling benchmark for how he was likely to be perceived when he tried to step out of Pelham's shadow, but he had managed to convince her with the persuasive skills that had elevated him to such high office.

His small network benefited from its connections on the ground and he had heard about Chen and his underground resistance movement. However, it was so well protected and secretive that he knew merely of its existence and not its location or capabilities. His people had engineered a meeting to reunite Julianne and Chen and the technically gifted Cantonese man had persuaded her to join his movement. Chamberlain therefore acquired a mole on the inside, but he had not forced her hand, preferring to act with subtlety. They had remained in contact, but it was too risky using social media. They had to communicate in the old fashioned way through cryptic phone calls. Even as Pelham's principal enforcer, he could not be certain that the P.M. himself had not arranged for Chamberlain's phone to be monitored. He wanted to see her again, so this anonymous coffee shop at the end of a narrow lane had become their unofficial liaison point. He knew the old lady was discreet.

"You look good Julianne." He tenderly brushed the wild strands of flaming hair from her face. They had not slept together since before her mission to find Harry, but today was about business. Hiding behind his shades, he never saw it coming. She reached out as if to embrace him but her right hand launched a stinging blow to his face. He grasped her wrist before she could strike again and gently began to twist. She grimaced and he let go. She rubbed her sore wrist and began to sob gently.

"What was that for?" His voice carried a steely edge and he took off his sunglasses, peering at her intently.

"If you had seen what I had seen!" she cried. "Tell me you had no part in it."

"A part of what?"

"Everything! What that monster is doing to this country. I saw what happened to those poor people, men, women and children alike. Families ripped apart and exterminated for no other crime than being born outside this country. I saw the boat at Pembroke. It's genocide. They'll hang you as a war criminal!"

Chamberlain gazed deeply at Julianne, his penetrating eyes burrowing into hers. "Listen to me Julianne. I am not responsible for what happened. I'm as sickened by this as you are. But I have to fight from the inside. It's the best way. If I resign in protest the same thing will happen to me as the other ministers. I can't do much from a wooden box six feet under. I asked if you still believed in me Julianne and you told me you did. I need your faith. Please understand.

Whatever my position, there are forces at work that are way beyond my realm of influence. I have to accept whatever fate awaits me but until then I will work hard to oust him."

She eventually calmed down and wiped her eyes with a napkin on the table. "If I believed for one minute you had any part of this, I would never speak to you again."

Chamberlain flashed his media friendly smile and her features softened. He knew that she found his charisma hard to resist, and he used it to his advantage. He studied her as she talked. Julianne still remained a little cautious when talking about the Resistance, and he did not press her. She knew very little about the technical capabilities of the movement, and it was difficult to assess from her limited analysis just how much of a threat the network of cyber warriors was to the regime. Chen would provide far more useful information but tactically it was not feasible. It would alert them to his knowledge of their existence. At least Julianne had been discreet, and he believed her when she assured him they had no idea of his knowledge. It was certainly not in her interests to tell anyone about him, because the group would expel her immediately. He decided to ask her about their new arrival.

"So why Harry?"

She sipped at her coffee. "He can give us a capability we don't currently have. A face and a voice to the Resistance. In the same way the faceless bureaucrats on the big screens espouse the government line, we hope that Harry can provide a viable counterpoint."

"Interesting," replied Chamberlain, a little condescendingly. "The government is in total control of the media. Just how is he going to get his message out there?"

Julianne hesitated, as if she were weighing up whether to tell him. "We have developed an alternative system to the Internet that allows us to send messages outside government firewalls. I don't know much about it, but I understand it allows us to bypass the censorship by operating independently of the Net. If it is developed further we may even be able to send messages outside of the country. Harry could be at the forefront of that."

"Now you have my attention," he said, genuinely intrigued. Chamberlain made a mental note to investigate further. The Conservative regime was dominant militarily but a propaganda war could expose some vulnerability in its iron-clad armour.

"You know he hates you," she said casually. "Harry almost died on that ship. He holds you as culpable as Pelham. If we get this project off the ground it will be hard to stop him being critical."

Chamberlain reached into the pocket of his jogging pants and pulled out a scrap of paper that he unfolded on the stained laminated table. "This is too important to let personal feelings get in the way. I never liked Harry but I have a grudging respect for his qualities, not least his tenacity. Which is why I want him to have this." He passed the scrap of paper to Julianne.

She looked at the paper curiously; just a single name and a set of random alpha-numeric codes scrawled on it. "What is it?"

"Duncan Cavendish. Look up the name. A colleague of mine found some highly interesting information on him, but I need Harry to find more and use this alternative media to expose the truth about who Pelham really is. The code is the access to the newspaper archive database. Access to the newspapers is restricted, as you know, but this will get you in. It will take some research but I think the world deserves to know what drives the man. If he manages to piece together the full story on Pelham, as far as a propaganda war is concerned at least, it could be a knockout blow."

Chamberlain glanced at his watch. "It's wonderful to see you again Julianne. I have to go but I promise we will spend longer together next time. These are dangerous times, and we have to be discreet." He put his sunglasses back on and drew the hood back over his head, and kissed her passionately on the lips. "I'll be in touch." He then swept out of the coffee shop, leaving her staring after him, a torrent of mixed emotions raging inside her.

# CHAPTER 50

Living in such a contained environment did not particularly suit Harry, but he had to admit he felt safer than at any time in the last four months. Since he had fled the Kent farmhouse back in July he had lived under the constant stress of being arrested or shot as an enemy of the State, particularly when he had tried in vain to flee the country. People around him had not been so lucky; Joe, Omar, Joszef and Martha, even Amir. This underground bunker, despite its bizarre location, had the feeling of permanency to it. Kessler had assured him that no-one outside their network knew of the underground bunker, even though it was on the doorstep of the Parliamentary buildings.

They gave him a few days to assimilate into his surroundings, which even possessed a basic gymnasium and an electronic library and media room. He actually felt able to relax, at least in body if not in spirit, and he found the camaraderie amongst the team quite refreshing. There was a shared respect for the Czar and a commitment to their goal that bordered on zealotry. No doubt this motley collection of cyber-criminals from overseas had lost someone, family or friend, as a result of Pelham's policies. They rarely spoke when they worked, but appeared to converse easily in the few waking hours they shared outside the work environment. There appeared to

Harry to be few signs of conflict, despite the diverse nationalities and the fact that there were only five women, including Julianne, in the group.

Most of the operators were content to work long hours as there was little else to do, and in any event it gave them a sense of purpose they lacked when off duty. They were not unfriendly to Harry, just diffident, but then he was considerably older and culturally worlds apart from them. Neither did they appear to be stir crazy, which was a testament to their discipline because after two days Harry was beginning to feel like a laboratory rat. He began to wonder why he had been brought here, especially as Julianne was often conspicuous by her absence, and Kessler had not been that explicit when he gave Harry the tour. He only knew what Julianne had told him in the pastor's cottage and on the road; but she had said little in front of Kendrick, and he realized she had only scratched the surface of what this network did.

On the third day, however, Chen approached him as he worked out on one of the treadmills, anxious to get his strength back, his right thigh still full of scar tissue and pulling as he jogged in t-shirt and shorts.

"Ah, Harry, there you are. I have searched everywhere for you," he joked with typical gallows humour. His voice was breezy and casual. "Are you ready to get to work?"

"Sure," Harry wheezed. He was glad of the excuse to escape the treadmill, realizing how unfit he had become, and he had to admit to missing Julianne. He followed Chen into the mess hall, not much larger than an average kitchen, and took a cup of water from the large water barrel in the corner. Chen pointed to Harry's right thigh which was still a ghastly, blotchy shade of purple.

"How's the leg? It looks ugly."

"I'll live. So what have you got for me? Kessler explained a little but I'm still clueless."

"Understandable," smiled Chen. He tugged at the nicotine patch just below his throat. "Damn things," he complained. "Worst thing about being down here is I can't smoke." He looked at Harry earnestly. "The government is in total control of the radio, television, the Internet and the social media. The ISPs have initiated a class court action against the government to protest at their regulation, but we all know how that will end. But even if the government is in control, that doesn't mean information can't flow outside of these media. Pelham's regime believes it has the monopoly on the dissemination of information and to a large extent it has. But there is another way."

"There is?" replied Harry, intrigued.

"In Kent I worked on creating an alternative to the centralized Internet controlled by the ISPs, and now by government. I did not complete my work but with Kessler's vision and some incredible brains in our group, we have made great progress. The system works on the basis of a decentralized peer-to-peer network, in which we can talk to other parties on the system. We are still using the same fibre optic cables that are used by the ISPs but riding on the back of them. They transmit so much data that our network piggybacking on them is like a fly landing on a galloping thoroughbred. We are too small to be noticed, yet our system allows us to share files through our own alternative registry, similar to the Domain Name System but working outside of it."

"But how can you talk undetected if you are using the ISPs?"

"Good question Harry. Each of the contacts in our system is hosting a portion of the equivalent DNS system and it allows us to create our own communications network. Think of it as similar to the system of secret notes passed on by couriers during the French resistance of World War Two. Without a method of communication we would be isolated and powerless, which is precisely what Pelham has forced on any group that opposes him, before he destroys them one by one. Our system is secure because the ISPs cannot take us down whilst we are hosting on our own servers." Chen paused, picking at the nicotine patch.

"The problem is we only have a handful of contacts hosting their part of the network, less than twenty, which means our network is rudimentary at best. It is evolving and we hope it will spread exponentially as more people join the resistance network and they make contact with other dissidents through the system. The one weakness we have is that the bulk of the network is hosted here so if we were wiped out that would be the end of the network. Our communications are encrypted and sent in timed packets which are destroyed within thirty minutes of opening, so it's difficult for the ISPs to intercept or to read the contents of the packages even if they discovered them. The trouble is that we have been unable to bypass the firewalls in place that prevents anyone from emailing or sending data outside of the country, except privileged Party members and those on the inside. We believe we are close to solving that issue. This government has subverted the consciousness of the people and only by getting the message outside our borders can we truly hope to influence international opinion. If we can break through the firewall, you can be our spokesperson, the face of the Resistance. You've seen first-hand what Pelham's regime is capable of, the atrocities. You know about the five-year plan. Yours will be a credible and compelling voice."

Harry nodded, leaning back in his tatty plastic chair. He did not claim to understand the engineering behind it; that was Chen's field, but the prospect of being able to broadcast a resistance message was tantalizing. He allowed himself the luxury of daring to hope that there was another way to fight this regime.

# CHAPTER 51

With a heavy creak the steel door to the mess hall opened and in walked the debonair figure of Kessler. He flashed a boyish smile and joined them around the Formica table. "What did I miss?" he said, his tall, athletic frame spilling over the small foldaway chair he settled in.

"I've taken him through our communications network," replied Chen.

"Good god, man, I hope you didn't bamboozle him with all that technical stuff." Kessler turned to Harry and took up the baton. "But it's not just the communications. I described our team as some of the best hackers and spammers in the business. This government is heavily reliant on its computer systems for its infrastructure. The U.K., whether it was the last Labour administration that I served under, or this current abomination, has never taken cyber attacks seriously. I told you what happened when I asked for more funding for the Cyber Reserve Unit. There is too much in-fighting between departments and they have no coordinated systems to prevent or defend against a cyber attack. That, and their arrogance, is their weakness. We have already instigated a few small attacks and the results have been better than I could have hoped for. As we develop our capabilities we can strike larger targets and really hurt this regime. At the moment we have been able to disrupt a few parts of the secure government Intranet by using DDoS - distributed denial of service - attacks by flooding their servers with huge amounts of spam, effectively blocking traffic to the site.

"The way we do this is by creating and introducing viruses over the Internet. These viruses infect computers and tablets and any other device that uses the Net. When an infected device is turned on it becomes a zombie machine that we can manipulate to attack and flood government websites with spam, choking the servers and preventing departments from communicating with each other through the Net. As far as the zombie device is concerned, the only difference they see is that their processor runs slower, as an unseen application in the background that follows a remote command to send packets of random illegible data does its work. Even if the government's cyber defence system could see where the data was coming from, there would be thousands of points of origin. Yes they can build more effective firewalls to block the data, but that would take time and skill they don't have. As for striking back, the targets are too disparate to yield any effective attack and even if they managed to close down one machine or even several hundred using their cyber strike capabilities, there will always be thousands more to take their place." He paused, smoothing his impeccably pressed shirt.

"It's caused them a lot of inconvenience but perhaps no more than that. Unfortunately one of my initiatives was to break up the government Intranet into a series of smaller independent sub-sites that could still talk to each other, but would ensure that any attack was isolated to the sub-site without affecting the whole system. Now I have to work on how to overcome my own creation. There's irony for you.

"However, that's just the start. Our real target is Britain's infrastructure, its military systems, energy, water, transport, banking and finance, the larger corporations that support Pelham. These are all legitimate targets. There are two ways in which we can cause damage. The first is cyber espionage. However, espionage only really works if we have a buyer for the classified information we can steal, or if the information we take can help us with the second method."

"Which is?"

"Sabotage. The military field of battle has traditionally been land, air and sea, and more recently space. But I believe that the wars of the future will be won and lost in the realm of cyberspace. Not all governments understand that it is potentially the most damaging war zone. If the programs we are close to completing work as intended, we have the potential to cause untold devastation on a scale far greater than any guns, rocket launchers or any other weapons the rebel forces have at their disposal.

"The use of software for cyber espionage and theft has been around for as long as the Internet. But the use of viruses to sabotage critical infrastructure is a more recent phenomenon. The first major attack of this kind was the Stuxnet worm which was used to attack Iran's nuclear facilities back in 2010. Not only could the malware gather and relay back information but it could also subvert industrial systems using programmable logic bombs planted in the system, waiting for its command to be executed. Despite this, there has been a huge expansion amongst developed nations of placing their critical systems onto networks that rely on remote computer-based instructions. Once a hacker can get into those systems he can countermand the instructions from the authorized network and cause chaos from a remote and anonymous location. It could be something as simple as overriding the instructions for a valve to open and close on an oil pipeline. Can you imagine the damage caused if the valve shuts off or fails to open when a surge of oil is streaming down the pipe? The resulting blockage could cause the pipeline to fracture and then the government has an environmental and economic disaster on its hands." Harry nodded in understanding as the Czar, in full flow, continued his explanation.

"The low barriers to entry and relative anonymity of cyber terrorists have levelled the playing field between countries outside of their respective military powers. But it's not just the governments of smaller countries that benefit from this. Corporations and criminal cartels are also highly active in cyber warfare. I would not call us either of those, but we do have strong capabilities. No government has ever been toppled by cyber warfare alone." He gave a flamboyant grin. "But then I want to cement my place in history.

"We have not yet been able to get into the electricity or other power grids yet, and the banking and finance sector is also proving hard to crack. But a key focus is breaking the government's monopoly of the media. We have a number of projects in place, several of which are in advanced stages. If we can break through the firewalls that prevent us from sending data out of the country, then we can build an effective propaganda campaign, which is where, my friend, you come in."

Kessler was interrupted by a low beeping that emanated from a tiny device located on his stylish brown leather belt. He reached down and flicked it off, and exchanged glances with Chen. "Excuse me. I've been summoned to the operations centre. I'm on call day and night – if you can call it that here – in case of developments. It seems we have one. Come along, this could be a good learning experience."

Chen and Harry followed Kessler out of the mess hall and through the shadowy labyrinth of corridors that connected them to the main area of operations. Once again he heard a rumble from a tube train, this time more distant. When they entered the chamber through the heavy steel door, Harry sensed an air of excitement amongst the group. Nearly half of them were gathered around a console over which sat a young Oriental man. His fingers danced over his tablet in front of him. The group parted like a wave as Kessler came forward and the young man at the console peered at Kessler through his outrageously thick spectacles. "Mr. Czar, sir, I think we do it!"

Harry glanced at Kessler. His face was impassive until he saw the screen, and then Harry could sense the anticipation in his eyes. "Talk to me Hayashi," he said, a slight edge in his voice.

Hayashi described the scene on his monitor. It was taken from a street camera they had hacked into, and it was pointed at a huge video screen on the corner that towered over the high street below, in this case Leeds. It was typical of the reviled screens that had been placed in strategic areas of each town and city which constantly spewed government propaganda and misinformation. The street camera had no sound but Harry could see on the screen a choleric, red-faced Lawrence Pelham waving his finger at his unseen audience.

"Watch please," said Hayashi.

His fingers danced again over the tablet and as they watched the Prime Minister's irate face disappeared and the vast overlooking screen went blank. The street camera remained intact, the street was still there, but the vast screen was now dark. Hayashi continued tapping away and then the blank screen was replaced by a still image of Pelham delivering a speech but altered so that he was dressed in the garish, spotted uniform of a clown. This comical picture remained on screen for only a few seconds as Hayashi continued his work, and abruptly the real Pelham regained dominion of the screen, unaware that he had been rudely interrupted.

A muted cheer echoed around the chamber and Kessler clapped Hayashi heartily on the back. He stood and bowed stiffly as his compatriots bombarded him with handshakes and choruses of approval.

Harry turned to Chen, feeling disengaged from the euphoria around him. "What does it all mean?" he asked.

"It means that you have a lot of work to do to get your propaganda machine into operation. You're going to become famous; or even better, notorious..."

# REUTERS EDITORIAL NOVEMBER 15

The last couple of days have brought a succession of hammer blows to the Conservative government. The nation remains subjugated under the military force of the regular army, the Order Police, and the People's Independent Army, all of them fiercely loyal to Pelham and his inner sanctum. The sporadic pockets of resistance remain fractured and ineffective, and the military remains focused on ruthlessly crushing any challenges to its authority. However, even this dictatorship cannot be totally impervious to public opinion, and given the extraordinary turn of events of the last few days, there will be some concerned debates in the corridors of power.

While its military rule has been irrefutable, the regime has taken a body blow in the propaganda war. The giant screens positioned menacingly over every high street in the country have long been regarded as a symbol of the Party's despotic hold on power, as they use the tool to justify their actions in an attempt to win the hearts and minds of the non-immigrant population; to inform but to threaten, to persuade and to warn against insurrection, and to espouse their world view on citizens with little choice but to listen.

However, three days ago, in unison across the country, the screens went blank. The polluted rantings from various icons of the government media machine were suddenly cut off in mid-flow. For an hour the screens remained black and silent, and every town was spared the tyrannical din for the first time in many months. All over the country, reports came in of muted cheers from sections of the public; many of whom were marched from their homes daily and forced to stand in town squares to watch the screens. In many places, however, those celebrations were met with retribution from patrolling forces intent on any excuse to exert their power. Accounts quickly filed in of a number of scuffles, resulting in several deaths and an unspecified number of injuries that the State media was quick to pin on rebellious factions intent on causing trouble.

After an hour, those screens suddenly flickered to life again, only it wasn't a Tory spokesman on screen. It would appear that they had been usurped. The voice and face at first was unfamiliar to the vast watching public, but it was quickly identified as belonging to Harry Clarke, a former political correspondent. Clarke just happened to be on the government's most wanted list for the murder of Graham Matheson just days after Matheson had resigned from his post in the newly formed Cabinet. Clarke is also wanted for being a leading member of the terrorist network that was destroyed by the government in July. At that time he mysteriously escaped and now it appears he has resurfaced, at least in virtual form.

Clarke wasted no time in setting out a catalogue of crimes by the ruling Party, interspersed with a raft of statistics that ranged from the number of people displaced by military forces to the amount of political dissidents that had mysteriously 'disappeared' since Pelham had taken power. It was the images that resonated with viewers, however. Across the country, those images brought gasps of shock from the assembled masses, and even the authorities paused in their persecution of citizens to stare up at the screens as appalling pictures and film of life under a military-backed dictatorship flashed across the screen. These ranged from photographs of protesters clutching bleeding heads after a beating by masked PIA foot soldiers to films of immigrants of all ages being herded like cattle onto cages on the back of the reviled camp transportation trucks, exposed to the teeming rain.

Amongst the torrent of misery, however, were even more disturbing images that Clarke claimed to have witnessed personally. He introduced a piece of footage by explaining that it was taken on a smartphone by a young Kashmiri boy who was now missing. He said the film was taken inside one of the so called *'Sonderzüge'* trains heading toward the coastal ports, in this case Pembroke. There had been rumours, quickly refuted by State media sources, that the conditions inside the train were crowded and insanitary, but hearing about the conditions and seeing them projected on giant screens is a major psychological shift. The poor quality but clearly authentic film portrayed a dark, airless carriage where unfortunate immigrants were squeezed together so closely there was little room to breathe. They had been packed together to maximize the number of people in each carriage, which was locked on the outside. The Kashmiri boy, with remarkable calm, described the appalling conditions and explained that they were on the third day of the journey without food or water, the only ventilation coming from a tiny half-closed grille on the top corner of the carriage.

These people had no information; they had no idea where they were going or how long they would be incarcerated, or the fate that awaited them when they finally arrived at their destination. By that third day many people had already perished, yet they were packed in so tight they remained upright amongst the press of bodies, survivors forced to stand shoulder to shoulder with the corpses, some of whom were undoubtedly family or friends. The film shows some of those corpses close up, eyes turned upwards and their skin a grey, ghostly pallor, already in the first stages of *rigor mortis*. The boy provides a colourful description of the stench, as the only place for people to relieve their bodily functions is a small bucket in the corner which most cannot reach anyway. The conditions are beyond inhumane, and the cries of agony and misery are something that, unlike the smell, the viewer is not spared from.

The footage continues as the victims are unloaded from the carriages by gun-toting soldiers pulling people from the train and pushing them to the dirty ground. Many of them are too exhausted to stand, but the soldiers drag them to their feet and force them to stand in line while severely traumatized families huddle together for comfort. In one barbaric scene, a soldier is seen repeatedly striking an old man in the head with a baton while the man raises his hands in a vain attempt to protect himself, before a final blow sends him crashing to the ground where he lies twitching.

The broadcast then cuts to a succession of still images. At first glance, it is difficult to see exactly what is being shown. It is dark and the figures in the picture are ill-defined, but as more images cycle through and repeat, the commentator carefully explains that these were taken on a cargo ship off Pembroke. It soon becomes clear what is being shown, and the images of dead bodies piled high in the container is even more disturbing than the film taken inside the trains. A short film of the bodies is taken, and as the camera pans around, it can be seen that the container is just one of many piled high on the ship.

The broadcast, accentuated by Clarke's calm depiction of events, in stark contrast to the usual belligerent ranting from Party officials, was so shocking in its brutal intensity that it immediately brought a storm of protest in social media circles unprecedented so far in

Pelham's administration. The government has made it clear that any dissent and criticism of its policies in the social media would not be tolerated, and until now most people have desisted for fear of the consequences. The broadcast, however, encouraged ordinary people to protest in the hundreds of thousands, and surely even this regime does not have the resources to track down and punish every individual who has the temerity to criticize the government.

The broadcast prompted a fresh wave of civil unrest, although demonstrations were limited and rapidly quelled by government forces. Anyone showing any sign of dissent against this regime puts themselves at considerable risk. Participants in protest gatherings know that inevitably they will be met with violent retribution. The social media storm at least offered some degree of privacy and given the volume of protesters, some protection, at least for a while.

The transmission continued through the night and for most of the following day, and ran in a continuous repeated loop, not only to reinforce the message, but to reach new audiences who had not seen the screens the first time. The broadcasts were loud and interspersed with sobering statistics on the number of people missing, sent to deportation camps and who had died of the anthrax-like disease that had ravaged those camps. Clarke talked in detail as a witness to the execution of hundreds of immigrants and the macabre act of loading the corpses into containers, and confessed that it was one statistic he could not offer, not even as an estimate. It was impossible to know just how many people had died this way, but he referred to it as a level of genocide never before seen in this country.

At first soldiers blocked access to the screens, although that did not prevent people watching from afar using binoculars and cameras with powerful zoom lenses. The volume was set as high as it had been previously, and Harry Clarke's damning words resounded accusingly across the streets. It took nearly forty-eight hours of indecision by the government to finally give the order. Unable to find the source of the intrusion into their network, and unable to cut the power centrally to their creation, Party officials had to wrestle with the decision to destroy one of the regime's most potent weapons, now that it had been turned against them. The capital and technological investment had been huge, but it was unclear whether the regime could regain control of the system. Like a prize bull that had suddenly turned and charged at its master, they had to put down their valued asset. Military forces were ordered to fire on the screens, and throughout the country, the screens were permanently dismantled or silenced by bullets and missiles.

The public relations damage had already been done when the screens were destroyed. The events of the last few days have thrown Pelham's administration into sharp focus. None of the reforms that Pelham promised have yet materialized and ordinary people are suffering under Pelham's repressive regime, even those that he purports to represent. Life in Britain's dictatorship is harsh and precarious. No-one is truly safe anymore. Pelham has created a paranoid society where survival is the primary motivation, forcing people to subjugate their beliefs and ethics, the qualities that make us civilized humans, to get through another day. Bribes and corruption are commonplace as 'public servants' seek to profit from their newly-elevated authority. History has taught us that corruption is rampant in repressive societies, particularly where food and other supplies are running low, as the economic sanctions, now in their third week, continue to bite. It is a tightrope that people walk however. Paying a bribe to a public officer even for basic necessities is still illegal, and people face the risk of being arrested and thrown in jail if they choose the wrong officer.

The threat of arbitrary incarceration is an ever-present danger, not just for the many immigrants still waiting for their deportation notices, but also for dissidents who have had the courage to speak out through the social media. They risk the dreaded late night knock at the door and the prospect of joining the swollen ranks of the 'disappeared.' The horrific images seen on the screens over the last few days has exposed this regime to scrutiny like no other event, and it could be the ripple that turns into a wave of dissent. Only time will tell, but it is clear the nation is now at a very important crossroads.

# CHAPTER 52

The mood in the main operations centre was buoyant, and even Kessler had unbuttoned his collar and tie and joined the team for a glass of cheap wine. In the ten days he had been underground, Harry noticed how Kessler maintained a discreet distance from his team, as if the lines of hierarchy were boldly drawn and demanded compliance. Today was not a day for such authority, and Kessler was perched on the end of a chipped wooden desk in front of the large screen, sipping at his wine, surrounded by his team of hackers and spammers. A procession of rapidly changing numbers rolled across the screen.

"Lord, what I wouldn't give for a nice glass of Beaujolais," he smiled. "I guess this UN food aid rubbish will have to do." He raised his glass in Harry's direction and Harry sheepishly raised his own in response. "Here's to our new-found celebrity and quite possibly the most wanted man in Britain right now. Congratulations Harry."

The assembled group turned to Harry and raised their glasses and Julianne, standing behind him, squeezed his arm affectionately. Harry was a little taken aback at the impromptu celebration and muttered his thanks. Chen, standing by Kessler's side, addressed the group. Every member of the Resistance was present.

"The numbers you see on the screen are indicators of social

media chatter. We have been able to hack into the government's so-cial media monitoring post and they measure the volume of instant messaging, texting, Tweets, blogging and every other form of distrib-uted electronic messaging. We don't have access to the breakdown by type of social media but I don't need to interpret the numbers for you. The volume of chatter is staggering. When you consider that so many people closed down their social media channels either voluntarily or under duress, the figures are even more remarkable. If Pelham thought that pulling the plug on the screens would quieten the chatter, he could not be more wrong. All of these people risk arrest and detention once the monitoring post identifies their source, but there is relative safety in numbers. Not even the government can arrest several million people at once, can they?"

He paused, his gaze sweeping the room. "Comrades, we have created quite a stir, but we still have a great deal of work to do to turn a ripple into a wave. We have no idea yet whether any of the so-cial media has breached the government's firewalls and gained inter-national attention, but you can be certain that the authorities will try to contain it. Even so, the people have spoken and we owe them a duty to keep up the pressure. So let's enjoy the moment for now and then straight back to work. Well done everyone."

It was the closest thing Harry had heard to a motivational speech since he had been here, but he had developed a new-found respect for the men and handful of women who worked diligently in this little warren under the noses of the enemy. They were an exception-ally self-disciplined group, and required little direction or incentive to work on their projects. He revelled in his role as their spokesman to the outside world, happy that once again he could make some contribution in the battle against this tyrannical regime. His broadcasts had been far more effective than anyone in the Resistance had anticipated. They had been filmed by Chen and two of his team and the simple recording of Harry talking had been interspersed expertly with the film they had secured from Amir's camera and other video footage that illustrated Harry's message. The script itself had been all Harry's and once it had been edited and Hayashi had uploaded it to the screens, the roughly three-hour film ran in a continuous loop. The broadcast was simple but stunningly effective.

As the team returned to work and the operations centre once again became a hive of activity, Chen sauntered over to join Harry and Julianne. He picked at the nicotine patch below his throat like an itchy scab. "Jesus I need a cigarette. Can I have a word? Would you mind if we stepped outside?"

Harry and Julianne both nodded their assent and they passed through the heavy steel security door, which hissed like an airlock as they passed out into the dark network of passageways outside the main bunker. A distant rumble cascaded along the passageway as the three stood outside and Chen spoke between deep draughts of a precious illicit cigarette. "We have achieved much more than we dared hope for, but the screens have been disabled. We can try and distribute the film through the social media channels but after the incident with the screens the Ministry of Information will be vigilant. Wherever our film pops up they will react quickly by deleting it or closing down any site or account that hosts the film. People would be taking a big risk by hosting the film on their individual social media accounts, as they could get targeted, but that still leaves thousands of other business sites that could potentially distribute it. Of course these sites face similar risks to individuals if they host our film – they could get shut down and permanently lose their Internet presence if the Ministry discovers it and retaliates. Despite the restriction on content as a result of the media clampdown, these sites still need to operate on the Net in order to do business. The bottom line is that the film is only just the start. We need to keep the momentum going if we are to sustain the propaganda advantage of the last few days."

"How do we do that?" asked Julianne, flapping at the smoke that gently drifted past her.

Chen smiled, baring his yellow teeth. "I have been negotiating anonymously with a number of sites through our own network and many are willing to host the film. The majority are not, through a combination of fear and corruption. Many businesses have been offered tempting incentives like generous tax breaks if they support the government's policies. The film has had huge impact but the regime will seek to suppress it where they can and without widespread distribution its impact will be diminished. We need an alternative system."

Chen was interrupted by a crescendo of noise from the Jubilee Line forty feet below. Every time Harry heard the noise it felt like the whole warren that was now his home would collapse. Chen calmly waited for the clamour to die down before he continued. "DMB. We have been experimenting with digital multimedia broadcasts for international audiences. DMB was developed in South Korea twenty years ago and has been around commercially for some time, although there are still some countries where it is not widely available. It uses digital radio transmission technology in the very high and ultra-high frequency range. Along with several experts in our network, we have been developing an extremely high frequency band to send content to all mobile devices, one that works outside the normal frequencies and therefore is not in the range blocked by the government. The challenge for us is that once we begin transmitting, we need people to tune in on their mobile devices to the frequency we are transmitting at. It's like launching a new media platform or website. In order to reach your intended audience, you need to advertise widely, and even then it takes time to build critical mass. Our problem is that we need to advertise under the radar because as soon as the authorities become aware of the broadcasts they will seek to block the broadcasts by jamming them, typically by broadcasting a signal on the same frequency. The EHF band we are working on is specially designed for broadcasts over a wide geographical area and test transmissions have been highly successful."

"Cut the technical crap, Chen. What does it mean in practice?" snapped Julianne impatiently.

Chen gave a condescending smile, as if he were humouring a child. "The result is that as long as the mobile devices are tuned to the correct frequency, they can receive our broadcasts, both in this country and internationally. We don't know yet how good the reception quality is over large distances, and we don't know how easy it will be for the government to jam our signal if and when they find the correct frequency. It's a cat and mouse game I'm afraid. The technology is promising though, and we are hoping that if the broadcasts reach an international audience it will have sufficient impact to spread like wildfire so we reach critical mass quickly and it prompts an international outcry when nations see their countrymen as corpses piled high."

Chen took a long drag of his cigarette and puffed out a number of smoke circles. "I think of this as our equivalent of the BBC World Service. The Service has always been seen as the voice of reason, listened to with hope by millions of people escaping tyranny from their own totalitarian governments across the world, an alternative to the heavily censored and sanitized State run media. It's somewhat ironic that the BBC World Service now belongs to a regime that is contrary to everything it has traditionally stood for. The next step is for you to keep making the content, and make it convincing. The screenings have shown that there is huge potential for the propaganda war, and it's the only way we are going to be able to force this government out."

Harry suddenly felt a crushing weight of responsibility on his shoulders, but it was mixed with a huge sense of anticipation. This regime could not be toppled by military force, at least not from within its borders. The way to defeat it was to provide information to help the world understand the abuse of power perpetrated by the State. It might take time, but surely Pelham's position would eventually become untenable, just as so many dictators had found in the past. It was a long road ahead, however, and whether he liked it or not, he had been placed at the forefront of the fight as the face and voice of the propaganda war. As they headed back to the operations centre, Julianne grasped his hand with genuine empathy, as if she understood his thoughts.

# CHAPTER 53

Although the bunker was claustrophobic because of its location, Harry had to admire the way the group had utilized the limited space they had. He was now much more familiar with the layout, and it reminded him a little of a cave network in Borneo he had read about. It was a warren of interconnected underground caverns that created a unique habitat. The bunker was similar, and boasted more than just the basic living and operational areas. Apart from the recreational rooms, the bunker also possessed a studio where Chen and his colleagues had filmed Harry, and it was here that Harry now spent the bulk of his working time. They had given him a tablet and he used it to research and draft his dialogue in preparation for the next filming.

Chen had excitedly advised him that they were close to making a test digital multimedia broadcast and so he was under pressure to write more dialogue. They had agreed to use the footage on Amir's phone again, even though it repeated their earlier screen broadcast. The DMB was aimed internationally and the film would be new to an overseas audience and retain its shock value. Unfortunately they had little other direct film of abuses committed by the regime, although they were attempting to source more incriminating footage through Kessler's network of contacts. He was acutely aware that the propaganda war would not be won on words alone. They needed to provide direct evidence to support their claims. Today's society was a multimedia society, and the message needed to be conveyed visually to secure any lasting impact.

He rarely found it difficult to draft the script but he knew the messaging had to be carefully worded and he found himself constantly restructuring and revising his text. Harry was in a more reflective mood today, and in the relative loneliness of the cramped studio, his thoughts inevitably wandered to Tamara and Byron. He still had no idea of their fate. The thought of them brought dark feelings of impotent rage, and it was a relief when Julianne appeared.

As she entered the studio she eased her lithe frame into the plastic chair across from his desk. She flashed an alluring smile. "You know," she began, "I always had a strong faith in you but it took me a while to convince Kessler and Chen to go after you. I think I have been fully vindicated by the success you've achieved." She reached over and squeezed his hand, and her soft fingers felt warm to the touch. "But I didn't want you back just for that."

Harry sighed and put down his tablet. She was always hammering at his defences when he felt at his most vulnerable, when thoughts of Tamara and Byron invaded his mind. She was a constant temptation and he had to admit it felt good having her back in his life. He had let Tamara down so many times before, but it felt to him that any act of betrayal now would be worse because she was not around to know about it. He gently removed her hand and changed the subject. "How's Kendrick?"

Her voice turned steely, an undercurrent of anger evident. "He's recuperating on leave. I understand that Grayson his boss was apoplectic with rage that you had been allowed to escape, but when he saw Kendrick's injuries he didn't suspect a set-up. He just thinks that Kendrick screwed up."

"I feel terrible about it," replied Harry sombrely. "He sacrificed a lot for me and I shot him. I've never shot anyone before."

Julianne's voice turned softer. "It was all part of the plan. Kendrick's a survivor. He'll be okay."

She hesitated before continuing. "Harry I need you to listen to me. I have something very important for you."

The earnest look in her hazel eyes convinced Harry to put down his tablet. She looked tired, and those beautiful almond-shaped eyes had fine lines radiating from them. She handed him a scrap of paper with a set of alpha-numeric numbers she had copied down.

"What is it?"

"It allows access to the restricted newspaper archive portal. Try it and see."

Harry tapped in the web address for the portal, which before the Conservatives came to power was a free information service accessible to all. The website appeared and requested a code to continue. Julianne brought her chair round adjacent to Harry's and he could feel her hot breath as they looked at the screen together. He tapped in the code from the scrap of paper and immediately the portal, with which he had once been so familiar, popped up.

"Type in *Duncan Cavendish.*"

"Who?"

"Just do it!" she said impatiently.

Harry obliged and scoured the impressive three-dimensional graphical site for various articles about the disgraced biologist. He found it a little suspicious that most of the articles about him had been blacked out, but he had no idea why. "What exactly am I looking for?" he asked.

"There." Julianne pointed at one of the various picture cubes floating around on screen. He tapped it with his finger and the article and supporting photograph dominated the entire screen. It was a screen-shot of a national newspaper from way back in 1988. Like the others the bulk of the text had been deleted, as if they carried some incriminating confession. The headline alluded clearly to his white supremacist leanings and his long jail term, but the censor had made a surprising omission in failing to scratch out the photo. Julianne was pointing to the boy pictured standing proudly next to Cavendish, the man's arm draped around his shoulder.

Harry sat back and let out a low whistle as he finally got it. "But Pelham was orphaned," he said, struggling to comprehend.

"Was he?" countered Julianne. "What evidence do you have of that?"

"None, just that it was generally considered common knowledge, even in the House. Of course Pelham never talked about his parents but everyone, even the media respected that. They just thought that maybe he found it too traumatic." He stared closely at the photo, rubbing at the stubble on his chin. Of course it could have been doctored, he thought, but why would anyone do so? No, the boy in the photograph was undoubtedly Lance Pelham.

"Where did you get this code?"

Julianne hesitated and he noticed a slight flush in her cheeks. "I have been put in touch with a contact within government. The code was passed to me."

Harry looked hard at her and Julianne averted her eyes. "Is it safe?"

Julianne glared back at him and her eyes were suddenly full of fire. He had seen that passion before. It was part of what had drawn him to her in the first place. "Is anything safe?" she countered harshly. "You have to trust me on this Harry. We have so much to gain. We can expose Pelham for the person he really is - it's worth the risk and my contact in government agrees. In fact she is taking a far greater personal risk by talking to us. No I'm not sure it's safe and I don't even know if she can be fully trusted, but we owe it ourselves to try. In fact you and I are meeting with her tomorrow."

Harry looked at her incredulously. "Kessler and Chen would never allow it!"

"Then we don't tell them. We are not prisoners here. We can come and go as we please within reason."

Harry had to admit that the thought of going 'upstairs' was rather appealing. Julianne spent a lot of time on the surface and he had to admit to feeling a little envious. He knew many of the operatives in the bunker had not surfaced for several weeks, but he was becoming a little stir crazy. The thought of feeling the wind on his cheeks – not the harsh wind stirred up from a distant passing train whistling through the tunnels – was hard to resist. "So what do you hope to achieve by meeting your mole in the government?"

Julianne looked thoughtful. "You probably know your way around the portal. Find out as much as you can to build up a picture of Pelham's childhood and influences. My contact is doing the same but I understand has some inside knowledge that will help us fill in any gaps. It would form the basis of a sensational broadcast."

Harry scanned the portal. "When do we meet your mole?"

Julianne's face brightened. "Does that mean you will come?"

"Yes I'll come. I think Kessler will have something to say about it though."

"He will only know after we have left. We're doing this for the Resistance."

"Let's hope Kessler sees it that way."

Julianne's ruby lips flashed into a confident smile. "I'll handle Kessler. We meet at 6.30 tomorrow morning. Find as much out as you can from the portal before then."

# CHAPTER 54

It was a sharp November day and the wind that Harry had yearned for blew an icy chill that stung his face. It was after six in the morning and still dark, but the first faint rays of the coming sunrise filtered through the low, dense grey clouds. The air carried the threat of a winter as cold as the summer had been hot. As he and Julianne melted into the shadows, cautiously making their way to the coffee shop at the end of a narrow lane near Westminster, he sensed a palpable menace in the damp air. The slick, rain-swept streets were deserted apart from the odd rat scurrying from one storm drain to another, and the ubiquitous presence of soldiers patrolling the streets, armed and alert for trouble.

They were in breach of a curfew that had been restored after the incident with the giant screens, and the deserted streets rendered them an easy target. The level of tension had increased significantly even since he had last been above ground. The regime was clearly intent on a show of force, and their presence was intimidating. They had been given tacit approval to act without accountability to suppress any further demonstrations of dissent. No-one dared risk being detained by soldiers in the current volatile climate. Anyone outside without a valid reason, particularly during curfew, risked being stopped and searched. That could inevitably lead to detention, which under the emergency powers granted to military forces in the last few days by Parliament would be for any length of time they saw fit. He could feel his heart pounding in his ears as they hid in the shadows, waiting for the next opportunity to move ahead without being seen. If they were spotted now, it would be over. How long would it be before they were forced to reveal the location of the underground bunker? He knew he would not respond well to torture. Along with the suppression of freedom of speech, the regime had suppressed freedom of movement, and Harry now understood Kessler's reticence in allowing anyone out of the bunker. No doubt they would face Kessler's wrath when they returned.

He allowed himself the luxury to reflect on their exit from the bunker. Despite the lack of natural light there, the concept of night and day was rigidly adhered to. Although the operations centre was manned on a twenty-four hour rolling basis by three roughly eight-hour shifts, the night shift was the least busy. Harry had hardly slept and did not need an alarm to wake him from his dormitory camp bed. He had gently crept out and met Julianne in one of the narrow corridors that led out of the bunker through a steel door. The dark passageway they walked along led to the same steep ladder they had descended when they arrived. In the darkness Harry could barely tell when they had reached the surface. Julianne was out first and swiftly disabled and then opened the magnetized metal grille. She emerged onto solid ground inside the abandoned chapel. Harry swiftly followed.

"How the hell did you do that?"

Julianne was taciturn. "Trade secret Harry. I just don't like the idea of being a prisoner down there," she explained as she helped Harry out of the hole before replacing the grille.

They had left the chapel through a small back door that opened out into a tiny enclosed courtyard. From there they could peer through a tiny hole in the brickwork to confirm there were no soldiers in the immediate vicinity.

Julianne had assured Harry that the coffee shop was not far, but they still spotted a few soldiers on patrol. Now, as they pressed against the slick wall of the narrow alleyway leading to the café, Harry stumbled in the dark over a large but yielding shape. Julianne's flashlight briefly played over the amorphous figure, revealing the pale, bloated face of a bearded Jewish man still wearing the traditional yarmulke on his head. In the middle of his forehead, just below the skullcap, a large scarlet hole, ragged and dirty, revealed his demise. Perhaps he was trying to escape the purge against immigrants that had intensified in the last few days, or maybe it was retribution for breaking the curfew. Julianne nodded in understanding at Harry's urgent look and they hurried on, alert and watchful. Harry's nerves were as taut as chicken wire and when they reached the coffee shop he let out a deep sigh of relief. The scruffy brick building was dark and apparently unoccupied, and he saw Julianne gasp in surprise when she found the door locked. She softly rapped on the door, glancing anxiously around her, and after an age they heard the sharp report of several bolts being drawn back on the other side.

The door opened and immediately a shrivelled old woman ushered them in and locked the door behind them. "She's already here Miss Julianne," hissed the old lady, leading them through the grimy shop past the counter into a small, gloomy room at the rear of the shop.

"Thank you, Hilda," Julianne whispered back. The only light came from a bare light bulb hanging on the end of a frayed electrical cord, and a tinny rattle came from the exposed pipework in one corner. The sole window had been boarded up but the room was not empty. Sitting at the scratched Formica-topped table was a young, athletic looking woman, her blonde hair tied back in a bun, accentuating her flawless skin and inviting features. A red woollen coat buttoned half way up hugged her shapely figure. She immediately stood up, a little embarrassed, as if unsure why she was there. She shook hands stiffly with Julianne, and Hilda brought some coffees as the trio introduced themselves.

"Rachel Thomas," she said warmly, turning to shake Harry's hand. Her grip was firm but her manicured hands were soft. Despite the early hour, Harry noticed that Rachel had applied her make-up perfectly, and it enhanced her delicate beauty. Harry found it hard not to stare at her and he sensed Julianne cast heated glances in his direction every now and then.

There was a hint of amusement in her clear blue eyes as she addressed Harry. "You have caused quite a stir Mr. Clarke. The Prime Minister is deeply unhappy with you."

Harry smiled at the understatement, and it set the tone for a more relaxed meeting. Rachel explained her position in the government and why she felt her conscience could no longer tolerate the transgressions committed by the administration in which she worked.

Her voice quivered as her long fingers danced over her tablet. "I cannot just resign in protest. If they found me here, especially if they knew who I was meeting, I would be finished, and I don't just mean my career."

Julianne nodded curtly. "We understand the risk you're taking.

Anything we say or publish will never get traced to you."

Rachel gave a wan smile, unconvinced, but nevertheless laid out her tablet on the table and talked them through her findings. As they talked, Julianne made notes on her tablet and Harry shared the results of his own research the evening before. Harry was able to interpret some of Rachel's findings with his knowledge of Pelham when he was a political correspondent. In turn Rachel was able to put into context a number of remarks made by Pelham from their analysis of Harry's findings. Like a vast jigsaw puzzle, they were able to piece together Pelham's life history in a way that the media had never attempted, and when they had finished they stared at each other in disbelief.

# CHAPTER 55

The trio's combined efforts in piecing together the collage of facts about Pelham and his family explained a great deal. Pelham's natural father was a gifted human biologist who had specialized in the study of various pathogens and how they affected the cell structure of human tissue. The experiments he conducted were designed to assist in the creation of new and stronger antibiotics that could bolster the body's natural immune system and slow down or even stop the cell destruction caused by these pathogens. It appeared to be a noble cause, but Cavendish had a dark side that failed to reveal itself until much later, in part because he insisted on working solo on his projects. He had enough power and influence for the Bedfordshire based biotechnology research institute that supported his work to comply with his demands. Back in the eighties, he was as close to a celebrity scientist as one could be.

However, he still retained sufficient anonymity to lead a double life as a white supremacist. There was no suggestion in the articles they reviewed that Cavendish marched through ethnic neighbourhoods chanting obscenities, fist pumping the air like the brainless thugs of the neo-Nazis from the English Defence League, the primary extreme far-right movement at the time. Cavendish was altogether more dangerous because of his brilliance.

His crime was far more insidious and the consequences devastating. He needed to test his antibiotics in live conditions using human control subjects. He managed to contaminate the water supply to a small district in Luton known locally as a Muslims' enclave. This was apparently achieved by causing sewage to seep into the water table through a pressurized valve separating the fresh water and sewage. Ordinarily the fresh water would flow under pressure through the valve and flush out the sewage pipe, but a drop in pressure caused the water to flow in the opposite direction, thereby contaminating the fresh water supply with sewage. No doubt if they probed further they would have found a sewage worker on trial for aiding and abetting Cavendish. The resulting contamination, affecting over two thousand people, caused an epidemic of diarrhoea and vomiting. Hundreds of inhabitants were hospitalized and there were over twenty deaths, mainly among the young and elderly.

Cavendish's team had turned up like the cavalry with his experimental drugs, and despite some spectacular successes at treating the illness, a Muslim elder became suspicious when they made a number of enquiries and could not find any hospital that had sent them. This led to an investigation by the elders, the result of which led Cavendish to be charged and tried for homicide and various other charges under the *Offences Against the Person Act*. His white supremacist activities were laid bare and the testimony of several Muslim elders was instrumental in ensuring a guilty verdict.

Cavendish was incarcerated when Pelham was a boy of twelve. Despite his affluent upbringing and his father's political connections, he had clearly lived in an atmosphere of bigotry and hatred against ethnic minorities, in particular the Muslim community from which

arose the damning testimony that sealed his father's fate. It was unclear what had happened to his mother but the boy was sent away to
live with a high-ranking but older Conservative M.P. Gordon Pelham
and his wife. The Pelhams were childless and the boy was adopted
as their own and took up the family name. The transition to a new
family went unnoticed by the Press, particularly as Cavendish had
kept his private affairs a closely guarded secret, not just his political
leanings but the existence of his family. No-one really knew or cared
much where the adopted boy came from, only that Pelham senior
finally had the son he had always longed for. When the boy sailed
through Eton and later Oxford with stellar grades, the Pelhams
proudly received the plaudits just like any set of parents whose child
had exceeded their expectations. Many people, and more importantly the media, hardly recalled that he had been adopted at all.

Throughout his career, Pelham had remained tight-lipped about
his background. His adopted parents died in a mysterious car accident in 2001. At the time Pelham was twenty-four and starting out on
his burgeoning legal career before taking up politics. Coincidentally
it was less than four years later, in 2005 that two major milestones
occurred in Pelham's life. His natural father apparently committed
suicide at Pentonville Prison in London, although Harry could find
no reports that linked him to Pelham. That did not surprise Harry.
At that point, Pelham was just another bright City lawyer and there
was no reason for anyone to question or even be interested in his
background. He doubted Pelham even attended the funeral.

In the spring of that same year, he ran as a Conservative M.P. in
Watford and won the seat by a narrow margin despite Blair's Labour
retaining power in the general election, and the fact that Watford had

a significant immigrant population. His natural charisma and ability to connect with the audience rapidly gained him popularity, and his tough talking on immigration and protecting British jobs resonated with a large section of the white middle and working class, who saw their prosperity and way of life being eroded, a condition that was exacerbated by the biting recession a few years later. Although several of his speeches were inflammatory, one political commentator described his delivery as 'mesmerizing.' It was those oratory skills and his shrewd tactic of restraining his true viewpoint to keep within the framework of the Party philosophy that led to his rapid ascent through the Tory ranks. The rest was history, and his glittering political career was well documented, even if many references critical of the man had been deleted or blacked out.

Rachel looked up from her screen. "It was only when I was close to him that I understood how vitriolic his hatred was toward immigrants in general but Muslims in particular. Now I know why. He must have been carrying that hate for decades before he finally achieved the power and opportunity to seek retribution for his true father. It also explains the Aryan Project."

Harry looked at her sharply. "The what!?"

"The Aryan Project." She flicked back to an article they had read about the opening of a new government research facility in an industrial estate in Watford. It drew their attention because it referred to the facility being in Pelham's constituency. Its stated purpose was wider than merely research into vaccines for infectious diseases. The article mentioned that one of the laboratories had been earmarked for investigating pathogens to attack the rat infestation that had gripped so many of Britain's cities. "This facility is where the Project is located."

Rachel explained the horrors she had witnessed at the facility, all in the name of creating the Perfect Race. The memory brought bitter tears to her eyes, especially as she had seen so many children torn from their families to be the subject of inhumane biological experiments.

Harry and Julianne listened sombrely as she described what she had seen. "It was the moment I realized he was a monster. What really affected me was the look in his eye when he saw those poor children being experimented on. There was no compassion, just a quiet sense of satisfaction that he had the power to decide their fate."

Harry frowned, deep in thought. "Yes I recall the five year plan discussing the concept of racial purity. It is not the first time that a dictator has held aspirations for a Master Race, but the medical technology is far more sophisticated. It is still an abomination. If he can orchestrate the type of mass killings I saw in Pembroke and to sink to the depths of experimenting on children, then he is capable of....." 

*"My God!"* Julianne stared at him, mortified. Her face was set like alabaster, but her eyes were wide with horror.

Harry merely nodded in understanding. His fingers danced over the three dimensional images of the papers and without looking up, addressed Rachel. "We need proof. Try and locate a technical article that describes the effect of the pathogen on the rats. We need to know what the symptoms are and how the rats eventually die."

Rachel worked furiously at her tablet and Harry remained busy on his own. It did not take him long to locate a recent article that described the mysterious 'anthrax-like' disease sweeping through the camps. Although it was over three months old, it was the most recent article he could find on the subject, describing conditions in the deportation camps during the searing heat of midsummer. Apparently the severe clampdown on the media had precluded any further articles on the subject, but Harry had what he needed. The illness had no known origin but the symptoms were described in detail.

Harry quoted from the article. "The mysterious bacterium that has spread through the deportation camps attacks the victim's internal organs through the bloodstream, causing swelling and fluid build-up, putting the organs under intense pressure until they eventually fail and collapse. The victim could die from a multitude of causes, ranging from liver and kidney failure to fatal heart attacks or even fatal brain haemorrhage. The external signs, apart from severe coughing spasms that usually bring up blood as the organs break down, the severe muscle cramps and intestinal pain is the presence of ugly skin lesions that break out all over the skin." He turned to Rachel. "Do you have anything on the rat pathogen?"

Her face was sombre, as if she had already guessed what Harry was looking for. She too quoted from an article, this one found in the *Journal of Molecular Biology*. "Scientists are working on a solution to the huge increase in the rat population that has infested our cities. They are close to finding a suitable pathogen that introduces hostile bacteria into the rat's gastro-intestinal tract that causes significant edema, an accumulation of fluid and swelling around the organs which places them under severe pressure and eventually causes severe damage to and eventual failure of the main organs. Early tests indicate that the rats often die from a huge heart attack or brain damage. Like anthrax, the pathogen can be transmitted through spores carried by the rats, making it easy for the disease to be carried to their nests, which are often inaccessible through normal extermination processes." She showed her tablet to Harry and Julianne – it held a picture of a dead rat, its bloated body strafed with angry red skin lesions.

Julianne's face drained of colour, and Rachel gasped in horror at the realization. Harry merely nodded in confirmation. "Joszef was right. This is our proof that the disease is man-made. *He's using the rat pathogen on humans.*"

# CHAPTER 56

Rachel broke the heavy silence first. "They must have engineered the disease at the same facility as the Aryan Project. It's in Pelham's constituency."

Harry nodded, his teeth gritted. "Now you know why I am so desperate to reach my wife and child. The last I heard they were interred at Salisbury Camp."

Julianne touched his arm and Rachel muttered. "Jesus I'm sorry Harry."

Harry's tone was gritty. "We know he is a committed fascist with a particular hatred of the Muslim population, and we can reveal his background to the world to help them understand why. As for the disease; as far as I know the world believes that it is an unfortunate natural contagion with an unknown origin, much like the SARS and H1N1 viruses. New diseases occur frequently in the modern world as the global climate becomes more imbalanced, but the State's media censure has made it difficult for journalists to independently investigate. I'm not even sure there are any independent journalists left, only those in prison like my friend Bernard Maxwell. I can claim on the broadcasts that the disease was engineered, but the Ministry of Information will merely dismiss it as an outrageous, groundless accusation. They'll produce a stack of evidence to show how they are supplying medicines and vaccines to the camps and looking for a cure. There is nothing in these files that connects Pelham. We need some solid evidence to show that he is directly implicated in the creation of this pathogen."

Rachel leaned forward. "What type of evidence?"

"Email correspondence that shows a direct line to Pelham, that he gave directions, perhaps to the laboratory or to figures within his regime. We need any files or media that implicate Pelham. It is not enough to be from his ministers. He could claim that they acted without authority even if it undermines his leadership. It has to be directly from Pelham. If we can find it then surely the UN will get off their backsides and bring in a task force. He will surely be finished."

Julianne sipped at her coffee, which had now gone cold. "How are we going to find evidence like that?" she sighed. The Resistance had proved capable of limited sabotage and spreading viruses to attack enemy cyber-based systems, and had also achieved some success at hacking into those systems. The giant video screens they had taken control of were a case in point. However, despite Kessler's boasts that no computer system was impenetrable, they had failed to breach the strong security protocols that protected central government.

Rachel spoke up, her eyes bright. "We have to do it the old-fashioned way and break into his office."

Both Harry and Julianne shot her an incredulous look, but she continued undeterred. "Yes you heard me right. We break in. I happen to know that his office is not as secure as it should be, and at two in the morning there is a change in shift between the security guards that patrol his office. Most of the guards are complacent because they don't expect trouble in a million years. He has lent me the holographic entry card to his office and I've been able to walk into it unchallenged before. I will need to steal it. Once inside we can lock the office and copy what we need. We have to try and access his computer if we can. From what he has hinted at, I believe he has a number of powerful corporate sponsors working in the background supporting him. We have to try and get hold of that list if we can, because his control runs deeper than you think. The support of these sponsors makes his position unassailable. They may be vital to bringing him down."

"Is that really feasible?" asked Julianne.

"I have to think about it," Rachel cautioned. "If I can get us into the office we need to consider how we can access his computer. Maybe you have someone in the bunker that can do that."

Julianne and Harry glanced at each other. How the hell did she know about their operation? As if she had anticipated their unasked question, Rachel said hastily. "It's okay, if anyone knew about the bunker they would have attacked it already. Its proximity to the Houses of Parliament makes it an ideal access point. You know the construction area around Westminster Tube station runs very close to the Houses of Parliament. That may offer us a way in, but I will need to do some research." She glanced at her watch and then said curtly, "This meeting is over. I have to go before I am missed." She slipped a thumb-sized SD card into Harry's hand. "Some film for your broadcasts Harry. I could never be associated with this and you're more famous than me. Call it a gesture of goodwill. I'll be in touch."

She abruptly stood up and took the long pashmina scarf draped over the chair, wrapped it around her neck and swept out of the room without looking back.

Julianne broke the heavy silence that passed between her and Harry. "Rachel's very attractive isn't she?"

Harry was flippant. "I hadn't noticed. How did you find her?"

Julianne swallowed hard. "Does it matter? The real question is can we trust her?"

Harry's expression was hard. "I'm wondering the same about you. Rachel knows the location of the Resistance. You remember what happened when the military found out the location of the compound in Kent? She may be on our side but what if she is compromised? How does she know our location? Are there others that know too? The implications are serious Julianne. Kessler needs to be informed."

Julianne's eyes were wide. "No, Harry," she implored him. "Kessler won't understand. He's too dogmatic. He may be a computer genius but he doesn't appreciate the subtleties of working inside enemy lines. Please Harry, let's keep this between ourselves for now."

Harry let out a deep sigh. "You're playing a dangerous game Julianne. I hope this doesn't explode in your face. I will keep my counsel for now but we have a formidable enemy as it is. Let's not make another one out of Kessler."

Julianne smiled and ran her soft fingertips along his cheek. "Thank you Harry. We make a great team."

Rachel pulled the collar of her heavy winter coat over her scarf and bent her head down against the wind which blew directly into her face as she emerged from the alleyway. The swirling current whipped up piles of loose garbage, papers spinning and flapping, and discarded cans rattled as they rolled along the wet ground, propelled by the strong wind. The rain stung her face as she hurried along, keeping a watchful eye for patrolling soldiers. She had the right papers in case she was stopped, but she really didn't want to have to explain what she was doing so far from the Parliamentary buildings at this early hour. She did not notice the black car with its single occupant parked further down the street.

Behind the tinted windows of the black car, the occupant peered through a powerful telescopic lens. It felt like the blonde figure in the red coat bent against the heavy drizzle was in the car with him. The occupant scratched his stubbly chin. A poor shave was a prerequisite in the security business. It made him look meaner and more fearsome, as if a person would think twice before challenging him. He pulled out his smartphone and dialled a familiar number, but as usual the video at the other end was turned off. However a curt voice answered quickly.

"Yes?"

"Hi it's me." The recipient of his call had banned him from ever using names, not that he even knew his.

"What do you have for me?"

"She's just left. She met both of them."

There was a short pause at the other end. "Good. Keep me informed."

The line went dead and the man sat back and smiled to himself. These so-called charismatic politicians had no social graces when it came to dealing with their subordinates. He knew his employer was in the inner sanctum even if he had never met him in person. He glanced out of his tinted window and spotted a soldier sauntering toward him. That was his cue to leave and he gunned the engine, kicking up piles of debris as the car quickly pulled away. He saw the soldier in his wing mirror briefly raise his rifle and then decide against it, and he breathed a sigh of relief.

# CHAPTER 57

As the grey dawn broke, the risk of being seen was so much greater. Harry and Julianne no longer had the benefit of the fleeting shadows of the early morning twilight, and fifteen minutes remained before curfew was officially over. The disused chapel was not far, but they stayed alert as they dashed out of the alley using any object they could find to seek cover. When they reached the disused chapel Harry sighed with relief as Julianne reached for the metal grille. Before she could engage the lock, the chapel door creaked open and a soldier slipped inside. Julianne jumped away from the grille and the soldier immediately raised his rifle at them.

"Stop where you are," he commanded. His reedy, high-pitched voice carried a tremor. Harry and Julianne froze and raised their hands. Harry studied the soldier. His face was sallow and riddled with teenage acne. He could not have been older than eighteen. His eyes were wide with fear and his bony fingers trembled over the gun. His combat uniform hung loosely on his skinny, almost emaciated figure. "What are you doing here?" he shouted, his voice hoarse and hands now visibly trembling. Harry and Julianne exchanged glances but stood rooted to the spot. The boy was clearly terrified and that fear made him unpredictable and volatile. A wrong move and he was liable to panic. Harry noticed the safety catch on his rifle was off.

Julianne responded in a gentle, soothing voice. "We're just out for a walk. We forgot about the curfew."

"I don't believe you!" croaked the soldier. "Where are your papers?"

Julianne motioned as if she were about to take them out and under the soldier's keen gaze she slipped her right hand into the inside pocket of her coat. "Slowly," hissed the soldier nervously. She pulled out a wad of banknotes and unfolded them. The boy's sunken eyes grew even wider when he saw the money. Julianne's tone was calm and measured. "You look hungry. I'm sure you could use this money."

The teenager gulped, clearly conflicted, his gaze fixed on the money. "They haven't even paid us for three weeks," he said. "How are we supposed to support our families? My Mum and Dad haven't eaten properly for ages."

The rifle lowered slightly and Julianne perceived this as an encouraging sign. "What's your name?" she asked softly.

"Private Dawson," he replied coldly.

"Well Private Dawson," she began, waving the money enticingly, "Do we have an agreement? We both go our separate ways and you get to feed your family. How about it?" Her tone was soothing, and the boy wavered. He looked around sheepishly as if a fellow soldier was about to catch him accepting the bribe.

The soldier nodded to a broken pew several feet away. "Put the money there."

Julianne complied and the boy moved to grab the money. Harry intervened. "Are we free to go?"

Dawson raised his rifle at Harry, his nervousness evident. "Shut up!" he shouted. "I'll tell you when you can go!" Harry stepped back, hands raised. The tension in the air was electric. He quickly snatched up the cash and began to back away toward the chapel door, still covering his targets with his rifle. Then everything happened at once in a blur of motion.

The metal grille in the stone floor of the chapel flung open and a figure dressed in a black balaclava raised its head above ground level. An arm holding a bulky handgun quickly followed and Private Dawson, momentarily distracted by the easy money in his hand, failed to react in time. Three shots in quick succession struck him directly through the heart, the sound muted by the small barrel of a silencer. The soldier jerked like a marionette and collapsed face first to the ground, blood spilling over the stone floor. He twitched a few times and then lay still as his blood continued to slowly pool around his lifeless form.

As Harry watched in horror, the figure climbed fully out of the hole and took off the balaclava. To his surprise he saw it was one of the few women in the bunker. He had only exchanged a few words with her, an Eastern European girl with cold grey eyes. Her expression was blank as she holstered the bulky gun and straightened her mousy hair. "Quickly," she snapped. "Help me hide the body before anyone else comes in.

"What the hell!" began Harry but her icy expression cut him dead.

"Now is not the time," she replied fiercely. "Help me." Harry helped the woman drag the corpse into a dark, secluded corner of the wrecked chapel. The skin already felt cold to the touch. It was probably a pointless exercise because the blood had created drag marks, an easy clue to any soldier looking for their missing comrade.

"The rats will feed on him," she said casually. There was no time to remove the blood, and the acrid smell of gunpowder was evidence enough. The three of them quickly descended through the metal grille and down the ladder to the subterranean passageway. When they had passed through the dark passageways for a few minutes, Julianne broke the heavy silence. "Olga, why did you have to kill him?"

Harry could not see Olga's face in the darkness but her steely voice betrayed her feelings. "Of course I kill him. What else I do?"

"Olga, he was leaving," Julianne persisted. "He was no longer a threat."

Harry sensed Olga stop and spin around to face Julianne. "What if he find comrades and come to chapel?" The hostility in her voice cut through the turgid air.

Julianne began to protest again but Harry put a firm hand on her arm. They soon reached the thick outer doors of the bunker which opened with a hydraulic hiss. The light from inside momentarily blinded them before they passed through. "Follow me please," commanded Olga. She led them through the main operations centre and into Kessler's office. Olga was ushered out and shut the door. When the Czar looked up from his papers at Harry and Julianne, his large brown eyes blazed with an intensity and suppressed rage that Harry found unsettling.

"What the hell were you playing at?" he snarled, his voice quivering with anger.

The ferocity in Julianne's voice equalled Kessler's. "He was leaving! For Christ's sake he was just a kid!"

The Czar stood up straight and puffed out his chest. His impressive physique bristled with indignation. "In case you hadn't noticed he was an armed soldier. You led him straight to our entry point. As soon as he saw you in the chapel he was expendable. Do you really think he was naive enough to walk away counting his money without telling his comrades about the chapel? Come on Julianne you're more sensible than that. This is a dirty war and there will be casualties, some justified and most of them not."

Julianne could not refute Kessler's cold hard logic. "Did you have him killed?"

Kessler clenched his fists. He's like a grenade ready to explode, thought Harry, standing on the fringes of their heated exchange. His temper was legendary and right now Julianne was pushing him to the limit. "Yes I had him killed!" he yelled. "I saw the monitors. If the Army found out about our entry point they could easily trace us here. How long do you think our magnetized grille would hold them? I was not prepared to take that risk and so I sent Olga to eradicate the problem. She's a former Olympic marksman and a part-time assassin for the Belorussian State Security Committee. I needed to make sure there was no mistake. Call it a necessary evil. The question is what were you even doing upstairs? This was not an authorized excursion. I hope you have a good explanation."

"I don't have to explain myself to you," spat Julianne.

Kessler thumped his desk, sending a stack of papers flapping to the floor. "Yes you damn well do! I am running this operation and it is my job to eliminate any threat to it. I've given you plenty of latitude Julianne, do not abuse it. Now, I will ask you again, what were you doing upstairs?"

Julianne remained obstinately silent, her eyes like lasers as she fixed her stare on Kessler. Exasperated, the Czar turned to Harry.

"Are you going to tell me?"

Harry was conflicted. "This is not my call. All I can say is that what we are doing is in the best interests of this organization and for the country."

"Surely I should be the judge of what is best for the Resistance," Kessler shot back. "You, Harry, are especially at risk. You're famous now. The day we took over the screens to make your broadcasts was the day you became a marked man. Can you imagine if a soldier arrested you, what a coup that would be for them? They would hand your head on a platter to Pelham."

"I'm prepared to take that risk."

Kessler's temples throbbed with fury and beads of sweat broke out on his dark face. "Well I'm not." The Czar addressed them like naughty schoolchildren brought to the Principal's office. "Your mission was unauthorized and if you are not prepared to tell me its purpose then you make my decision easy. You are both banned from leaving the bunker."

Julianne glowered at Kessler. "You can't do that! This is too important!"

"Then tell me!" he persisted. "I will not have secrets in my operation."

Harry spoke calmly in order to diffuse the hostility. "All in good time, Anatoly. I promise this could turn into something big, but you have to trust us."

Kessler tore his eyes away from Julianne and glared at Harry. "You left the bunker in secret and now you ask for my trust? I stopped trusting people a long time ago Harry, because they abuse your trust, just like you and Julianne did today. If I believed you were plotting against us you would have suffered the same fate as the soldier. You're too valuable to lose. You put yourself and our operation at great risk by stepping out. The ban stays until you're ready to disclose everything. Now get out!"

Julianne stormed out of his office to the tiny gym where she stripped down to grey T-shirt and shorts and began pounding the heavy canvas punch-bag with ferocious intensity. Harry presently caught up with her and could not help but admire her lithe figure slamming the punch-bag until it swung wildly and the perspiration streamed down her face.

"Now you see what kind of man Kessler is," she said breathlessly, barely pausing in her assault on the bag. "He's as much a dictator as the Prime Minister!"

Harry was thoughtful. He too did not relish the idea of being imprisoned in this underground chamber. "Yes I'm beginning to see that."

# REUTERS EDITORIAL NOVEMBER 28

The pressure on the British government has intensified further over the last few days with more startling revelations about its activities. These revelations, coupled with previous allegations of genocide, were of such magnitude that they caused a storm of protest across many countries and led to the resumption of the emergency debate on the crisis by the UN Security Council in New York, following its original meeting in October.

After the government had silenced the huge screens several weeks ago following the hacking incident, it appeared they had successfully blocked another avenue of dissent. However, it was only a temporary reprieve for this increasingly isolated regime. It appears that the unidentified dissidents found a new and highly effective medium in which to transmit their activities, using digital media broadcasts (DMB). DMB is a digital radio transmission technology that allows multimedia broadcasts to be sent to phones, tablets and any other mobile devices. Because it acts outside the normal frequencies it falls outside the transmission range blocked by the current media blackout operating in the U.K. In addition, it has been impossible to trace the source of the transmissions because they originate from a virtual private network which conceals the original location.

The broadcast was far more effective because it reached beyond the shores of the nation itself, allowing the international community a rare glimpse of life inside this closed country other than official State broadcasts. The transmission frequency at which the film was broadcast meant that very few viewers picked up the original transmission. However, news of the broadcast went viral in minutes, and soon its audience had outstripped many mainstream transmissions as it repeated itself in a continuous loop.

The transmission was once again presented by the sober, reflective figure of Harry Clarke, who has rapidly ascended to iconic status as the face of a burgeoning media rebellion. Even so, he studiously avoided any mention of the organization he represents. His commentary was rational, objective and articulate. He made no threats against the regime but merely provided a factual commentary to the images, which lent the film an even greater potency. Although the footage was amateurish, clearly filmed secretly on a smartphone, the graphic and disturbing images of human experimentation garnered immense impact. Clarke explained that the images were taken in a secret government facility, known as the Aryan Project, a name that conjures up memories of the reviled activities of the Nazi Party.

The analogy is ironic, given the further revelations regarding Lawrence Pelham's past, something he has always kept a closely guarded secret. Clarke claims to have discovered the real identity of this mysterious leader, who despite his craving for media attention has always jealously protected his family background. This has often led to wild, distorted speculation and several defamation actions. Clarke's assertion that Pelham is the offspring of a former white supremacist, Duncan Cavendish, who died in prison nearly twenty years ago, could be considered another piece of idle speculation. The former political correspondent has offered nothing to lend credence to the claim; yet his articulate and restrained presentation arguably lends a certain gravitas to the claims, like a star witness in a high profile trial.

His final and most damning allegation was that the disease had been engineered in the laboratory as a form of ethnic cleansing in the deportation camps. This is a staggering claim. There have been many cases of governments using chemical weapons on their subjects, but the deliberate, calculated production and distribution of an artificial pathogen, if proved, would place Pelham's regime into a category of barbarity that arguably makes immediate UN action essential.

Indeed, Clarke's accusations held such weight that they reached the inner circle itself, with Giles Chamberlain in his capacity as Party spokesman forced to issue a vehement denial. He dismissed the revelations as a bitter and acrimonious attack with no foundation in truth, made by a terrorist enemy of the State, a fugitive wanted for murder and whose testimony could hardly be considered credible. Chamberlain also rejected the film as "lurid sensationalism" and a "ludicrously amateurish fake creation." Even so, his haughty denial of these "wild and baseless accusations" was not convincing enough to ease the troubled conscience of the UN.

During a heated debate, the Secretary-General Kobie Emosi was harshly criticized for his mishandling of the 'British crisis.' He came under fire for his failure to mobilize a task force to land on the island and act as a peacekeeping force. There were several calls for him to resign amongst the delegates, a move unprecedented in recent times. His defence was eloquent but unconvincing. There were far too many political factors at play, he explained. The British Prime Minister had been intransigent and dismissive in his attitude to intervention by a UN peacekeeping force, and Emosi reminded the Council of the strength of the U.K.'s military forces. He asserted that he had no wish to commit the UN to the quagmire of a potentially long and drawn out military conflict that could result in incalculable casualties for both sides, including innocent civilians inevitably caught in the crossfire. The Secretary-General continues to believe that negotiation and mediation remain the best strategies, although there has been little evidence of direct talks at the highest level, merely a regular dressing down for the U.K.'s representative on the Council.

However, after the latest revelations, support from the U.K.'s allies has become more muted. Both the United States and India remain allies of the U.K., at least for now, and following India's recent secession as a permanent member of the UN, they have a power to veto any proposed action by the Council. In partnership with several non-permanent members from Europe, they rejected outright a military solution just over a month ago when the Resolution for the U.K. problem was last debated. Now they are adopting a more realistic stance. The Indian representative stated that "whilst we fear that a military presence could escalate the crisis, the unfortunate conduct of the country's ruling Party has made it a real possibility." That has been the clearest rhetoric yet regarding the waning support for Britain's ruling powers.

The UN representative for China called for immediate and decisive action, stating that if the claims were true, they were "a monstrous affront to human dignity" and that the British regime had "engaged in a level of barbarity rarely seen." When the U.K. representative retaliated by questioning China's own record of human rights abuses and its trade in organ donations, the meeting almost descended into chaos.

In spite of the dwindling level of support for the U.K., its allies maintained their adoption of the veto power to block any resolution on peacekeeping or military action against Britain. As a result, the UN was unable to reach firm agreement on a strategy to address the problem. The meeting ended in recriminations with several delegates from Muslim and African states vehemently complaining that the UN's procrastination was condemning innocent civilians to death for every day it failed to act. If the claims made by Harry Clarke are true, this complaint has substance. What is perfectly clear is that as the first Christmas under the current administration approaches, and the economic sanctions begin to bite hard, the U.K. is bracing itself for a long, hard winter.

# CHAPTER 58

The parliamentary debate had been conducted with a level of intensity unparalleled in Pelham's tenure as Prime Minister. As he left the floor of the House he stormed into his elegant wood-panelled office and slammed the door so hard it strained at the hinges. Chamberlain quickly followed and paused outside the door, smiling discretely to himself. Behind the mahogany door the sound of smashing glass resounded and Chamberlain waited a few moments before he knocked and entered. Pelham had another glass in his hand, ready to hurl against the wall, but he refrained when he saw his deputy. His face was flushed and tiny dark lines radiated from under his tired, dull eyes. His famously boyish features were strained and his jaw was set. Chamberlain thought he looked every inch a man under severe stress.

"That damn bitch," he growled, referring to the BNP Opposition Leader Jane Forster. "How dare she question my leadership!"

Chamberlain was pragmatic. "It's her job Lance. I've told you before not to take these things personally." In fairness, Chamberlain had to admit, it felt like a personal attack on the Prime Minister, especially when the BNP leader had questioned the veracity of the allegations regarding his background. The Prime Minister had sidestepped the question by stating firmly that his background was completely irrelevant. However, that had not stopped a few catcalls from the Opposition benches suggesting he clear up the position with the House. Chamberlain had observed this exchange with detached amusement. In the previous six months of Pelham's tenure, the Opposition Party had raised barely token challenges to his unassailable authority. The furore of the last few days, allied to the intense pressure exerted by the United Nations, had rapidly weakened Pelham's position. Like a pride of lions turning on its wounded fellow animal, they had sensed vulnerability and had attacked. Pelham had not expected such a defiant stance but Chamberlain had to grudgingly accept he had fended them off well. The debate had commenced with Prime Minister's question time, a tradition Pelham had retained to demonstrate at least some vestige of democracy. However, taking their cue from their leader's aggressive stance, the Opposition Party had grilled the Prime Minister for several hours, while loyal Tory Party members sneered and shouted insults at their political opponents, forcing the Speaker of the House to restore order several times.

Jane Forster supported the general anti-immigrant policies that formed the cornerstone of the Conservative Party's manifesto, but had pledged to challenge the Prime Minister on the way in which he implemented those policies. In practice she had rarely done this. At this debate, however, she had been quite vocal in her concerns that Pelham's policies had pushed Britain into its deepest crisis since the last World War. Shouting over the jeers ringing out from the Tory benches, she stated that recent incidents and the reports leaking from the country's shores into an international arena had lowered the standing of the United Kingdom in the eyes of the world.

Forster had been a member of the BNP for over twenty years

and leader for nearly three. The Party had been fractured by in-fighting and a lack of direction. Even as the nation fell into deep recession and the general attitudes of the country became one of simmering resentment against immigrants, the BNP was too divided to take full advantage. They continued to lobby for change through the judicial process, advocating firm but voluntary incentives for immigrants to leave. However, a number of senior figures in the Party, including Adam Griffiths, protested that the BNP was far too moderate, and they eventually broke away to form the more extreme group known by its acronym as FREE, which had metamorphosed into the People's Independent Army under Griffiths' leadership.

The power vacuum created by the breakaway group directly led to Forster's ascendancy to the leadership. Chamberlain had been surprised. He did not dislike the woman, but although she was an ambitious and respected figure, he had never envisaged her as a true leader ready to ascend to the pinnacle of the Party. In spite of the factions and infighting prevalent in the Party, the BNP continued to accumulate votes as the tide of public sentiment swung in their favour. Forster had steadied the ship and brought stable and struc-tured leadership. Her fierce ambition ensured she stamped out any dissent within Party ranks, and it was widely considered that her strong leadership allowed the Party to emerge as a credible oppos-ition to the government. Until now the Opposition had been muted, but today Forster had imposed her considerable physical presence in a fractious, at times ill-tempered debate.

Chamberlain had not seen such an overt challenge to Pelham's authority since he had come to power, and the P.M. was as mad as hell. He pouted and slammed his tablet onto the large old-style writing bureau. "Get me Rachel," he ordered brusquely.

Chamberlain's fingers danced over his device in compliance with his boss. "Lance, our approval rating has taken a huge hit since the broadcasts. The BNP has seen a chink in the armour and is trying to cash in."

The Prime Minister kicked the broken glass on the carpeted floor away from the drinks cabinet and poured himself a large Scotch. "She has the audacity to question the wisdom of my actions, just because the sanctions are starting to hurt." He took a long gulp of Scotch and slammed the empty glass down with a bang. "We are all making sacrifices. I never promised that the transition to a better Britain was going to be easy. Just because we have a temporary shortage of food and provisions because of those bureaucrats at the UN; the diet will probably do her some good," he grumbled, making an oblique reference to the BNP Party Leader's much-publicized weight issues. "That's the trouble with people like her. As soon as things start getting tough, she begins to question everything that we have stood for. Neither she nor her Party has any mettle. They are too blind and weak to see the wider picture."

Chamberlain persisted. "Of course I agree, but we have the UN Human Rights Council condemning us and demanding an investigation into human rights abuses in the country. We're not North Korea. We cannot remain impervious to this. At some point we will have to respond and co-operate. We need to show to the international community that we are making concessions, such as granting an amnesty to a few political prisoners as a gesture of clemency, or demonstrating that we are working hard to improve conditions in the deportation camps."

"Why the hell should we?" Pelham shot back. "I told the electorate back in June that we faced a long hard road, and that it would take extraordinary strength and discipline. I also said that the future of the country is too important to consider the rights of the individual, particularly criminals." He poured another Scotch and eyed his deputy accusingly. "You wrote the speech for me, remember?" he said scathingly. "I will never submit to terrorists and they will never be released on my watch."

"Yes I did, Lawrence, but this is about damage limitation." Chamberlain could barely mask his irritation. "We have just spent the last three hours fending off accusations that we are engaging in human vivisection to create some 'Master Race,' as Forster put it. I have hundreds of foreign journalists trying to beat down our door seeking information about the claims made in the film. You know these days that perception is everything, and we risk being isolated not just from the rest of the world but from the very people we were elected to represent."

"Be careful, Giles. You're starting to sound like a socialist."

Chamberlain snorted in frustration and was formulating a harsh response when they were interrupted by a gentle tap on the door. "Come in!" barked Pelham.

Rachel walked in, looking distinctly uncomfortable, but Pelham immediately brightened. "Ah, Rachel," he began, "I need you to be even more creative than you usually are." He gave a wicked grin and Rachel blushed as Chamberlain stared at her. "Two things. Firstly I want you to research and dig up some serious dirt on Jane Forster. Jesus surely she has some immigrant background. The woman is descended from Afrikaans for heaven's sake. There must be something. She has outlived her usefulness and we need her removed from power. Do your homework and see what scandals you can find out about her."

"Yes sir," she said quietly.

"Then find out what that bloody idiot Harrison-Jones is doing about finding the source and closing down those DMB transmissions," he said, referring to Christopher Harrison-Jones, the Information and Technology Minister. "I partly blame him for this leak. We need to make sure it doesn't happen again or his next job is going to be at one of the deportation camps."

"Anything else sir?"

Pelham gave her bottom a playful smack and he grinned at her. "I told you, there's no need to call me sir. We know each other too well for that."

Rachel turned even redder. "Yes s-- Lance," she replied sheepishly.

Pelham's face turned dark again. "And please find out from Griffiths why the hell that terrorist Harry Clarke is still alive and making those broadcasts. They should have tracked him down after he sabotaged the screens. Make it clear to him that finding and eliminating that piece of scum is his number one priority. I am beginning to wonder about his leadership abilities."

He flopped down in his luxury swivel chair and tapped away at his computer while Chamberlain sat down on one of the easy chairs to the other side of the desk. He gave an almost imperceptible nod to Rachel while Pelham had his head down tapping away. Pelham finished his note, signed off from the PC and stood up to go.

"Oh, Lance, did you check your schedule for tonight's media briefing?" said Chamberlain quickly.

"No no, where's my tablet?" he said absentmindedly.

"Can't see it," replied his deputy. "Just check on the computer. We have to go – video conference call with our UN representative in New York. Poor bastard has taken a grilling the last few days."

"Yes, okay," sighed Pelham. He sat back down in his chair to check the entry on the computer. He didn't notice that Rachel stood behind him, holding her tablet discretely so that the outward facing camera was positioned over his hands. He got up, buttoned his jacket and strode out of the door, quickly followed by Chamberlain who thrust his tablet in his hands. "I found it," he said simply.

As they left the Deputy looked back at Rachel and she was suddenly alone in Pelham's office. She stood motionless, as if too paralysed to act on this sudden opportunity. She knew she did not have long and she sat in the soft folds of the leather chair in front of his PC, and placed the tablet upright on its stand on the desk. She studied the video she had just taken. It was awkward because the angle of the camera was over his shoulder, and his fingers obscured the keys he was tapping. She ran it at least fifteen times before she had developed a mental picture of the words he had tapped in.

Her heart was hammering furiously as her fingers wavered hesitantly over the keys. Based on her analysis of the video, she had a good idea of the password but it was still not definite. A sickening feeling settled in her stomach when her first log-in attempt failed and the PC warned her that she had just two more attempts. While she was glad that Pelham had rejected the clumsy and error-prone retinal verification scans in favour of an old style password approach, she knew that three failed attempts would cause the computer to go into security mode and immediately dump the information to a secure cloud server, delete its hard disk files and set off the klaxon alarms. When her second attempt failed she almost panicked and fled the office, conscious that any of Pelham's support staff could come knocking at any time. It took a great effort of will to analyze the video again and try a third time. Her fingers trembled and cold sweat gently rolled down her brow. Rachel pressed the last digit and her finger hovered over the 'Enter' key, her body tensed and ready to bolt. She closed her eyes and pressed down, but no alarms sounded. Instead the screen flashed white and a welcome message appeared. She was in!

Rachel quickly reviewed the file structure, committing it to memory, as she flicked through the folders. She had what she needed, a way in. Now was not the time to interrogate whatever lay beneath the folders with their cryptic titles. Rachel scribbled down the folder names to save precious time for when she was next able to access the files. However, as she saw one folder entitled *Deportation Camps'* she quickly drilled through various sub-folders to find the records she needed. Information on the deportation camps was ring-fenced to Ministers and their immediate support staff by a powerful firewall, and so access was beyond Rachel's authority. But she had checked her facts and knew who to look for. The records were extraordinarily detailed, encompassing who arrived at each camp. She found the camp she needed and then checked the records. There was no trace of the person she was looking for. With trepidation, she checked the mortality records and entered the name in the search bar. There it was. Rachel's heart sank. It would be hard but he needed to know. She quickly signed off and left the office. As she stepped briskly down the corridor, she spotted an aide scurrying toward Pelham's door. Her timing was perfect but it failed to lift her sagging spirits.

# CHAPTER 59

When Julianne approached Harry, she almost lost her nerve. Since they had been confined to the bunker they had rarely spoken. She resented being held a virtual prisoner in this man-made network of urban caves, and she knew Harry felt the same. Chen had tried to broker a peace with Kessler but it was of little use. Harry continued to release a number of propaganda broadcasts and the reports that filtered through suggested he was having an impact in the international community. Kessler was pleased, but the mutual antipathy that had grown between them precluded any form of recognition on the part of the Czar.

Harry was working in the studio editing his latest digital broadcast as Julianne entered. She gave a weak smile. "How are you Harry?" she asked earnestly.

Harry looked up, a little confused. "Okay I guess........?"

Julianne fumbled for the right words. She hated the thought that she was the one who was bringing this news. "There's no easy way to say this Harry, but it's about Tamara."

Harry instantly ceased his editing work and looked up sharply at her. Julianne fought the urge to bolt out the door. "She passed away in the camp."

At first Harry said nothing, did not even look up, but finally he replied, almost casually, "How do you know?"

"Rachel was able to get a message to me. She was able to check the mortality logs at the Salisbury camp and found Tamara's records," she explained gently.

Julianne watched Harry fight to maintain his composure, a losing battle. Julianne rubbed his shoulder comfortingly as he slumped down in the battered plastic chair and put his head in his hands. She heard him give a small cry of grief which developed into heavy, choking sobs. He stood up, the tears flowing. Julianne embraced him whilst his body shuddered.

"What about Byron?" he said between choking sobs.

Julianne momentarily pulled away. "I-I don't know. She didn't say."

His voice rose and the look in his eyes frightened Julianne. She had seen such a look in Sean's eyes just before he would beat her. "She didn't say?" he spat. "Didn't she think it was important enough? My son is out there alone in a plague infested concentration camp and she forgets to check on him?" He picked up his chair and slammed it against the wall with such venom that the plastic spine shattered. In the confined space Julianne backed away, mortified by his primal anger. However, just as suddenly his rage subsided and he fell back into her arms, his body wracked by uncontrollable shaking from raw grief.

She comforted him like a child until he was calmer, glad he was back in her arms, even under such tragic circumstances.

Finally Harry looked earnestly into her eyes. "H-how did it happen?"

"She died from the camp disease. Christ, they don't even have a name for it. But there was no mention of Byron. That's a good thing Harry; it means he must surely be alive."

Harry sounded tired. "I wish I could share your optimism. Even if he is still alive he's out there in one of Pelham's filthy camps all alone. He must be scared and hurting badly. I have to find some way to get to him. That's all I care about now."

"I know this is hard but we must be patient. Even if the Czar is no more than a playground bully, the progress we've made, what you've achieved, has been remarkable. It has vindicated our efforts in finding you. I know we're on the verge of a breakthrough."

"How would you know?" Harry snapped. "My son is out there lost and alone. How can you tell me to be patient?"

Julianne shrank back, surprised by the ferocity in his tone. "I didn't mean it like that." She paused, and then made her decision. "Look, Harry, there may be a way to get Byron out. I haven't told you everything about my trips upstairs."

"What do you mean?"

"I made some high-level connections – before I found you," she added hastily.

"How high?" Harry frowned, curious to know more.

"About as high as they get." She muttered sheepishly. "Giles Chamberlain."

Harry needed to muster all his self-control not to explode. His expression was dark and accusatory. "What the hell have you got us into?"

Julianne put a placating hand on his face. He swatted it away, his eyes narrowed in suspicion. She backed away like a wounded animal. "It's not like that. Hear me out!"

Julianne explained how she met Chamberlain while Harry listened silently, struggling to comprehend this sudden turn of events. She tried to convince him that Chamberlain was not the monster

Pelham had turned out to be, but was trying to effect change from within. She relayed how he was working covertly within the inner circle to effect change and find a way within the intricate political machinery to have Pelham removed from power. At times Harry shook his head disbelievingly.

"Look at how he gave us the codes for the newspaper archive. Why would he do that?" Julianne said.

"Chamberlain is a pernicious bastard who has only one object-ive in life, and that is to further his own ends," Harry responded harshly. I have no doubt that he wants to see Pelham impeached, but not for any altruistic reasons. If anyone is more of a sociopath than Pelham it is that Ox-bridge tyrant."

"It's different now. He's changed," Julianne protested. "Giles told me he had seen the carnage and the suffering that Pelham's regime had caused, and he would do everything in his power to stop it."

"It's not just Pelham's regime," he corrected her acidly. "It's the Conservative Party's regime of which he is the Deputy Leader. He is second-in-command to the most brutal leadership in the country since the Romans. He is as culpable as anyone. There are millions dead or dying because of the Police State the Tories have created. He's a mass murderer of the worst kind."

"No, he is *not* like that," she retorted. "He's a kind and gentle man who found me when I was at my lowest ebb." Her voice rose. "After you left me remember?"

Harry's eyes narrowed in suspicion as he studied Julianne's face. It was there hidden in the depths of her hazel eyes and the way she looked, the imperceptible twitch of the mouth that he had seen at the farmhouse with Sean. She was holding back.

"You slept with him didn't you!" It was more a statement than an accusation.

Julianne's mouth twitched even more and her eyes lowered.

"God dammit I knew it!" he shouted. He kicked the broken chair in frustration, freshly enraged by Julianne's betrayal. "Julianne, I don't even know you anymore. You're going to get yourself badly hurt, but you'll also take the rest of us down with you. When you no longer serve his purpose, you'll be sent away as a political prisoner just like the rest of us. I will try and put your name on the Remembrance Wall if they don't get me first. Tell me he doesn't know where the bunker is because Rachel knows and she could be easily compromised."

"I would never put the Resistance in jeopardy. This is my life!"

"That wasn't the question," Harry shot back. "Does Chen know about this?"

Tears glistened in Julianne's eyes. "No, of course not."

"Good," he said harshly. "Keep it that way. If Kessler found out he would feed you to the rats."

"Please Harry!" cried Julianne, rubbing her cheeks as tears streamed down. "He can get your son out. That has to be worth everything we're fighting for hasn't it? Everything I've done has been for the Resistance."

Harry snorted with derision. "Once again I find myself in a position where I have no choice but to trust you. Byron means more to me than any damned Resistance. Finding him means everything to me, and sitting in this dungeon making anti-government videos is not going to get my son back."

"Does that mean you will help me break into Pelham's office?"

Julianne asked hopefully. Rachel has everything planned."

"Yes, but only because I want my son back. Tell me the details later. I can't bear to look at you the moment." Harry stormed out, leaving Julianne stung by the brutality of his words.

As Harry strode to the mess hall through the dark, metallic corridors, his mind swirled with a mass of conflicting thoughts. The vision of his dead wife burst into his mind, like a photograph. He pictured her happy and contented, but he knew it was false because he had failed her. Harry should never have lost her in the first place, but his infidelity and drinking had doomed their marriage. He had not consumed alcohol for a long time, his abstinence the result of circumstances rather than any self-discipline on his part. If there was any time to fall off the waggon it was now. He was suddenly overcome by a deep feeling of sorrow that sliced through him like a hot knife, and he collapsed to his knees, grieving for the only woman he had ever truly loved.

# CHAPTER 60

Despite the physical proximity of their surroundings, it was several days before Julianne saw Harry again. Even then she had to seek him out. Since she had told him about Tamara's death, he had been as reclusive as it was possible to be in the cramped conditions of the bunker. She had allowed him the space to grieve for his former wife in his own way. However, events were moving rapidly and she found him in the studio, hunched over his tablet. She had enjoyed having him in her arms again, whatever the circumstances, and she guiltily hoped it would lead to more, but it might well have been a hundred years ago, so remote and unassailable did it seem now.

When she entered he looked up, his eyes sad and reflective.

"How are you Harry? I was worried about you." She attempted a smile, but it felt false.

"I'm fine Julianne." His tone was clipped and businesslike. "What do you want?"

Julianne grimaced, hurt by his tone. She swung the heavy steel door shut. "I've been speaking to Chen. He's going to help us get out. I'm going insane here. The thought of even a few hours above ground is exciting."

Harry frowned in surprise. "Why would Chen help us? His loyalty is surely to Kessler."

"Kessler doesn't know us like Chen does. He trusts us. Kessler doesn't. The information we gained as a result of our incursion outside was an acute embarrassment for the government and for Pelham in particular. It was a propaganda triumph. Chen sees the value in that. He has always been the one to advocate a non-violent solution, to pressurize the government by spreading awareness across the globe about the regime, hoping the cavalry will march in and liberate us. He confided in me that he was concerned about the Czar; he saw some parallels with Sean." Julianne wrinkled her freckled nose in distaste at the thought of her former lover.

"His team is close to a breakthrough in being able to hack into major infrastructure systems and sabotage them. Knocking out the screens was just the start. They will soon be able to take out utilities, transport and possibly even political or military targets. Chen is concerned about the level of power they could wield. If it is not used responsibly innocent lives will be in the firing line. He is not sure that Kessler is too concerned about making the distinction between legitimate targets or not. He may be super-intelligent but that man carries a lot of anger."

"I understand that but if it comes to it, can you be certain that Chen will come through for us? It's hard to know who to trust down here."

"Come on Harry. You know Chen is rock solid," retorted Julianne, gently rebuking him.

"I guess you're right," conceded Harry. "Being confined down here like a Morlock is affecting my judgement. When do we leave?"

"Tonight at one. We have a specific rendezvous time with Rachel at two. We must not be late because we have a limited window of opportunity to avoid Security and we need to allow enough time to get through the tunnels. Tonight is our best chance; we may not get another for weeks." She tentatively touched his shoulder. He did not react, but the muscle underneath his plaid shirt was taut, as if frozen.

"Are you ready, Harry?"

"I'm ready to find my son," he answered bluntly. Harry returned to studying his tablet. Julianne lingered uncomfortably and finally said, "Get some sleep. I will see you at one."


Chen studied the monitors in the Operations Centre. The chamber was never entirely devoid of people. Although Kessler was strict about maintaining a circadian rhythm amongst his team, supported by a multitude of old-style clocks throughout the bunker, there were always some individuals who liked to work at night, particularly when they were in the middle of a project. There were several reasons for this. Despite Kessler's best efforts, the lack of natural daylight played havoc with people's body clocks, and once the rhythm of night and day was lost it was difficult to retrieve. Some of his team would have worked overnight even if they were above ground, because they fitted the stereotypical profile of the hacker, unfettered by constraints of time, operating at all hours in preparation for an attack when their prey least expected it.

It was probably why many of their team felt comfortable in this underground bunker. Some of them hardly saw daylight even before they arrived here, immersed as they were in cyberspace, eschewing the physical space of the outside world. Many of them had led a solitary existence, brilliant at what they did but obsessed too. The Resistance had brought these people together into a community of like-minded individuals, providing at least some human companionship and more space than they had occupied when hidden away in a bedsit or dark basement. There was limited interaction between the residents of the Resistance. No defined social structure had yet emerged, despite the close proximity in which people lived. It worked well that way; there was less chance of a conflict that could be catastrophic in the closed society they had created.

Chen had begun to feel more unsettled recently, like a caged hamster peering out through the bars, longing to explore the world outside its enclosed universe. He studied the daily intelligence briefings and knew just what conditions were like on the surface, so he knew the risks of leaving the bunker. That did not stop him yearning to feel the sun on his face again, or even just the rain falling. He yearned for the sumptuous taste and aroma of a Sichuan hotpot or Zhangcha duck, dishes from his native province of Sichuan, instead of the tasteless freeze-dried rations that they had to scavenge from UN food drops. It was a desire that reached beyond the bounds of logic. He knew that Julianne and Harry's mission was hazardous, but he could not help feeling a twinge of envy. It was at times like this that he could do with smoking ten or fifteen cigarettes at a time. His abstinence from his precious tobacco, other than the occasional illicit smoke, only added to his despondency.

He glanced over at the three people in the room, all silently hunched over their workstations. Two of them, Nikolai and Bogdan, were Romanians, both from the same small town nestled in the foothills of the Transylvanian Alps that had developed a reputation as an axis for online fraud. He could not remember its name, but Bogdan had once proudly boasted that the town had earned the nickname 'Hackerville.' They were the closest thing to friends the Resistance had, yet they were still solitary figures who conversed only occasionally and then in monosyllabic tones. The third man was Chinese, but he was worlds apart from Chen, both culturally and physically. Wei hailed from the Jilin Province, a predominantly rural area in the far north of the country. The southern Chinese people often referred to them disparagingly as 'peasants.' There was still a great deal of discrimination in China against its own people despite the nation's explosion onto the world stage in the last three decades and its billion people dispersing to all four corners of the globe.

Physically the man was heavy and ponderous, his bulky figure a testament to the way in which the Chinese population had embraced western culture, including its fast food. There was no fast food in the bunker, and Wei's sallow skin hung in a wrinkled heap around his neck as he became involuntarily thinner. Even so, he was the antithesis of Chen's lean, wiry frame. Chen knew the cigarettes kept his weight down. Since he had lived in the bunker, with less opportunity to smoke, his weight had started to creep upwards....

The thought of smoking stirred him into action. He waved to Nikolai. "Watch the monitors. I'm going for a long walk. I could be gone awhile." The young Romanian man grunted in acknowledgement, understanding what a 'walk' really meant, and Chen stepped out through the heavy steel door.

He glanced at his watch and walked along the dark, silent passage, the pitted, metal pipes and ducts running along the walls and ceiling glistening with moisture under his flashlight. He passed the heavy metal entrances to the two large dormitories and mess room and continued on to where the passage widened out and turned at right angles to the spider-shaped network of caverns that comprised the main section of the bunker. He heard the scrabbling of a rat and shone his flashlight ahead on the floor. A pair of frightened, crystalline eyes stared back, caught in the intense white light, and the rat scurried away. Chen sighed with relief; these dirty creatures had become more audacious in the last few years. They didn't always run away.

The passage opened out onto a large steel platform raised above the tunnel hollowed out around it. In the suffocating gloom Chen's flashlight picked out a pile of cardboard boxes stacked high and an assortment of discarded equipment strewn carelessly over the floor. This included excavation tools such as shovels, drills and hammers used in building the platform but abandoned long ago. This open platform, enclosed by a rusting guardrail, was now the storage area for the bunker. The boxes mainly held UN food parcels retrieved from the surface.

Chen always felt skittish coming here, as if someone or something would jump out at him from the darkness. It was always so quiet, away from the comforting activity of the bunker, except when a tube train rumbled past somewhere below, which would not happen at this late hour. The only sound was the steady *drip drip* of water deep within the dark shadows.

The peace was shattered by a sharp clanking sound, like metal on metal. He whirled around, and caught in the beam was a figure. He immediately raised his beam to the face and Julianne blinked rapidly, shielding her eyes from the harsh glare.

"Put it away," she rebuked him. "You're blinding me."

Chen snapped off his flashlight, plunging them back into darkness. "Sorry. I always get nervous around this place."

"Yes you are. Now turn it back on. Harry should be here by now."

Chen switched on his flashlight and seconds later Harry emerged from the dark tunnel. Chen immediately directed them down a set of metal steps toward a tiny passageway that led off from the main corridor. It seemed to lead nowhere but Chen strode forward confidently, his flashlight playing over the clammy walls.

Chen's voice sounded flat in the enclosed space but he whispered anyway. "This is the only way out of the bunker into the tunnels that lead toward Parliament. You can't get above ground anymore without Kessler finding out. He has put an alarm on the grille at your usual access point, and the cameras are being monitored. He either doesn't know or doesn't care about this exit because it leads nowhere, so he would never expect anyone to want to escape through here. But then you are not trying to get above ground, at least not yet. You might even be able to make it back before he realizes you're gone."

They could barely squeeze through in single file and the wall felt cold to the touch. Harry could imagine these walls suddenly closing in and crushing them to death. It was strange how such unfamiliar, claustrophobic places played havoc with the mind. He breathed deeply, following his companions, but was relieved when the narrow tunnel emerged into a small cave-like chamber. Chen swung the flashlight around the chamber, and the stark white light picked out two tunnels that led into blackness.

"Follow the left tunnel for about four hundred metres. You will reach an access hole but stay vigilant or you will fall down it. It just appears, and it's a five metre drop onto the concrete sewer system. Being covered in shit will be the least of your problems. There is a vertical ladder that will take you down to the lower level close to the Jubilee line. You will probably be walking parallel with the tube tracks for a while."

"Thanks Chen. I have Rachel's instructions from there." Julianne gave Chen a brief hug.

"Hang on a minute," interjected Harry. "Are you saying that we have to walk along the sewer?"

Chen grinned widely, his yellow teeth revealing tobacco stains in the harsh glare of his flashlight. "Of course. I hope you didn't wear your Sunday best."

# CHAPTER 61

It felt like a first date. Waiting for someone that might not turn up, stomach fluttering, anxiously checking the time, wondering if the arrangements you made had been properly understood, and even if they were, would your date bother to show? All of these thoughts crossed Rachel's mind, only the implications of being stood up were far more serious than the humiliation of a failed date. Rachel had placed herself at great personal risk to be here, and as she lingered near the wall vent in an obscure corridor, she checked her watch and looked around anxiously for any sign of security.

At this late hour there were few security personnel stalking the subtly lit corridors. They swung their batons and whistled tunelessly to alleviate the boredom, never really alert for trouble. The security cordon that had been placed around Parliament, especially since the escalation of the troubles had made the Gothic structure a virtually impenetrable fortress. The last thing they expected was to confront an intruder. They were used to people working behind closed doors throughout the night, mainly interns working on projects with impossible deadlines for their masters. The politicians were never that dedicated to public service. Even so, being discovered lingering in the corridors was likely to arouse suspicion, so she stayed watchful.

Rachel had left the Prime Minister snoring gently in his bed and hurried over. She did not even have time to shower, to wash off his stench of corruption. It was times like this she felt truly disgusted with herself; but even as he laid on top of her, thrusting and grunting enthusiastically, she told herself it was for the greater good. In truth, however, she was deeply afraid of him. To spurn his advances now could be calamitous. He always slept like a log after he had gorged himself on her body, and she figured she had at least an hour to return back to his bed. She was thankful his security team were discreet, especially as she often came and went at odd hours. If she slipped back while he was still asleep he would never know she had left.

She nervously fingered the holographic key-card she had stolen from his jacket pocket. The Prime Minister was a creature of habit and as soon as he fell asleep she knew exactly where to look. He sometimes lent it to her if she was required to enter his office to run an errand. It was a measure of trust he placed in few people, one of the advantages of being his mistress.

Her thoughts were interrupted by a dark shape that turned the corner and headed in her direction. She immediately strode confidently toward the figure as if she was in a hurry, and as they passed closer she gave a cheerful wave. "Hi George," she said brightly, recognizing the portly, ageing night watchman.

George swept a hand through his thinning hair, a reflex gesture when he saw an attractive woman, as if it would make a difference. "Evening Miss Thomas. Pulling another late one? You work too hard Miss."

"The demands of the State never stop, even at night George."

He smiled coyly back. "I'm about to knock off. Goodnight Miss Thomas." They both moved on, and as soon as George had turned the corner in the corridor she moved back to the area around the air vent. She had already unscrewed the retaining bolts in readiness, so it would be easy to take off. It was nearly two o'clock. They should be here imminently.

Her mind cast back to the blueprints for construction work around Parliament Square carried out five years ago. It had taken a great deal of time-consuming research to locate them in the Parliamentary archival database. The idea had come from an architect friend, Pierre, a former lover who had suggested that many historic buildings in England had tunnels and passageways that often led into the bowels of the building. He quoted the example of Nottingham Castle, which sat on a spur of rock riddled with tunnels, caverns and cellars that had been used by members of the Royal family to escape capture during the Plantagenet era. That had set her thinking. There was no way to break into this fortress through the usual channels. Pierre had suggested that the renovations to the Westminster Tube station in the past few years might show something. The work included refurbishment of the steel and concrete foundations around Big Ben and Portcullis House, and also affected the structure of the Parliament building. Rachel had found the blueprints and Pierre had been able to cast an expert eye over them, finding a possible entry point. The problem was there was no way of knowing if that entry point had now been blocked.

That fear now gripped her as she glanced at her watch again. The security guards would be changing shift and the window of opportunity had now arrived. However it was three minutes past two, which meant that they were late.

The tunnel seemed to stretch endlessly in the light of Julianne's torch as she played it over the slimy concrete walls. It appeared to narrow and occasionally they stumbled over small blocks of masonry that had fallen away from the wall. Time seemed to move at a slower pace in the confines of the tunnel but presently they reached the access hole and climbed carefully down the steel ladder into the sewer tunnel five metres below. Their boots splashed as they reached the ground. The stench was overpowering, and Harry found it hard not to throw up immediately. Gagging, he held a hand to his nose until the smell became just that bit more bearable, their senses adapting to the fetid air. The tunnel was like a huge pipe, and Harry found himself trying to walk wide-legged against the lower curve of the wall to avoid the flowing black water. That water contained the stinking waste of a city which had tripled in size in the one hundred and sixty years since the sewer system had been constructed, and the sewer had been modernized only sporadically since then.

They reached a junction where the tunnel led right and left. Julianne, leading, waved her flashlight to the right. They realized that they had been in a tributary and now joined the main sewer flow, the intensity and depth of the water increasing dramatically. The flow of the water was powerful after the recent rain, and it was knee high, pushing them along so that they had to fight to stay balanced. Harry did not wish to contemplate the thought of losing balance and falling face first into the sewer water and he had to stay highly focused. When he stumbled once he grabbed at the wall for support, and its wet, slimy feel made him faintly nauseous. He was gently bumped by soft objects moving fast in the flowing water, trying to close his mind to the thought of what they might be. A heavier object bumped into him and he heard a high-pitched squealing as it passed by. Julianne's light played upon a pair of pink eyes, the rat thrashing desperately in the water to stay afloat as it drifted past at the mercy of the fast-moving current.

"We are directly under Big Ben now," she yelled back to Harry over the roar of the water, amplified in the confined space. "Great," retorted Harry sarcastically. "So what?"

"It means we are close to the access shaft."

Less than three minutes later, Julianne let out an excited shout as her flashlight fixed on a section of roof that had been excavated to form a black shaft that led upwards, and which housed a rusty metal ladder. She could see a small black sign that read "Access Shaft 35."

"This is the number Rachel gave me. We are on the right track." She glanced at her watch. "We have to hurry though. Rachel warned us not to be late." She put the flashlight in her breast pocket and confidently began to clamber up the shaft on the steel ladder. Harry quickly followed, relieved to escape the free-flowing water with its foul contents. No sooner had he climbed a few rungs when he heard a metallic groan and felt the ladder move imperceptibly away from its concrete support. He was already too far up to jump back down into the blackness. Harry hung on, blindly trusting that the ladder would hold and clambered up as quickly as he could. The ladder felt more solid further up. He could not tell where Julianne was but shortly she called down. "I'm up!"

Harry kept going and Julianne shone her flashlight down to him. She hauled him up and they sat and rested for a moment. Julianne's flashlight revealed a small, square tunnel that was too low to stand in. To his relief it was dry, however.

"Not far now," Julianne reassured him. "We're now directly under the Parliament building." She whispered this as if they could be heard, but her voice echoed down the dark passage. "We crawl from here."

Harry followed Julianne blindly on his hands and knees. "Why no light?"

"This is the ventilation tunnels for the building. Rachel told me to turn off any lights from here as we could alert Security."

They followed the tunnel in complete darkness but Harry could feel a slight incline as the tunnel tapered upwards. It suddenly turned acutely and they had no choice but to follow, the crawlspace too tight to even turn around. However, Harry saw a faint light at the end of the tunnel and they soon reached a point where they turned upwards into a vertical shaft. They were able to stand up, and the source of the faint light was immediately in front of them, a small ventilation grille. Knees aching, they hurried to the grille and looked out through the slats. Suddenly a figure blocked their view. The figure quickly unscrewed the grille and lifted it aside. For a horrifying moment they thought that a security guard had found them but the hands that reached in were distinctly feminine.

"Thank God," muttered Rachel, helping Julianne through the small opening. "I thought you weren't coming. Hurry up!"

# CHAPTER 62

They moved quickly to reach the corridor that ran past the Prime Minister's office. Rachel led them, checking each corner whenever they changed direction through the maze of corridors. It was not far but the corridors of power were a labyrinth to the uninitiated. As they turned one corner Rachel suddenly stopped short and frantically waved them back. They squeezed into a shadowy alcove behind a supporting pillar while Rachel casually engaged the security guard in light conversation as he ambled past. Her body blocked his line of sight from the alcove and he shuffled by, swinging his baton lazily. As he did so he sniffed the air curiously.

"When are they ever gonna fix those bloody drains eh?"

Rachel gave a nervous laugh. "Yes it's an outrage," she agreed. He lingered a little more and finally took his cue to move on. When he was gone she hurried on. "Quickly, he may be back," she hissed. "He might follow your scent."

"You didn't tell us we'd be wading through the sewer," Harry whispered harshly.

"With a bit of luck you'll be wading through it again in another fifteen minutes," Rachel retorted quietly. They reached the P.M.'s carpeted outer office and Rachel swiped the holographic card over the reader on the wall. A lock clicked open and they stepped in to the inner sanctum of his office, locking it behind them. It was dark and the shutters were drawn, but in the gloom Harry spotted a light stand in the corner. Harry went to turn it on.

"No!" hissed Rachel. "The glow might be seen through the shutters. It will arouse suspicion."

Harry shrugged while Rachel quickly sat in the plush leather chair by Pelham's desk and fired up the computer, working from her flashlight only.

As the computer scrolled through the security protocols, Rachel prayed silently to herself that the codes were still valid. It had been nearly a week although she knew Pelham was quite blasé about such things, born of the arrogant belief that no-one would have the temerity to challenge him in so blatantly. She carefully tapped the codes as her two partners-in-crime stood either side. The cursor lingered for a while, blinking. *It was taking too long!* Rachel let out a deep breath as the computer flashed white and the welcome message appeared. She immediately set to work, highly focused on her task, acutely aware of their limited window of opportunity to extract the information they needed. She pulled out her SD card and began reviewing the files. "Tell me what you need Harry."

Harry pulled up a chair from behind his desk and looked over the mass of folders. Some of the folder names were cryptic and gave little clue as to its contents. It would take hours to interrogate the computer and find the right information. They had minutes.

Rachel, however, pulled out a crumpled piece of paper and smoothed it out on the desk. "These are the folder names. I've been studying them to get a better idea of what might lie beneath them. I'll copy what I can but focus on these files." She pointed to a number of highlighted entries on the paper. "I think these are the most likely to implicate Pelham."

"I first want evidence that he allowed the disease to spread through the camps."

Rachel swiftly opened the folder entitled "Deportation Camps" that she had accessed previously when left alone in his office, and they saw a folder entitled 'Cleaning.' Its apparently innocent name aroused Harry's suspicion. It felt like a veiled reference to ethnic cleansing. His intuition was confirmed when they scrolled down the list of file names, which were much less ambiguous. "Check that file," said Harry, pointing at the screen. It was a record of email and social media correspondence between Pelham and Dr. Heath, the Head of the Research Facility in Watford that Rachel had visited. As they scanned its contents they quickly realized they had hit the jackpot. The correspondence related to the timed release of the pathogen and the process for distributing it to the deportation camps, clear evidence that the disease was manufactured.

Scrolling down the text, they saw that the correspondence also alluded to the Aryan Project. There was too much information to assimilate now. No doubt, Harry surmised, the files would also provide details of the atrocities committed at the U.K. ports such as those he had witnessed in Pembroke. "Copy the whole folder," he instructed Rachel. This would be a goldmine for him to analyze back at the Bunker.

They then moved to another folder which was less oblique, named 'Financial.' In the folder was a sub-folder titled 'Contributions' and within that was a file called *Corporate Sponsors*. They clicked on the file and a white spreadsheet bounced onto the screen, casting their faces in a ghostly glow. Julianne peered over their shoulder as the trio viewed the list of sponsors with figures by the side. Harry was stupefied. "Is this really what I think it is?"

Rachel stared earnestly back at him. "I believe it is exactly that. I knew he had extensive contacts but even I did not believe that his network was so comprehensive. No wonder the man is such a narcissist." Laid out before them in glorious detail were the names of some of the wealthiest and most powerful men and women in the country, movers and shakers of the highest order, mainly from the industrial and business world, but also from sports, entertainment and the arts. The column to the right of each name was assigned a financial sum, and the total at the bottom came to a staggering figure. The next column referred to where money had been deposited. Most of the sums appeared to have been funnelled to offshore bank accounts.

A separate list revealed the companies which had supported Pelham and it too had similar columns. The combination of support from wealthy individuals and corporate benefactors had provided Pelham with the resources to shape the country in whichever way he desired. As Harry looked down the screen, oblivious to the fact that he was an intruder in the office of what was plainly the richest as well as the most powerful man in Britain, he realized the colossal task that awaited any opponent to Pelham. Whilst he refused to believe that all of these benefactors, among them some famous and highly respected public figures, would endorse the methods that Pelham had used to reshape the country, they clearly believed in the principle of his five-year plan, and that made Pelham more formidable and dangerous than Harry had ever imagined.

Rachel copied the folder containing the list of sponsors and anxiously glanced at her watch. "We should go now."

"No," protested Harry. "I want to see the records for the Salisbury camp. I need to know what they did with Byron."

Julianne laid a gentle hand on Harry's shoulder. "Harry I know how important this is to you but we don't have the time."

Harry's restrained tone held an undercurrent of anger. "I need to find out what happened to Byron!"

In a dark corner just below the stuccoed ceiling a tiny light blinked on unnoticed. A miniature pinhole camera built into the wall flickered into life and its lens moved silently and imperceptibly until its gaze was fixed on the intruders.

# CHAPTER 63

Rachel handed Julianne the small SD card containing the vital information that would expose the government. Her svelte fingers hovered over the keyboard, anxious to turn off the computer and get the hell out of there. Harry was insistent, however. "I need to see what they did with my son. I'm not leaving without that information."

Julianne's tone was soothing. "Harry we might already have that information on the files we copied. Rachel is right. We have already been here too -..."

She was interrupted by the sound of the mahogany door being flung open. The gloom was instantly banished by a harsh yellow glow from the elegant chandelier in the middle of the ceiling. The trio of intruders could only stare, blinking at the door, frozen like a rabbit caught in the headlights.

It took a moment for their eyes to adjust, to recognize the figure that strode confidently through the doorway. The tall, athletic frame of Giles Chamberlain emerged. Behind him stood two burly, broad-shouldered guards, walls of solid muscle dressed all in black, curiously at odds with Chamberlain's stylish tan-coloured jacket. They reminded Harry of the night, so long ago it seemed, when he had taken illicit photos of Graham Matheson and his Hispanic male lover outside the *Libertarian* nightclub, following which he had been chased by two bouncers. The men blocking their escape were also bald with goatees, each sporting a pair of sunglasses and an earpiece. Harry thought of saying to them, 'Come on guys; sunglasses indoors in the early hours of the morning? Really?' Somehow he did not think they would share his humour. Indeed the main difference from the bouncers at the *Libertarian* was that these men were holding semi-automatic pistols and looked quite capable of using them.

Rachel quickly composed herself, but she could not hide the tremor in her voice. "Oh, hello Giles, I wasn't expecting you. I was copying Pelham's files for you as we agreed."

Chamberlain's expression was hard and his gaze was unwavering. "Really? Are you sure they were for me Rachel? Then what are these two doing here?" His tone matched his look. One of the security men moved forward. Harry noticed a ragged zig-zag scar along his chin. It was the only thing Harry could notice that prevented them being clones.

"Yes, yes," stammered Rachel, clearly intimidated. "They were for you."

Chamberlain laughed harshly, brushing away her feeble explanation. He turned to her accomplices. "Julianne, it's nice to see you again. Oh, and Harry, it's been a long time. You have been acquiring quite a reputation, and certainly ruffled a few political feathers I can tell you. I feel almost inclined to ask for your autograph." He laughed again, this time baring his teeth like a hyena as he turned to Rachel. "Were you planning to tell me about this little nocturnal escapade?"

Rachel gave a nervous laugh. "Of course, Giles, we are all in this together."

Chamberlain stopped chuckling and his voice was steely. "In what together, exactly? All I can see is a group of intruders in the Prime Minister's office rifling through his files. As the Deputy Prime Minister it's my duty to inform you that your actions constitute treason."

Julianne's pale face flushed red. "What the hell are you talking about?"

Chamberlain pointed to the small SD card in Julianne's hand just as she tried to slip it into her pocket. "Give me the card Julianne."

Julianne balled her hands into a fist, as if to protect the card. "No chance," she said savagely.

Chamberlain gave a curt nod and his two security men instantly raised their pistols in perfect synchronization and trained them at her head. "Give it to me!" he yelled.

Shocked, Julianne tossed the card to Chamberlain and the guns returned to their owners' side. Chamberlain gave a wide grin as he slipped the card in the breast pocket of his tailored jacket. "This will come in very useful. I've been trying to figure out Pelham's corporate sponsors for a while. It looks like you may have done the job for me. Now I have to decide what to do with you."

Julianne moved threateningly toward Chamberlain but Scarface stepped in front of his boss, a formidable human shield. Julianne hesitated and retreated under the guard's unyielding presence and blank expression, eyes hidden behind the sunglasses. Instead she shouted angrily at the Deputy P.M. "You're a double-crossing bastard Giles! You told me you would get Byron out if Harry helped you!"

Harry turned and stared hard at Julianne. Giles merely gave an ironic smile as if he were humouring a child. "You must have misunderstood. But I am not heartless. Maybe there is a way that Harry can be reunited with his son." He gave another swift nod and the other beefy subordinate, his neck lost in the muscle mass of his overdeveloped shoulders, quickly strode toward Harry as if he were set to walk right through him. When he was within arms-length he coshed Harry in the jaw with the solid metal grip of the pistol. The pain shot through Harry like a lightning bolt. Harry heard something crack and he staggered back, the strong acrid taste of blood filling his mouth. The bodyguard wasted no time in wrestling a stunned Harry to the ground and, with his knee on his back, wrenched both arms and snapped on a pair of handcuffs over his wrists. He hauled him upright and stood him in front of Chamberlain so their faces were inches apart.

"I really am glad you came, Harry. Lawrence is obsessed with finding you." The Deputy P.M.'s tone carried real menace. "He will be enthralled when I deliver you to him. I can't guarantee what he has planned for you. That's out of my hands. My only promise is that it won't be pleasant."

The guard grabbed Harry's hair with his left hand, the pistol in his right pointed at Harry's temple, and he half-dragged his prisoner out of the office. Julianne cried loudly, realizing where the battle lines had been drawn. "Harry, I'm so sorry, I didn't know!"

Harry's voice was slurred from the force of the blow to his jaw. "I warned you Julianne. You were insane to trust him!" he shouted back as he was bundled away.

"Harry please understand!" Julianne implored him. "I did what I thought was right!" She buried her face in her hands, tears streaming down from a combination of rage and ignominy. Harry was right. What had she done? Would she ever see him again?

Chamberlain turned to Rachel. "I would suggest you go back to our glorious leader as you clearly prefer his bed to mine."

Rachel bit her lip angrily. "Is this what it's all about? You think I rejected you?"

Chamberlain's laugh was more like a sneer. "Don't inflate your own importance Rachel. There are forces at play far more significant than our petty flirtation. If you're lucky he might still be asleep and you will have a reprieve, at least temporarily. I will decide what to do with you later. Now please leave!" Rachel, her cheeks burning, and feeling the heat of Julianne's hostile stare, tearfully rushed out of the office.

Scarface retreated to the corner, and Chamberlain and Julianne faced each other. His voice turned suddenly softer. "I know you're angry at me. I don't blame you for that. Politics is never straight-forward. It can sometimes get messy and complicated. Everything I have done is still consistent with our plan."

"You used me!" said Julianne, her voice choked with anger and humiliation.

"Oh come on Julianne, don't be so melodramatic. We all use other people. It's a part of the human condition. Didn't you use Harry to support the Resistance?"

"That's different. He knew exactly what he was getting into!"

"I may not have been completely transparent but I do still care about you, if you can believe that." His hand moved slowly toward Julianne's face as if to caress it but she swatted it away. His smirk faded and his expression turned hard. "Sometimes that just isn't enough."

"What are you going to do with me?"

"You've been of great assistance to me Julianne, and you still can be. But circumstances have changed. The rules have changed. You are free to go, but unfortunately I will have to send you back down the sewer." He gave a thin smile. "You're not at your best today. I'm going to have to fumigate this office and remove any trace that anyone was here." He waved his hand flamboyantly.

"When you return to the bunker you will do as I say. I own you now. Our aspirations have not changed. The Resistance can help me oust Pelham, which is what you wanted anyway. You can still help to make that happen. You will report to me on their activities but you will work for me."

"And what if I refuse?" Julianne countered defiantly.

Chamberlain let out a short, almost sympathetic laugh. "The one thing I admire about you apart from your smoking hot body is your spirit, but sometimes your resolve is misguided. Face the facts, you have no choice. I can make it known at any time that you have compromised them. What do you think Kessler will do? He would probably have you killed, and no-one, least of all me wants that. I have no intention of destroying the Resistance. They can achieve a lot for me, but we had to remove Harry from the picture. He was proving too influential and he would have dragged me down along with Pelham. I can't afford to take that risk."

Julianne could not restrain herself any longer. She launched herself at Chamberlain and clawed at his face. Chamberlain was caught by surprise and stumbled back. Scarface immediately rushed in and tore Julianne away and pushed her to the floor. He raised his fists to beat her but the Deputy shouted "No!" The guard hesitated and Julianne scrambled away behind the Prime Minister's desk.

Chamberlain gingerly touched his face. His skin was shredded below his left eye and when he checked his hand there was a small drop of blood on his fingertips. "Get her out of here!" he ordered the guard angrily. The black-suited figure hauled Julianne up and squeezed her left shoulder in an iron-like grip, pushing her out of the office. Chamberlain followed behind until they reached the ventilator grille through which she had entered the building. Scarface lifted the grille and roughly bundled Julianne into the shaft. "Remember, Julianne, you're duty is to me now. I will be in touch."

Scarface finally took off his sunglasses and peered intently through the grille until she had disappeared out of sight. "Get this grille sealed off," instructed Chamberlain. He hesitated, thinking hard. "On second thoughts leave it alone. It might come in useful someday." The Deputy P.M. strode confidently down the corridor toward his own office, patting his jacket pocket containing the SD card with its treasure trove of information. There was much work to be done, but he could feel that the tide was turning in his favour. It was not yet three in the morning but he had never felt more alert.

# CHAPTER 64

Several days had passed and Rachel still had no idea what was being planned for her in the halls of power. She had been torn between the attentions of the two most powerful men in the country, one who had shocked her with his complete disregard for human life, and the other who had betrayed her after she spurned his advances. She had known deep in her heart that like a pawn surrounded by the queen and knights on the chessboard, she would eventually be outmanoeuvred and at the mercy of forces beyond her control. She had skulked back to Pelham's bed as Chamberlain had ordered, her mind a whirl of possibilities, none of them promising. The Prime Minister had no such problem. He was still snoring peacefully when she returned and lay there the rest of the night, torturous, racing thoughts dashing any hope of sleep.

She had peered at herself in the mirror the next morning and she looked deathly pale, her eyes dull and puffy. Pelham had jokingly commented that her look might be explained by the demands of his insatiable appetite, but he had to concede that she appeared tense. The business of running the country and perpetuating the atrocities that Rachel had witnessed personally or heard detailed accounts of continued as if nothing had happened.

Now she was on the road taking in the breathtaking beauty of the Pennines. Although it was early December, the weather had blessed the inhabitants of the towns and villages nestled in the valleys and dales of this vast range of fells. These barren, moor covered hills were often described as the backbone of England. It was cold, and the higher peaks were capped with gleaming white snow, but the sun shone in a clear winter sky, and only a few wispy clouds huddled around the peaks, drifting lazily against a china blue canvas.

The day before, Pelham had insisted that she take a rest, mistaking her tension for overwork. He had been attentive as ever, maybe a little more distant than usual, although she was probably imagining it. He had strongly suggested that she take the town car with a driver and head off to Alston Moor in the Cumbrian Northern Pennines, where his family owned a beautiful cottage. She had refused the services of the driver, but had accepted the offer of the car. Armed with the necessary paperwork to pass through the various checkpoints she would inevitably encounter along the way, she had set off early that morning, happy to escape the fierce political arena that had weighed her down like an anchor.

The car seemed to climb effortlessly up the winding road in the lee of the hills, and it felt almost like a carefree summer's day. For Rachel life was anything but carefree. At least for a while she could escape her worries and enjoy the raw beauty of the grassy hills and jagged rocks of this sparsely populated region.

She smiled ironically to herself as she thought about the years ahead. One day the historians would chronicle the seismic transition of this once great nation and Pelham's role in the chaos and devastation. She hoped the scholars would not judge her too unkindly. Her role as concubine to one of the worst mass murderers in political history was probably assured, but she hoped they would not consider her a willing participant in the crimes. Maybe they would understand she had been placed in an impossible situation and lacked the courage to fight back.

Rachel had spent the last few days anxiously waiting for the inevitable storm to arrive. She had developed an almost stoic acceptance of whatever fate was in store for her, so jaded and spiritually drained had she been by her exposure to the inner circle of this despotic regime. Even so, she found that waiting for something to happen shredded her nerves. The silence was deafening. She just wanted to get the consequences of her actions over with as quickly as possible.

Yet Pelham had shown nothing but his usual kindness toward her. She had seen Chamberlain only once in the preceding days and he had merely given her a knowing smile, his eyes dancing with detached amusement. Clearly he had not told Pelham about the break-in to his office. She thought optimistically that maybe it was never going to come out and everything would be alright. As she considered it more, she rationalized that it was not in Chamberlain's interests to reveal exactly what had happened.

She had, however, remained as wound up as an eight-day clock and Pelham had insisted on this little sabbatical. Whilst she felt some discomfort at fleeing Parliament, she rationalized that it was for the best. She stopped at the small, isolated garage near the picturesque village of Alston to collect the keys to the cottage as Pelham had instructed. She was vaguely curious as to why the cottage keys were at the garage, but the gruff ruddy-faced owner had been expecting her. He had broken off from talking to a tall, lean but morose-looking man whose eyes were hidden behind mirror-shaded glasses. The man was dressed in dark but elegant clothes but his attire, completed by a long trench-coat, was oddly conspicuous in these parts. The owner handed her the keys and checked over her car unsolicited, even looking under the chassis, while she grabbed a coffee from a small machine inside the tiny cashier's booth, conscious that the tall man was staring in her direction.

She had put him out of her mind and continued on her journey, not wishing to waste time as darkness was less than an hour away and the shadows were starting to lengthen. The small Lexus climbed up the winding road, its engine revving higher as the gradient increased until the road reached the top of the barren, windy fell. As she slowed, the sweeping vista of the Pennines revealed itself to her. It was a quilt of green and brown, a vast expansive valley that stretched into the distance, in the middle of which a narrow blue ribbon wound its way and ended at a deep azure lake glittering in the winter sun. The scene seemed surreal, like a vast watercolour landscape she might see at the Victoria and Albert Museum. She had stopped to admire the scene, sitting on the hood of the car despite the chilly freshness. The air was cold but pure, and she felt cleansed, as if the breeze had blown away the filth of the atrocities that had blighted this beautiful country. To look at the peaceful landscape laid out before her, it was hard to believe the country was in such turmoil.

Shivering, she got back into the Lexus and began her descent into Alston Moor. The road was narrow and pitted in places, the potholes filled with water and harder to spot. It curved around the side of the fell, cut into the edge like a mountain pass. A small metal barrier that prevented a drop into the valley below curved around the edge of the road. She focused on the twisting road, taking her time. Out of the corner of her vision she noticed the sharp icy blue light of the Blue-tooth communications device flick on, and a familiar voice filled the air. In the confines of the car his tone was rich and smooth, as if he were delivering a speech to his supporters. There was, however, a plaintive, melancholy feel to the voice as he addressed her directly.

"Rachel, I feel I have failed you in some way. I had high hopes for us. One day Helen would be removed and you would take her place as my First Lady. We could have achieved so much together. I trusted you Rachel but you didn't return that trust." The voice paused, and Rachel could tell it was a prerecorded message. "I know what you did. I tried to understand why and I wanted to believe that you did it for the right reasons. But the facts don't lie. I have to confess I am hurt and disappointed. You were my one treasure in the dirt that we wallow through every day. You made my life so much better. I will miss the fun we had together; you are such an accomplished lover. That's why it hurts me so much to do this."

She stared incredulously at the blue light from where the disembodied voice emanated. The car lurched slightly and she stepped on the brake to slow down. Her foot went right through and the car began to speed up as the downward gradient became steeper. She pressed frantically on the brake pedal but there was no pressure, her foot hitting the floor with no effect.

Pelham's voice cracked with emotion. "You breached my trust Rachel, but worst of all I find that you are plotting against me. I cannot allow anyone to do that, not even you. There is too much at stake. Please believe me when I tell you how difficult this was for me. I really wish there had been another way."

The voice paused as the car continued to gain speed down the narrow road and she desperately fought for control. The car bounced against the granite wall of the fell and lurched to the other side, clanging hard against the barrier, her only protection against plunging off the steep sides of the fell.

"Goodbye Rachel," said Pelham with an air of finality.

The blue light flicked off and the voice was gone. The car bounced heavily, the grey wall outside her right hand window a blur as the car sped down the road. Her foot frantically pumped the pedal in vain. Then she saw it. Ahead the road curved steeply around, hugging the mountain in a 'U' shape. Although the metal barrier followed the sharp turn to prevent a hapless driver plunging over the precipice, the severity of the bend demanded a driver slow down and virtually crawl around it. Rachel had no such luxury. For a split second she thought about jumping out of the car, but the road was too narrow and the rock wall flashing past was too close. Even if she managed to open the door, there was no clearance and she would be crushed by her own car. With rising panic she tried to steer the car in a jagged motion to reduce speed but it had little effect. The momentum of the car was too great. As she saw the barrier rapidly advance, it felt like the car was stationary and the barrier was rushing up at her.

With one desperate pump of the pedal she realized it was too late. With a shriek of grinding metal the car struck the barrier, which folded under the weight and speed of the metal projectile. Suddenly there was only air under the vehicle. Its momentum carried it level for a fraction of a second, and then gravity took over. The front end of the car dropped downwards and the car plunged two hundred feet onto the rocks and bushes at the base of the fell. The car came to rest, its front end crumpled by the impact, and immediately exploded into a fireball. The noise of the explosion echoed through the valley, sending a huge flock of birds retreating into the safety of the air, their black wings suddenly filling the sky like a portent of doom.

# REUTERS EDITORIAL DECEMBER 5

As bitter winter winds whistle through the troubled land, Britain's first Christmas under Lawrence Pelham's despotic rule promises little seasonal cheer. Estimates of the number of inmates at deportation camps have proved difficult to verify, but independent sources claim that the figure could be as high as two million. This does not account for the number of casualties of the war of attrition that Pelham has forged on those who fall foul of the *Minorities Registration Act*. These include immigrants who have perished in the camps, rebel fighters killed by government forces and political prisoners.

If the chilling allegations of mass exterminations in British ports are true, that number is swelled significantly by unknown numbers of victims.

For all these classes, there is insufficient information to make anything more than uninformed guesses at the true numbers. In any event it means there are still several million people living on borrowed time, waiting to be transported to deportation camps, spared so far only by the lottery of having too many people for the infrastructure to handle.

Those who remain at liberty are faced with a period of deep austerity, considered by many to be worse than the Second World War. The country has been crippled by sanctions and yet Pelham stubbornly refuses to allow a UN peacekeeping force into the U.K. This is despite pressure not only from the Opposition but allegedly from members of his Cabinet too. Indeed there are rumours circulating that suggest deep divisions in the ruling Conservative Party, but Pelham's dogmatic and forceful approach has ensured that any dissent is quashed with minimal debate.

The UN continues to struggle for a positive way forward. Following the heated emergency debate on the U.K. crisis which yielded little but recriminations it decided to suspend Britain from UN membership. In the current climate this is considered no more than a symbolic gesture but it is an indication of the level of seriousness that the UN regards the situation. It is an unprecedented move that was not invoked even after the Russian annexation of Ukraine over a decade ago precipitated another Cold War.

Already isolated by most of the international community, and fast running out of allies beyond his borders, Lawrence Pelham also risks isolation within his own Party. His strength so far has been in his ability to command both the regular Armed Forces through the Chief of the Defence Staff, Sir Terence Harding, and the People's Independent Army. Bolstered by the State Security Service and the State Secret Police, and allegedly supported by powerful corporate sponsors, the Prime Minister wields an inviolable level of power.

History has shown that this is not always enough for a dictatorship to survive. It needs only a few cracks and divisions to appear from within and the whole foundation is undermined and starts to crumble. Only time will tell if Pelham falls in the same way. While there are rumours of discontent concerning the state of the nation, no-one yet has had the courage to openly stand up to Pelham, for fear of the consequences. Indeed, that is often why dictators retain power for so long. No one wishes to be first to take a stand because they are likely to pay the ultimate sacrifice. But once a martyr has appeared, there will undoubtedly be others and Pelham could face a mutiny.

As sanctions bite and winter takes hold, news of the atrocities continues to filter through to ordinary people, despite the government's attempts at suppressing the media. The evidence suggests that popular support for Pelham is waning, even amongst the hard-core element that vehemently supported his vision and promises. Few, however, will wish to stick their heads over the parapet. The official Opposition, the British National Party, which has since the election in May failed to enforce any accountability on the ruling Conservative Party, is now on the offensive. The BNP has tacitly distanced itself from the reported atrocities. In a recent statement, BNP Leader Jane Forster claimed that whilst her Party supported the general principles of the Conservatives relating to immigration, it was not aware of the alleged atrocities and would never condone such activities. In addition, Forster claims that the BNP is seeking to work with any aid agencies allowed in the country to provide its support in combating the anthrax-like disease still rife in the deportation camps, as well as to provide better living conditions. The barracks were not built with any form of heating and are ill-equipped to protect against the cold. The British winters have been particularly severe in recent years, and the long-term forecast suggests the trend is set to continue. Refurbishment is urgent because it is bitterly cold even now, and the first reports of hypothermia cases have already begun to surface.

Against the backdrop of this political interplay, the man at the centre of allegations against the Party and Pelham in particular has suddenly fallen silent, almost as quickly as he emerged with shocking revelations that rocked the free world. Indeed, Harry Clarke's broadcasts alone have done more to sway the tide of sentiment and repulsion of the international community against the country than any military insurgency.

Whilst the country is still technically embroiled in a civil war, Pelham's forces reign supreme and there is little sign of organized opposition emerging as a serious threat. Most rebel forces remain in hiding although surprise 'terrorist' attacks have increased in number as the rebels continue to engage in a covert offensive. The superiority of Pelham's forces alone will not be enough, in the final analysis, to maintain his authority. Political observers have almost universally acknowledged that Pelham has sown the seeds of his own downfall, but the question for the watching world is how far this modern dictator will be allowed to continue his heinous program. The time is surely near when the UN at last says 'enough is enough' and is forced to take its last resort option of military action. However, against strong, highly trained and well-equipped forces, the UN risks being dragged into a destructive, expensive and potentially disastrous campaign; yet every day of inaction sentences more innocent people to a barbaric death. As the season of goodwill approaches, Britain is a nation ravaged by hate and conflict.

Yet amidst this depressing backdrop, there are encouraging signs that the British people, so long culpable of political apathy stemming from a long history of democracy, are pushing back. Despite the heavy police and military presence on the street, protests are increasing, more and more from the indigenous population whose lives have been blighted by the despotic ruling Party and the warped vision of their dictatorial leader. These green shoots of hope may yet signal the beginning of the end of Lawrence Pelham's reign as the Dictator of Britain.

\*\*\*

## Connect with Paul online

Website: http://www.paulmichaeldubal.com

Twitter: @pauldubal

Facebook: Paul Michael Dubal

Goodreads: Paul Michael Dubal

I.A.N.

www.independentauthornetwork.com/paul-michael-dubal.html

Praise for Paul Michael Dubal's
## CRIMES AGAINST HUMANITY

*"A heart pounding, pacy thriller that explores a difficult subject with compassion"*

*"An intricately woven plot – it's action packed and fast paced, the characters really come alive"*

*"Good twists and turns - it's a very entertaining and hard to put down read"*

*"The author successfully combines suspense and in-depth research of a controversial topic"*

Where it all started... **THE DICTATOR OF BRITAIN**

*"A scarily real apocalyptic vision of a near future Britain"*

*"A first class political thriller superbly researched"*

*"A great mix of high octane adventure and thoughtful social and political commentary"*

www.ingramcontent.com/pod-product-compliance
Lightning Source LLC
Chambersburg PA
CBHW070826260626
47170CB00007B/2277